PUCK PACT

EAST COAST
BOOK 3

KRISTEN GRANATA

PUCK PACT

KRISTEN GRANATA

PREFACE

A Note from the Author

There are several scenes in this story where the heroine's boss sexually harasses her and other female employees. The scenes are not overly graphic, and it is always stopped before it gets too far.

Furthermore, if you are triggered by hospitals, please proceed with caution.

If you'd like specific details before reading, you can always reach out to me on social media, and I'll be happy to give you some spoilers. Your mental health is important to me.

This book is a standalone in my East Coast series that follows characters from *Heart Trick* and *Odd Man Rush*. You don't have to read those stories in order to follow along with this one, but I hope you love the characters enough to check them out!

To all the girlies scrolling on BikeTok. This one's for you.

1

AARYA

"I can't believe you're reenacting porn videos with your fake boyfriend."

Cassidy smirks as she texts Trenton from across the VIP room. "It's strictly for research purposes."

I purse my lips. "Yeah, sure. You're only doing it because you want to write about it in your romance books. It has nothing to do with the fact that you're having the best sex of your life with a gorgeous hockey star."

She grins. "It really is the best sex of my life."

"Well, good for you. You deserve it after limp-dick Sheldon."

It sucks seeing your best friend get cheated on by a guy who didn't deserve her in the first place. I've plotted his death in seven different ways. Just waiting on the green light from her to make my move. I'm confident I can make it look like a painful accident.

Cassidy bumps me with her shoulder. "Who was the best sex of *your* life?"

"I refuse to assume that I've had the best sex of my life yet. If the best sex I've had is the best sex I'll *ever* have, then I might as well go fling myself into traffic right now."

"I thought you had fun with that guy from the Bronx."

"Eh, I'd give him a solid six. At least he didn't rub my clit raw like the rest of them. I don't understand why they think they have to treat it like they're buffing out a scratch on their car. It's sensitive. Fucking take it easy, DJ Scribble."

Cassidy tilts her head back as she laughs. "Some of them really are clueless unless you teach them."

"Maybe you've got the right idea. Maybe I have to start showing men videos of what I want them to do in the bedroom. It's working wonders for you."

"Make a PowerPoint presentation."

"Now there's an idea." I heave a sigh, glancing over the railing at the dance floor below. "I'm so sick of these dating apps. The guys are all the same. They take you to their apartment—most of which haven't seen a Swiffer duster in months—and they all do that same jackrabbit maneuver for exactly three minutes until they come."

Cassidy cringes. "Maybe you should take a break from those apps. You're burning yourself out."

I spin around and lean my back against the railing. "At this rate, I'm better off staying in and using my vibrator. She's never let me down."

While Cassidy goes back to texting her fake boyfriend, a man steps inside the VIP room, garnering all of my attention.

Tall with dark features, he's wearing a black button-up with the sleeves rolled along his muscular forearms, and a pair of jeans that hug his thick legs. He towers over the rest of the hockey players around him as he nods hello to them before lowering himself to sit beside Trenton. His large body looks disproportionate to the velvet couch under him. The length of one of his black dress shoes looks like two of mine stacked together.

SZA's *Big Boy* immediately starts playing in my head.

I know hockey players are generally big guys, but I can't imagine this one gliding across the rink on ice skates. He looks more like the chopping-a-tree-in-the-woods type. Better yet, *he's* the damn tree...and I'd like to climb it.

I nudge Cassidy with my elbow. "Hey, who's the guy who just walked in and sat down next to Trenton?"

Cassidy glances up from her phone. "That's Alexander Krum. He's the captain of the Goldfinches. They call him Krum Cake."

There's nothing that looks "crumb cake" about this guy. More like a rich chocolate cake with a silky-smooth chocolate frosting. The kind you pick apart with your hands, and suck the remnants off your fingertips so that you get every last drop.

Delicious as sin.

"Well, I'll call him sex on a stick."

Cassidy laughs as she slips her phone into her purse. "Come on. Let's go say hi. I haven't met him yet."

We're out celebrating the Goldfinches' win tonight. I haven't seen a single hockey game in my life, but if the players look like this Alexander Krum Cake guy, a girl might start watching.

Trenton stands and wraps his arm around Cassidy's waist as he introduces us to Alexander. "This is Cassidy, and her best friend Aarya."

Alexander pushes to his full height and shakes Cassidy's hand. "It's nice to finally meet you. I'm halfway through your book. It's excellent."

I choke back a laugh. I can't picture this giant, menacing man reading a sappy romance novel.

Cassidy's mouth falls open. "You're reading *Say You'll Stay*?"

Trenton beams. "All the guys are."

My best friend is a badass bestselling romance author, and I love seeing her get the recognition she deserves whenever someone tells her how much they love her writing.

Cassidy gives me a playful shove. "Would you look at that? Professional hockey players are reading my book, yet my own best friend hasn't."

I scoff. "I've read your sex scenes."

"Not the same thing."

Alexander's head tilts as he sets his dark-brown eyes on me. "Why haven't you read her books?"

I shrug. "I'm not into reading. And I can't stand that Hallmark channel romance bullshit."

His eyebrows jump. "You think love is bullshit?"

"I didn't say *love* is bullshit. I just don't buy into all that romantic crap. It sets these unrealistic expectations for women. No guy is going to do the things you read in a book. It's damaging for a young girl to read that and assume a man is going to come along and sweep her off her feet."

He crosses his arms over his chest as if I've personally offended him. "Men can be romantic."

3

Getting yourself off and asking, "Was it good for you?" right before you call her an Uber doesn't constitute as romantic, buddy.

I huff out a laugh. "I've never met a man who has done *any* of those things in her books."

"Then you haven't been spending time with the right kind of men."

Here we go. The *I'm different than other guys* speech. Why do men bother pretending like they're not all the same? Why go through all that work, just to end up an *I told you so* the very next day?

I roll my eyes. "There are billions of people in the world—there's no way that there's one end-all-be-all for each of us."

It's foolish to think that you can love one person for the rest of your life. That's a long-ass time, and people get bored of each other after a while. It's the reason the divorce rate is so high.

Another one of Trenton's teammates chimes in. "Come on. You can't tell me there's no such thing as love." He gestures between Cassidy and Trenton. "Just look at these two love birds. They're fucking adorable."

I inwardly cringe. The guys don't know that Cassidy and Trenton are only pretending to date. Something about helping Trenton's image after he got traded for some bullshit that went down with his old team in Seattle. The guys are oblivious to the fact that their goalie isn't actually in a committed, loving relationship with my best friend.

Cassidy gazes up at Trenton. "What do you think? Do you believe in soulmates and the *romantic bullshit* I write?"

"I believe in love." Trenton brushes a strand of hair from her face. "I believe in caring about someone so much that you'd do anything for them. I believe in putting someone's happiness over your own. I believe in showing them every single day how much they mean to you, even if it's in little ways to let them know you're thinking of them. So, whether romance means flowers and jewelry, or taking a lavish trip to Greece, or simply showing up when they need you, I think the right person will do those things for you when he loves you. And if it's real, no one and nothing could take that love away."

Damn. It's a beautiful notion. And if I didn't know better, I'd believe him. But I'm a realist.

Alexander turns to me as he jerks his thumb toward Trenton. "The way he's looking at her? *That* isn't fake romance bullshit. *That* is real love."

4

I'm about to argue my point further, but Cassidy locks eyes with me, and I can see the sadness reflecting in them. In the midst of their fake dating situation, Cassidy has developed very real feelings for the star goalie, and all this talk about true love isn't helping.

So, I bite my tongue and pat Alexander on the shoulder. "Whatever you say, Big Man." Then I hook my elbow around Cassidy's and tug her away from the group before they can see the tears welling in her eyes. "Let's go dance."

We head downstairs and make our way onto the dance floor.

Once we're in the middle of the sea of sweaty bodies, I lean in and shout over the music. "You okay?"

"Yeah, that was just..." Cassidy shakes her head, her voice trailing off.

"Intense?"

She laughs. "Exactly."

"I don't know, Cass. From where I was standing, Trent looked sincere. I think you two need to have a conversation about how you feel."

"He was just faking it. And I will not be the one who catches feelings in this scenario."

"Not even if he catches feelings too?"

"I don't know." She shakes her head as if to wipe the idea from her mind. "I don't want to talk about this anymore. Let's just have fun tonight."

Now *that* I can do. "Got it, boss."

We let the music take over as we move to the rhythm of 90s R&B pumping through the speakers. We let loose and forget about the weird world of fake dating and hockey players for a while.

It's not long before Trenton appears behind Cassidy, wrapping himself around her. I flash her a knowing smile, and back away to give them space.

But I back up into a wall of heat.

"Would you like to dance?" Alexander's voice is deep, and his breath is hot against my neck.

I glance over my shoulder to meet his dark eyes. "You're asking consent to dance? What a gentleman."

"A man should always ask permission before he touches a woman."

I spin around and wrap my hands around the back of his neck, pushing my body flush against his. "Permission granted."

My best friend is a hopeless romantic, and I hope for her sake that

Trenton is good to her so she can be in the committed relationship she wants to be in. Me on the other hand? I'm only interested in one thing, and something tells me that one night with this gentle giant of a man might be well-worth my time.

Alexander's hands settle on my hips as we start to move. My backless halter dress leaves little to the imagination, and any other guy would've trailed his fingers down my spine, or slipped them underneath the fabric. But not this man.

And the fact that he hasn't only makes me want him to do it more.

I lift my chin and bring my lips to his ear. "Any man in here would've asked me to go home with him by now."

He chuckles, low and deep. "I'm not that kind of man."

"Please. Every man is that kind of man."

"You're too young to be this jaded."

"I'm realistic, not jaded."

He pulls back to look at me. "Either you've been burned by someone, or you've never been in love. So, which one is it?"

I roll my eyes. "Oh, fun. You're psychoanalyzing me now. Do you want me to lay down on the couch upstairs while you take notes and ask me about my childhood? I'm sure we can find a clipboard for you around here somewhere."

He smirks. "Defensive too. Someone sure did a number on you."

I press a palm against his chest and push him backward a few steps. "Just because I don't want to be married with two kids and a white picket fence doesn't mean I have trauma. I don't want to be tied *down*, just tied *up*. So, if you're not going to do it, I'm going to find someone who will."

His large hand wraps around my wrist, tugging me back into his arms. "Have you been tied up before?"

"Is that an offer?"

"That would take a certain level of trust. You shouldn't let just anyone tie you up."

"Are you saying I shouldn't trust you?"

"You shouldn't. You just met me."

"I can handle myself." I arch a brow. "The question you should be asking is: Can *you* handle me?"

One corner of Alexander's mouth tips up, and a dimple sinks into his cheek. "I have no doubt."

Confidence oozes off this man, so sure of himself that he could give me exactly what I'm looking for. And that deep voice filled with promise sends a shiver of need down my spine.

"You talk a big game. You should put your money where your mouth is."

His fingertips dig into my hips. "You're so willing to give up this beautiful body without making a man earn it first. It should be a privilege to touch you. Something a man works for, to prove himself worthy."

"If I waited for a man to prove himself worthy of me, I'd die a lonely old woman."

"Let me take you on a date."

"Or we can skip the boring part and you can take me home." I drag my lips along the side of his neck, nipping at his earlobe. "I don't want your honor or your chivalry. I just want you without your clothes on."

A low groan leaves him, rumbling in his chest.

Still, he doesn't say *yes*.

"You have a lot to say about me, but what about you?" My teeth graze the stubble along his jaw. "At least I'm living my life. I see something I want, and I take it. I think something, I say it. But you're so concerned about being a proper gentleman that you're missing the fun. You think you're in control, but you're just restrained. Repressed. What kind of life are you living if you're always holding back?"

His lush mouth tips into a frown, and when I look into his eyes, I know I've struck a nerve.

I take his hands and guide them over the swell of my ass. "I *want* you to touch me, and I know you want to. So why bother depriving yourself? For one night, why don't you just let go?"

He rests his forehead against mine, his chest and shoulders heaving as he fights for his breaths. I can almost hear the silent debate warring in his mind.

Come on, Big Man. Let go.

"Take me home," I whisper against his lips.

But those words that've never failed me once, not ever, have the effect of a cold bucket of water on this man.

He shakes his head as he pulls back, hitting me with a regretful look. "I'm sorry. I can't."

Then he turns around and disappears through the crowd.

And I'm left standing there wondering how in the hell I just got rejected.

2

ALEXANDER

I EASE OPEN THE FRONT DOOR AND CREEP INSIDE MY HOUSE, making sure to close it quietly behind me before gently laying my keys on the entryway table so they don't make too much noise.

But it's no use.

The jingling of metal followed by the pitter-patter of feet echo in the hall.

"Daddy!"

I flip on the lights just in time to see a flash of unruly dark curls as it crashes into my leg, followed by our dog, Ellie, jumping up to plant her front paws on my ribs.

"Daddy, you're home. I waited up for you."

"Even though I told her not to." Annie, my nanny, leans against the wall and shakes her head as she gives me an apologetic smile.

I chuckle as I push Ellie down so I can hoist Giuliana into my arms. "That's okay. I'm in the mood for some bedtime snuggles anyway."

Giuliana wraps her arms and legs around me like a koala, laying her head on my shoulder. I close my eyes, relishing in her love and letting her warmth soothe my troubled heart.

"Can we lay in the big bed together?" she asks.

"Sure. Why don't you take Ellie into my room and get it ready for me so I can say goodnight to Annie and lock up the house."

Giuliana squeals, not in the least bit tired as she springs from my arms. "Bye, Annie! Come on, Ellie. I told you Daddy would let us snuggle in his bed."

I shake my head as they run into the hallway, thick as thieves. "She doesn't want to snuggle. She's only using me for my bed."

Annie grins. "She's a master manipulator, and she's only three."

"I'm terrified to see how smart she'll be when she's a teenager." I chuckle. "How was everything tonight?"

"Fine, as always."

Annie is a longtime family friend who I kept in touch with after my parents passed. When she found out about Giuliana three years ago, she jumped at the chance to help me. I was an unexpected parent, and became an unexpected single parent when Giuliana's mom relinquished her rights. Annie was there for me when I had no one, and she has become an important part of our family. Sometimes, I think my mother sent her to me because she couldn't be here herself.

Annie slides on her coat, but before she opens the front door, she turns around to face me. "You know you're allowed to have a personal life, Alexander." She lowers her voice as she glances toward the hallway. "Being a father doesn't mean you're not allowed to do things for yourself every once in a while."

Heat creeps into my cheeks, as if she can see the evidence of Aarya all over me. "I just want to be here for Giuliana. That's my priority."

"As she should be. But your happiness is a priority too. Don't let yourself feel guilty about it. Your parents would tell you the same if they were here."

I pull her in for a much-needed hug. "Thank you, Annie."

"I just want to see you happy." She presses her palm to my cheek. "That's all."

I nod. "I know."

I watch her until she's safely inside the guest house in our yard, and then I make my way into my bedroom to see my favorite girl.

Giuliana is sprawled out in the middle of my bed with Ellie beside her—

head on a pillow like the human she thinks she is. I pause in the doorway, my chest expanding as my heart swells at the sight.

"How was hockey, Daddy?" Giuliana rubs a silky piece of fabric on her blanket. "Did you play good?"

"I did." I flop onto the mattress beside her, brushing her curls away from her face. "How was your night? Did you take good care of Ellie while I was gone?"

"Uh-huh. Annie let me hold her leash when we went on a walk." She scrunches her nose. "But then she took a really big poop and we needed to go back to the house to get another bag because it was a two-fer."

I tilt my head back as I laugh. "Two-fer? Is that what Annie said?"

"Yup. It was disgusting."

"Sounds like it." I twirl one of her curls around my index finger. "Did you wash good in the bath tonight?"

Giuliana rolls her eyes. "Of course, Daddy. I'm a big girl now. I know how to wash myself."

"Oh, excuse me. I'm so sorry. I forget how big you are sometimes because you look so tiny in my big bed. Maybe if you slept in your own kid-sized bed, I'd be able to remember."

Her bottom lip juts out. "But yours is so much better than mine."

"Our mattresses are exactly the same, except mine is bigger because *I'm* bigger."

She snuggles closer to me, nuzzling her head against my chest. "I just don't want you to be lonely in this big bed all by yourself."

"Lonely?" I pull back and glance down at her sweet face. "Where did you hear that word?"

"At school."

"What do you think it means?"

"It's when you don't have anybody to sleep in your bed with." Big round eyes blink up at me. "Makayla's mom sleeps in bed with her dad. Robby said his mom sleeps in bed with his dad. Stella has two moms and no dad, but her two moms sleep in the same bed together."

Ah, I see where this is going.

"Even I have someone to sleep in bed with." Giuliana reaches behind her and runs her fingers through Ellie's fur. "You're the only one who sleeps alone, and that means you're lonely."

I press a kiss to the top of her head. "Just because I sleep alone doesn't mean I'm lonely, angel girl. Lots of people only have one mom, or one dad. Some people don't have a mom or a dad, and one of their other family members raises them. Everyone's family looks different."

"So, you're not lonely then?"

My chest squeezes at her question. "No, baby. How could I be when I have you?"

"I'm not gonna be around forever, you know. I'm gonna go to college one day. And you can't come with me. Parents aren't allowed at college."

I chuckle as I pull her close and wrap my arms around her. "That's a long time away, so let's not think about that just yet."

"I'm just keepin' it real, Dad."

My eyebrows shoot up. "Keeping it real?"

"Uncle Mac taught me that one."

"Of course, he did."

McKinley is the only one of my teammates who knows about my daughter. He was there the day Giuliana's mother showed up at my door with a positive pregnancy test, and he has kept the secret ever since. It's not that I *want* to hide Giuliana from my friends, or that I'm embarrassed of her, or even that I don't trust them. But Giuliana is my whole world—the only thing that truly matters to me. I've been trying to shield her from the spotlight I'm forced to be in. She didn't ask for this lifestyle, and I intend on keeping her out of it for as long as I can.

Which is why I don't allow myself to be photographed with women, or indulge in one-night stands like some of my other teammates. I can't risk not being here when Giuliana needs me because I'm too busy getting my dick wet somewhere in the city. It's bad enough that hockey takes me away from her as much as it does, but at least I can rationalize that it's my means to support her, not some extracurricular choice.

I roll off the side of the bed and kick off my shoes. "I'm going to wash up for bed, and then it's time for you to go to sleep."

"In the big bed, right?"

I smirk at the sight of her pouty face. "Yes, in the big bed."

She grins as she burrows under the covers.

After I brush my teeth and change into my pajamas, I slip into bed and watch Giuliana sleep for a while. It calms me, watching the rise and fall of her chest as she breathes in and out through her tiny parted lips.

The truth is: I *am* lonely. Being a single parent is isolating enough. Add in the schedule of a professional athlete, and it's doubly as hard to have a personal life and make a true connection with someone.

My loneliness is the only reason I can think of as to why I almost gave in to Aarya tonight.

God, what I would've given to be able to succumb to her for just one night. She's gorgeous, and feisty as hell. The attraction was there. Those lush lips and her sinful curves, accentuated by that barely-there dress she wore. How easy it would've been to say yes and indulge myself. To lose my sense and forget about my responsibilities, forget who I'm supposed to be, forget about what's right and wrong.

But I don't have the luxury of acting on my desires. Not anymore. Not even for one night.

Plus, Aarya made it clear she wants nothing to do with a serious relationship, and that isn't the type of woman I need to be entertaining. I don't want to be another notch on someone's belt; an accomplishment to boast about; some shiny object people want to show off.

I haven't gotten laid in an embarrassingly long time. My teammates would think I was crazy if they knew just how long. And it's not for lack of options. I'm a twenty-nine-year-old professional athlete with willing women literally throwing themselves at me wherever I go.

But I want more. I want to find love. A relationship. Someone I can turn to when life gets hard. Someone I can care for.

I want what my parents had.

And I want that for Giuliana too.

I have to hold out until I find it.

My mind whirls into the late hours of the night, and when sleep finally comes, I dream about Giuliana skipping through the waves on the beach in Tuscany with a mother who loves her.

3

AARYA

"Aarya, see me in my office when you're finished with the tour."

My stomach twists, but I force a smile as I turn to my boss. "Yes, sir."

I love my job as the education officer here at the gallery. I get to meet new people every day, and talk to them about the artwork I love so much.

My boss, on the other hand, makes me want to crawl out of my skin. But I need this job, and it's going to open the door for me to own my own gallery one day.

One day.

Sometimes it feels like that day will never come, but the more I save up, the more of a possibility it becomes.

After I say goodbye to my tour group, I make a beeline for my boss' office. Get it over with and rip it off like a band aid.

I tap my knuckles against the door frame. "Hey, Carter. You wanted to see me?"

His blue eyes light up when they land on me, traveling down my knee-length sweater dress. "Come in. Close the door."

I step into his office and make sure to leave the door cracked open enough so my coworkers can see inside if they passed by.

"Is everything okay?" I ask, standing behind one of the chairs in front of his desk.

"Yes, everything is fine. I just wanted to tell you how great you did with the Sanderson School tour the other day. They left glowing reviews on the website, and made sure to name their tour guide."

I smile and let out a breath of relief. "Thank you. They were an energetic group. They had so many good questions."

Carter rises from his chair and rounds his desk. I resist the urge to back away from him as he comes closer, the relief I just felt now dissipating.

When he reaches me, he lifts his hand and brushes my hair off my shoulder. "You're so good at your job, Aarya."

I lean back a fraction of an inch. "Thank you. I do love it here."

The reminder more for myself to stop me from kneeing this guy in the balls.

"I'd love to see you in a different role here. A higher title." He twirls a strand of my hair around his index finger. "There are a few positions I'm considering you for."

My heart races, my fight or flight response kicking into high gear as he continues to touch me. "Uh, yes. I'd love to be considered for Susan's job when it becomes available at the end of the year."

Several employees and I are gunning for Susan's education officer spot, as sad as we are to see her go. It would mean more money, more responsibility, and more experience for me—all of which I need before owning my own gallery.

Carter inches closer. "Yes, I think you'd be a perfect fit for that role. You and I would have to spend a lot of time together to discuss your ideas and discuss the direction of the education department."

I swallow past the dryness in my throat. "Of course, sir. That sounds great."

"Aarya, I told you: You can call me Carter." He leans in, his cheek brushing against mine as he whispers, "As much as I love it when you call me *sir.*"

I clamp my mouth shut so I don't spew vomit all over my boss.

I *need* this job.

I force another fake smile. "Well, I should get back to work. I have another tour coming soon."

Carter opens his mouth to say something else, but he's cut off when Chanora sticks her head into the office. "Aarya, your tour is here."

"Ah, see?" I let out an awkward laugh. "Right on schedule."

I all but run out of the office, and clutch Chanora's arm as we scurry down the hallway. "Is my tour really here?"

"No, they're not due for another twenty minutes. But I had to get you out of there before he started bringing up all the *positions* he wants to put you in again."

I shudder at the thought. "There has to be something we can do about this. It's getting worse every week."

She shoots me a dubious look. "Girl, you know what happened to the last person who tried tattling on Carter."

"I know, I know."

Carter fired Kelly without a warning in front of all the other employees at a staff meeting, then blackballed her from working in other galleries in the area. I was a newbie at the time, with no idea what was happening, but Kelly gripped my arm on her way out the door and said, "Get out now while you still can."

I didn't understand what she was referring to then, but I sure do now.

One day, I'll be rid of my boss.

One day, I'll be my own boss with my own gallery.

One day.

I just have to hold on a little longer.

"Thanks for coming with me."

I link arms with Cassidy as we walk along the path leading to the mansion before us. "No problem. You know I'm always down to be your wing woman."

Getting to hang out with a bunch of hot hockey players isn't the worst way I could spend my night.

She side-eyes me. "I was hoping it wouldn't be weird between you and Alexander."

"Alexander who?"

She laughs. "Okay, because you're clearly over him rejecting you the other night."

"I am." I flip my hair over my shoulder. "Besides, he's the one who should feel weird seeing me look this good after turning me down."

Cassidy reaches out and presses her finger against the doorbell. "You do look hot."

McKinley swings open the door with a wide smile before letting his icy-blue gaze roam over the both of our bodies. "Damn, ladies. You're looking gorgeous tonight."

I pat him on the shoulder as we step inside. "I'll make sure not to tell your goalie that you just checked out his girl."

"Shit," he mutters. "Sorry, Cass. Totally didn't mean that."

She giggles behind me. "I'll take a compliment wherever I can get it, Mac. Thanks for having us over."

"Of course. Everyone's in the game room downstairs. Make yourselves at home. Can I get you anything to drink?"

I nudge him with my elbow. "What are you boys drinking?"

"Corona with lime."

"Then we'll take two."

I follow Cassidy down into the basement, keeping my eyes from roaming around the room in search of Alexander.

Truth be told, I'm feeling slightly nervous about seeing him tonight. It's not every day I get turned down by a guy when I give him an open invitation to sleep with me. But Cassidy needed me by her side so I'm brushing it off and holding my head high.

Alexander can eat his heart out. It's his loss anyway.

Trenton pulls Cassidy in for a kiss when we get downstairs. "Hey, Aarya. How are you?"

"I'm good. Can't complain." I squeeze his shoulder. "Great game the other night. I heard it was a shutout. I don't know what that means, but Cassidy said it's a good thing."

He bites back a smile, ever the modest player. "Thanks."

I spot Alexander crossing the room to make his way toward us, so I grab Cassidy's arm. "Oh, look! Mac has air hockey."

Cassidy drags her heels as I pull her toward the table. "No. I'm not playing against you. You remember what happened last time."

Trenton smiles as he looks between us. "What happened last time?"

"She hit the puck so hard, it flew off the table and almost broke the window at the bar we were at." Cassidy shoots me a playful glare. "Aarya is like Monica from *Friends*. Nothing is ever just a game with her."

I roll my eyes, feigning innocence. "There's nothing wrong with a healthy dose of competition."

"I'll play with you."

My head whips around to Alexander, who walks up alongside Trenton.

Cassidy pats him on the shoulder. "Good luck, buddy. You're going to need it."

"Hey, where are you going?" I pout as Cassidy pulls Trenton toward the other teammates by the pool table.

My traitorous best friend wiggles her fingers over her shoulder, leaving me alone with Alexander.

He smirks. "Hi."

I blink up at him wearing a blank expression. "Hi... remind me who you are again?"

His smirk grows into a full-blown grin, because he knows I know damn well who he is. "I'm Alex, Trenton's teammate. We met at the bar the other night."

God, he looks good. He's wearing a white T-shirt with a pair of well-fitting jeans. His muscular arms are on display, complete with thick corded veins traveling up his forearms. Everything about this man is big and strong. I bet he could—

No. *No!* Focus.

"Oh, you're the one with the weird nickname. What was it..." I tap my finger against my chin. "Twinkie? No. Apple pie? No. Wait, I got it— Cupcake!"

He tosses his head back as he laughs. "Close enough."

I smirk as I spin around and grab one of the neon green mallets and set it on the table. "So, you want to play?"

"Sure. But first, I owe you an apology."

I purse my lips as I look away with a slight roll of my eyes. "That's not necessary."

"It is to me." He heaves a sigh, shoving his hands in his pockets. "I shouldn't have left you on the dance floor so abruptly the other night. I should've stayed with you to make sure you got home safely, or offered to give you a ride. I'm sorry I left you like that."

He's sorry for...not making sure I got home safely?

My eyebrows pinch together and my chin jerks back. "Oh."

"What?"

I shake my head in disbelief. "That was totally not the apology I was expecting."

"What were you expecting?"

"I don't know." I lift my hand and let it fall. "Maybe: *I'm sorry for giving you blue balls. I was such an idiot for turning you down.* Something to that effect."

He coughs out an incredulous laugh. "You want me to apologize for *not* sleeping with you?"

"You should be sorry about it. You missed out on what could've been a very fun night. Plus, you had me so turned on, I had to go home and use my vibrator—only it died halfway through, leaving me *very* frustrated."

"That sounds..." He swallows. "Terrible. Forgive me."

I hike a shoulder. "I'll think about it."

"Why don't we make a wager?" He gestures to the air hockey table. "Let me make it up to you."

"It's going to have to be a damn good wager."

"If I win, you'll have to let me take you on a date."

My eyebrows shoot up. "*That's* what you want if you win?"

"It's not like I need money." He tilts his head. "I'd much rather have something that my money can't buy. Plus, I'd get to prove you wrong at the same time, and show you that romance truly does exist."

I fold my arms over my chest, leaning my hip against the table. "Fine. I agree to your terms. Only because you won't win."

"And you? What do you want if you win?"

"*When* I win..." I pause until I think of something. "I want the money you'd spend taking me on said date."

"Really?"

I hike a shoulder. "Not everyone makes hockey player money, Big Man. It'd be nice to have a little extra cash on hand."

"Okay." He sticks out his hand between us. "You have a deal."

I place my hand in his, and give it a firm shake. "Game on, Pound Cake."

Alexander presses the power button to turn on the table lights and air. The plastic puck rattles against the table as we take our respective sides.

I slam the puck to the right, and it ricochets off the wall at lightning speed before sinking into Alexander's goal.

His eyes widen as the digital number changes from zero to one in my favor. "Why do I feel like I just got hustled?"

I grin. "One, nothing."

His eyebrows pull together, all humor wiped from his features as he crouches down and sends the puck sailing back to my side. I block it, but he sends it right back and into my goal.

"Tied up," he says.

"Not the kind of tied up I was hoping for tonight."

He chuckles. "You won't be able to distract me. I'm laser focused when it comes to this game."

I lean over the table, and his eyes immediately drop to my overflowing cleavage. "You sure about that, Carrot Cake?"

His Adam's apple bobs before he clears his throat. "Just hit the damn puck."

"A date sounds so boring, you know?" I knock the puck across the table. "Two people sitting across the table from each other, rattling off random facts about yourself like you're reading from a resume. I can think of a way to have much more fun."

"It sounds like you haven't been taken on a proper date." He hits the puck back to me. "And I can't figure out for the life of me why a fierce woman like you would let a man get away with anything less."

His words pierce my armor, tugging at something deep inside me.

I've never had faith in finding love. I learned at a very young age that men will only disappoint you.

I shake my head and block Alexander's next several attempts. "I'm not into any of that fluffy romance shit."

"How do you know you don't like it if you've never experienced it?"

The green puck slides into my poorly blocked goal.

Fuck. Two to one.

I slam the puck harder this time, and Alexander's eyes follow it as it bounces off the surrounding walls.

I need to regain control here. "I was thinking about you, you know. Right before my vibrator died."

His dark eyes fly up to mine.

The plastic disc sails right into his goal, and I smile. "Don't you know how rude it is to get a girl all worked up just to leave her hanging like that?"

His jaw clenches as he sets the disk on the table and slides it over to my side. "I didn't mean to do that."

"No? You didn't think putting your hands on my body, squeezing my ass, rubbing me against your cock would have an effect on me?"

I score another goal.

Three to two.

I block his next shot, and keep going. "I imagined the way your tongue would feel between my thighs. Something tells me you're an expert at making a woman come. Am I wrong, Big Man?"

"I've never had any complaints."

"No, I bet you haven't. I bet you've got the size too, don't you? I thought about how big you must be. The way you'd feel inside me. Wondering if I'd be able to take all of you our first time together."

I sink the punk into his goal *again*.

Alexander's cheeks are flushed, and I catch him discreetly adjust his pants before he tosses the puck onto the table.

I'm turning myself on with all this talk, but it's worth it to see him get flustered.

The puck sails across the table while I push him further. "You like being in control. You're probably dominant in the bedroom too."

His eyes narrow as he tries to block me out.

"I'd let you dominate me. I like being choked, spanked, and called a good girl as much as the next person." I smirk. "But I'd bet my life's savings that you'd let me dominate you too."

I sink another goal, and keep going.

"You'd get on your knees for me, and let me boss you around. You're always so in control, it'd feel good to give in to me, don't you think?"

Another goal.

He's barely volleying the puck at this point, his pupils are dilated and glazed over.

I reach across the table to knock the puck onto his side. "I bet you'd be such a good boy for me, Alexander."

Final goal.

Seven to two.

The table shuts down, our mallets floating to a stop somewhere in the middle. But Alexander's eyes don't leave mine, wild and heated. What I wouldn't give for him to snap. Grab me and have his way with me right here on the air hockey table.

"I didn't turn you away because I'm not attracted to you. You know that, don't you?" Alexander's chest heaves as he stalks around the corner of the table and steps closer to me. "I think you know I'd love nothing more than to have you in my bed. To kiss you. Taste you. To *feel* you. I'd give you everything you need, and have you begging for more. And I'd give you more. I'd give it to you until your legs shake and your voice is hoarse from screaming my name, over and over again." He stops when he's in front of me, tipping my chin up so he can speak against my lips. "Because I've thought about you since that night too. I took myself in my hand to the thought of you on top of me, riding me, owning me, taking every last drop of me."

Wetness pools between my thighs, and warm desire coats my insides.

"But I won't touch you if you aren't mine, Aarya. If you let me do the things I want to do to you, you won't be doing them with anyone else. No one but me. And it wouldn't be for one night."

I tilt my head, trying to grasp at any semblance of control I have left. "You're so sure you'd have me coming back for more?"

"I'm certain of it."

The unwavering verity in his voice has me convinced as well.

But I won't put myself out there to get rejected by the same man twice.

"Too bad you're nothing but a tease, Big Man. You talk a big game but you can't back it up, which is why you now owe me some cash." I step back from him, walking backward. "You might be the king of the ice, but down here with us mere mortals, you just got schooled."

4

ALEXANDER

IF YOU ASKED ME WHY I'M OUTSIDE OF AARYA'S ART GALLERY, waiting for her to get off work, I wouldn't have an answer for you.

Actually, I'd tell you it's to pay her the money I owe her from our bet. But I could've easily sent her a check in the mail. The money isn't the only reason I'm here.

Maybe I'm a glutton for punishment, teasing myself with something I can never have.

Maybe I'm just a fool.

Probably both.

I haven't been able to get this woman out of my head since the moment I heard her sassy mouth the night we met, and the last encounter we had at McKinley's house only brought me closer to breaking all of my rules.

Would it be so bad for one night? Hell no. I have no doubt Aarya would be every one of my fantasies come true.

But a woman like her would chew me up and spit me out after she's finished with me. I'd want more, and she'd only discard me after she got what she wanted. I can't get invested in someone who doesn't want me, the real me, someone who isn't looking for the thrill of a night with a pro athlete.

I come with too much baggage to be careless over one night of sex.

Which is one of the reasons I lost the air hockey game on purpose. Aarya doesn't truly want a date with me, and she obviously needs the money. I didn't want to take that from her just to force her to go out with me.

I push off my bike when I spot her exiting the gallery. Her long dark hair cascades over her shoulders in loose, bouncing waves, complimenting her light-brown skin. Thick eyebrows arch over her dark eyes, and red lipstick makes her plump lips pop, offsetting the black sweater dress clinging to her lush curves. Her black leather ankle boots clack against the pavement as she steps outside.

Damn, she's sensational.

She locks the front door and spins around, then gasps when she sees me.

I grimace, holding up my hands. "I'm sorry. I didn't mean to scare you."

"Fuck." Her eyes are wide as she clutches her chest. "You can't lurk around late at night dressed in all black and sneak up on a woman."

"I wasn't lurking. I was standing here in plain sight. I thought you saw me." I rub my palm against her back. "Are you okay?"

She flinches at my touch and jerks away from me. "I'm fine. You stalking me now, Cheesecake?"

"I wanted to give you the money I owe you. I would've called you, but I didn't think you'd answer if you didn't recognize the number, so Cass told me where you worked."

"Traitor," she hisses. "Who says I'd have answered even if I did recognize the number?"

"Touché." I chuckle. "Let me give you a ride home."

Her eyes dart to my bike. "*You* have a motorcycle?"

"Yeah, why do you say it like that?"

"I expected you to drive a Camry or a minivan. Something safe and reliable."

"That sounds like an insult."

"It's not an insult if it's the truth."

"Come on." I hold up the spare helmet I brought for her. "Let me give you a ride."

She spins on her heels. "Thanks, but I'll walk."

I follow after her. "I can get you there quicker."

"I refuse to get on that thing."

"I'm a very careful driver."

24

"No such thing on a motorcycle."

I frown. "You walk home alone often?"

"Every night."

"That's not safe."

"I can handle myself, Big Man."

"Do you know how many women get abducted every year in this country?"

"What about motorcycle accidents, hmm? Do you know those statistics as well?"

I guide her to the inside of the sidewalk so I'm the one closest to the street. "I do, and you're safer on a bike than you are walking at night in Jersey City."

"Listen, Fruit Cake. I'm less than a ten-minute walk from my apartment building. So, if you can skip the lecture about stranger danger and get to the paying me part, I'd really appreciate it."

I twist my backpack around in front of me, and yank on the zipper before reaching for the envelope inside. "Here you go."

She lifts the flap and her eyes double in size as she sifts through the cash. "Alexander, this is too much."

"You asked me to pay you what I'd spend on our date."

"You don't drop two grand on a date."

"Says who?"

She sputters. "Says...says...anyone. That's crazy. What could you possibly spend that much money on?"

"Guess you'll never find out because you won't go on a date with me."

She's not wrong. I wouldn't normally spend that much on a date, but she sounded like she needed the money, and I felt bad.

She rolls her eyes as she stuffs the envelope into her purse. After a moment, her demeanor turns sincere. "Thank you. Seriously, I really need that money, so I appreciate it."

"Do you mind if I ask why you need the money?"

"I love my job, but my boss sucks. I'm saving up to open my own gallery one day." She huffs out a laugh and shakes her head, running her hands up and down her arms. "It's far off in the distance, but it's a dream of mine."

I slip off my jacket and wrap it around her shoulders to keep her warm. "Here."

She dodges me. "I'm good."

But I place it on her shoulders anyway. "It's cold. Just wear it."

She leaves it like that, hanging off her shoulders instead of sticking her arms inside and zippering it up.

Brat.

"Why does your boss suck?" I ask.

"He's a misogynistic pig who thinks it's okay to sexually harass his female employees."

My feet falter. "I'm sorry, what? He's sexually harassing you?"

She shrugs like it's no big deal. "He hasn't forced himself on me or anything."

"But he's making you feel uncomfortable?"

"He's not the first man to make a crude comment or two, and he won't be the last. I just have to bide my time until I can get out of there and open my own place."

I glance over my shoulder, tempted to head back to her gallery. "Your boss still in there?"

"No, he left earlier. And you are not going to march in there like some overprotective meathead and fight him. I don't need to get fired."

I clench my jaw, grinding my teeth. "Fine. But you'll tell me if he ever puts a finger on you."

"Like I said before, I'm a big girl and I can handle myself. Thank you for the money, but you don't need to worry about me."

It makes me wonder who *does* worry about her, if anyone. It's obvious that she's been taking care of herself for a while now. Was it her family or someone else who made this woman think she's all she has in this world?

I change the subject so I don't upset her. "Cassidy told me you were coming to the game tomorrow night, so I figured you needed something to wear." I reach back into my bag and pull out my yellow and black jersey with the number sixteen etched onto it.

"Is this yours?" She takes it from me, holding it up in front of her body.

"It's one of mine, yeah."

She glances up at me before tearing her eyes away too quickly. "Thanks."

"Do you know anything about hockey?"

"Not unless it's air hockey."

I grin. "I think you'll enjoy it. You seem to have a competitive streak in you, and hockey is an exciting game to watch."

Aarya slows down as we approach a tall apartment building. "Well, this is me." She hands over my jacket. "Are you sure about this money? It's...too much."

"Consider it an investment on your dream." I hike a shoulder. "Besides, you won it fair and square, remember?"

She graces me with a genuine smile, wide and beautiful as it lights up her face. "Thank you."

Affection warms my chest. "Goodnight, spitfire."

She shoots me a wink. "Night, Bundt Cake."

5

ALEXANDER

"You ready for this?"

I heave a sigh as I stride toward my lawyer. "I just want to get this over with so I can go back to pretending like this asshole doesn't exist."

Peggy clicks her tongue against the roof of her mouth. "It's bad karma to talk about a dying man, you know."

"After all the shit my grandfather did, I think Karma will overlook my comments." I swing open the glass door and gesture for Peggy to walk in ahead of me.

"Just keep your cool," she says, lowering her voice once we're inside. "Let me do the talking."

I felt nothing when my grandfather informed me of his cancer diagnosis. Not sadness. Not grief. Not regret. I didn't feel satisfaction either—I'm not a monster. But it felt like it was any other day. Like I'd overheard someone else's conversation as they passed on the street.

So, when his lawyer called and mentioned something about discussing my grandfather's will, I wanted no part of it. My grandfather hasn't offered me anything my entire life. Why would he leave me anything in his death? And why would I want anything with his name tied to it anyway? But his lawyer hounded me until Peggy convinced me to meet with him.

Most grandparents are loving, generous people. They create strong bonds and fond memories with their grandchildren. They're like extensions of a child's parents. But Lorenzo Aorta isn't like most grandparents. He didn't bat an eye when he pushed my mother away for marrying someone he didn't approve of; or when he refused to welcome my father into his family despite the wonderful man he was; or when he pretended that I didn't exist for the first sixteen years of my life. My father was from Germany, and Lorenzo couldn't stand the fact that my mother married someone outside their circle. He's an old-fashioned man with old-fashioned beliefs. Italians marry Italians. Money marries money. He's deep-rooted in ethnocentrism, passed down among generations.

Even after my parents died and I was forced to spend two years living on his estate until I turned eighteen, he barely uttered two words to me until I moved out.

To be honest, I didn't care that he didn't accept me as his grandson—but he hurt my mother, and I will never forgive him for that.

Lorenzo's lawyer, Frank, stands when we walk into his office. "Alexander, thank you for meeting with me. You're a difficult man to get a hold of."

I scan the room, surprised to find that my grandfather isn't here for this meeting.

I clasp Frank's outstretched hand for a quick shake. "Let's make this quick. I have a game tonight."

Peggy digs her elbow into my ribs before we lower into the chairs facing Frank's desk.

"Yes, of course." Frank drops down into his leather chair and slides a manila file folder across the top of his desk. "Your grandfather named you in his will, and he asked me to share a copy with you. Look it over, and let me know if you have any questions."

I hand the file to Peggy. "I don't want anything from Lorenzo. I told you this on the phone."

Frank swallows as he tugs on his collar. "I understand that, but there's something you need to know concerning the villa in Tuscany."

My eyes snap up to his. "My parents' villa?"

Frank grimaces. "Technically, the villa is in Lorenzo's name. He—"

"No, it belonged to my parents. They owned it, and they left it to me when they passed."

Granted, I wasn't old enough to inherit it when they passed. They had it in their will that it would become mine on my thirtieth birthday, a present they thought they'd be here to surprise me with.

Frank clears his throat. "Your grandfather holds the title. It's under his name."

My chest heaves with my shallow breaths as I fight to keep my cool.

Son of a bitch.

Peggy's eyes scan the paperwork inside the folder. "It looks like he's leaving the villa to you as long as you abide by this contract."

Blood roars in my ears as my blood pressure spikes. "No. He can't do that. My parents had it in their will that I inherit the house. He can't override that. He can't take the house away from me."

"He's not trying to take it from you." Frank holds up his hand. "Why don't you take a moment to look over the contract."

Peggy lifts a small white envelope from the folder. "There's a letter here addressed to you."

"I don't want to read his letter." I pinch the bridge of my nose. "Just tell me what I have to do so I don't lose the villa."

Peggy hands me the contract. "You have to disclose your financial portfolio and investments with the aforementioned advisor."

My eyebrows press together. "I have my own financial advisor. Why does he want me to use his?"

"He wants to make sure you're set up for retirement," Frank says. "You're a young athlete with a lot of money. Lorenzo wants to make sure you're able to handle the financial responsibility of the villa so it stays in the family."

I snort. "Family."

The word burns on my tongue like acid. I had a family, but they were taken away from me too soon. This pathetic excuse of a grandfather has never been my family.

"There's more," Peggy whispers. "Keep reading."

My eyes land on the last stipulation, and my mouth goes dry. "Married?!"

Frank leans forward in his chair. "Look, Alexander—"

No wonder the coward didn't want to be here for this meeting. He knew I'd choke him out and speed up the process of his death.

"What the hell does being married have to do with owning a house?" My eyes bounce between Frank and Peggy. "This is absurd."

"He wants to ensure that you sign a prenup, so you'll be able to protect your assets. It'd be a bonus if you married someone within the same income bracket as you, but not many women make what a pro-athlete makes, so that's not a requirement. Either way, he feels like a married man will be less likely to knock up a random woman in a hotel room and let her take him for all he's worth." Frank clears his throat. "His words, not mine."

I swallow past the lump of bile in my throat, shifting my eyes to my own lawyer. "What can we do about this, Peg?"

She gives me a small shake of her head. "Not much, kid. Your options are to do what this contract is asking you to do, otherwise he won't give you the deed to the villa."

My heart sinks. I want to crumple this contract and stuff it down Frank's throat. But that would mean losing the villa, and I can't bear the thought of never stepping foot inside of it again. Of never sitting by the garden my mother loved. Of never feeling the old leather of my father's office chair under my fingertips. Of not being able to share it with Giuliana someday.

Losing the house feels like losing my parents all over again.

And maybe that's what Lorenzo truly wants. Maybe he can't stand the thought of a half-breed living off of his legacy.

Well, fuck that and fuck him.

I consider myself to be a pretty even-keeled guy. Nothing ruffles my feathers. Not even on the ice. I'm in control of my emotions, and I articulate them well. I'm the voice of reason between friends. The captain of my teammates. The one people come to for help. It's a rare occasion when I deem something worth fighting over.

But this? This is the one thing I have left of my parents.

And I'll be damned if I let this man take it from me.

I rise from my chair. "And if I agree to these terms, I get the villa? No more tricks up his sleeve, no strings attached? I show my finances, get married, and he'll sign it over?"

I say it like marriage is as easy as picking out a car, and not one of the most important things I'll ever do in my life.

"This isn't a trick, Alexander." Frank pushes out of his chair and buttons his suit jacket. "If you agree to the terms, then you have until your birthday to fulfill the requirements."

"We have a deal."

Peggy gasps beside me as she shoots out of her chair. "Alex, wait. Let's think about this."

I know what she's worried about because it's the same thing on my mind. But I won't give up on my dream of having a future spent in that villa, creating the same beautiful memories with my own family that I once made there.

This is insane. Ridiculous. Foolish.

But I'd be willing to sell my soul to the Devil himself if it meant getting that villa in my name.

I snatch a pen off the desk. "Where do I sign?"

"You good, Krum?"

I fly around the back of the net, glaring at Trenton. "I'm fine."

I'm anything but fine.

I missed six of the ten shots I took during warmups and Trenton wasn't even blocking the goal. I've been fired up ever since I left Frank's office earlier. I should've known better than to schedule a meeting with him on game day, but I wasn't expecting *this*.

I can't lose the villa.

That is the only thought on a loop in my brain. But this game is about to start, and I need to figure out how I'm going to focus.

"You lucky bastard." McKinley skates by me and smacks me on the pads with his stick. "Your girl looks hot in black and yellow."

My girl?

My eyes follow his gaze until I spot Aarya's dark hair and bright-red lips. She's sitting next to Cassidy behind Trent's net—and she's in the jersey I gave her with the number sixteen clear as day on it.

I forgot she was coming tonight. For a moment, my entire mood shifts. A surge of pride courses through me as I skate past the glass that separates us, letting my gaze speak for me.

Damn, she looks good.

She shoots me a wink as her plump red lips pull into a smirk, and I grin.

"There he is." Trenton smacks my helmet. "Now get your head in the game and let's fucking go."

We head back into the locker room, and I'm soaring on a high, feeling the adrenaline pumping in my veins like it always does before a game—only now it's turned all the way up.

She's wearing *my* number, with *my* name sprawled across the back.

Aside from the rare occasions Annie has snuck Giuliana in to watch me play, this is the only other time someone I know is wearing my jersey.

As we're waiting in the tunnel for the announcer to call each of the players out onto the ice, I slap Jason's shoulders from behind. "Let's go, boys. We're undefeated. We're going straight to the championship this season. This is our year. I can feel it."

The team shouts and chants, the air electric with the pre-game buzz.

Until it all comes crashing down when I'm announced onto the ice. My eyes find Aarya as I circle the rink, and then I watch as she yanks my jersey up and over her head before stuffing it inside her purse.

What the hell?

I can't make out what she's saying to Cassidy, but I catch Cassidy shake her head as Aarya crosses her arms over her chest.

Why would she wear it only to take it off?

What just happened?

Something inside me snaps.

I can't even get the woman to wear my jersey, let alone go on a date with me, yet I somehow need to get married before I lose my parents' villa.

How in the hell is that going to happen?

Anger courses through me, the years of resentment towards my grandfather I've shoved down now bubbling to the surface.

Without thinking, I skate over to the boards in front of Aarya and bang my stick against the glass. "Put on your jersey."

Aarya locks eyes with me and shakes her head, mouthing, "No."

I clench my jaw, hurt and confusion rolling off me in waves. "Put. It. On."

She arches a brow and says, "Make me."

If the game wasn't about to start, I'd climb back there and put the jersey back on her myself.

But I don't have time for this bullshit, or whatever game she's trying to play.

All the pent-up frustration I've been experiencing lately, all the stress, all the heartache... I'm about to take it out on the ice.

Once the puck drops, I'm all over the rink. My job as the Center is to assist and make the plays happen, finding openings for my teammates to score. I'm fast and I pride myself on being two steps ahead of everyone else. But tonight, none of my passes meet their intended targets, I haven't made one successful shot to the goal, and I even got a two-minute penalty for boarding.

Maybe for another player, this could be chalked up to a bad game. But I'm the captain, and I have a responsibility to my team. Yet my anger has me in a chokehold and no matter how hard I try, I can't shake it off.

Somehow, by the grace of God, we come away with a win. The boys played their asses off and stepped up when I couldn't. And I let them know that when we get back to the locker room.

McKinley slings his arm around me. "It's okay, Krum. We all have our off days. No one's perfect, not even you."

I shake my head. "I let you down."

"Hey, enough of that." Jason nudges me with his elbow. "It's one game, and we still won. Don't beat yourself up about it. Go home and get some rest. Tomorrow's a new day."

Those are the same words I'd offer a teammate. I'm just not used to being on the receiving end of them.

After I shower, I hop on my bike and head home, eager to see my favorite curly-headed girl.

Still, thoughts plague me while I ride.

Get married or lose the villa. It doesn't seem fair or logical.

Adding insult to injury, a beautiful woman didn't even want to wear my jersey tonight. And it stings a little more than I'd care to admit. Hundreds of people wear my name across their jerseys all across the country, but not one of them is ever truly there for me.

No one to love me.

No one to claim me.

I belong to no one.

6

AARYA

"Remind me why I let you convince me to do this?"

Cassidy grabs onto my elbow as my arms flail. "Because it's for a good cause."

"Well, I'm going to need someone to raise money for *my* cause when I bust my ass and end up in the hospital."

Cassidy laughs as I steady myself. "Just hold onto the boards until you get your bearings."

For some reason unbeknownst to me, I laced up a pair of stiff-ass rental ice skates to attend a child's birthday party.

Granted, said child was being bullied at school until Trenton got wind of it, and showed up at his school to invite him to the ice-skating rink so they could play hockey together with the entire team.

Little Toby's story *may* have warmed my cold, black heart a little.

My feet slide out from under me and my body jerks awkwardly until I grasp onto the boards for support.

Cassidy skates around with Trenton for a bit, while I cling to the perimeter of the rink, my legs wobbling like a newborn giraffe.

"I take it this is your first time skating?"

My shoulders jump at the sound of the unfamiliar voice behind me. I grimace as I twist around to make eye-contact with the stranger. "No, I'm actually one of the professional athletes. Can't you tell?"

The man chuckles as he holds out his hand, palm facing up. "Come on, let me help you. I'm Mr. Sykes, Toby's teacher."

"I would take your hand, but I'm too afraid to let go of the boards."

He slips his right hand around my waist, coaxing my left hand into his. "There you go. You can do it."

I shift, trying to put some space between us without falling to my icy death. "Shouldn't you be helping the kids?"

"You seemed like you needed more help."

I huff out a laugh. "Awesome."

"And if I'm being honest, you're beautiful. So, I guess my reason for skating over to you is a selfish one."

"You're sweet." I side-eye him. "Not my type, but sweet."

Mr. Sykes raises his eyebrows. "It's the teacher khakis, isn't it?"

I scrunch my nose. "It's the elbow patches on your jacket, but the khakis aren't doing you any favors."

He nods as he laughs. "I love your honesty. I—"

His words are cut off as a giant man cuts across the ice, headed directly toward us, and skates to a stop, spraying ice onto Mr. Sykes' pants.

I arch a brow at him.

I haven't spoken to Alexander since jersey-gate last week. When Cassidy saw me wearing his jersey, she filled me in on what it really meant...

"WAIT A SECOND—WHOSE jersey are you wearing?" Cassidy asks.

I shrug like it's nothing. "I'm showing my support for Krum Cake."

Her eyebrows jump. "Since when?"

"Since he stopped by my gallery last night and dropped off his jersey."

"Oh, he just stopped by to give you his jersey?"

I flip my hair over my shoulder and avert my eyes. "Yeah, he came by the gallery."

"Why would he give you his jersey?"

"I don't know. Geez, what's with the Spanish Inquisition?"

She coughs out an incredulous laugh. "Oh my god."

"What?"

"You like him."

I scrunch my nose. "I don't like him. I barely know him."

"Says the woman wearing his jersey."

I lift my chin. "It looks cute on me. That's all."

"And I'm sure it's going to be on his floor later."

I roll my eyes. "It's just a jersey."

"It's never just a jersey. He gave it to you because he wants to see you with his name sprawled across your back."

I pause. "But he wants me to show my support for the team."

She shakes her head. "Think about it, girl."

"Oh, hell no." I tear the jersey up over my head and stuff it into my purse. "I'm not someone's property. I don't need him to impart his insecure masculinity on me."

HOMEBOY WAS *PISSED* that I took off his jersey.

And I liked it.

I enjoyed seeing that side to him, catching a glimpse of the unhinged version of the respectful and composed man he's shown me thus far. I half-expected him to show up at the gallery again, demanding to know why I took off his jersey.

Mr. Sykes sputters. "You're Alexander Krum. Wow, I'm a huge fan." He completely lets me go and holds out his hand to shake Alexander's large one—and I yelp as my legs fly out from under me.

In a flash, Alexander catches me before I hit the ice. He hauls my body against his, pulling me close as he wraps his arm around me. "Easy, spitfire. I've got you."

I clutch his black hoodie in my fists, not because it feels so damn good being pressed against him but because I'm afraid for my safety. The ice looks very cold and hard, and I don't want my head bouncing off of it.

God, this man smells good.

"Thanks for bringing her to me," Alexander says, shaking Mr. Sykes' hand. "I think some of the kids were looking for you over there."

Mr. Sykes clears his throat, catching the hint. "Yes, of course. It was nice meeting you both."

I smack Alexander's chest as the poor teacher skates away. "That was rude."

"You looked like you were uncomfortable. He had his hands on you."

"Much like your hands are on me right now."

He gazes down at me. "Are you uncomfortable?"

I roll my eyes to mask the way my body reacts when this man touches me. "Just get me to the sideline or whatever you people call it in hockey. I think I'm done skating for the day."

"Nah, I'm gonna teach you to not be afraid on the ice." He swivels to face me and takes both of my hands in his. "I won't let you fall. You can trust me."

"I'm not athletic. You're going to be disappointed."

"Disappointed by you?" He smiles. "Never."

Heat creeps into my cheeks, but my nerves take over as he starts to skate backward, pulling me with him. My ankles wobble and I grip his hands like the lifelines they are.

"Besides, I was doing Mr. Sykes a favor," he says. "He wouldn't have known how to handle a woman like you."

"Didn't expect you to be the jealous type." I smirk. "Though I kind of liked seeing you the way you were at the game last week."

"That was..." His entire demeanor changes as he shakes his head. "You can give the jersey back if you don't want it. Figure you won't want to keep it since you couldn't stand wearing it for more than five minutes at the game."

There's a hint of disappointment in his voice, and a dejected, faraway look in his eyes.

Shit. Is he actually hurt by this?

I tip my head. "Cassidy said wearing someone's jersey is how an athlete claims you. And I'm not interested in being claimed."

He grunts. "It's actually the other way around."

"What do you mean?"

"It's a way for *you* to claim the athlete. Wearing his name, donning his number like you're proud to represent him. It's nice to know someone out there in the stands is there specifically for you."

My stomach drops. I shouldn't care what this guy thinks. Hurting a man's feelings is my favorite pastime. But this man hasn't been a total dick, and he genuinely looks like he's upset about this. He was genuinely excited for me to wear his jersey, and I stuffed it in my purse like I was ashamed of him.

"I didn't mean to make you feel like I was embarrassed of you. That's not what I was thinking."

He shakes it off like it doesn't bother him, though I can see it all over his face that it does. "I had other things on my mind that night. Normally, I can shove it down until after the game, or use it to fuel me, but I guess I let it get to me."

"What happened?"

He pulls me around the far end of the rink, glancing around as the wind rustles his thick hair. "It's...family stuff."

"Ah, good old family trauma." I chuckle. "Wanna talk about it?"

"You'll think it's crazy."

I snort. "I've seen my fair share of crazy."

"Not like this."

"Try me."

He sucks in a deep breath before blurting it all out. "My parents owned a villa in Italy, and when they died, they left it to me. I love that house. I vacationed there my whole childhood, and I always envisioned having my own family one day to make memories with there like I did when I was a kid. But I just found out that my evil grandfather holds the title, and if I don't get married before my thirtieth birthday, I'll lose the house."

My skates knock into each other as I jerk to a stop. "What the fuck?"

"Told you it was crazy." He huffs out a sardonic laugh. "There are a few other hoops I have to jump through, but none of them are as insane and archaic as the marriage thing. I don't have a girlfriend, let alone a wife, but if I don't find one soon, then I'm going to lose the house, which is ridiculously unfair and completely ludicrous. I turn thirty in less than eleven months."

"This villa is that important to you?"

"That villa is all I have left of my parents. When I'm there, I feel connected to them. I can't lose it."

Sadness pricks at my heart. "When did your parents pass?"

"When I was sixteen. They were riding around Italy on my dad's motorcycle, and a drunk driver hit them. Killed them on impact."

My eyes widen. "Shit, I'm sorry."

Alexander tugs on my hands and continues to pull me around the rink. "You're doing good. Now try putting one leg in front of the other, kind of like you're walking, but glide instead."

I'm a little unsteady at first, but I'm able to do as he says.

"Why would your grandfather try to take the house away from you if he knows how much it means to you?" I ask.

"Because he's a piece of shit."

I grunt. "Clearly."

"He hated that my mother married someone he didn't approve of, and when I was born, he never accepted me as his family."

I can relate to that, more than he realizes. I don't normally share my family history with anyone, but for some reason it comes bubbling out of me.

"My father didn't want to accept me either. He broke up with my mom when she told him she was pregnant with me, so I didn't even get to meet him." I let out a bitter laugh. "Turns out he was married to someone else with a real family of his own the whole time."

Alexander frowns. "I'm sorry."

I hike a shoulder. "It's their loss. You and I are two bomb-ass people and they're missing out. Plus, your grandfather is almost dead so, he's about to miss out on everything in the general sense anyway."

One corner of his mouth ticks up.

"And I'm sure you have women lined up at your door to date you. Finding a woman to fall in love with you shouldn't be too hard."

His eyes meet mine, sadness swirling in their dark depths. "Most women only want to date me to say they're dating a pro hockey player."

"Yeah, I guess that's a hard thing to deal with."

He heaves a long sigh. "So now, I don't know what I'm going to do. But I have until I turn thirty to do it."

"You should just do what Cass and Trenton were doing and hire someone to fake marry you."

Alexander hits me with a blank stare. "What?"

My eyes widen and I clamp my hand over my mouth.

Oh, fuck.

I wasn't supposed to say that.

"What are you talking about?" he asks again.

"Nothing." I shake my head. "Nothing. I... I didn't say anything."

He pulls me over to the side of the rink, skating to a stop. "You said something about Trenton hiring someone...to do what?"

I grimace and my shoulders droop. "You have to swear you won't tell them that I told you. It was supposed to be a secret."

He glances across the ice to where Cassidy and Trenton are helping Toby take shots at the goal. "I won't say a word."

I run my hand through my hair and let out a frustrated sigh. "When Trenton got traded to the Goldfinches, Celeste thought it would be good for his image if he pretended to date Cassidy. You know, show the world that he's over the drama with his cheating ex and his old teammates. So, for the first few months of their relationship, it was all fake."

Alexander's eyes bounce between mine like he can't believe what he's hearing. "How does one pretend to date someone?"

I shrug. "Celebrities do it all the time for publicity reasons. They'd go on dates and get photographed together. Boom, the world thinks they're dating."

"Did Cassidy get paid to do that?"

I chew on my bottom lip to stop myself from laughing. "Oh, she got paid in a different way."

He arches a brow. "Tell me."

I lower my voice, making sure there aren't any children around us. "She used him as her sex muse for the romance book she recently published. She'd send him ideas and he'd act it out with her so she could write about it."

Alexander rubs his jaw as he fights a smile. "Not a bad deal for him."

"Nope. And now look at them. They're so in love, it makes me sick."

"Damn, I had no idea."

"Maybe you should talk to Celeste and see if she can find you someone who'd be interested in marrying you to help you keep the villa."

He shakes his head. "It'd have to be someone I could trust. I can't do something like that with a stranger."

I hike a shoulder. "It's worth a shot. And who knows? Maybe you'll fall in love with her the same way Trenton and Cassidy did."

"Falling in love isn't as easy as you're making it sound."

"It wouldn't be worth it if it were easy. Isn't that what they say about love?"

His eyebrows hit his hairline. "That sounded awfully romantic coming from you."

I roll my eyes. "Relax, I read that on a greeting card once or something."

He grins. "Uh-huh. I think you've got a big heart underneath all that sass. But don't worry, I won't tell anybody."

A small smile breaks free in spite of myself. "Good. I need to keep my street cred."

7

ALEXANDER

"All right, boys. Let *The Very Manly Book Club* meeting commence."

I scrunch my nose. "*The Very Manly Book Club?*"

"We needed a name," McKinley says.

"That's *not* going to be the name of our book club." I hold up my hand. "And who made you the president?"

"I did." McKinley puffs out his chest. "You can be the team captain on the ice, and I'll be the captain of our smut books."

Jason nudges him with his elbow. "You have to read more than just the sex scenes in order to be the president of our club."

Trenton chuckles from the row behind us. "You *did* read more than just the sex scenes, right?"

McKinley scoffs. "Of course I did."

Jason arches a brow. "What was the main character's name?"

McKinley flashes a triumphant grin. "Scarlett."

"Nice job, Mac." Trenton rubs his palms together. "All right, so what did you guys think about the book?"

Trenton is our new goalie. He got traded from his Seattle team after his fiancée cheated on him with one of his teammates. With us, he doesn't have to worry about that kind of disgraceful behavior. The Goldfinches are our family, and we'd never do anything to hurt our brothers.

"What I want to know is: What did *you* think of the fact that your girlfriend wrote a book about four dudes getting with one chick?" McKinley waggles his eyebrows as he gestures between the four of us. "Because it sounds like she's hinting at something here."

Jason punches McKinley in the arm since he's sitting closest to him. "Focus on the book, dipshit."

"I think this was Cassidy's best writing yet," I say. "She made a foursome believable. I was fully invested in each of their relationships."

Jason's eyes narrow. "What do you mean *she made it believable?*"

I hike a shoulder. "It's not like that stuff would happen in real life, multiple partners like that."

"It could." Jason averts his eyes as he flips through the pages of the book in his lap. "It's not talked about as openly as monogamous relationships, but it's out there."

"Mormons are polygamous," McKinley says.

"That was back in the nineteenth century." I pinch the bridge of my nose, like I often do when talking to McKinley about history. "Polygamy isn't allowed anymore, and most Mormons don't still practice it."

Trenton nods. "I think that's why these 'why choose' books are so popular. It's a taboo subject that you don't see every day."

"They're popular because they're hot as fuck." McKinley points to his pants. "I had a boner the entire time I read this book. I had to stop and jerk off, like, every chapter."

Coach turns around from the front seat of the bus. "Something you should keep to yourself, Mac."

Several of our teammates clap and cheer in agreement.

McKinley coughs out a laugh. "Oh, come on. Don't act like you guys are any better than me. Reading these romance books is the equivalent of watching porn."

"Cassidy gets turned on while she's writing." Trenton bites back a smile. "I love being her research for these scenes."

My chest warms seeing Trenton so happy after everything he's been through. And Cassidy is a sweetheart. Finding true love isn't easy when you're in the public eye like we are, and they give me hope that one day something might be out there for me too.

McKinley flips to a page he has tabbed in his paperback. "The camping scene in chapter twelve? That was probably my favorite sex scene in the whole book."

Jason and I nod in agreement. The group scenes were *hot*. In real life, I'm a one-woman kind of man. But when you're reading romance? Anything goes.

Trenton glances around our group. "I also liked the friendship between all the guys. How they were so open with each other, and you could tell that they really cared about each other. It's like they were a family."

"I don't know how they were okay with sharing the girl they were in love with." I grimace. "Would you be able to watch your girl go down on your best friend?"

Trenton shakes his head hard. "Hell no. I don't play well with others."

"That's because you two are possessive as fuck." McKinley laughs and then lets his head fall back against the seat, his bright-auburn curls bouncing back as he does. "I don't know. I've never been in love, but I think if you're in a tight-knit group like that, and you're all into it, and everyone trusts each other, then I might be able to get into sharing."

Trenton swings his gaze to Jason. "You're quiet over there, Stams. Could you watch Kourtney get railed by another dude?"

Jason hesitates before answering, like he's actually giving it some thought. "I think it depends on the dynamic between the people involved. Would I want to watch Kourtney go up to a random dude in a club and bang him? No. But if it was a person we were both comfortable with, and it was something she was interested in exploring together, then I don't know if I'd be able to say no to that."

That surprises me. Jason is wholly in love with his wife. They were high school sweethearts, and I can't imagine him being okay with her wanting to be that close with someone else.

Trenton's eyebrows hit his hairline. "You'd have sex with another dude if she wanted you to?"

He hikes a shoulder. "If it felt right, why not?"

"Have you done that before?" I ask.

"No, I haven't felt a connection like that with another man. But it's not something I'd be opposed to."

McKinley pats him on the shoulder. "Why do I feel like you and your wife are into some kinky shit?"

He chuckles. "It's not about kink. Kourtney and I are honest with each other about who we are and what we want. We're open-minded."

McKinley nods. "I've been with men before."

Trenton's mouth falls open. "I didn't know that."

I'm shocked listening to my friends reveal such honest pieces of themselves. I love how open-minded and inclusive our team is. That's not easy to come by, especially in the world of sports.

Jason shifts in his seat as he continues to talk. "I think it's more about the connection you have with a person than it is about their gender. So many people are stuck in thinking that they can only be attracted to one kind of person. You always hear women say things like, *He has to be tall*, or men say, *I'm not into dudes*. But if we opened our minds to the possibility of falling in love without those restrictions, imagine the kind of love we could find."

"Kind of like falling in love if we were all blindfolded," I say. "You wouldn't be able to focus on what they looked like, or the color of their skin, or what their genitals looked like. You'd have to go on how they made you feel."

"Exactly." Jason offers me a grateful smile. "Love knows no bounds. We're the ones who put restrictions on ourselves and limit ourselves."

"Love is love." McKinley nods. "I totally agree."

We all sit in silence as the bus travels down the road, a bunch of hockey players lost in our own philosophical thoughts about love and its many forms.

Until McKinley's voice breaks through the quiet. "So, about that camping scene. Have any of you ever thought about getting your dick pierced?"

Trenton cringes. "I've heard about how it can increase your pleasure, but I don't think I could go through with the initial pain."

"What about anal plugs?"

Coach whips around again. "Mac, I'm about to stick an anal plug in your mouth if you don't shut the fuck up. Take a nap or something."

We stifle our laughter so as not to upset our coach.

McKinley leans in and whispers, "Someone should try putting an anal plug in *his* ass."

Jason elbows him in the ribs again. "Don't piss him off."

"The storyline was good though." I return our attention to the book before Coach really snaps. "I was on the edge of my seat when their relationship became public and everything was falling apart."

"I loved how Scarlett was scared of what her family would think throughout the entire book, and then she was forced to face her fears and tell them," Jason says.

Trenton smiles proudly. "It was important to Cassidy to make sure Scarlett was more than just a toy being passed around. She put a lot of care into writing her character."

"She had a lot of character growth, and it was beautiful to watch." Jason lowers his voice. "I teared up during that scene when her mother told her she would love her no matter what."

Jason and I both lost our parents, and I know he must've been thinking the same thing I was while I read that scene. It made me think about all the incredible things my parents are missing out on in my life, and the moments *I'm* missing out on not having them with me. They'd be so proud if they could see the things I've accomplished, that the dreams I used to talk about actually came true.

Once the book club meeting ends, McKinley turns his attention to me. "Hey, Krum Cake. Anything new with you and Aarya?"

"Nope."

It's been months since we've spoken. I need to focus on finding someone serious—and keeping the villa in my name. I don't have time to waste on someone who doesn't want the same things I do.

"I don't know how you resisted her." McKinley sighs. "She's like a Middle Eastern goddess."

I wince at the reminder. "It doesn't matter. There's no point in spending one night with her when it won't lead to anything."

Trenton grunts. "She's like a praying mantis. She'd chew you up and spit you out the second she was done with you."

"I'd let her. She gives off dominatrix vibes." McKinley waggles his eyebrows. "Same thing goes for Trent's PR agent, Celeste. She looks like she'd make you get on your knees and crawl to her."

Jason rolls his lips between his teeth, hiding a smile, like he's in on some private joke. "I can get her to stuff a ball gag in your mouth and shut you up for a while."

McKinley flips him off, and we laugh as the two bicker.

"At this rate, I'll never find a woman to settle down with," I murmur more to myself than to my friends.

Jason's eyebrows pinch together. "You're still young, man. You've got plenty of time to fall in love. It'll happen when it's meant to happen."

"I don't have time." I shake my head and squeeze my eyes shut. "You don't understand."

The clock has been ticking over my head like a time bomb. Every day I get closer to my birthday is one day closer to losing the villa.

McKinley swings his legs into the aisle, leaning his elbows on his knees. "So, help us understand. What's going on?"

The guys watch me as I wrestle with what to say. I need to be their unwavering captain. The picture of stability. Not someone with this circus of a personal life.

But being vulnerable with them helps to lead by example. We lean on each other on and off the ice, and if I can't trust them, then they won't trust me.

"My grandfather is dying, and he changed his will to take my parents' villa away from me."

Jason's head snaps to me. "What? Why?"

"I don't know. Just another way to fuck me over." I scrub a hand over my jaw. "I always imagined I'd retire there. Bring my wife and kids there for summer vacation. But my grandfather put a stipulation into his will that if I'm not married by the time I turn thirty, I won't be able to inherit it."

Trenton's head jerks back. "That's ridiculous."

I nod. "You guys know I want to find someone and fall in love. But now it feels like I have limited time, and if I don't find it, then I lose the house."

"Can you fight it?" Jason asks. "If your parents left the villa to you, isn't there anything you can do to reverse his changes?"

"Nope." I glance out the window at the trees blurring together as we pass them by. "My grandfather has major money and connections, and the will is iron-clad."

"Damn, that sucks," McKinley says.

"You could always hire someone to pose as your fake wife."

All three of our heads turn to Trenton.

He glances toward the front of the bus and gestures for us to be quiet with his finger against his lips. "That's what Cassidy and I did in the beginning. She posed as my girlfriend for the media."

"What?" McKinley shouts.

"Shh, you idiot," Jason whisper-yells. He leans closer to Trenton. "Are you saying Cassidy isn't really your girlfriend?"

McKinley's mouth flaps open. "But you're getting married in a few months."

I'd be just as shocked as they are if Aarya hadn't spilled the secret to me at the skating rink.

"We are getting married." Trenton's gaze drops to his hands in his lap. "Everything between us is real now, but we didn't start out that way."

I rest my forearms on my knees, mimicking the other guys as we huddle together in the aisle so no one else hears us. "How did it start?"

"Celeste thought it was a good idea to get some good PR surrounding me after the bullshit with my old team. So, when those paparazzi pictures surfaced of Cassidy and me in our parking garage, it seemed like the perfect opportunity. Celeste wrote up a contract, had Cassidy and Aarya sign an NDA. Cassidy wouldn't sign the NDA without being able to tell her best friend what was going on."

"She told *her* best friend, but you didn't want to tell us," McKinley mutters.

"I'm sorry, Mac." Trenton looks around the group, making eye-contact with each of us. "I'm sorry for lying. It just... sounded so silly, faking a relationship, as if I couldn't find someone to love me for real. I guess I was embarrassed."

"You have nothing to apologize for," I say. "We all do what we think is best at the time. Just know that we're your friends and you can tell us anything. We will *always* be here for you."

The guys take turns asking questions about Trenton's arrangement, but the possibilities continue to zoom through my head at warp speed like they have from the moment Aarya told me about this.

I can't invite a woman into my world, my home, my private life. My daughter's little bubble has to stay safe. Something like this could jeopardize everything I've been working so hard for.

"So, what do you think, Krum?" Trenton snaps me out of my thoughts. "Maybe Celeste can set you up with something similar to make sure you get to keep the villa."

I rub the back of my neck. "I don't know, man. Where would I even find a woman willing to do something like that?"

"Why not Aarya?" McKinley asks. "You know she's attracted to you."

"And Cassidy has known her for years, so she's not some random person off the street," Trenton adds.

"Yeah, but she doesn't do relationships. I couldn't even get her to wear my name on her jersey, let alone take it as her last name. What's going to make her want to pretend to be married?"

Trenton grins like he already knows the answer. "You just have to give her some incentive."

Money. She does need the money—she said so herself. If I offered her a good amount...

"No." I shake my head hard as if to shake the idea right out of my head. "I can't. It's more complicated than that."

"How so?" Jason asks.

I glance around the group, not missing McKinley's knowing stare.

Trenton shared something personal with us. I should be able to do the same. I should be surrounding Giuliana with love, not hiding her from the people who are important to me.

I blow out a long breath through my lips. "I have a daughter."

The entire bus turns around in their seats, including Coach. It's pin-drop silent as I find the words to explain why I've kept this from the guys for so long.

"She's three now. Her name is Giuliana." A smile tugs at the corners of my mouth. "She's the best thing that's ever happened to me."

"Three." Jason pauses like he's trying to make sense of it all. "Why did you wait so long to tell us?"

"I've been trying to keep her away from the spotlight. You know how the paparazzi can get. That's not the kind of life she deserves to grow up in."

"That I get," he says. "But what about *us*? You could've told us. We would've kept that secret for you."

I nod. "I know you would've. It's hard to put it into words. Maybe a part of me felt embarrassed—not of her, but of the fact that I had a careless accident with a one-night-stand. That her mother didn't want to stick around to be a part of her life."

"Fuck her," McKinley blurts out. "She doesn't know what she's missing out on. That is for *her* to be embarrassed about."

Coach nods. "We are a family, Krum. And your little girl is a part of our family now."

Emotion swells in my throat. "Thanks, Coach."

Trenton smiles. "We can't wait to meet her, man."

And then I smile too. Because regardless of whatever shit my grandfather threw my way, I know everything will work out in the end. I have my team, my friends, and my baby girl.

And that's all that matters at the end of the day.

8

ALEXANDER

"Why can't I come to the wedding?"

I ruffle Giuliana's curls. "Because there aren't going to be any other kids there. You'll be bored, and up way past your bedtime."

Her bottom lip juts out as she bounces onto my bed. "No fair. I'm four now. I can stay up later."

I adjust the tie around my neck, double-checking it in the mirror before I sit down beside my daughter. "I'm sorry, baby. But you're going to have so much fun with Annie tonight. And I'll be back in time for breakfast tomorrow."

"Can you bring home a rainbow bagel for me?"

"Of course."

She climbs onto my lap and I wrap my arms around her, breathing in her sweet scent. "You still smell like you did when you were a baby, you know that?"

She rests her head on my shoulder. "I don't remember being a baby."

"No, we don't really have memories from when we're that young."

She lifts her head and brings her big round eyes to meet mine. "Are you going to have a wedding one day like Uncle Trenton?"

Unease twists my gut. "I'd like to."

"So why don't you get married then?"

"Because I have to find someone to love first."

"Well, are you looking?"

I chuckle and press my lips to her forehead. "Sometimes. But I'm busy with hockey and being your dad. If it's meant to be, then the right person will find me."

She furrows her brows. "That's not how it works, Daddy. You have to go find her. The prince always has to go on an adventure and that's where he meets the princess."

"You think I need to go on an adventure?"

She nods. "You can bring Ellie and me as your sidekicks. Like Olaf and Sven."

I lift her in my arms as I rise from the mattress, and walk into the hallway. "And what kind of adventure should we go on?"

"I don't know. I'm just a kid. You need to figure that part out yourself."

I laugh, deep and loud, the way this girl always makes me laugh. "Okay, I'll think about it."

"You *need* a princess, Daddy."

"You're the only princess I need, baby." I smack another kiss to her cheek before setting her down on the kitchen counter. "Now, let's go over the rules while I'm gone."

Giuliana's shoulders droop. "No chocolate before lunch, and Annie is the boss."

I nod. "Just because you're cute doesn't mean you get to be in charge. Respect the grown-ups. You got me?"

"Yes, Daddy."

Annie lifts Giuliana from the counter. "Doesn't Daddy look handsome all dressed-up?"

My girl nods. "Just like a prince."

I arch a brow. "Maybe lay off the Disney movies for a while. Watch a documentary or something."

Annie laughs. "Roger that."

"I love you, baby. Be good and have fun." I shoot Annie a wink as I grab my wallet and keys off the counter. "Thanks, Annie. Call me if you need anything."

"We'll be fine," she calls after me.

Guilt pricks at me like it always does whenever I go somewhere without my daughter. I make a mental note to take her somewhere fancy where she can get dressed up like a princess for a night.

Since I told the team about Giuliana, they've embraced her with open arms. And she's practically obsessed with her new uncles. She asks to see them almost every night for dinner, and begs me to FaceTime each of them at bedtime. Another wave of guilt rushes over me as I think about how long I've deprived her of having a bigger family.

By the time I get to the wedding venue, I've turned off *Dad Mode* and turned on *Best Man Mode.*

I was honored that Trenton would ask me to stand beside him on his wedding day. He went through so much losing his best friend and teammates after the scandal on his former team, and it means a lot to know that he trusts me as his best friend now.

A sleek black limousine pulls up to the front as I approach the building. The back door swings open and a gold stiletto steps out. My eyes travel up the ankle attached to it, followed by the bare leg revealed through a high slit in an emerald-green dress.

My heart nearly stops as Aarya stands from the vehicle, smoothing her hands over the silky material hugging her curves. Her long, dark hair cascades over one shoulder, leaving the other bare, begging to be kissed and licked and bitten. The front of the dress twists in the middle of her breasts, full and luscious, yet another place I can't help but imagine my mouth venturing to. Her brown skin shimmers in what's left of the sunlight as it sets on the horizon, illuminating her like the goddess she is.

I haven't seen her since I told her about my marriage predicament. Trenton and Cassidy have been busy with wedding planning, and it's been a while since we've all gotten together for a fun night out. I thought I'd be fine seeing her after all this time, that my body wouldn't have the same reaction to her as it once did. But I'm a statue watching her from afar while she helps Cassidy out of the limo, gathering the train of her dress so it doesn't hit the ground.

"You got a little drool there, bud." McKinley steps beside me and hands me his handkerchief. "Right there on your lip."

I snap out of my daze and turn to face him. "I almost forgot how beautiful she is."

He nods, glancing over my shoulder and raking his eyes over her. "And you're the lucky bastard who gets to be her partner tonight."

I shake my head. "It's going to be a long night."

"THE BRIDE and groom would like to ask the bridal party to join them on the dance floor."

I suck in a deep breath. I managed to keep my staring to a minimum during the ceremony, doing my damndest to focus on my Best Man duties. But now that the reception has commenced, all bets are off. Trenton and Cassidy are occupied, as are the rest of the guests. Each of my teammates have their plus ones, and Aarya and I are the only ones without dates. It's inevitable that we'll be spending some time together.

"You ready to dance, Big Man?" Aarya downs the remainder of the champagne in her glass before she stands and holds out her elbow, waiting for me to take it and lead her onto the dance floor.

"Of course." I smirk as I rise and link our elbows together. "I've been waiting for this moment all day."

She quirks a brow as I spin her in a circle. "And why's that?"

"So that I can do this." I wrap my arms around her waist and pull her against me, relishing in the feel of her soft curves. "I've been dying to dance with the most beautiful woman in the room."

She shakes her head on a laugh as if she doesn't believe me, and clasps her hands at the back of my neck.

"You look absolutely exquisite, Aarya."

A deep-flush crawls into her cheeks. "You clean up pretty well yourself, Sponge Cake."

"You know, eventually you're going to run out of cakes to call me."

She hikes a shoulder. "I Googled ideas leading up to the wedding, so I should be good."

"So, what you're saying is, you've been thinking about me."

"Whatever helps you sleep at night." Her eyes roll. "How's the search going, by the way? Any luck finding a wife?"

"No." My mood sours at the reminder. "Not that I've been trying. The whole idea of paying someone to marry me sounds insane. And how much would I even offer for something like that? One-hundred-thousand dollars should suffice, but what if she wants more? How do I put a limit on that?"

She chokes and coughs. "I'm sorry, what?"

"I mean, I can do more if you think that's not enough."

"More? That's a lot of money." She shakes her head on a laugh. "Shit, I'd marry you for one-hundred-thousand dollars."

I'm reminded of the fact that Aarya is saving up for her own gallery, and then the idea smacks me in the head like an obvious sign I didn't see coming.

Thoughts race through my head. We're both attracted to each other. It'd be so easy to parade her around town and send the message to my grandfather's lawyer that I'm officially on my way to owning the villa. Plus, she's in my friend group, so it'd be a hell of a lot easier to trust her.

I've been so worried about finding someone to pose as my wife; someone I know; someone that could help me pull this off. Yet maybe she's been in front of me this whole time.

I arch a brow. "You would?"

"That's not what I meant. For a hundred grand, I'm sure a lot of people would be interested."

"I'm not talking about other people." I dip my head and bring my lips closer to her ear. "I'm talking about you."

She cranes her neck to tilt her head and look up into my eyes. "I don't think you could handle being my husband. I need someone who can keep his wife satisfied."

The champagne on her breath mixes with her sweet vanilla scent, making an intoxicating combination for my senses.

"I'm not paying someone to sleep with me."

"No, but don't you think your wife would want to? How long can you expect a woman to pretend to be in a committed relationship with you and not fulfill her needs?"

This isn't something I've thought of.

And she's not wrong.

The song ends before I can explore this new level of anxiety further, and blaring bass pumps through the speakers as the DJ gets the party started.

"Thanks for the dance, Big Man." Aarya reaches up and places a chaste kiss on my cheek before scurrying off to dance with Cassidy and their friends.

I shove away my thoughts as I head to the bar to grab a beer and join Trenton and the rest of the guys back on the dance floor. This night isn't about me, and as the Best Man, I need to make sure that the groom is well-taken care of.

I replace Trenton's empty bottle with a full one before slapping him on the back. "How does it feel to be a married man?"

His smile consumes his entire face, his eyes sparking as he gazes at his wife in the middle of her friends several feet away. "Fucking amazing."

"I'm happy for you, man. You deserve this."

He wraps his arms around me in a bear hug. "Thanks, Krum Cake. You're my best friend, you know that?"

"Always got your back."

"And I've got yours." He grips my shoulder as he pulls back to look at me. "You and Giuliana."

Warmth blankets my chest, squeezing my heart. "I appreciate that."

McKinley dances over to us, his auburn curls bouncing as his hips shake. "Why are you standing all the way over here? Go dance with your wife."

"Just having a heart-to-heart with my brother here." Trenton wraps one arm around my shoulders and the other around McKinley. "Hey, Stamos! Get over here."

Jason pries himself away from his wife and heads over to us, closing off our huddle. "What's up?"

"I just want to say thank you for being here for me, and not just tonight. I really love you guys."

Jason leans closer to me. "How many beers has he had so far?"

I stifle a chuckle. "Not enough to be having this talk right now."

"Hey." Trenton cuts us off. "I'm not drunk, but it's my wedding night and I'm allowed to be all up in my feels."

"Amen to that." McKinley breaks away first and drags him onto the dance floor. "Let's party, bro. Cassidy has some hot friends I need you to introduce me to."

"You okay?"

Aarya waves me away, squinting one eye as she tries to clasp her shoe strap around her ankle. "I've got this."

By the looks of her on the floor in the empty ballroom, and knowing how much she's had to drink tonight, she most certainly doesn't got this.

I crouch down on the floor beside her. "You sure about that? Because your shoe is on the wrong foot."

She leans back and slumps against the wall. "Fuck it. I don't need shoes."

"Come on." I slide my hands around her and lift her into my arms, scooping up her shoes with me as I stand. "I've got you."

Immediately, her arms wrap around the back of my neck and she rests her head on my shoulder, nuzzling against the crook of my neck.

She's not blackout drunk, but I'm not confident she'd make it to her room without taking a tumble. I'll sleep better knowing she's safe in her bed.

I carry her to the elevators in the lobby, and step inside the first empty one that opens.

"You smell good," she slurs.

The elevator door closes and I glance at the buttons on the panel. "What floor are you on?"

"Seven-oh-seven. Or maybe it's seven-oh-eight. The key is in my purse." She pauses and lifts her head. "Where's my purse?"

"I don't know. I didn't see it with you while you were attempting to get your shoes on."

She groans and lets her head fall back against my shoulder, muttering something incoherent.

"I'll look for it for you, don't worry. Let's just get you to bed first." I slap the button for the eleventh floor.

"How am I getting to bed if I don't have my key?"

"You'll sleep in my room."

She hums against my neck, sending a delicious tingle down my spine. "You going to sleep with me after all, Big Man?"

I bite back a smile. "While you're drunk? Never."

"You're better than me. I'd totally take advantage of you if you were drunk."

"I don't doubt that."

The door slides open and I carry Aarya down the hall to my suite.

Her head pops up as I step inside. "Your room is a hell of a lot nicer than mine."

"Then I guess it's a good thing you lost your room key." I lower her onto the foot of the bed. "Let me get you something comfortable to change into, and then I'll grab a water bottle and some Tylenol from the lobby while I look for your purse."

She groans as she struggles with the zipper behind her back. "Just get me out of this dress."

I toss a pair of my sweats and a T-shirt onto the bed beside her, then pull her up until she's standing in front of me. She shuffles in a circle and I tug the zipper down her spine until it reaches her tailbone, exposing her smooth skin. My fingers tremble as I let them linger there, ghosting my knuckles along the dip of her lower back. She shivers under my touch, pushing her ass back against me. Then she pulls down the top of her strapless dress, shimmying it down past her waist until it pools at her feet.

She's standing before me in nothing but a black satin bra and a matching thong.

Our eyes catch in the mirror across the room, and she lets her head fall back against my chest, every part of her bare skin pressed against my body as she watches me, waiting for me in silent invitation.

"You're flawless," I whisper, my lips brushing against the cusp of her ear. "Absolutely stunning."

She pushes her ass against my growing erection over my slacks. "I want you. And you want me too."

I grip her shoulders and step back, needing to put distance between us.

She pouts with an adorable whine. "Why do you keep pushing me away?"

I spin her around and cup her face so she's looking into my eyes. "Aarya, you have no idea how much I want to give in to you. And you have no idea how difficult it is to restrain myself whenever I'm around you, because the only thing I can think about is tasting your lips, and all the ways I wish I could make you come."

Her eyes widen and her lips part.

"But I need something more. More than just one night of passion. I want to be part of something bigger, something meaningful. And I'd love to see if we could have something like that, but you've made it clear that you only want one night from me." I shake my head. "I'm worth more than one night, and I think you are too. I just wish you could realize that."

Her eyes turn glossy as she blinks up at me. "Marry me."

My throat goes dry. "What?"

She's drunk. There's no way she just said—

"You need someone to marry, and I need a hundred thousand in my bank account. Why don't you fake marry me instead of a stranger?"

"I...you can't."

"You've done nothing but reject me since the day we met. I'm putting myself in a vulnerable position right now, so please don't make me regret it because I won't beg for this more than once." She takes my hands and squeezes them. "We can help each other."

On one hand, it sounds perfect. But then Giuliana's innocent face fills my mind. How would someone like Aarya fit into my home? Could I really bring her into my daughter's life, knowing it's all a lie? I thought this was what I wanted, but now that it's real, I'm not so sure this is a good idea.

I tug Aarya into me, engulfing her in a sincere hug. "You've had a lot to drink. Why don't you sleep on it, and we'll talk about it in the morning."

"Fine, but I already told you: I'm not that drunk." She presses her palm against my chest and pushes out of my hold. "Also, you should know that I don't like hugs."

I chuckle. "Just think about it, please. For me."

"Okay, Big Man. We'll talk in the morning."

I slip my T-shirt over her head, and she pulls out her strapless bra from underneath before tossing it onto the floor. Then she crawls into bed, forgoing the sweatpants, and tucks her legs under the covers.

I lean over and examine her hair. "Let me take these pins out of your hair."

"You don't have to do that."

"Let me. You'll have a headache if you sleep in them."

I don't tell her how I know, that Giuliana complains about her head hurting if she falls asleep with clips in her hair. I lower myself onto the mattress beside her and pull out each bobby pin one by one, setting them down on the nightstand beside her. Then I massage her scalp, shaking out her hair to relieve the pressure.

"God, you have the best hands," she murmurs.

I let out a small chuckle. "Let me go find your purse, and then you need to drink some water."

"Forget the purse." She tugs my arm. "Snuggle me."

With those big brown eyes looking up at me, there's not much I'd say no to.

"The spitfire likes to snuggle?"

She grunts. "Don't tell anyone."

"Your secret is safe with me."

I climb onto the bed behind her and pull her body close, wrapping my arm around her midsection. She fits perfectly against me, and I let out a long breath as she groans, mumbling nonsensical things into the pillow.

I feel her body drift off to sleep within seconds, and all I can think in the stillness of the room is...

This could be the perfect solution, or an absolute disaster.

9

AARYA

I GROAN AS I PEEL MY EYES OPEN. "WHY IS IT SO BRIGHT IN here?"

"Because it's noon."

I jump at the sound of Celeste's voice beside me. "What are you doing here? Oh my God. Did we...? Shit. How drunk *was* I last night?"

She laughs. "Girl, if we had sex last night, you'd remember it. I'm phenomenal in bed."

I push myself up until I'm propped against the headboard. "Where's Alex?"

"He had to leave early this morning, but he didn't want to leave you alone." She shrugs. "So, you're stuck with me."

"I'm relieved it's you, honestly." I cover my face with both hands. "I don't know if I could face him after last night."

She sits up on her knees and gasps. "Did you two finally fuck?"

"No," I whine. "But I'm pretty sure I begged him to."

She cringes. "Ew."

I bury my face under a pillow. "I know!"

"Well, it obviously didn't deter him because he left you an adorable note on your nightstand."

I jump up and clutch my head. "Whoa. Too fast."

"Easy, champ. Drink the water with the Tylenol he left you."

I slip the pills into my mouth and wash them down with several gulps of water. Then I lift the notepad and run my finger over the small, neat printed letters on the page.

Good Morning, spitfire...

Sorry I couldn't be there when you woke up, but I wasn't sure how much sleep you'd need to recover after last night (or if you'd want me in your space). You have the room for as long as you need it. Hoping you remember what we talked about last night. Here's my number when you're ready to talk. No pressure.

—Insert whatever baked good nickname you come up with here

I slump back against the headboard and heave a long sigh.

"He's a gentle giant," Celeste says quietly.

"That he is." *A gentle, caring, respectful giant.* "I...think I proposed to him last night."

"I heard."

My eyebrows lift. "He told you?"

"More like he asked me to help if you had any questions."

"This is insane right?" I lift my hand and let it drop on the comforter. "Pretending to marry someone for money."

Celeste turns to face me and crisscrosses her legs. "People enter into arranged marriages all the time. It's not as strange as you think."

"Arranged marriage." I huff out a laugh. "Two words I never thought I'd be contemplating."

"Let me tell you what I know, and maybe it'll help you make your decision. If you want to make some good money, this is an easy deal. And the man in question? He's one of the best guys I know. There is no doubt that you'd have everything you could ever want and need while you're married to him. He'd make sure you were well taken care of, and never for a second expect anything in return."

I groan again. "How is this helping me make a decision?"

"Just telling you the facts, babe." Celeste squeezes my knee. "You just have to decide if one-hundred-thousand dollars is worth being tied down. Because even though you're not marrying for love, you have to be all in. You have to make it look legit—which means playing the part of the committed wife. And I know that's not something you're into."

I frown. "I just...I don't know if I can do this. I never saw myself as a wife."

"Maybe that's because you haven't met the right person yet. Or maybe you're not into marriage, and that's okay too."

"Are you?"

"I never say never to anything in life. You don't know where life will take you, or how you'll grow and change, or who you'll meet."

I nod, letting Celeste's words sink in.

She nudges me with her shoulder. "Do you think you'd be able to do something like this?"

"How long would we have to be married for?"

She twirls a long strand of red hair around her index finger. "That depends on his grandfather's will. Alex's lawyer would have to take a look at the details. Long enough to make it look legit, I'd guess."

Anger flares in the pit of my stomach. "What kind of person does that to his own grandson? The man is dying. Why does he care what happens to the villa?"

Celeste grunts. "My parents would sell me in exchange for a villa. Some of us have shitty families."

I raise my hand above my head. "Ditto."

"Let me guess." She takes a swig of coffee from her mug on the nightstand. "You have daddy issues. He left when you were little and now you don't trust any man you meet."

I choke out a laugh. "Spot on."

"But you've got some mommy issues in there too." She closes one eye. "I'd say she didn't handle the breakup well and dated a string of losers, who you hated."

I nod. "Impressive."

She flips her hair over her shoulder. "It's a gift."

"Enough about me. I think you need to tell me what was going on between you, Jason and his wife last night. I saw the three of you dancing together, and I've gotta be honest: It was hot."

Her pale cheeks tinge a rosy pink color as she laughs. "Cinderella doesn't help the Fairy Godmother. It's the other way around."

"Uh-huh." I side-eye her. "I've got a gift too, and it's spotting bullshit."

She flicks her eyes up to the ceiling and shakes her head. "We're just friends. We have been for a long time. They're married, and I'm the third wheel. That's how it always was, and that's how it always will be."

"Okay." I hold up my hands in surrender, not wanting to push her into talking about something this personal. "What do you say we order room service and enjoy this hockey player suite a little longer?"

"I'm in."

"So, now that you have the full story, what do you think I should do?"

My black Maine Coon cat, stretches out across my lap, offering me nothing but a big, bored yawn.

"Thanks for your help, Dash."

Celeste and I spent the afternoon stuffing our faces with warm, fluffy breakfast foods while watching Christmas movies on the giant flatscreen. But now that I'm back in my apartment, alone with my thoughts, I have to sit down and make a serious decision.

Naturally, I pick up my phone and text the group chat to procrastinate.

> Me: How does it feel to be married, Cass?

> Cassidy: No different really...

> Cassidy: But married sex is HOT!

> Cassidy: Which I hear you might be learning about soon enough

> Celeste: Oh shit. Did you decide to fake marry Krum Cake?

Me: I don't know. Still thinking about it.

Cassidy: I think you should do it.

Me: For reasons other than going on double dates with you and Trenton?

Cassidy: Absolutely. I think this could be really good for you.

Cassidy: Like in a social experiment kind of way

Me: My life is not a science project

Cassidy: I'm just saying... I think being in a relationship could be good for you.

Cassidy: Plus, how could you say no to Alexander? He's such a good guy.

Celeste: I second that. He has those puppy dog eyes.

Celeste: And have you seen the badunkadunk on him?

Cassidy: True. It's nice.

Cassidy: Trenton's is nicer though

Cassidy: Sorry, that was Trenton 😬

Me: Eww tell your husband to get out of our group chat

Cassidy: Anyway, I know you could use the money, so it's a win-win.

Me: Well I'm not a dog person so his eyes have no effect on me

Me: And yes, he has a dump truck for sure

Me: He's a biker boy AND a hockey player... doesn't seem fair

Celeste: How are you not a dog person? They're literally the best animal ever.

Me: I can name 3 other animals that are cooler than a dog

Celeste: Go.

Me: Dolphin. Elephant. Lion.

Me: Boom.

Cassidy: But you can't have any of those animals as pets

Me: WHOSE SIDE ARE YOU ON?!

Cassidy: The side of any dog

Cassidy: I bet your cat still hasn't come out to greet you since you got home from work

Me: He's in my lap, thank you very much *insert picture*

Me: He's a king. He doesn't sit and fetch for me like a peasant

Me: AND your opinion doesn't count. Your bird literally pecked her brother to death

Celeste: RIP Candy 🙏

Cassidy: Your cat would literally eat your decomposing body if you died

Cassidy: No loyalty

Me: He's a survivor who does what he has to do

Celeste: Let's bring it to a vote. All in favor of Aarya fake marrying Krum Cake say "I"

Celeste: I!

Cassidy: I!!!!! 🦝

Celeste: I think you already know the answer

Celeste: You might as well just text him

I let my head fall back against the couch with a groan.

The bottom line is: I'd be crazy to turn down one-hundred-thousand dollars. I think living with the regret of not doing it might be worse than doing it.

Which is why I lift my phone from the armrest and type out a text to Alexander.

Me: I have questions...

Me: But I think I'm in.

10

ALEXANDER

"Daddy, this is your best braid yet."

I smile down at my work. "I think you're right, baby."

Thank God for the girl dads of YouTube who post hair tutorials. Learning how to style Giuliana's curls was one thing, but learning how to do a French braid is something else entirely.

I spin her around so she's facing me on the bathroom counter. "Let's go through our checklist one last time. Do you have your toothbrush?"

Giuliana pops up one finger in the air. "Check."

"Do you have your pajamas?"

"Check."

"What about mini-Ellie? Did you pack her?"

"Check." Her little lips turn into a frown. "What if I miss the real Ellie? I've never slept without her before."

"I know your first sleepover is a big deal, but I think you're going to have so much fun that you won't even have time to think about real Ellie. And any time you miss her, you can squeeze the stuffed version of her."

"You promise you'll snuggle her in the big bed?"

I stick out my pinky. "I promise."

She twists her tiny finger around mine and kisses her thumb. "What are you going to do tonight, Daddy?"

"I'll be here hanging out with Ellie."

"Will you miss me while I'm gone?"

"Of course, I'm going to miss you. I always miss you when we're not together. But I'm so excited for you to have fun with your friends from school."

As much as I hate the thought of my little girl being old enough to have a sleepover at her friend's house, I'm beyond excited to have Aarya over for dinner.

My body has been buzzing with nerves since she texted me last night saying she wants to talk about the fake marriage agreement.

Have I thought about how I'm going to tell her that I have a kid? No.

Do I think Aarya will be cool with it? Also no.

But I texted Cassidy and asked for Aarya's favorite meal, so I'm hoping that my cooking can convince her to do this with me.

Annie leans against the doorframe with Giuliana's coat in her hand, and her eyebrows jump. "Wow, I think that's your best braid yet."

I puff out my chest. "Thanks. I'm getting better at it."

"Practice makes you better. Right, Daddy?"

I lift Giuliana off the counter and set her down on the tile below. "Right. There's no such thing as perfect but—"

"You can always try your best," she finishes.

Annie shakes her head on a smile. "All right, Giuls. Say goodbye to Daddy. It's time for your big girl sleepover."

"Big girl sleepover! Big girl sleepover!" she chants.

I crouch down in front of her and cup her sweet face. "Use your manners while you're there, and make sure you don't eat too much candy so you don't get a bellyache."

"I'll be the bestest girl, Daddy. You'll see. I'm gonna do so good at my big girl sleepover."

"I know you will, baby." I wrap her in my arms and hold her tight, inhaling a lungful of her sweet scent. "I love you so much."

"I love you more."

"Nope, impossible. I love you the most."

"I love you more than all the grains of sand in the entire world."

"I love you more than all the blades of grass."

"I love you to infinity."

She squeals as I lift her into my arms and hold her above my head like an airplane headed into the hallway. "To infinity and beyond!"

We let Giuliana have a moment with her dog before Annie takes her hand and leads her onto the porch.

Annie shoots me a wink. "Have fun tonight, Alexander."

My stomach clenches in a tight ball. "Will do."

Fun.

Nothing about this messed up scenario is fun.

Maybe if Aarya were coming over for an actual date, and not to discuss the large sum of money she'll be getting if she agrees to enter into a marriage of convenience with me...

But no. Thanks to my grandfather, my life can't be that simple.

I straighten up the bathroom after Annie and Giuliana leave, then vacuum Ellie's hair off every square inch of the house before making sure everything is tidy in our bedrooms. Not that I'm expecting Aarya to venture into my bedroom tonight, but she might want to check out the space she'll be living in at some point.

I pause in the doorway of Giuliana's room. Pinks and purples; Disney princesses; baby dolls and puzzles. I try to imagine Aarya having a tea party dressed in a pink tutu—because apparently, we're not allowed to dress down for tea parties in this house—but I can't picture it.

This isn't going to work. Introducing Aarya to Giuliana's world will be like forcing a square peg into a round hole.

What the hell am I doing?

Nerves swarm me like bees, stinging me everywhere and causing panic to constrict my throat.

My phone vibrates in my back pocket, and my shoulders jump. Cassidy's name lights up the screen, and I scramble to swipe my thumb across it.

"Hey, Cass. Everything okay?"

"Yeah, just checking in on you."

"Pfft. I'm fine. You don't have to check on me." I rub my sweaty palm against my jeans. "I've got everything under control here."

"You're out of breath. You just got finished anxiety cleaning your house, didn't you?"

"Yes, yes I did."

She chuckles. "It's going to be okay, dude. You've got this. You're charming and handsome and sweet and—"

Trenton's voice blares through the speaker. "And your ass is almost as nice as mine."

"In your dreams, Trent." I laugh, releasing some of the tension in my shoulders. "I'm just nervous because either way, her decision holds a lot of weight. If she says no, I'm right back where I started in jeopardy of losing the villa. If she says yes, I have to figure out how to keep her happy, protect my daughter, and convince the world that this is legit, all at the same time."

"I know it's a lot of pressure," Cassidy says. "But you have to keep reminding yourself of two things. One: You're doing this in the name of your parents, because they wanted you to have this house."

I nod. "And two?"

"Aarya is my best friend in the entire world. I've known her forever, and I wouldn't let either one of you venture into this scenario if I didn't trust that everything will work out."

I blow out a long stream of air through my lips. "I wish I shared your optimism."

"I know she doesn't seem like it, but Aarya is a big softie under all that snark. She wears her attitude like armor, but it's only to protect the big heart she has underneath it."

"That helps. Thanks, Cass."

"Text me if you need me. You got this, Krum Cake."

Thirty minutes go by after Cassidy's pep talk, and I'm feeling calmer than I was. The house is clean, Giuliana is taken care of for the night, and the food smells delicious. I've handled everything within my control, and I have to let go of whatever I can't. One step at a time. We're not walking down the aisle tomorrow. Tonight, we're just having a conversation. Two friends having a casual dinner.

I can do this.

The doorbell rings and my heart stalls out.

I can't do this.

Ellie lets out a loud bark, and I pat her head. "Quiet, girl. Don't scare her away."

Flipping the dish towel over my shoulder, I make my way to the front door and take a deep breath before swinging it open.

Aarya is in a black sweater that falls over one shoulder, accenting her brown skin and midnight hair. Dark-denim jeans hug her curves, tucked into black boots. Her signature red lipstick has me biting into my own bottom lip, wishing I could sink my teeth into hers instead.

"Wow," I breathe out. "You look incredible."

"And you have a dog." She peers around me. "A big dog."

"She's very friendly." I glance over my shoulder at Ellie, who's sitting patiently several feet away, tail sweeping back and forth against the floor. "She's blind and half-deaf, so she might bump you with her nose."

"Is she a rescue?"

"She is. Nobody wanted her, and they were going to put her down. I couldn't let that happen." I step aside and hold open the door for her. "Please, come in."

She shoves a white box against my chest as she walks inside. "I brought dessert."

I glance down at the square box, and a smile stretches across my face.

Crumb cake.

Ellie's nose goes up in the air as she picks up Aarya's scent. She moves toward our new guest, and nudges her leg with her nose. Then she jumps up on her hind legs, her tongue lapping at the air.

"Down, girl." I gently tug her down, and flash Aarya an apologetic look. "I'm so sorry. She never does that."

"It's okay." Aarya brushes off her sweater. "I have a cat, so she probably smells him."

I almost blurt out the words, *Giuliana has been dying for a cat.* She's been asking for a kitten ever since her friend Makayla got one last month. But we have our hands full with Ellie, and I don't know the first thing about cats.

Instead I say, "You're not a dog person, I take it?"

Aarya scrunches her nose. "Not really. They're slobbery and gross." She glances down at Ellie. "No offense."

"That's okay." I stroke the top of Ellie's head. "I think cats are snotty and mean."

Ellie sneezes like she agrees.

Aarya scoffs. "They're independent and elegant."

Well, we're off to a great start here.

73

I lead her down the hall and into the kitchen. "Would you like a glass of wine?"

"Hell yes." Her eyes bounce around room. "I was surprised when you sent me your address. I didn't realize you lived in the suburbs."

"It's quieter here. Not many people know where I live."

"It's definitely more private." She perches on a stool at the island. "It smells amazing in here. Where did you order from?"

I glance at her over my shoulder as I reach for a glass in the cabinet. "I didn't order."

"You know how to cook, Big Man?"

"I do." I pull out the cork from the wine bottle with a pop, and fill the glass before sliding it over to her. "My mother taught me. I was always in the kitchen with her growing up."

She smiles as she wraps her fingers around the glass stem and raises it to her lips. "Did you make one of her recipes tonight?"

I gesture to the pots simmering on the stove. "Spaghetti and meatballs."

"No way." She hops off the stool and scurries over to the stove, peering over the pot simmering on the burner as if she doesn't believe me. "Oh my god. This is my favorite meal."

"I asked Cassidy what you liked to eat."

Her eyebrows hit her hairline. "Why wouldn't you just ask me?"

I hike a shoulder. "I wanted it to be a surprise."

"You didn't need to go through all this trouble. We could've ordered a pizza."

All this trouble? It's just dinner. Has no one cooked her a simple meal before?

"Feeding you is the least I can do if you're really going to do this with me."

She arches a brow. "You offered me one-hundred-thousand dollars. That's more than enough."

"It's just money."

"Says the man who has plenty of it."

"That's not what I meant." I pause and inhale a slow breath. "This is a big deal. If you agree to marry me, your whole life will change. You'll be forced into the spotlight, and the media will watch and judge every little thing you do, or don't do. It'll be a lot different than the life you know now.

And sure, the money is great, but I don't want you to think that's the only thing you'll be getting from me. We're in this together, and even though the marriage will be fake, the way I treat you won't be. I'm going to make sure you're happy and taken care of in every way possible because you're helping me keep my parents' villa. I'd be devastated if I lost it, and you're giving me a way to keep it. So, this is more than a business transaction to me. As far as I'm concerned, I'll never be able to thank you enough for helping me."

Her dark eyes bounce between mine like she's trying to decipher whether I'm feeding her bullshit.

I let her look, because she won't find it.

Her voice is low when she finally speaks. "I almost talked myself out of coming here tonight."

"I'm really glad you didn't."

I reach out and twist one of her loose curls around my index finger, unable to stop myself from touching her in some way. I want to hug her, to wrap my arms around her and hold her against me so she can feel just how much I appreciate her for being here. But Aarya is like a skittish animal, and I don't want to scare her away being too much too soon. I can be...intense. And that's not what she wants. She's doing this for the money, so I need to keep things as objective as I can.

I drop my hand and turn to twist the knob and shut off the flame under the pot. "Besides, if you cancelled, you would've missed out on this amazing dinner I slaved over."

"Amazing, huh?" She lets out a laugh and some of the tension leaves the room. "I'll be the judge of that. Where are your plates? I'll set the table."

I direct her around the kitchen while I drain the water from the spaghetti and mix in the sauce. Then we carry everything into the dining room. Ellie trots over to her bed, and lies down not too far from the table.

"Your house is beautiful," she says, taking the seat across from me.

"Thanks." I watch as she twirls the spaghetti around her fork. "You say it like you're surprised."

"It just doesn't give off single hockey player vibes."

"What kind of vibes does it give off?"

Her eyes roam around, bouncing off the furniture. "I would've guessed that a guy named Dan lives here. He's an accountant, or something in finance. He has a wife named Brenda, and they have two kids—Sawyer and

Jackson. They take the kids to baseball practice. Maybe Dan's the coach. Brenda is definitely a PTO mom. She bakes for all the school events and Dan spends his Sunday's golfing."

I blink at her. "That is oddly specific."

She grins as she lifts her fork to her lips. "Like I said, this place isn't a bachelor pad."

She's not too far off base.

This would be the perfect time to tell her about Giuliana...

"Oh my god." Aarya clamps her hand over her mouth as she chews. "This tastes so fucking good. Holy shit."

My eyebrows lift. "Yeah? You like it?"

She cuts a meatball in half and shoves it into her mouth with the spaghetti still in there. "I can't believe you made this. This is the best sauce I've ever had."

"I'm glad you think so." I watch her with amusement as she moans over the meal I made, pride bursting from my chest. "But what I don't understand is, out of all the meals that exist in the world, why are spaghetti and meatballs your favorite?"

She twirls another forkful of spaghetti. "My mom never cooked unless it was a frozen pizza or something she could pop in the microwave. But I'd see families sitting down to have a meal together on TV, and it seemed like they were always eating a big bowl of spaghetti. They just looked...happy. And I guess that's something I never had—big family, homemade dinners. My father was off having that with his real family while my mother and I ate ramen every night."

I swallow as I set my fork down on the table. "I'm sorry he left you both."

She hikes a shoulder as if she's unfazed by it. "He's a lying piece of shit. I'm glad he left before I met him."

I could never dream of doing that to Giuliana. It makes me sick just thinking about it.

She clears her throat, bringing me back to the present. "So, how long would we have to be married for? I was talking with Celeste, and she said it would have to be long enough to seem legit. But who determines what's legit?"

"I'm not sure." I pick up my fork again. "There's nothing in the will that states how long I have to be married for. It just says I have to be married in order to get the house. So, I think that works to our advantage."

She nods as she chews. "I think six months to a year would seem solid enough. You always hear about celebrities getting married and divorced quickly."

I choke on a piece of spaghetti. "You'd be willing to do this for a year?"

"You don't want your grandfather reneging on the stipulations, do you?" She sips her wine before she continues. "We have to show him that we're serious, until we're not. You're getting this house and there's nothing he can do about it. It's go big or go home."

A smile tugs at the corner of my mouth. "There's my spitfire."

She rolls her eyes and hides her smile behind the wine glass. "Honestly, I'm doing this for purely selfish reasons. One-hundred-thousand *and* home-cooked meals like this? One year will be a drop in the bucket."

I chuckle. "You'll have to let me know what other meals you like. I'll make sure the fridge is stocked while I'm at away games."

"Would I have to come with you to away games?" She chews her bottom lip. "I don't know how often I could take off of work."

I sit forward, leaning my elbows onto the table. "You do what you're able to do. I'd love to have you there, whether it's away or a home game. But if you're not into it, then it's not a big deal."

She spins the stem of the glass, staring down at it. "What about sleeping arrangements? Would we be sharing a bed?"

"I have a nice-sized guest room. Several of them, actually. You can take your pick, and make it your own. You'll have your own bathroom and as much privacy as you want."

"Okay, because—" She pauses and holds up her index finger. "Do you hear that?"

I glance around the room, straining to hear what she's hearing. "What?"

"It sounds like buzzing."

My phone.

I jump up from the table and bolt into the kitchen. There's only one person who could be calling me right now. Sure enough, there are two missed called already on the screen while the phone rings in my hand a third time.

I swipe my thumb across the screen. "Annie, what's wrong?"

The sound of Giuliana's wailing blares through the speaker. "*Daddy!*"

My stomach drops to the floor. "What's wrong? What's going on?"

"Giuliana fell while they were jumping on the bed," Annie says. "Her arm hurts. I'm on the way to the hospital. We should be there in eight minutes."

My heart pounds in my throat. "I'll meet you there. It's okay, baby. Daddy's coming. I'll see you soon."

Shit, shit, shit.

Aarya's voice reminds me that I'm not alone. "Everything okay?"

I shake my head and swallow around the lump in my throat. "I'm sorry, but I have to go."

She steps into the kitchen and touches my arm. "Hey, what's wrong?"

I shove my phone into my pocket, and look into her worried eyes. "I have to go be with my daughter."

11

AARYA

His daughter?

A daughter.

Alexander has a daughter.

I can barely form coherent thoughts in my mind, let alone out loud. "W-hat?"

He stalks out of the kitchen and heads for the foyer. "I don't have time to explain right now, but I promise, I'll explain everything to you later."

It's like I'm underwater, and everything sounds garbled.

He has a daughter?

He slips his arms into his jacket and snatches his keys off the entryway table. "I think her arm is broken, and I have to go to the hospital. You can stay here for as long as you want. Finish eating, or take it home—whatever you want. But I have to go."

My mouth flaps open and closed as I blink up at him.

He leans down and presses his lips to my forehead. "I'm really sorry, Aarya."

And then he's out the door. I stare at it for a few seconds until Ellie's wet nose bumps into my leg.

I glance down at her. "Did you know he has a daughter?"

She sits and cocks her head to the side.

"Some help you are." I dig into my purse for my phone and send a text to the group chat.

> Me: Am I the only one who didn't know that Alexander has a daughter?

Celeste: 😥

Cassidy: He told you?

> Me: You traitors!!!! 🔪 🔪 🔪

> Me: And you didn't think to tell me this because...?

Cassidy: It wasn't my secret to tell

> Me: I'm your best friend. You tell me ALL the secrets!

> Me: Even when you're not supposed to.

> Me: I'm your one.

> Me: OMG... am I not your one anymore now that you're married?

Celeste: 🍷

Cassidy: He wanted to be the one to tell you.

Cassidy: Trent says he kept it from the team for a long time too. He's really private about her.

> Me: Ask Trent if he knows he married a traitor

Cassidy: Yes, but she can suck a golf ball through a straw so it's worth it

Cassidy: Sorry, that was him

Celeste: You look like you'd give good head, Cass

Cassidy: Thanks 😊

> Me: Can we focus please?!

Me: A fake wife is one thing. But a fake step-mom?

Cassidy: Are you still at his house?

Me: We were having dinner and then he got a call and left

Me: His daughter got hurt and is on the way to the hospital

Celeste: Oh no, what happened? Is she okay?

Me: I don't know

Me: I didn't even know he had a daughter until 30 seconds ago

Cassidy: Trenton is texting him now, I'll find out

Celeste: Poor thing. He's probably so worried about her.

Me: Have you guys met her?

Cassidy: Only once at her birthday party last month.

Celeste: She's really cute

Cassidy: Wait, where are you now?

Me: Standing in the middle of his house with his dog

Celeste: I love Ellie! She's the best

Me: He's a dog person and he has a kid. Those are some pretty big red flags if you ask me

Cassidy: Stop it. Those are the greenest flags I've ever seen

Me: Who's the baby mama?

Me: Oh fucking Christ... IS HE MARRIED?!

> Me: Please tell me he's not married

Cassidy: Breathe, babe. He's very much single

Cassidy: This isn't the same scenario as your father

Celeste: Baby mama is nonexistent, but you should let him be the one to tell you about her

> Me: How could he completely omit the fact that he has a child?

> Me: Who does that?

> Me: When did he plan on telling me—when I moved my things into the spare bedroom?

Cassidy: I know this is triggering for you, but hear him out before you make any rash decisions

Celeste: Don't give up on him just yet, girl

Ellie's whimper pulls my attention from my phone.

I follow the sound, and spot her in the kitchen lying down beside an empty bowl on the floor. "You thirsty?"

I fill up the bowl in the sink before placing it back down in front of her. She laps at the bowl until it's empty, so I refill it again.

"Drink up. But I'm not taking you out on a walk and picking up your shit, so you can forget it."

I can't help but think about my father in this situation. He hid his real family from my mother for years—and he hid us from them. What kind of sick person can live a double life like that? How can you lie *that* much and be okay with it?

Does he ever think of us? Of me?

Alexander doesn't seem like that kind of guy. Then again, who knows what he's capable of? I don't truly know him, despite what Cassidy and Celeste have to say.

Questions swarm my mind. I should leave. I should run out of here and never look back.

But my stomach ties itself in a knot as Alexander's worried face flashes in my head. He was here, cooking a meal for me, when he could've been with his daughter...wherever she was. And now she's hurt. Who knows how long he'll be at the hospital for. I should get this all cleaned up for him.

I clear off our plates from the dining room table, and rummage through the kitchen cabinets until I find containers with matching lids. I scoop the leftover food into them, and stick them in the fridge. Ellie lies down at my feet while I scrub the pots in the sink and load everything into the dishwasher.

Cleaning helps me relax.

Once the kitchen is spotless, I venture around the rest of the house. I'm technically not *snooping*. I'm just...looking around.

The living room is next to the dining room, huge with a vaulted ceiling and a plush sectional couch in front of a mammoth-sized flatscreen, of course. It's too dark to see outside the French doors leading out to the patio, but I can only imagine how lavish the backyard looks.

Ellie follows close behind me as I make my way down the hallway, passing a bathroom and several guest rooms until I get to the two closed doors at the end of the hall.

Peeking inside the first room, I flip on the lights and let out a small gasp as Ellie pushes her way between my legs and prances into the room, jumping right on the bed.

An explosion of pink assaults my eyes. Dolls in dresses; teacups and saucers; frilly pillows; and tiny pink shoes. I stand frozen in the doorway, not wanting to enter the innocent space, as if I'll mess it up somehow just by being in it.

I try to imagine the large hockey player in this room—having a tea party or reading her a bedtime story—but I can't. I can't picture it because I'm still in disbelief that this is his reality. Every interaction we've had replays through my mind. But not once has he mentioned or even alluded to having a little girl.

How can he keep her a secret?

My chest squeezes, and it's all too much. I back out of the room and opt for door number two instead.

Alexander's scent hits my nose the second I step inside. Everything is neat, simple, and monochrome, much like the living and dining rooms. It's like his daughter's room is where the only ounce of color is stored in the entire house.

On his nightstand sits a picture frame, and my feet carry me over to it before I can stop myself. Reaching out, I lift the black frame, and I can't help the smile that spreads across my face.

Thick, dark curls and big brown eyes. Pudgy cheeks and little shark teeth. Her tiny hands wrap around the back of Alexander's neck as she smooshes her face against his, squeezing him so hard you can feel it just by looking at the picture. She's a mini-him. She's adorable. And the pure joy emanating from his face is breathtaking.

The thought of something bad happening to her twists my insides. No wonder he ran out of here like the house was on fire.

Where is her mother?

Questions continue to assault me as I leave his room and close the door behind me. Ellie doesn't seem to want to budge from the little girl's bed, so I don't bother to try to move her.

I head back to the living room and slump down onto the couch. *Damn this thing is comfortable.* I stare down at my phone and type a text to Alexander before deleting it, then retyping it, over and over again.

What do I even say?

I shouldn't bother him while he's tending to his daughter at the hospital.

Eventually, my heavy eyelids droop closed.

Five more minutes and then I'll leave.

"I THINK SHE'S AWAKE, DADDY."

My eyes pop open, and I'm met with a tiny human and a large dog— both sitting way too close to my face.

Because I'm still on Alexander's couch.

Fuck!

"Look. she's awake! I told you!"

Alexander's hushed voice enters the room. "I told you to leave her alone and let her sleep."

The girl frowns as he scoops her into his arms. "But she's awake now."

"She's awake because you woke her." He glances down at me and gives me an apologetic smile. "I'm sorry. I held her off for as long as I could."

Sitting up, I turn my face away as I wipe around the inner corners of my eyes. "I'm so sorry. I must've fallen asleep."

On his couch.

In his home.

With his kid here.

Ellie jumps onto my lap and her tongue slides along my cheek.

I scrunch my nose in disgust as I push her away. "Ew, dog."

Alexander's daughter giggles. "That's how she says *good morning*."

My hair is a mess and I no doubt have smudged eyeliner around my eyes. This is not how I want anyone in this room to see me, least of all the gorgeous hockey player who's looking down at me with amusement dancing in his eyes.

"I should go." I fling the blanket off my legs—don't remember putting that on myself last night—and jump up from the couch.

"Wait, we made pancakes." Alexander's daughter reaches out for me. "I cut yours into the letter A for Aarya, and I put it on my princess plate. And you have to sign my cast. See? I broked it jumping on the bed at my friend's house last night. You were sleeping when we got home so I couldn't show you."

I pause, lifting my eyes to the bright-pink cast on her little forearm. "Does it hurt?"

She nods. "It hurt-ed really bad when I fell. But the doctor said it's a hair fraction, so it's not too bad."

Alexander rolls his lips between his teeth. "A *hairline fracture*."

"Yeah, that's what I said."

He presses a chaste kiss to her cheek before setting her down on the floor. "Why don't you go finish setting the table, and give Aarya a minute to wake up."

She disappears into the kitchen, leaving me alone with Alexander.

He shifts from one foot to the other, running a hand through his hair. "I'm sorry. She has no patience when someone is asleep. You should see her on Christmas morning."

"What's her name?"

"Giuliana."

"Pretty."

He takes a step forward, but I move backward. "Aarya, I owe you an explanation. I know this is probably a bit shocking—"

"You think?"

He grimaces. "This isn't how I wanted you to find out."

I cross my arms over my chest. "*Did* you want me to find out? Because you haven't said a word to me about that little girl."

"I know. Once you told me you wanted to do the whole fake marriage thing, I planned on telling you. But then last night happened the way it did, and..." He lifts his shoulders and lets them fall. "I'm sorry you had to find out that way."

"Why have you been hiding this?" I dip my head and lower my voice. "The world has no idea you have a child."

"And I'd like to keep it that way." He glances over his shoulder in the direction of the kitchen. "I don't want her to have to deal with the paparazzi, the media, or anything else that comes along with my hockey life. I know it'll happen eventually, but I'm just not ready for that yet. I want to keep her protected for as long as I can."

"Daddy, hurry." Giuliana sticks her head through the doorway. "Aarya's pancake is getting cold."

Alexander flicks his eyes to mine. "You don't have to stay if you don't want to. I understand if—"

"Come on, kid." I breeze past Alexander and head toward the kitchen. "Let's see this princess plate you're talking about."

Just because I'm pissed off at her father doesn't mean I have to upset Giuliana too.

Her eyes light up as she reaches out for my hand. "You're sitting next to me over here. I always use the princess plate for breakfast, but you're a guest and Daddy says we're supposed to treat guests extra special, so I let you have my plate. Who's your favorite Disney princess?"

"I, uh, I don't know. I never really liked Disney movies when I was a kid."

Giuliana freezes as she cranes her neck to look up at me. "Why?"

"I'm not really a princess kind of girl. I don't like the idea of needing to be saved by a man."

She tilts her head like she's processing what I said. "The princesses can do the saving. Elsa and Anna save each other, and they're sisters. I don't have a sister, but I'd like one. Do you have any sisters? My friend Makayla has a brother, and he's really cute but he drools a lot."

Giuliana rattles off question after question, and I'm not sure which one I'm supposed to answer first, or if they're rhetorical, but I'm starting to lose track of them.

She climbs onto the stool at the island, grunting as she maneuvers around her cast. Then she pats the cushion of the stool next to her. "This is your stool." I sit, and she inches her stool closer to me until it knocks into mine. "Look! It's a capital A for Aarya. Daddy let me use a butter knife to cut it out. He always cuts my pancakes into special letters and shapes. Do you like it?"

I nod. "It looks great. Thank you."

Alexander steps into the room, side-eyeing me, while his daughter keeps talking.

"I like to dip my pancakes into the syrup like this." She dunks one end of her pancake into a small cup of syrup. "But Daddy likes to pour the syrup on top." When she brings the pancake to her mouth, a string of sticky brown liquid drips onto the counter and her lap, but she doesn't seem to mind. "Daddy is a really good cook. He makes the best pancakes, but we also have a waffle iron."

Alexander lifts a coffee mug and gestures to the Keurig. "How do you take your coffee?"

"Black, please."

He scrunches his nose. "No sugar, or creamer?"

"Nope."

"Daddy says I'm not allowed to drink coffee because it'll give me too much energy," Giuliana says, now with syrup somehow on her nose.

I nod. "You do seem to have a lot of energy."

She grins, revealing all of her tiny teeth, as if I gave her a compliment.

Alexander sets down a mug in front of me. "Can I get you anything else?"

I snatch the cup and wrap my fingers around it, relishing in its warmth. "I'm good."

He turns around and pours pumpkin spice creamer into his own mug that says *Number One Dad*.

I arch a brow. "You like pumpkin spice?"

"I do." He clinks his mug against mine before taking the seat on the other side of his daughter. "And I don't think I like your tone."

I snort. "I just find it interesting that the big, tough hockey player likes pumpkin spice coffee creamer."

Giuliana giggles. "He has dress-up tea parties with me too."

Alexander gasps, clutching his chest. "My own daughter just threw me under the bus. Whose team are you even on?"

She squeals with laughter. "I'm on Aarya's team now."

"You little traitor." He reaches over and tickles her stomach, causing her to let out an ear-piercing shriek. "That was supposed to be our little secret."

I can't help but stare at the scene in front of me.

Less than twenty-four hours ago, I was contemplating marrying this man for one-hundred-thousand dollars. It was supposed to be a simple arrangement. A business transaction, really.

But now...how am I supposed to live here?

Like *this*. With *them*.

A pretend husband is one thing, but a pretend family?

I can't do this.

Giuliana's voice breaks through my thoughts. "Do you like your pancake?"

I tear one of the legs off the letter "A" and stuff it into my mouth. "I love it."

She beams. "We're going to the park today. Can you come with us?"

"Oh, uh, no. I'm sorry. I can't."

Her bottom lip juts out. "Why not?"

My eyes fly to Alexander's, unsure of what to say.

Alexander covers her hand with his. "Aarya has to work today."

"What's your job?" she asks.

"I work in an art gallery."

"Do you paint?"

I shake my head. "People come in to look at paintings, and I give them a tour around the gallery. I teach them about the artists."

"Can I come see your gallery?"

I hike a shoulder. "Sure. Do you like art?"

"I love art. I like to draw and color and paint. We paint at school, and my teacher says I'm a natural. That means I'm really good at it."

I smile. "Maybe your artwork will be in a gallery someday."

She whips her head around to look at Alexander. "Daddy, can we go to Aarya's gallery today?"

"Not today, baby. We're going to the park so we can spend some time together before I leave for my game tomorrow."

My eyebrows push together. "Who stays with Giuliana when you're out of town?"

"I have a nanny. She lives in the guest house." He points somewhere over his shoulder. "She was one of my mom's close friends."

Sadness pricks my heart. He doesn't have family to help him with his daughter, and she doesn't have grandparents, or a mother.

I glance down at Giuliana as she dips another piece of pancake into the syrup, getting it all over her fingers, happy as a pig in shit.

Who did he have a child with, and why isn't she here helping take care of her kid?

After I finish my A-shaped pancake, I ball up my napkin and push back from the island. "Well, thank you for breakfast. I should get going."

Giuliana shoots up onto her feet. "You're leaving already? But I want to show you my room."

Alexander grabs her waist, pushing her back down until she's sitting on the stool. "Easy. You have to be careful."

I bring my dish to the sink so I don't have to look into Giuliana's sad eyes.

Puppy eyes just like her damn father.

"I need to head home and get ready for work," I lie. "But maybe you can show me your room another time."

"You'll come back?" she asks.

Alexander watches me like he's wondering the same question.

"Sure. You can give me a tour of your room, and show me some of the artwork you made."

Without warning, she dives off the stool and into my arms. I stagger backward, catching her so she doesn't tumble onto the floor.

She wraps her arms and legs around me like a little koala bear, squeezing me with all her might. "I can't wait."

Bile creeps into my throat, making it hard to swallow.

Fuck, I have to get out of here.

I set Giuliana down on the stool, and bolt out of the kitchen.

"Have you seen my shoes?" I ask to no one in particular as I lift the blanket off the couch to check underneath it.

"I took them off while you were asleep and put them by the front door." Alexander grips my elbows to steady me as I spin around and bump into his chest. "Your things are all by the front door."

I push out of his grasp, and storm into the foyer. My boots are beside the door, and my purse sits beside a tote bag on the entryway table.

"I packed leftovers for you," he adds, gesturing to the containers inside the tote.

"Thanks." I shove my feet into my boots and grab everything off the table, rushing as if I'll be trapped here if I don't get out of the house right this second.

Without looking back, I tear open the door...and then I'm gone.

12

ALEXANDER

"And you haven't heard from her since?"

I shake my head as I swing my backpack onto my shoulders. "Nope."

"Have you tried calling her?" Jason asks.

"I don't want to pressure Aarya to talk if she's not ready to. She ran out of the house like she couldn't get away from me fast enough. Meanwhile, Giuliana hasn't stopped asking me if we can visit her art gallery."

The kid is relentless.

"It's been a week, man." McKinley claps me on the back as we step off the plane. "You should reach out, just to see where her head is at."

Trenton puts up his hood, flicking his eyes to mine. "Cassidy has been in the writing cave, so she hasn't spoken to her much either."

"That's okay, I don't want to put her in the middle. I'll just give Aarya a call."

"No harm in trying," Jason agrees.

We say goodnight, and then I hop on my bike to head home.

Only, I don't head home.

Being at an away game helped keep me distracted, but now that I'm back, I don't think I can look my daughter in the eye while I lie to her about why Aarya hasn't been back to see her room.

Aarya doesn't have kids, so I don't expect her to know that you can't tell a child that you're going to do something unless you plan on doing it. But she did, and now I need to end this so I don't have to keep stringing Giuliana along.

I know Aarya wants to back out of our plan. I guess I just need to hear her say it.

After the twenty-minute ride into Jersey City, I park my bike in front of the gallery and pull off my helmet. Running a hand through my hair, I step onto the sidewalk and peer through the window.

Aarya is talking with a man at the front desk. At first glance, it looks harmless. But her arms are wrapped around her midsection, and her shoulders are hunched—nothing like the sassy, confident woman I've become accustomed to. Whoever this man is, he's entirely too close to her, and something about the way he's looking down at her has the hairs on the back of my neck standing up.

I rap my fist against the glass door, admittedly a little too hard, but it gains their attention, and I don't miss the relief flashing in Aarya's eyes when she spots me.

The man walks over and unlocks the door before cracking it open. "Gallery is closed. Come back tomorrow."

I stick my foot through the opening before he can close the door. "I'm not here for the gallery."

His head snaps to Aarya. "Do you often have visitors here after hours?"

Her eyes widen as she scurries over, clutching her purse to her chest. "No, I don't. He...he's..."

She stammers, so I step in. "I'm here to pick her up. We have plans."

His eyebrows hit his hairline as gets a good look at me. "Oh, shit. You play for the Goldfinches."

He knows me, so I need to be careful. "And you are...?"

"Carter Stevens." He sticks out his hand as he puffs up his chest. "This is my gallery."

Ah, so this is Aarya's boss who's been harassing her.

I crush his hand in a firm shake as anger spikes in my gut. "Nice to meet you."

"How do you know Aarya?" he asks, pulling his hand back and rubbing it with the other.

Good. I hope it's broken.

"She's my girlfriend." I slip my hand in hers and tug her through the doorway until she's safely outside beside me, away from this creep.

Carter's eyes narrow on her. "I didn't know she was with anyone."

"Well, now you know." I tilt my head. "It was nice meeting you, Carl."

"It's Carter."

"Right, right." I turn to face Aarya. "Ready to go?"

She nods, and offers her boss a quick wave. "Night, Carter."

"We'll finish our conversation tomorrow then," he says.

"Sure."

I can guarantee they won't be finishing whatever conversation they were having.

I unbuckle the spare helmet attached at the back of my bike. "Put this on, and don't argue with me."

Aarya swallows as she takes the helmet and pushes it over her head. I tilt her chin to adjust the buckle underneath, lowering my voice so her boss can't hear me. "Did he touch you?"

She eyes him over my shoulder. "No."

I jerk the bottom of the helmet, forcing her eyes back to mine. "Look at me, Aarya. Did he touch you?"

"No. Just get me out of here."

I shrug out of my leather riding jacket and put it on her, zipping it up to the top. It's colder when you're riding, the air temperature dropping the faster you go. Though we won't be going too fast around the city streets, and the ride to her apartment will be quick, I make a mental note to get her proper riding gear as the winter temperatures continue to drop here in New Jersey.

I mount the bike and lift the kickstand, planting both my feet on the ground. "Hold onto my shoulders." I reach back and flip down the passenger foot pegs. "Then swing your left leg over to the other side."

Aarya does as I say, mounting the bike behind me.

"Now wrap your hands around me and hold on."

Her hands slide around my waist, and I pat her hand. "You ready?"

"No."

"I promise, I won't go fast."

She presses her body against mine, squeezing me tight. "Okay, I'm ready."

I turn the key in the ignition, hit the kill switch, and press the start button. The engine rumbles to a start, and Aarya's fingers dig into my ribs. It's too loud to talk her through this, and I don't have mics synced up through the helmets—another thing I add to my mental list of things I need to do. All I can do is get her home safely, and show her that riding with me won't be as scary as she thinks it is.

I pull out onto the road, and she grips me so tightly that I can barely breathe. But I don't mind the feel of her holding onto me like this. Like she knows I've got her. Like she trusts me.

I want to show her that she can.

I take it slow, easing around each turn and staying in the lane instead of splitting like I would if she weren't on the bike with me. After whatever just happened with her boss, my only focus is getting her home and finding out what that piece of shit did.

Within minutes we arrive at Aarya's apartment. I park and prop the bike on the kickstand before sliding off the seat and turning off the engine. I don't take nearly enough time to appreciate how adorable she looks sitting on the back of my bike as I wrap my arms around her and scoop her off the bike. When her shoes hit the pavement, I tug her close so I can unclip the buckle under her chin and pull off the helmet for her.

Her chest heaves as she stares up at me, eyes wide and her wild hair all over the place.

"Well?" I pull off my own helmet and set both of them on my seat. "What do you think?"

"That wasn't so bad."

I chuckle. "I told you, I'm a safe driver. Maybe next time you won't have to squeeze all the air out of me."

She grimaces. "Sorry."

"That's okay. It's still better than Mac. He jokes about putting his dick in my ass the whole time he's behind me."

That earns a smile out of her. "Not surprising."

I stare down at her, needing to know what happened with her boss. "You okay?"

She averts her eyes. "Yeah, I'm fine."

"Hey." I tip her chin. "The truth."

She heaves a sigh. "Carter wants to promote me."

"Is that what *you* want?"

She hikes a shoulder, glancing around at the quiet neighborhood around us. "I'd want it if there weren't any strings attached."

My anger flares. "Did he imply that there were strings attached?"

"He always implies things. Maybe he'll stop now that he thinks I'm dating the captain of the Goldfinches."

"He'll definitely stop if I put my fist through his teeth."

"Easy, Big Man." She pats my chest. "Never would've thought you'd be one for violence. Then again, it turns out that there's a lot I don't know about you. A bike. A daughter. Seems like there's a lot you're hiding."

"Well, I'd like to discuss that with you." I slip my hands into my pockets. "That's why I came to the gallery tonight. I was hoping we could talk."

She nods like she figured as much. "Let's go upstairs."

I lock up the helmets and follow Aarya up to her apartment on the sixth floor.

"I used to live in Cassidy's building, but I'm trying to save as much as I can so I downsized." She glances up at me as she turns the key in the lock. "It's not a big fancy house in the suburbs."

"It's fine. I don't judge."

I glance around the small space as we walk inside. The kitchen and living room are open in one area, and the bathroom and bedroom are off to the side. The furniture is minimal, and there's a small TV across from the dark-gray couch.

"I eat, I sleep, and I shower. This place serves its purpose." She tosses her purse onto the bistro table near the kitchen and stuffs her keys inside it. "Fair warning, I have a cat. He isn't friendly and he hates everyone, so don't be offended if he doesn't let you pet him."

I glance around looking for him. "Giuliana has been begging me to get a cat."

"How's her arm?"

"The cast is a pain in the ass. She's itchy and sore and uncomfortable."

She nods. "I broke my ankle in middle school. That shit sucked."

I shake out of my jacket and lay it over the back of the chair. "How'd you break it?"

"My mom was dating one of her asshole boyfriends at the time, and I got in between them when they were arguing. He pushed me and I rolled my ankle."

"Jesus." The more I hear about her past, the more I understand why she views men the way she does.

"My mom really knew how to pick them." She shrugs like it's nothing. "Want anything to drink?"

"No, thanks."

She gestures to the couch, and we take a seat on opposite ends. I spot something furry and black moving along the back of the couch out of the corner of my eye.

"No sudden movements," Aarya whispers.

I smirk. "Animals usually love me."

"Well, you haven't met *this* animal." She watches her cat with caution as the cat approaches me. "Dash must've had a bad experience with a man because whenever he's around one, he—"

Dash, the vicious monster that he is, climbs his way down my shoulder, along my chest, and curls up in a fluffy ball in my lap.

Then he lets out a singular *meow.*

I run my fingers along Dash's silky fur. "You're a secret sweetie pie just like your mom, aren't you?"

He nuzzles his head against my arm.

"I..." Aarya's mouth hangs open. "Is he purring?"

I let out a low chuckle. "He sure is."

"I have never seen him like this before." Aarya shakes her head. "You're like the animal whisperer."

"I think maybe you haven't been around the right kind of men." I lift my gaze to hers. "The cat *and* the woman."

She rolls her eyes. "Says the man who lied about being a father."

"I didn't lie." I scratch behind Dash's ears. "I just...kept her a secret from everyone for a long time."

"Why?"

"I chose to be a hockey player, and the spotlight comes with the territory. But Giuliana doesn't need to be put through all that. Plus, it'd only raise questions about her mother."

"And where *is* her mother? Why isn't she here helping you raise that little girl?"

I let my head fall back against the couch as I stare up at the ceiling. "I'd had a little too much to drink one night after an away game, and I went home with someone I'd met at a bar. I wasn't careful. It was foolish, and reckless. I wasn't thinking. I didn't think I'd hear from her again until she showed up at my door and told me she was pregnant." I swallow, choosing my words wisely. "She wanted no part of being a mother. I wasn't ready to be a dad either, but I couldn't let that baby go. So, I made sure she had everything she needed until Giuliana was born, and then I never saw her again. She signed the contract my lawyer wrote up, terminated her rights, and it was like she never existed."

It's not a lie. I just omitted specific details, not ready to share them with Aarya yet.

Aarya stares down at her hands in her lap as she listens. "Do you think she'll ever change her mind?"

"No." I hike a shoulder. "Will she ever regret it? Maybe she will. Maybe she won't."

As I watch Aarya's face, it dawns on me that this might be a sore subject for her, whose father made the same choice to leave his child behind.

I lift Dash in my arms, and scoot us to the other side of the couch. He jumps into Aarya's lap and paws at her while he stretches.

Aarya's eyes are on me while I lower myself beside her, and take her hand into mine. "Whether your father thinks about you or not, I can tell you with absolute certainty that he's missing out on you." She averts her gaze, but I tip her chin and bring her right back to me. "I'm sorry I didn't tell you about Giuliana. I hope you can understand why. I'm just trying to protect my daughter."

She nods, the questions swirling in her dark eyes as they bounce between mine.

"I know this isn't what you signed up for when you agreed to fake marry me, so I get it if you want to back out." I offer her a small smile. "Giuliana and I are a package deal."

"She's the reason you want to keep the villa, isn't it?"

"Now that she's old enough to remember it, I want to take her there. I want her to have the same kind of memories I have. I want her to feel close to my parents, even though they're not here to meet her."

Aarya covers my hand with hers. "They're with you both every day."

I stare down at our contact, emotion constricting my throat. "I just want Giuliana to have a full, happy life. She doesn't have a mother, or grandparents. I'm trying to be all of that for her, but it's hard sometimes."

She squeezes my hand. "You're doing better than you think."

I huff out a laugh. "She hasn't stopped asking me when she's going to see you again. The kid has the memory of an elephant."

Aarya frowns as she stares down at the sleeping cat in her lap. "I don't know if I'm cut out to be a step-mom. Even a fake one."

Disappointment sinks into my gut. Though I already knew what her answer would be, it still stings to hear her say it out loud.

"I get it," is all I can say at this point. "Thank you for hearing me out."

I push off the couch and move toward the table for my jacket.

"What if I'm not good at it?"

I turn around and meet Aarya's worried gaze. "What?"

She places Dash on the couch before she stands, and wrings her hands in front of her. "I don't want to mess up your kid."

I tilt my head. "How would you mess her up?"

"I don't know." She holds her arms out wide before letting her hands fall and smack against her legs. "I don't know the first thing about kids, or how to change a diaper, or what they eat. I curse a lot—I know you're not supposed to do *that* around them—and I definitely don't watch Disney movies. The color pink repulses me. I'm not motherly at all, in case you haven't noticed."

Affection warms my chest at her concern. "Giuliana doesn't wear diapers, so you're in the clear there."

"I don't even know how old she is."

I take a step toward her. "She's four."

"What if she chokes on her food? Or on a toy? Google said kids put things in their mouths, and I won't know what to do if she's choking."

I take another step toward her. "You Googled it?"

"Yeah, that's why I haven't called you all week, because I was trying to learn as much as I could so that I could convince you that Giuliana would be safe around me. But there's so much you need to know, and I don't know if I'll be good at any of it, and she was really sticky that day with the syrup, and—"

I close the distance between us and wrap my arms around her, pulling her against me.

"Why are you hugging me?" Her voice is muffled against my chest as her body stiffens.

"Because I can't stand here listening to you tell me all of this and not hold you."

She tries to push out of my grasp. "This isn't necessary. You don't need to comfort me."

"This is more for me than it is for you."

She stops squirming, but doesn't lift her arms around me.

We stand in the silence of her apartment, with Dash weaving through our legs, and I hold onto the only shred of hope I have of keeping my parents' villa.

I rest my chin on the top of her head. "I didn't know the first thing about children when Giuliana was born, so it's been a learn-as-I-go experience. Annie has been a huge help. I'm not sure I would've survived some of the harder days without her. But you've put more thought and care into being with Giuliana than her own mother did, so I'd say that's a good start. Plus, she's already obsessed with you."

Aarya pulls back and looks up into my eyes. "Really?"

"For the last week it's been, *Aarya's hair is so pretty; can you do my hair like Aarya? Can we visit Aarya at her gallery? I'm going to paint a picture for Aarya so she can hang it in her gallery. Is Aarya coming over today? I want to show her my room.*" I shake my head. "It's been exhausting."

A slow grin spreads across her face, like she's happy to hear that Giuliana has been talking about her. And something deep inside me settles into place.

Maybe this can work after all.

I cup her face, my thumb stroking her cheek. "All you have to do is be yourself. That's the only version of Aarya I want. But if you don't feel comfortable with this, then there is no pressure. You can tell me no, and I'll walk right out your door, and we'll go back to being friends."

She arches a brow. "Friends?"

"Your best friend married mine. I'd like to think we're friends now too."

She chews on her bottom lip giving me a sly look. "We're about to become a lot more than friends, Funnel Cake."

My eyes widen. "Does that mean...?"

She nods. "I'm in."

Relief crashes into me like a tidal wave, and I scoop her up into my arms and spin her in a circle. "Thank you."

She grunts as I set her down, and shoves me away. "That's two hugs in one night."

"The spitfire doesn't like hugs?"

She squares her shoulders. "Hate them."

Dash paws at my leg, missing out on the fun. I pick him up and he nuzzles into the crook of my neck.

Aarya shakes her head. "Looks like Giuliana is getting that cat she's been wanting."

13

AARYA

"Cheers, ladies."

I lift my martini glass. "To Kourtney, for coming out and living out all of our bisexual, polyamorous fantasies."

Kourtney covers her mouth and tries not to spit out the wine she just sipped. "Do *you* have bisexual fantasies, Aarya?"

I hike a shoulder. "No, but you and Celeste are hot, and I wouldn't mind watching."

Celeste grins. "We are pretty damn hot, if I do say so myself."

Cassidy wraps her arm around Kourtney's shoulders. "I'm just so happy you felt comfortable enough to come out to us. We would never judge you."

Kourtney rests her head against Cassidy's shoulder. "That means the world to me. I wish my father felt the same way."

Sadness pricks my heart. Kourtney recently came out to her parents and told them that she wants to be with both Jason *and* Celeste—her husband and their childhood best friend. It shocked all of us, but in the end, her happiness is what matters most to us. Her father, unfortunately, did not share our sentiment. They haven't spoken since she told him.

"Forget about us." Celeste waves her hand and turns her attention to me. "Let's talk about you. I need all the details about what's happening between you and Krum Cake."

I spin the stem of the glass. "Well, we have to go on a few dates and make our relationship public. He'll do a press conference and announce that we've been dating for a while, so the world thinks we're already an established couple, which shouldn't be too hard of a sell since our best friends married each other. Then I'll move into his house; we'll have a short engagement; and we'll get married." I hike a shoulder. "We talked it all out on the phone the other day, so we have a plan."

Celeste blinks at me. "You're giving me nothing."

My eyebrows press together. "Those are all the details I know."

"I want to hear about the tension between you. Give me angst, give me passion, give me longing glances because you both want each other but you don't want to blur the lines of your agreement."

I cough out a laugh. "I think you're reading too many of Cassidy's books."

Kourtney nudges Celeste with her elbow. "They haven't even gone on their first date yet."

"I don't care. I've seen them in the same room together. I see something there." Celeste snatches her purse off her chair and digs inside her wallet until she pulls out a fifty-dollar bill, slamming it on the table. "I bet you're going to fall in love with Alexander Krum before you file for divorce."

Cassidy squeals. "Me too!"

My mouth flaps open. "Are you kidding me? We're not falling in love."

Cassidy pulls out two twenties and a ten. "Ante up, bitch."

Kourtney shakes her head on a sigh as she reaches for her purse. "Sorry, Aarya. I love love too much to not take this bet."

I roll my eyes. "You guys are romanticizing this. Nothing about this situation will lead to love. We're just two friends helping each other out. That's it."

"Two friends who are very attracted to each other." Celeste winks. "I see the way you look at him with those *fuck me* eyes of yours."

I grunt. "Yeah, a lot of good they're doing."

Cassidy squeezes my shoulder. "But now you know why he turned you down that first night."

Learning about Giuliana *did* help heal my bruised ego, understanding why Alexander doesn't do one-night-stands.

"I don't know the first thing about kids." I down the rest of my martini and set the empty glass on the table. "Or being married. This is a disaster waiting to happen."

"Marriage is whatever you want it to be." Kourtney laces her fingers with Celeste's. "I'm with a man *and* a woman. That's not traditional marriage, and that's okay. We make it right for us."

Celeste nods. "Plus, Alexander has a nanny. I'm sure she'll be able to help you with anything you need to know. You won't be alone."

"I think you're going to make a great pseudo step-mom." Cassidy smiles. "Though I have to admit, I'm shocked you're agreeing to this."

"I shocked myself." I lift a shoulder and let it fall. "I don't know. Something pulled in my chest as I looked at that little girl. I saw myself in her, knowing there's a parent out there who didn't want her just like mine didn't want me."

The girls reach out and cover my hand with theirs. "Maybe there's a reason you came into each other's lives," Cassidy says.

She knows I don't believe in any of that *meant to be* bullshit, but I don't remind her of that.

Kourtney's eyes glisten. "You're going to make a difference in her life, Aarya. You bring so much to the table you're not giving yourself enough credit for."

"I don't know about that. She's all tutus and Disney princesses, and I don't mesh with that lifestyle at all. My mother didn't give me the best example. How will I know what to do?"

"Because you have the biggest heart," Cassidy says. "You forget I've known you for over two decades now. I know who you are, and you are not your mother."

The waiter stops by our table, eyeing our empty glasses. "Another round?"

"Yes, please." I hand him my glass. "And keep them coming."

He arches a brow, amusement shining in his brown eyes. "Are we celebrating something tonight?"

I let my eyes trail up his muscular arms, his skin a smooth, dark-brown. His full lips tip into a smirk when he catches me checking him out.

Cassidy wraps her arm around my shoulders. "She's getting married."

Cockblock.

"Damn, that's a shame." His eyes rake over me as he shakes his head. "I mean, congrats."

I grimace as he walks away with our glasses. "I don't think I'm going to be able to survive a whole year without sex."

"I don't think you'll have to wait too long." Celeste grins. "Another fifty bucks says you fuck Krum Cake within the first month of living together."

Cassidy whips out more cash. "Oh, I'm totally getting in on this one."

I cross my arms over my chest. "The man has willpower made of steel. I literally undressed in front of him on the night of your wedding, and served myself up on a platter."

"You were drunk," Kourtney says. "Alexander is too much of a gentleman to take you up on that offer."

"I feel like he's not a gentleman in the bedroom." Celeste waggles her eyebrows. "He gives off Dom vibes."

"Daddy Alex," I murmur, and my skin heats at the thought.

God, now I'm imagining his large hand around my throat.

"Makes you wonder how long it's been since he's had sex," Cassidy says. "Giuliana is four-years-old, and I haven't seen him with anyone since I've known him."

Celeste's jaw drops. "You think he hasn't had sex in four years?"

We glance around the table at each other, wondering the same thing.

"I'm marrying a monk." I groan, and let my head fall against the table. "Figures."

"You know, they say the man you drunk dial is the man you truly want to be with."

I roll my eyes. "Good thing I'm not drunk."

Celeste laughs. "Then why is your left eye closed?"

I flip her off as I lift my phone to my ear. "I'm just calling him because I have some questions about our agreement."

Kourtney touches my shoulder as we all say goodbye. "Are you sure you don't want a ride home?"

"No, I'm good." I wave. "Night, ladies."

"Love you!" Cassidy calls before getting into the car with Trenton's driver.

The phone rings until Alexander's raspy voice comes through the speaker, sending a delicious shiver down my spine. "Hello, spitfire."

"Hi, Birthday Cake."

He chuckles. "How was your girl's night?"

"It was good. I didn't have sex with the waiter though."

"Oh? And did you *want* to have sex with the waiter?"

"He was good-looking, and he was definitely checking me out." I stifle a yawn. "But if I'm about to be a married woman, I can't be having sex with random waiters."

"That's right. You can't."

"Which brings me to the reason for my call." I heave a dramatic sigh. "When was the last time you had sex?"

"Me?"

"Yeah. We were discussing it at dinner. If Giuliana is four, and you don't have one-night stands, then was the last time you had sex with Giuliana's egg donor?"

He coughs out a laugh. "Where are you right now?"

"Walking home from *Patrizio's*."

"But that's a twenty-minute walk from your apartment."

"At least."

"And it's freezing out."

"I have a coat."

"Stay there. I'll come and get you."

"No way. You're all the way out in perfectville. It'll take you longer to get here than it will for me to walk home."

"I'm at the stadium. I stayed late to get an extra workout in." Rustling and movement sound in the background. "Send me your location, and I can be there in five minutes."

The call ends, but I don't send Alexander my location. I know it'll piss him off, and maybe that's why I do it. Maybe I just want to reiterate that I don't need anyone to protect me.

I walk until a sleek SUV pulls up to the curb alongside me. Alexander steps out and jogs around the front end to swing open the passenger side door.

My eyes trail the length of his long legs in a pair of gray sweatpants that should be illegal on this man. The matching gray hoodie and damp messy curls he's sporting give him a cozy yet sexy look. Fresh out of the shower, I bet he smells delicious. I want to bury my nose in the crook of his neck. Slide my hand into his pants and find out what he's packing.

Alexander points an index finger at me. "Stop looking at me like that."

"Can't help it."

"Is that the same look you gave the waiter?"

"Jealous?"

He steps into my space and tugs on the zipper of my jacket, pulling it all the way up. "Do I need to be?"

"I'd like to see you jealous." My gaze falls to his lush mouth. "I'd also like to see you on your knees."

He leans closer, his lips brushing the cusp of my ear. "That makes two of us."

Heat spreads throughout my entire body despite the cool night air surrounding us.

He places his hand on my lower back and guides me toward his truck. "Come on, let's get you home."

"Where's your bike tonight?"

He arches a brow. "Is that disappointment I hear?"

"No." *Maybe.* "I just haven't seen you on anything other than that crotch rocket."

"It's too cold to ride tonight. Besides, I wouldn't let you ride on the back of my bike if you're drunk."

I scrunch my nose. "I'm not drunk."

"Then why is your left eye closed?"

I slap my hand over my eye. "I'm just tired, okay?"

He grins as he tucks me into the passenger seat and closes the door.

Once he climbs in on the driver's side, he clips his seatbelt and pulls out into traffic. "Why do you walk everywhere? Do you not have a car?"

"I never needed one living in this city. I work nearby, and my friends live close. Why waste the money?"

"What if it's raining or snowing?"

"It's not a big deal."

"I can get you a driver. He can take you wherever you need to go."

"That's ridiculous. I don't need a driver to take me somewhere I can walk to in ten minutes."

"If the weather isn't good, or if it's late, or I can't get to you, then I'd like you to use a driver."

I shake my head. "You're going to be in trouble when Giuliana gets older, you know. You're not going to be able to control everything she does."

He grunts. "Don't remind me."

I watch him as he drives, the way his long fingers wrap around the steering wheel; the way his seat is pushed all the way back to accommodate the length of his legs; the way his eyes stay on the road, despite the fact that I wish they were on me.

The way his Adam's apple bobs in his throat when he swallows and says my name like a warning. "Aarya."

"You still haven't answered my question. How long has it been since you've had sex?"

"Why does it matter?"

"I'm just curious."

His jaw works under his skin. "It's been a long time."

My eyes widen. "Since Giuliana?"

His curt nod gives me my answer.

"But...why?"

He heaves a sigh as he flicks on his blinker. "I've been busy."

"You're a man. You're never too busy for sex."

"There you go again, with your jaded views on men." He pauses. "Some women are just as bad, you know. It's not the gender that makes people assholes."

My mouth falls open. "Did Alexander Krum just curse? Alert the media."

He smirks as he side-eyes me. "I curse from time to time."

"That was the first one I've heard come out of your mouth."

"You curse enough for the both of us."

"Does that bother you?"

"Not at all. It's part of your charm."

I snort.

When we reach my apartment building, Alexander double-parks out front. I reach for the door handle but he presses the lock button, locking all the doors.

"I'll get it." He gets out of the truck, makes his way around the front bumper, and unlocks the door with the button on the handle before opening it for me.

So chivalrous.

"Watch your step getting down."

I ignore his outstretched hand and jump down. "I'm good."

"I was thinking," he says, walking me to the building. "We should go on our first official date. Let the media get some pictures of us while we're out, and get the ball rolling."

I nod. "Sure."

"I have a game Friday night, but what about Saturday?"

"Works for me. Where do you want to go?"

"You leave that part up to me." He grins. "Looks like I'll get to take you on that date I've been asking for after all."

"Don't look so smug about it."

"Why not? I get to take a beautiful woman on a date and get photographed with her for all the world to see. I'm going to be a smug bastard."

I roll my eyes as I try—and fail—to fight the smile stretching my lips.

He reaches out and brushes his fingers against my cheek. "I like it when I make you smile."

I give his chest a playful shove, more so to put some distance between us than anything else. "All right, Big Man. Let me know what I should wear on this date of ours once you sort out the details."

"We'll take the truck. This way, you don't have to worry about wearing something conducive to straddling the bike."

"No, but it'll be conducive to straddling something else."

He groans as his head falls back.

I shoot him a wink as I head up the stairs. "Night, Pop Tart."

14

AARYA

Alexander shows up promptly at 6:55pm for our date.

He's leaning against his blacked-out SUV looking like an absolute snack in charcoal-gray slacks and a black button-down shirt with the sleeves rolled up. His thick hair is styled neatly instead of the usual messy mop from being smushed under his helmet.

I smirk as I make my way down the stairs of my apartment building. "Five minutes early just as I suspected."

"If you're not early, you're late." His dark eyes make a slow perusal of my long-sleeve black dress, and I don't miss the way his jaw ticks when he reaches my bare thighs peeking out of the thigh-high black boots. "You look incredible."

"Had to look good for the paparazzi."

He dips down and presses his lips to my cheek, letting his mouth linger by my ear. "So, this dress isn't for me?"

"Not unless you're planning on taking it off me, Big Man."

He glances up at the sky like he's saying a silent prayer.

But it's a lie. This dress is totally meant to drive him crazy.

He swings open the door to the back seat and before he follows me into the car. "Sam, this is Aarya, my girlfriend."

I flinch at the word *girlfriend*. It sounds so foreign. I've never been a girlfriend before. I know we need to use terms like this, but it's definitely going to take some getting used to.

"Hey, Sam." I wave at him in the rear-view mirror. "Thanks for driving us around tonight. Any chance you'll tell me where we're going?"

Sam chuckles as he pulls away from the curb. "But that would ruin the surprise."

"Damnit, he got to you too." I glare at Alexander. "I hate surprises."

He reaches out and squeezes my hand. "This will be a good surprise, I promise."

The way he's looking at me is as if he knows the reason I hate surprises is because I've only had bad ones.

I shift in my seat and stare out the window, trying to figure out where we're going. We take the Liberty Bridge into Manhattan, with endless possibilities there. I watch Sam's turns, trying to figure it out for nearly thirty minutes. But it's not until we turn onto 5th Avenue and slow to a stop in front of vast steps peppered with paparazzi pointing cameras in our direction that it hits me.

My lips part and my heart thumps a furious rhythm in my chest. "We're going to the MET?"

He nods. "I rented it out for the evening."

"You rented... the MET?"

He chuckles. "The whole museum just for us."

"I love this museum."

"I figured you would."

I blink between the museum and him, my brain not fully computing the fact that this man rented out the Metropolitan Museum of Art.

For *me*.

It's not dinner or a movie. It's not drinks at a bar. It's not a, "You up?" text at 1AM.

It's thoughtful and sweet.

It's clever.

It's one of my favorite places in the world, yet I've never told him that.

But I don't have time to let it all sink in, because we have to get out of the quiet vehicle.

"It's going to be a little bright out there," Alexander warns. "Just hold my hand, keep your head down, and don't answer any questions. Understand?"

I nod, nerves buzzing under my skin. "Yes."

Celeste leaked the news that Alexander Krum would be stepping out with his never-before-seen girlfriend, ensuring that our picture would make it onto the news to get the city talking. It's only now that it dawns on me that my simple life is about to become a lot less private.

Am I ready for this?

Alexander watches me with those keen dark eyes. "You ready, spitfire?"

"Ready," I lie.

Sam steps around the front of the SUV and swings open our door. Alexander slides out first, and there's a frenzy of clicks and flashes as the paparazzi descend upon us. I clasp Alexander's hand, and he tugs me close, guiding me up the museum stairs.

"Krum, who is this woman?"

"Is this your girlfriend?"

"How long have you been dating?"

"Kiss her!"

Flashes go off like lightning around us, making it hard to see. I grip tight onto Alexander, praying that I don't miss a step and fall in front of all these people.

"I don't remember there being so many stairs here," I mutter.

Alexander chuckles. "Almost there."

Finally at the top, we push through the glass doors and once it closes behind us, silence blankets us again.

A security guard greets us with a smile. "Good Evening, Mr. Krum. Enjoy your night."

Alexander shakes his hand. "Thank you, Billy."

"Wow." My eyes bounce around the entrance. "I've never seen it this empty before."

"It's all yours tonight." Alexander squeezes my hand, and I don't know if he realizes that he's still holding onto it even though the paparazzi can't see us. "Anywhere in particular you want to start, or should we just wander around?"

"Wander. Definitely wander."

He smiles as he leads me further into the museum. "I've never been here before."

"I used to come here all the time when I was younger. My mom would be dating some loser, and I wanted to get out of our tiny apartment. So, I'd come here and stare at the artwork for hours, in my own little peaceful world."

He frowns like that upsets him.

"I haven't been here in forever though. I've been so busy working that I haven't taken the time to come back. There are so many new exhibits I've heard about."

"Why do you love art?"

A small smile tugs at my lips as I gaze at the paintings before us. "I love how much it represents. An artist feels so much emotion—whether it's anger, sadness, heartbreak, joy, love—that they need to get out and express it in these incredible art forms. They say so much more than words can. It's like you're looking at a piece of someone's soul."

We stop walking, and Alexander turns his attention to me. "Have you created any art?"

"I used to paint." I hike a shoulder. "Nothing that great."

"I'd like to see it one day."

I roll my eyes. "In the words of my mother, it's just shitty kid art."

"I happen to like kid art." He dips his head to make sure I'm looking into his eyes. "And nothing you do is shitty, Aarya."

Warmth spreads throughout my body, but I clear my throat and avert my eyes from his intense gaze. "Come on, Big Man."

We spend the next hour walking around, and Alexander listens intently while I tell him about each of the exhibits. He asks questions like he actually cares, and I have to hand it to him, he's a great actor. It must be all the time spent listening to Giuliana's endless rambling.

I point up ahead at the room we're approaching. "This is my favorite spot in the entire museum. It's called—"

My feet stop and my heart falters.

The American Wing is a beautiful skylit courtyard with balconies and multi-levels filled with sculptures and paintings. I've seen it countless times during the day, but never at night—and never the way it looks right now.

A small round table covered in a white linen tablecloth sits in the center of the courtyard. Different sized LED candles flicker everywhere, casting a romantic glow around the table. A massive bouquet of red roses lays across one of the two chairs, and metal tins cover the plates at each place setting.

"What is this?" I whisper.

"This is dinner." Alexander's deep voice slides over me like hot butter. "I didn't get to enjoy the meal with you when Giuliana broke her arm, so I wanted a do-over. This looked like the perfect spot."

Dinner...inside the museum.

The museum he rented out for our date.

"Wow." I inch closer to the table, in awe at how beautiful the setup looks. "But the paparazzi can't see all of this."

"This isn't for them." He lifts my hand and presses a soft kiss to the top of it. "The pictures outside might be for them, but this night is for you."

My throat is tight, making it difficult to swallow. "This is too much."

"You're wrong." Alexander leads me toward my seat. "This is exactly what you deserve."

He pulls out my chair before I can get to it, and I lift the bouquet from the seat to my nose. "These are beautiful."

"I wasn't sure what kind of flowers you liked, but the color reminded me of your lips."

I smirk as I lower myself into the seat. "You looking at my lips, Big Man?"

He takes the flowers from me wearing a smirk of his own. "Only about as often as you look at mine."

So, all the time then. Got it.

I watch as Alexander pops the cork on a bottle of red wine and pours it into my empty glass. Then he reaches into his pocket and pulls out his phone, tapping on his screen, before soft music plays somewhere in the background.

"When did you have time to do all this?"

He hikes a shoulder like it's no big deal. "Before I came to pick you up. Dinner was delivered about five minutes ago, so it's hot."

He uncovers the plate in front of me, and my mouth waters at the sight of a perfectly-cooked steak, accompanied by potatoes and vegetables.

"You do this for all your first dates?" I ask, eyeing him as he takes a seat across from me.

"Haven't been on many first dates since I joined the Goldfinches, but I think all first dates should be something special."

I know he's pulling out all the stops tonight to make a show for the media, but something tells me Alexander is truly this romantic regardless of who's watching.

We cut into our steaks, and a serene quiet blankets us while we enjoy our meals together. I can't stop my gaze from wandering around the room, hoping to commit every second of this moment to my memory forever.

"How's the food?" he asks.

"So good." My eyes meet the concern in his. "Everything is so good, Alex."

A small smile blooms on his face as he lets out a quiet laugh.

"What?"

He shakes his head. "I just really like it when you say my name."

I didn't even realize I called him Alex.

"Not Big Man, not a silly hockey nickname. Just Alex," he explains.

And it's now that I realize, I'm not the only one who hasn't been on a proper date. If Alexander hasn't had sex since Giuliana was born, then he hasn't dated anyone either. He has isolated himself because he can't trust that anyone will want him for more than his pro hockey player status—and on some level, I get that. I don't let people in because it's easier to keep them out rather than giving them the opportunity to disappoint me.

We might be total opposites in some ways, but Alexander and I are similar in others.

I reach across the table and lace my fingers with his. "Thank you for making tonight so special for me. I really appreciate all the effort you put into this, Alex."

His fingers squeeze mine and his dark eyes glisten in the candlelight. "You deserve it."

"I know it's not easy letting people in, especially where your daughter is concerned. But I'm grateful that you're letting me." I let out a breath of a laugh. "Even if I'm totally not cut out for the job."

"I think you're going to surprise yourself with how perfect you are for this."

The way he's looking at me, surrounded by dozens of candles and the incredible backdrop of the museum, feels too much. Too real. Too much like I could get used to his belief that I'm worth more than a fun night between the sheets.

I pull back my hand and lift my knife again, busying myself with cutting another piece of steak. "We should discuss the contract."

He clears his throat and sits upright in his chair. "Was there anything you'd like to amend?"

Reaching behind me, I pull out the tri-folded papers from my purse and flip to the second page. "It says here that you're giving me the money upfront."

Alexander nods. "And?"

I give him a dubious look. "Don't you want to hold onto the money until you're sure I've held up my end of the bargain?"

His dark brows pinch together. "I'm not holding this over your head, Aarya. You're not enslaved to me. And I figured you'd want to get a head-start on finding a space for your gallery."

"But you're giving me the money to spend before we secure your parents' villa."

"Do you plan on taking my money and disappearing into the night, never to be seen again?"

"No, but—"

"Then we're good. You can take the money and get started on building your dream *while* we get my villa back."

I lift my wine glass and bring it to my lips. "Okay."

"How does the calendar I sent you look? I put a few away games in there, but you don't have to come to them if you can't get off work." He swallows and dabs the corner of his mouth with his napkin. "But I was thinking, with the money upfront, maybe you'd want to quit your job and—"

"I can't just quit my job."

"But your boss is harassing you. I thought you'd be happy to get away from him."

"It's not just about him. I have bills to pay, and finding a space for a gallery of my own will take time. I can't risk it."

His head tilts as he leans back against his chair. "Aarya, just so we're clear: You'll be living with me—all expenses paid. Anything you need money for, I will provide. If you want new shoes, or a manicure, or money for your phone bill, or hell, if you want a car, it's on me."

I cough out an incredulous laugh. "No fucking way am I letting you be my sugar daddy."

He purses his lips. "That's not what this is, and you know it."

"I have to stand on my own two feet. I can't just quit my job and live in delusion as if you're going to be my provider."

"But I am going to be your provider. I'm going to be your husband."

I lean in and lower my voice, even though nobody else is listening. "You're going to be my *fake* husband. What if I can't get the gallery up and running in time? What if our contract ends before the gallery comes to fruition? What if the gallery completely fails?"

"My money is yours for as long as you need it. I have more than enough, and I'm not going to cut you off just because the contract is over." His eyes narrow. "You're helping me keep my family's villa. I'm eternally indebted to you. Don't you see how important that is to me?"

"I can't ask you to do that for me." I shake my head. "I need a fallback plan."

"Let me be your fallback."

I grew up watching my mother trust the word of a man, promising to take care of her only to dump her on her ass the second he was done with her. We struggled financially and I swore to myself I'd never follow in her footsteps. As much as I want to believe that Alexander means what he says, I just can't allow myself to. What's to keep him from going back on his word once he has secured the villa?

"Thank you, but I'll be staying at my job for as long as I can, until it's the right time to leave." I wave a dismissive hand, hoping he'll drop it. "I make my own money and I can take care of myself."

His lips turn downward, and I know he's not happy with my response, but he doesn't push the issue.

We finish eating, and then he lays his napkin on the table as he pushes out of his seat.

He tugs my hand, pulling me up. "Dance with me."

"Don't you want to finish the tour?"

"We will. We have plenty of time for that." He pulls me close and rests his hands on my waist. "We have the place to ourselves for as long as you'd like."

I wrap my hands around the back of his neck and sway to the soft music playing in the background.

He dips his head and speaks low at the cusp of my ear. "I've had a hard time letting people in, as you can see when it comes to my daughter. Letting you into my personal life, knowing you're going to be a part of Giuliana's world, isn't easy for me. I've never told anyone this before, but her mother took advantage of me."

My head jerks back as I look up at him. "What do you mean?"

"I've always kept my drinking to a minimum because of what happened to my parents. The night I met her, I only had two beers. After that, my memory gets hazy." His Adam's apple bobs as he swallows. "And I always use protection during sex. Yet there was no evidence of a condom anywhere when I finally woke up the next morning. She was already gone at that point. But at the time I didn't think anything of it. I figured I let things get a little out of hand, and that was that."

I believe him wholeheartedly. Alexander is always careful and needs to be in control. Having a wild night of drinking and unprotected sex doesn't sound like him.

"Men get roofied too, you know. It's not as common as when it happens to women, but it does happen."

He nods, his eyes not meeting mine as he continues. "She showed up at my house with a positive pregnancy test a month later, and said she couldn't afford to keep the baby. Of course, I offered to take care of her medical expenses, and I told her I wanted her to keep the baby if that's what she wanted. I went to every appointment, gave her money for whatever she needed. Food; prenatal vitamins; I even paid her rent.

"I was there in the delivery room. I saw Giuliana come into this world, and it was the most incredible miracle I've ever witnessed. Then I had an away game the next day. But when I returned to the hospital to see them, they were gone."

I try to school my features so he doesn't see how horrified I am.

"I panicked. I searched everywhere for them. I called Giuliana's mother —Rachel—and texted her for two days straight. Then a letter showed up at my house. Rachel wanted money in exchange for Giuliana."

Anger spikes in my veins. "Are you fucking kidding me?"

"Rachel never planned on keeping her. She conned me. Strung me along the entire time just to get money out of me."

"And if you didn't want her to keep the baby when she first came to you?"

He blinks back tears. "She would've terminated the pregnancy and probably tried to con someone else."

"How much did you give her?" I whisper.

"I was desperate to get my baby girl away from her."

"How much, Alex?"

"Half a million."

I suck in a gasp, unable to contain my reaction. "That fucking psychopath got away with half a million dollars?"

He hikes a shoulder. "I would've given her anything she asked for just to hold Giuliana in my arms."

Jesus Christ. This poor man.

"Why didn't you go to the cops, or get a lawyer?"

"I was embarrassed. I felt like a fool. And nobody would ever believe that a woman could take advantage of a big guy like me." He shakes his head. "I was so fucking stupid."

"You're *not* stupid. That bitch deserves to get hit by a bus. Hell, let's find her. I'll do it myself."

One corner of his mouth curves up. "Easy, spitfire."

I rest my head on his shoulder and stroke the hair at the back of his head. "I know you wouldn't have Giuliana without that piece of shit, but I hate that she has her DNA."

He hums in response. "So, I know you've been through experiences in your life that have made it difficult for you to trust people, especially men. But I want you to know, just because that's the way it's always been doesn't mean that's the way it always will be. Not everyone is out to get us. You have Cassidy, and I have my friends. We've created a small circle of people we can count on. And I hope in time, you'll see that you can count on me too."

I don't know what to say, so I close my eyes and let his words sink in as he continues.

"I know you pride yourself on your independence, and I'm not trying to take that away from you. I just want to make things easier for you. It's okay to accept help sometimes—the kind of help that doesn't come with strings attached."

I heave a sigh and let my fingers run through the silky curls at the back of his head. "Please tell me you have some kind of weird deformity, like a tail or a third nipple. Or maybe you save your toenail clippings in a jar."

He blinks. "What?"

"You can't be this perfect all of the time. There has to be something wrong with you."

His head tilts back as he laughs. "So you're hoping I collect toenail clippings? That would make you feel better?"

I scrunch my nose in disgust. "I mean no, but I just want to find out what's wrong with you."

"Maybe there's nothing wrong with me. Maybe I'm just a normal guy."

I shake my head. "No way."

His arms squeeze around me, drawing me closer. "I think you're trying to find something wrong with me so you can stop yourself from liking me so much."

I roll my eyes. "I don't like you. I tolerate you."

His chest rumbles against mine with his laughter. "Sure, you do."

I hate the way it feels like he can see right through me. I do like him. As a person. As someone I'd consider a friend. As someone I can trust.

And that scares the shit out of me.

I step back from him, and tug his elbow. "Come on, Big Man. Let's go before your head fills up this entire room."

AFTER I SHOWED Alexander every inch of my favorite parts of the museum, we head back to the main entrance.

An even bigger crowd than before awaits us.

"I'm going to talk to them as we walk to the truck," Alexander says. "You can smile and say hi if you're comfortable. Otherwise, just hold onto me and keep your head down."

I stick my arms into my jacket as he holds it out for me, and my eyes survey the scene outside. "I can say hi."

Alexander slips his hand into mine and waves goodbye to the security guard. "Thanks for being here tonight, Billy."

"Anytime, Mr. Krum. Good luck out there."

I suck in a deep breath right as we push through the door and exit the museum. Cameras click and the shouting begins.

Alexander flashes the paparazzi a killer smile as he lifts his free hand to wave at them. "Have a good night, everyone."

"Krum Cake, who is this you have on your arm tonight?" someone shouts.

"This is my girlfriend, Aarya." He glances at me and his smile widens. "Isn't she beautiful?"

The shouting gets even louder, more questions being fired at us as we make our way down the stairs.

I try my best to lift my head and smile, but the flashes are so bright, I can't see a damn thing.

"Can we get a kiss for the camera?" another man yells.

Now would be the perfect opportunity to kiss me while everyone's watching. Alexander gazes down at me, a slight smile tilting his lips. His eyes bounce between mine before dropping to my mouth. I grip onto his arm, readying myself to put on a show in front of all of these people like we're animals at the zoo.

But he doesn't kiss me.

Instead, he leads me to the SUV and tucks me inside.

Disappointment flares in my gut during the ride home, but I shove it down. It's not that I wanted to kiss on camera; it's that Alexander finally had an excuse to kiss me, and he chose not to. This man will probably go the entire fake marriage without setting his lips on me once.

It's quiet in the vehicle on the ride back to my apartment, and as soon as Sam pulls over in front of my building, I hop out and toss a quick goodbye over my shoulder. "Thanks for tonight."

"Aarya, wait." Alexander chases after me as I quickly make my way across the sidewalk toward the stairs.

"I had a great time. Let's just leave it—"

Before I can finish my sentence, Alexander grips my wrist and spins me around to face him. "I didn't want our first kiss to be for them."

Them. The paparazzi.

"And why's that?"

"Because I want it to belong to me." He brushes his nose against mine. "Because I've wanted to kiss you since the first night we met." His hands come up to cup my face. "Because I don't want you to think I'm doing this for the cameras."

I fight to slow my racing heart. "No cameras around now."

His eyes drop to my lips.

I hold my breath, waiting for him to make the first move—needing him to be the one to do it.

And then his mouth covers mine.

One large hand snakes around my waist to hold me against him, while the other settles at the base of my head, sinking his fingers into my hair and keeping me where he wants me. His tongue surges between my lips, taking all of my air with him as he deepens the kiss.

All I can do is fist his shirt and try to keep up with him, my shoes barely touching the floor, completely at his mercy as he claims me. My entire body comes alive—my skin heating and desire pulsing between my legs. I can honestly say that I've never been kissed with such fervor, such need.

Possession.

I take both of his hands and guide them to my ass, letting him know what I want and granting him the permission I know he needs. He groans into my mouth as he squeezes two overflowing handfuls and hauls me against the front of the building. I lift my legs and cross my ankles around his waist as he lifts me, not caring that I'm in a dress or that anyone can see us. The only thing I can focus on is the fact that this giant, beautiful man is kissing me like his life depends on it.

He massages my tongue with his, sending shock waves straight to my clit. The kiss is slow and sensual, yet strong and demanding at the same time. That's exactly how Alexander is, an oxymoron of soft and hard, gentle and firm.

I suck his plump bottom lip into my mouth and bite it, eliciting another deep groan from his chest. I want more of those noises, want more of him to unravel until he's no longer in control of himself.

But he pulls back too soon.

I pout in protest, nowhere near ready for the loss of his mouth.

He drops his forehead against mine, holding me steady against the building while his chest heaves. "You're going to be my undoing. And I don't know how to stop it."

"Maybe you don't stop it." I trace his plump lips with my index finger. "Maybe you just let it happen."

He sets me down on my feet and hits me with a pleading gaze, like he's begging me to stop tempting him.

After what he shared with me tonight, now knowing what Giuliana's awful mother did to him, I realize how much he needs to be in control. I can't pressure him to take me upstairs and ravish me, as much as I want him to. That decision needs to be his.

For the first time ever, I don't want to be a man's lust-filled impulse.

I want to be his choice.

I give Alexander a playful shove and lighten the mood. "I guess it's time for me to go. I officially have a standing date with my vibrator every night since you took me off the market."

His eyes close as he stifles a groan. "You're not going to make this easy for me, are you?"

"Not a chance, Cream Puff." I shoot him a wink and jog up the steps of my apartment building.

"Hey, Aarya."

I spin around at the top of the stairs.

His eyes bounce between mine. "How did I do on our first date?"

"I think you've ruined me for all other dates." I shake my head, still in disbelief that this man went through the trouble of renting out one of the biggest art galleries in the world. "No one will ever be able to top the MET."

A sly grin spreads across his face, as if that was precisely his plan.

15

ALEXANDER

"Great game tonight."

I grin, clapping Trenton on the back. "I still can't believe you stopped that biscuit at the end of the second period."

He arches a brow. "You doubting me now?"

"Never."

Tonight's home game was great, and I can't deny it's because I'm still on a high from my date with Aarya this past weekend. The only time I've been able to stop thinking about kissing her was when I was on the ice tonight.

The way her mouth moved against mine, her tongue inviting me in, with her legs locked around my waist while I kissed her against the building?

Absolute heaven.

It's been forever since I've kissed a woman, but no kiss has ever compared to the fire I felt with Aarya.

Should I have kissed her? *No.*

Do I regret it? *Also no.*

But now it's going to be nearly impossible to keep myself from doing it again, and I need to be smart about the way we interact moving forward.

"Look at you, man." McKinley spins his towel and whips me with it. "You can't keep that goofy-ass smile off your face for more than two seconds."

I shake my head as I head into the shower, unable to deny it but not wanting to admit it out loud. I have to keep myself in check. This is nothing more than a fake arrangement to Aarya. Sure, she's been trying to coax me into something physical, but that's where it stops for her. I can't get attached. I can't delude myself into thinking she'll want more from me at any point.

It doesn't help that our pictures are plastered everywhere I look this week. The headlines read, "Krum Cake's Secret Girlfriend Revealed." I haven't bothered to scroll through the comments or read any of the articles, but it's out there in the world now.

But as I head out of the stadium after my shower, all the excitement drains from my body.

"Funny how your girlfriend is magically revealed after you find out about losing the villa."

My shoulders jump at the sound of my grandfather's voice lurking in the parking lot.

"Thought you were on your deathbed," I reply, schooling my expression to look bored despite the fact that he caught me off guard.

Lorenzo snickers. "I just wanted to drop by for a quick chat."

I unlock my SUV and toss my duffle bag into the back seat. "You could've called me for a chat."

"True, but then I wouldn't be able to see the look on your face when I give you this." He holds out a manilla envelope. "I have a feeling it'll be worth the trip."

Nerves clench my stomach as I take the envelope from him, but it's nothing compared to the way the muscles in my entire body seize when I pull out a picture of Giuliana.

She's holding Annie's hand as they walk out of her preschool together.

My blood runs cold. "What. The fuck. Is this?"

Lorenzo slips his hands into his pockets, a smug smirk on his wrinkled face. "This is your reminder of what's at stake if I find out you're fabricating a marriage to this new girlfriend of yours."

My jaw clenches. "Sounds an awful lot like a threat to me."

He hikes a shoulder. "Call it what you will. I just thought you could use some incentive."

"My daughter has nothing to do with this." My voice echoes off the low ceiling of the parking garage. "You're threatening to hurt children now? I always knew you were a piece of shit, but I didn't realize you were psychotic."

He laughs. "I'm not threatening your child. I'm simply letting you know that if I find a shred of evidence that you're planning on an arranged marriage to get around my will, I'll let the world know their favorite hockey captain has been hiding a lot more than a secret girlfriend."

I lunge toward him, but he side-steps me and wags his index finger in my face. "Uh-uh. Remember, there's always someone watching. Wouldn't want to tarnish your good boy reputation, would you? *Crazed hockey player assaults his elderly grandfather post-game.* How would Child Protective Services feel about that headline?"

This motherfucker.

My lungs constrict as I ball my hands into fists, crumpling the picture of Giuliana. "Get out of here. Now."

"I'll be seeing you, Alexander." He walks backward into the parking lot. "Oh, and by the way... your daughter is adorable. Looks just like you. Shame her mother didn't stick around."

My face heats and I can feel my pulse thumping in my neck.

Breathe. Deep breaths. Don't do anything stupid.

I watch Lorenzo until he disappears in a black car, and then I get into my SUV.

My chest heaves as I try to breathe, but I can only suck in short puffs of air. Then it happens.

Blurred vision.

Heart racing.

Sweaty palms.

No, no, no.

I haven't had a panic attack in years. I grip the steering wheel and squeeze my eyes shut, trying to gain control of my body. I rack my brain, retrieving the exercises from my memory.

I purse my lips and breathe in like I'm sucking air through a straw.

One, two, three, four.

Out through my lips.

One, two, three, four, five, six, seven.

Again.

And again.

And again.

The longer out-breaths slow my heart rate, and a calm crawls over my body. I blink to clear my vision, continuing my steady breathing.

"I'm in control," I say. "I'm in control."

Then I pull out my phone and make a series of calls. First, Annie, to make sure she and Giuliana are safe at home. Then, to Celeste to inquire about hiring a security team. Last, I call Aarya. She doesn't pick up, but there's a chance she might still be at work.

When I pull out of the parking garage, giant raindrops splat against my windshield. Instead of heading home, I make my way to the gallery. I'd bet money that Aarya doesn't have an umbrella with her.

Sure enough, I find her already walking home with her hood up and no umbrella. I pull over to the curb and roll down my window. "Get in!"

She squints through the rain, and jogs over to the passenger side door when she realizes it's me. She slides inside, and I crank up the heat to stop her teeth from chattering.

"I'm sorry I couldn't make it sooner."

"That's okay." She brushes a few wet strands of hair off her forehead. "I forgot to check the forecast before I left for work today. How was your game?"

"Fine." I pull back out onto the street, my eyes darting to the rearview mirror. "How was work?"

"Fine." She turns to face me. "You okay?"

"Yeah, I'm fine." I glance at each of the cars around me as we pull up to a red light. "How was work?"

"You just asked me that."

I flick my blinker on and check the rearview mirror again as I turn down the next street. "Oh, right."

Her head whips around. "What are you looking at?"

"What? Nothing."

"You're acting weird right now."

I run my fingers through my hair. "I'm sorry. I just—"

She grips my wrist and holds up my hand. "Your hands are shaking, Alex. What the fuck is going on?"

A long breath escapes me. "I'll explain when we get to your place."

She crosses her arms over her chest and watches me in silence until we pull up to her apartment building. I get lucky with a spot not too far down the block, so I use my jacket to shield Aarya as we make a run for it through the rain from the truck to her building.

Once she closes her apartment door behind us, she grabs a towel for each of us and tosses me one. "Start talking."

I run the towel over my hair as I pace the length of her living room. "My grandfather showed up to the stadium today. He had... he had a fucking picture of Giuliana."

Aarya's eyes widen as her hands drop to her sides. "What? How?"

"I don't know. He thinks we're faking this relationship, so he threatened to leak information about Giuliana."

"Why does he think we're faking it?"

"Because we are!" I scrub my hands over my face. "I haven't had a girlfriend since before Giuliana was born. Now, I suddenly have one after reading my grandfather's will? This was a terrible idea. Why did I think we could pull this off?"

"Hey." Aarya steps into my path, stopping me from pacing. "Where is Giuliana right now?"

"She's home. I called Annie before I came to pick you up."

"Okay, so she's safe. Right now, everything is okay."

I pull the crumpled picture out of my pocket and hold it out in front of her. "He found my daughter. He knows where she goes to school."

She takes the photograph from me, her eyes roaming over Giuliana's precious face. "He's just trying to scare you, and it obviously worked."

"Of course it worked. No one knows about her, yet this scumbag found her. He even knows that her mother isn't around." I shake my head, thoughts whizzing through my brain at warp speed. "He has someone watching us. Someone following us. If he knows where she goes to school, then he knows where I live. He probably knows where you live too. I know we said we'd wait, but I think you should move in with me now. I can't protect you from all the way out here. And I'm going to hire a security team. And—"

Aarya shoves at my chest. "All right, Big Man. Sit down."

"I don't want to sit. We—"

She tugs my arm, yanking me toward the couch. "I didn't ask."

I plop onto the couch, staring up at her. "Why are you so calm right now?"

She plants her hands on her hips, standing over me. "Your grandfather, he's just trying to get a reaction out of you. He wants you to fuck up so he doesn't have to give you the villa. But that's too damn bad, because he can't prove that we aren't dating. He can't prove any of this is fake. And he knows this, so he's grasping at straws and making idle threats about Giuliana because he knows she's the only thing that'll make you go crazy."

I blink. "But what if he—"

"What if he *what*? How can you prove someone is faking a relationship, unless there's explicit evidence? People fake marriages for citizenship and get away with it all the time. We've got this in the bag."

She's right. My best friend married her best friend, so it's only natural that we'd hang out and possibly hit it off. Our story makes sense.

Now Aarya's the one pacing the room. "The only physical evidence is our contract, and we can just shred it. You can delete it from your computer, and make sure it didn't get uploaded to the Cloud. Get rid of any emails with your lawyer. I'll have to erase my texts with the girls. I don't think he'd be able to get my phone records without a court ordered warrant, and he'd need just cause for that."

My chin jerks back. "Why do you know all of this?"

"I watch a lot of documentaries."

"What the hell kind of documentaries are you watching?"

"The murdery ones."

I shake my head as a small smile tugs at the corner of my mouth. I reach up and catch her hand to stop her from wearing out the carpet. "Come here, spitfire." She slumps down next to me, eyes wide, and I can see her brain moving a mile a second. "Thank you for calming me down."

She frowns. "You were shaking before. You looked... I didn't like it."

I cover her hands with mine. "I have anxiety. I used to get panic attacks a lot, but I went to therapy and learned some exercises to help me cope. I had a panic attack tonight, after my grandfather paid me a visit."

"You have those often?"

"No. Not since Giuliana was born. I was a single parent running on no sleep with a colicky baby, and not a single clue what I was doing. Sometimes,

I'd have a panic attack while she screamed her head off as I was holding her in my arms."

Aarya chews her bottom lip as she listens.

"That's when I reached out to my mom's friend, Annie, and she literally saved me. I learned so much from her, as well as from therapy. I guess my grandfather's will brought some of those old nerves back up again, and when I thought about him hurting her, I started to panic."

She nods. "Look, I know it's scary to think that someone's been watching us—especially Giuliana. But I think I have an idea that can help you tell your grandfather to fuck right off."

"I'm listening."

"Tell the world about Giuliana yourself."

"No. No way."

"Hear me out," she pleads. "You feel good when you're in control, right? And Lorenzo made you think that he's in control, but he's not. If you get ahead of him and be the one to announce that you have a daughter, then he can't hold anything over your head. He loses the power. And what does he have to use against you after that? Nothing."

I hear what she's saying, but that's a bigger ask than she realizes. "She's only four. She's not ready for this."

"Kids are resilient. Isn't that what everyone says about them? Fuck if I know, but maybe you're making this a bigger deal than it will turn out to be. Maybe you'll get to stop living under the stress of getting caught, and you can live freely with her."

For four years, I've stopped myself from doing the things I've wanted to do with my daughter. I couldn't chance being spotted at the park, so I built a park in our backyard; I couldn't take her to the beach, or to Disney World, or even give her a tour of my stadium before a game. If it weren't for Annie, she'd be like Rapunzel locked in a tower.

I let my head fall back against the couch and stare up at the ceiling.

Maybe Aarya is right.

Maybe I've been doing this all wrong.

I've been so worried about the media messing up Giuliana's life, but maybe *I'm* the one fucking up her life.

"Hey, look at me." Aarya grasps my face between her hands and jerks my head until I'm looking in her eyes. "Stop thinking whatever you're thinking.

You did what you thought was best for her, and she has had a wonderful life. But now it's time to take control and do things your way. You are not a bad dad."

I lean into her touch, letting my eyes close for a brief moment. "How did you know what I was thinking?"

"Because you're the only person I know who will have something bad happen, and think it's your fault."

I want to tell her how thankful I am that she's doing this with me. How good it feels to know I'm not alone in this. How much I appreciate her help.

My gaze falls to her lips. I want to kiss her.

God, do I want to kiss her.

And having her in my house is going to make fighting this ten times harder.

"I want you to move in with me. And no more walking around alone. You'll have your own bodyguard, and a driver to take you wherever you need to go."

Her eyebrows waggle. "A bodyguard, huh? Sounds fun."

I shoot her a glare. "My *wife* will not be having an affair with her bodyguard."

"Then I guess my *husband* better figure out how he's going to keep me from straying."

Without thinking, I grip her hips and pull her onto my lap. Her thick thighs straddle my waist, surrounding me in her scent as her hair falls around me. She braces her hands on the couch behind my head, unsure eyes bouncing between mine yet laced with desire.

I run my fingers through her soft hair, gripping onto the back of her neck as I pull her mouth down to mine. "My wife will not touch another man. She will not look at another man, flirt with another man, think about another man. She will not fantasize about any other man besides her husband. She belongs to me, and I belong to her. Is that clear?"

Aarya rolls her hips against me as her fingers toy with the hair on the back of my head. "I'm still a little unclear on all that. It doesn't seem very fair to me."

"Why not? The same rules apply to me. You're the only woman who consumes my thoughts. The only woman I long to touch. The only woman I fantasize about every night when I wrap my hand around my cock." I tip my chin and bite her plump lip. "The only woman whose name I whisper as I make myself come."

A small moan slips out of Aarya's mouth as she shudders against me, and that sound is my undoing. I push off the couch with her in my arms and flip her onto her back, coming down on top of her and kissing her hard.

My tongue surges inside her mouth, wrapping around hers. Aarya's legs come up around my waist, her ankles locking behind my back and letting me know that she's not letting me go anywhere. I thrust my hips against hers so she knows just how hard I am for her—only her.

I slip my hands between her body and the couch, gripping two handfuls of her ass while I grind against her. She meets my kiss with the same intensity, licking and sucking and biting, gasping for air as we consume each other. Her nails scrape down my scalp, down over my shoulders, and down the length of my back until her fingers slip underneath my shirt, searing my skin with her touch. All the while, her moans spur me on.

I could easily lose myself in her, lose my control. It would feel fucking incredible to let go and give in to this insatiable need to sink inside of her, to feel her pussy clenching around me while she screams my name.

Fuck, what am I doing?

I have to think about the bigger picture here.

I *have* to.

As much as my dick hates me for it.

I slow our kiss, my tongue licking inside Aarya's mouth in one final languid motion before I pull back.

Her thighs squeeze me, locking me in place. "Get out of your head, Big Man."

My forehead drops to hers as I steady my breaths. "I wish I could."

"I can help you with that." She lifts her hips off the couch and rubs her most sensitive spot against me. "Sex is a great way to clear your mind, you know. Maybe that's why you have so much anxiety. All that pent-up frustration is no good."

I chuckle and press a chaste kiss to her forehead before unclasping her ankles from around my body. "You're probably right."

"I have to ask." She pulls herself up to sitting, and brushes her hair away from her face. "Is it...is it because you don't trust me?"

My head tilts. "What?"

"Giuliana's mother took advantage of you just to get something out of you. You know that's not what I'm trying to do, right? Because the last thing I want is trick you into having a kid. No offense. I'm just saying, I want to make babies—minus the babies. Plus, I'm taking your money in exchange for helping you keep your villa. So, technically, I'm not using you. We're helping each other. Like partners."

"You are nothing like Giuliana's mother." My expression softens as I reach out and stroke her cheek. "And no, I don't think you're trying to take advantage of me."

"Then why won't you have sex with me?" she blurts out as her eyebrows pull together. "I've never had a problem getting laid before, and you seem like you're attracted to me. So, what's stopping you? Be honest. Because a year of us living together seems like a really long time to not act on what we're feeling here."

I let out a long stream of air through my nostrils. "You want to know the truth?"

She nods, squaring her shoulders. "I can take it."

This woman. She thinks it's *her*. Something *she's* lacking.

I clasp her hand and bring it to my chest, flattening her palm over my heart. "Because when I'm around you, I can't control this erratic beating, and it terrifies me. I like you, Aarya. I've been interested in you since the moment I laid eyes on you, and if you let me, I'd show you what it feels like to be with someone who truly cares for you. But you've made it clear that you don't want a relationship, and I have to protect my heart. I can't have you the way *you* want me to have you, and not have you the way *I* want to have you." I swallow past the emotion in my throat. "I can't fall in love with you and watch you leave after this contract ends."

Her lips part and her eyes widen. "But you're not going to fall in love with me."

"If you think I couldn't, then you don't see yourself at all."

She chews her bottom lip, her eyes searching mine like she doesn't understand what I'm saying. Like she can't fathom the idea of a man falling for her.

"I have to look out for Giuliana too. I haven't figured out how I'm going to explain you living with us, but I know she's going to become attached to you. I can't have her expecting us to be a family, expecting you to be in her life as anything more than what you are. I can control myself, but I can't control how she feels. So, we have to keep the lines clear when you move in."

"Which means keeping our hands off each other."

I nod. "Keeping our hands off each other."

Which may be the hardest thing I've ever tried to do in my life.

16

AARYA

"Hurry up with the popcorn. It's on!"

Kourtney, Celeste and I huddle together on the couch while Cassidy scurries over with two overflowing bowls of freshly popped popcorn.

The Goldfinches are at a press conference today, and there's a lot for the players to discuss. Not only are they in the middle of an undefeated season, but the world recently found out that defenseman Jason Stamos is in a polyamorous relationship with Kourtney and Celeste. And as of the other night, people also found out that Alexander Krum has been hiding a secret girlfriend. But the biggest bomb about to drop at this press conference revolves around a curly-haired little girl. Today's the day Giuliana steps into the spotlight.

My stomach has been in knots all morning for Alexander. Seeing him the way he was the other night when he showed up at the gallery, shaking and anxiety-ridden, was so unlike the calm, composed man he usually is. It breaks my heart to see all the hard work he put into hiding Giuliana go to shit all because of his spiteful grandfather and his conniving lawyer. Giuliana is too innocent to be caught in the crossfire of this situation, and Alexander doesn't deserve to have this choice stripped from him.

But I truly believe that taking control and being the one to announce this news will help Alexander in the long run.

Cassidy turns up the volume on the TV as the boys take their seats along the panel. The hockey questions start, but all I can focus on is Alexander in a suit.

Damn, that man is attractive.

Memories of his kiss flash through my mind for the gazillionth time today. It was so unlike him, so impulsive. There was no reason for him to kiss me. No one watching to catch it on camera. He did it because he wanted to. Because he couldn't stand not kissing me. It was intoxicating and I want more.

But I can't have more.

Alexander made it clear that we have to keep things platonic. While I don't understand how sex would lead to love, I do understand him wanting to set boundaries where Giuliana is concerned. After a year, this will all be over. I'll go back to my life, and they'll go back to theirs. The last thing I want is that little girl thinking I'm going to be her new mommy, only to rip it away from her in the end.

Celeste's fingers snap in front of my face. "You good, Aarya?"

My head snaps up as I blink back to the present moment. "What? I'm here."

She snickers. "You were thinking about that kiss again, weren't you?"

I rub my temples. "It's like my brain is stuck on a loop."

"A good kiss will do that to you," Kourtney says, smiling at Celeste. "Do you remember ours?"

Celeste beams. "I'll never forget it. I was shocked as shit that the girl I'd been in love with all throughout high school was actually kissing me."

"And now look at you." Cassidy heaves a dreamy sigh. "Together forever with Jason, after all three of you were best friends in high school."

"Having sex on a porn website," I add.

Kourtney's cheeks redden like it always does when we bring up the new website she built. We've been friends for over a year now, and she's the last person I'd ever peg for creating a porn-infused dating app. I'm more surprised about this than I am about the three of them being together—I saw that shit coming from a mile away, with all the flirting and stolen glances.

"Have you thought about making an account on the site?" Celeste asks.

I scrunch my nose. "I'm pretty much down for anything when it comes to sex, but posting it on the internet for anyone to see? I'm not sure if that's my kind of kink."

"You don't have to post it publicly." Cassidy shovels a handful of popcorn into her mouth. "You can see who you match up with first and then send private messages to them."

"That wouldn't be very proper for an almost-married woman like myself, now would it?" I roll my eyes. "I'm stuck in the world of celibacy for the next year."

"Listen!" Celeste gestures to the press conference on the screen. "They just asked Krum Cake about his new girlfriend."

Confident and composed as always, Alexander graces the cameras with a smile. "Aarya and I have been dating for the last six months. We met through mutual friends, and we wanted to keep things private while we got to know each other."

"How serious are things between you?" a reporter asks.

Providing them with the answer we rehearsed, he folds his hands on the table in front of him and says, "Very. We both want the same things in life, and we make each other very happy."

"Tell us about her," someone else calls out.

"She's beautiful, as you all saw from the pictures. But she's also incredibly smart, creative, and ambitious. She has a big heart, and a fierce independence about her that I love." Alexander's smile widens as he looks head-on into one of the cameras. "She's everything I've ever wanted to find in a woman."

My body heats as I shift on the couch, suddenly feeling stifled in Cassidy's enormous apartment.

The girls squeal, but Kourtney notices the look on my face. "You okay?"

I nod, forcing a laugh. "Yeah, that just wasn't something we rehearsed."

Celeste and Cassidy exchange glances, while I reach forward and chug the glass of water sitting on the coffee table in front of us.

"There's also something else I'd like to talk about today," Alexander continues. "Something I've been keeping from everyone—aside from my smoking hot girlfriend."

The press room erupts in laughter before falling eerily quiet, waiting to hear the next piece of juicy news.

"I have a daughter."

There's an audible gasp from everyone in that room, and my heart leaps into my throat. Cassidy reaches out and clasps my hand, giving me a supportive squeeze.

"Her name is Giuliana, and she's four-years-old." The questions start, but Alexander holds up his hand to silence them. It's shaking, and I wish like hell I could be there to soothe his nerves.

"For a long time, I didn't want her in the spotlight. I still don't, honestly. But I also don't want to hide the most important part of my life from the world anymore. I want to be able to take her to my games, and take her out of the house without worrying about who's going to see us together. I want her life to be normal—or as normal as it can be with a professional athlete for a father.

"I won't discuss her mother, so you can hold those questions. She's not in the picture, and that's all you need to know." Alexander gazes around the room as the cameras click. "I chose this lifestyle, and I know the media comes with the territory. But Giuliana is only a child, and all that I ask is that you respect her privacy."

McKinley leans over and pats Alexander on the back. "And anyone who doesn't respect his wishes has to answer to the team."

The guys laugh, and the spotlight shifts to Jason as he clears his throat. "Since we're coming clean with our secrets, I have one of my own I'd like to talk about today."

The girls and I watch as Jason professes his love for both Kourtney and Celeste, also taking the heat off Alexander's news for a while. He looks so calm sitting there listening to Jason, but I know deep down, he's feeling anything but calm. The memory of his panic attack twists my stomach, and I hate that I won't be there for him when the conference is over.

I can't begin to unpack why I care at all, so I shoot him a quick text, knowing he'll read it as soon as he gets out of there.

ME: Deep breaths, Big Man. I'm proud of you.

WE SPEND the rest of the afternoon celebrating Jason, Celeste, and Kourtney's polyamorous relationship being outed to the world.

But my mind keeps pulling me back to Giuliana.

Her life is going to be so different now, her sheltered little world about to triple in size. I feel a responsibility to help her maintain any semblance of normalcy. To protect her.

My mother never protected me from the cold realities of the world. She made sure I knew from a young age that my father deceived her, and didn't want me. I didn't have the luxury of living in a happy bubble. If there's anything I can do to shield Giuliana from pain and disappointment, then I'm going to do it.

Even if it means perpetuating her foolish notion that fairy tales and princesses are real.

I rise from the couch. "I have to go."

Three pairs of eyes snap up to me. "Where are you going?"

"I want to be there when Alex gets back."

For some reason, the thought of him in that big house by himself, panicking after he puts Giuliana to sleep, really bothers me. He's been nothing but sweet and kind to me, and he's in a shitty situation. He deserves a little kindness too.

Cassidy shoots up from the couch and rushes me, wrapping me in a bear hug. "I love you, Aarya."

I shove her off me. "Eww. Stop. Don't make this into something bigger than it is."

She nods, swiping a tear from the corner of her eye. "Okay, I won't."

I scrunch my nose. "You're such a freak."

AFTER WE MAKE A QUICK STOP, I ask my security detail to take me to Alexander's house.

It's weird having a bodyguard follow me everywhere I go, but Eddie barely speaks, and I don't mind not having to pay for an Uber.

I pause before stepping outside. Maybe Alexander wants to be alone. Maybe showing up here unannounced wasn't the best idea.

"You okay?" Eddie asks.

Yeah, just trying to muster the courage to get out of the car.

"I'm fine. Sorry. Thanks for the ride."

I hoist the bags out of the car and carry them to the gate before pressing the button on the keypad.

A woman's voice comes through the speaker. "Hi, can I help you?"

"Uh, yeah. I'm... I'm Aarya. Alexander's, uh, friend." I glance at the camera pointed in my direction. "I know he isn't home yet, but I was hoping—"

The gate swings open before I can finish. "Come in! Come in," the woman says.

As I walk along the path to the house, a short, brown-haired woman with olive skin waits in the doorway wearing a wide smile.

Giuliana pushes past her and runs to me, with Ellie hot on her heels. "Hi, Aarya!"

I can't help but smile as I set the bags down at my feet and brace for impact. "Hey, girl."

Giuliana jumps into my arms and Ellie smacks into my legs.

"Stop running with your cast!" The woman I assume is Annie scolds the duo as she scurries down the path toward us.

I stumble backward but regain my balance. "Come on, let's get inside before you catch a cold. It's freezing out here."

"I didn't know you were coming over today," Giuliana says, wriggling out of my hold and peering inside the bags at her feet. "You brought Chinese food!"

I offer Annie an apologetic look. "I'm sorry for showing up unannounced."

She waves me off and throws her arms around me. "It's so nice to meet you. I'm Annie."

Jesus, what's with all the hugging today?

I lower my voice so Giuliana can't hear me. "I saw the press conference, and I just wanted to make sure he was okay."

She cups my cheeks as she pulls back. "He's going to be so happy that you're here."

We head inside, Giuliana leading the way as she attempts to carry one of the shopping bags, dragging it mostly, and talking the entire time. "I love Chinese food. Especially the noodles. Daddy says we can't eat it too often because it isn't good for you. Did you get fortune cookies? Daddy holds them behind his back and makes me pick a hand."

Giuliana's rambling continues as we step inside, but I lose track of what she's talking about as she hops from one topic to the next.

In the kitchen, Annie gestures to a drawer. "Giuls, get out the silverware and set the table. I'll get the plates down for you."

"Yes, ma'am." Giuliana salutes her with her little hand.

Annie chuckles as she turns to face me. "I didn't get to listen to the whole thing because I was with her. How did Alexander do? Poor thing was so nervous."

"He did great. He answered their questions perfectly, and he looked like his usual cool and collected self."

Annie heaves a sigh. "Of course. He never lets anyone see past that."

We watch as Giuliana trots back into the kitchen and reaches for the plates stacked on the counter, humming a tune, completely oblivious to the way her life is about to change.

"I hate that his grandfather put him in this position." My jaw clenches. "That little girl doesn't deserve to be used as a pawn against him."

Annie squeezes my forearm. "I think you gave him good advice. You reminded him that he can take his control back. He's been feeling so helpless with everything his grandfather added to his will. If I could, I'd kill that man myself."

I let out a surprised laugh. "Hell, yeah, Annie. I like you already."

Her cheeks tinge red as she covers them with her palms. "Forgive me, I shouldn't have said that. Some first impression I'm making."

"Don't worry. I'm with you on murdering his grandfather."

Giuliana pops her curly haired-head into the kitchen. "Helloooo? Are we eating dinner, or what?"

Annie's head whips around. "I know you're not talking to us with that attitude, little miss."

Giuliana giggles. "Just joking."

Annie purses her lips. "Uh-huh. Get your butt in the dining room and find your manners."

Giuliana holds out her hand for me. "Come on, Aarya. You can sit next to me."

I watch as Annie serves Giuliana a small pile of lo mein, noting the way she cuts it up for her. Then she scoops a couple of broccoli florets onto the plate beside the lo mein, cutting it into smaller pieces as well.

Giuliana scrunches her nose. "But I don't want broccoli."

"You only have to eat these few pieces." Annie sets the plate down in front of her. "No broccoli, no fortune cookie."

She pouts, turning those big round eyes to me. "Do you like broccoli?"

I nod, having enough sense to lie as I flick my eyes to Annie. "I do."

As if Annie can see right through me, she puts a scoop of broccoli on a plate for me. "Good, then you can eat it together."

Giuliana lets out a whine, and I'm right there with her. I try not to let anything green infiltrate my diet, but something tells me Alexander is strict with the way Giuliana eats, and I won't be the one to mess this kid up.

I lift it off my plate by the stalk and shove the whole thing into my mouth, chewing and trying not to gag as I give Giuliana a thumbs up. "Eat it first, and then you can wash it down with the noodles after."

Her eyes light up as she copies me, both of us contorting our faces as we force a swallow. Then she mimics me as I shovel a heaping forkful of lo mein into my mouth.

Annie shoots me a wink from across the table. "You're going to fit in just fine around here."

I sure fucking hope so.

Halfway through our meal, the front door opens and Giuliana leaps out of her chair. "Daddy!"

"Hi, baby girl." His voice sounds tired, and when he finally comes into view in the dining room, I can see the evidence of his stressful day all over him. His tie is completely undone, as are the first few buttons on his collar. His hair looks like he ran his fingers through it a million times over, and his dark eyes have a dull hue to them.

"Aarya came over. She wanted to surprise you." Giuliana waves her arm, gesturing to me. "She brought Chinese food!"

Alexander's feet falter when his eyes land on me. For a split second, I worry that he'll be angry that I'm here intruding on his privacy. But his expression morphs, and his eyes light up the same way Giuliana's did when she saw me walking toward her house.

"Hey." I offer him a sheepish shrug because I don't know what else to say.

"Hey." His eyes bounce around the table before landing back on me.

Giuliana kicks out of his hold and slides down his body into her chair beside me. "Aarya and I ate our broccoli first. Then we washed it down with the noodles."

"Good girl, eating your vegetables." He bends down and presses a kiss to the top of her head before moving around the table to take his seat at the head of it.

"Daddy, tell Aarya she's a good girl too. She ate her broccoli."

I smirk as I lean back against my chair. "Yeah, Daddy. Call me a good girl."

My eyes widen as soon as the words leave my mouth.

Oh, fuck.

Annie chokes on her Pepsi.

Alexander's mouth opens but no sound comes out.

Giuliana looks up at her father, no doubt waiting for him to call me a good girl, and shit, I am too.

Instead, he pops up from his chair and bolts into the hallway. "I'm going to get changed before I eat."

This is *exactly* the reason I know I'm going to suck at this whole kid thing.

Annie steers the conversation back to something appropriate. "So, Alexander told me that you're going to open up your own art gallery."

I shake my head as I swallow. "Not for a while. I don't think I'm ready for that yet."

"I'm sure there's a lot that goes into something like that." She dabs the corner of her mouth with her napkin. "My husband used to fill every wall of our house with paintings. He hated watching television, so he'd sit in the living room and stare at the artwork instead."

It's not lost on me that she's speaking in past-tense, and that notion is confirmed when Giuliana says, "He died."

"I'm sorry to hear that." I glance at Annie. "What kind of paintings did he collect?"

"All kinds, but his favorite was abstract." She laughs, shaking her head. "It never looks like anything but a bunch of scribbles to me, but he swore he understood it."

I smile. "Some people have a knack for interpreting abstract art."

Giuliana slurps up a singular noodle. "What's abstract?"

"Art that uses shapes and colors instead of pictures of a specific thing." I slip my phone out of my back pocket and Google an example for her. "See this? This is abstract art."

She peers down at my phone. "That looks like scribble-scrabble. My teacher says we're not allowed to color like that."

Alexander waltzes back in the room, wearing those damn gray sweatpants and a black Goldfinches T-shirt. "People pay a lot of money for that scribble-scrabble."

Giuliana scrunches her nose. "People are bonkers."

Alexander shakes his head as he lowers himself into a chair. "Let me guess: Uncle Mac taught you that word?"

"Yup," she says with a giggle. "Bonkers."

"Your Uncle Mac is bonkers," Alexander mutters before redirecting his attention to Annie. "How was today?"

"Good, as always. She has one page of homework tonight."

Alexander's eyebrows lift as he swings his gaze to his daughter. "My big girl has homework?"

She scoots up on her knees, unable to sit still for more than a minute. "I have to trace letters "B" and "G" tonight. "B" says *buh*, like b-b-banana. And "G" makes two different sounds. Miss Kelly used my name as an example today. She said the word *game* starts with the letter "G," but so does Giuliana. That's just confusing. Why wouldn't they make it a "J" instead?"

Annie laughs. "The English language is very confusing."

Giuliana keeps us entertained for the remainder of dinner, but I can't help it as my eyes drift to Alexander. He gives his daughter his full attention, never once pulling out his phone or telling her to be quiet, and there's no TV on in the background.

It's a true family dinner—nothing like I've ever experienced.

Annie tries to clean up once we finish eating, but Alexander shoos her out of the kitchen. "You've done more than enough. You're officially off duty."

I bump him with my hip. "And you've had a long day, so go spend time with your daughter. I'll handle the dishes."

Annie watches us from the doorway with a faint smile on her lips. "I like this one, Alexander."

His dark eyes flick to mine. "Yeah, so do I."

Giuliana barrels into the kitchen holding two fortune cookies in each hand. "Daddy, do the thing!"

He lifts her into his arms and sets her down on the island before taking the cookies from her. He tosses them into the air, juggling them, while she squeals with laughter. Then he holds them behind his back and asks her to pick a hand.

She taps on his left arm, and he tosses a cookie at her. We watch as she tears through the wrapper and cracks open the cookie, pieces dropping onto the floor below—where Ellie is waiting to lick them up.

"It says..." Alexander flips the small piece of paper to face him. "Good luck and prosperity will follow you."

"What's pros-rare-ity?" she asks, totally messing up the word.

"Prosperity. It means success." He scoops her off the counter and sets her on the floor. "Which will happen if you keep eating your broccoli and doing your homework."

She rolls her big eyes. "My fortune isn't about broccoli, Daddy."

I laugh at that.

Alexander turns around. "Pick a hand, Annie."

She points to his right arm, and he tosses her a cookie. "You will always be surrounded by true friends." She crouches down and pulls Giuliana into a hug. "That's the best fortune."

Alexander spins to face me. "Your turn."

I tap my chin with my index finger. "Left hand."

He holds out my cookie with his palm facing up, and I tear into the wrapper. Fortunes are silly and meaningless. My mother always threw out the cookies with the takeout bags, so we never read them. But with three pairs of eyes on me, I know I have to read this one with a smile.

"A dream you have will soon come true."

"Your art gallery!" Giuliana wriggles out of Annie's arms and crashes into my legs. "Your dream will come true now."

"Maybe you're right." I pat the top of her head and toss the paper onto the counter. "Okay, it's your dad's turn."

Alexander breaks open his cookie. "The art of life is not controlling what happens to us, but using what happens to us."

I nod. "See? Can't be in control all the time, Big Man."

"Where did you get this food from?" he says with a laugh.

Yeah, these fortunes were oddly specific.

"Well, it was a pleasure meeting you, Aarya." Annie steps forward and wraps me in another hug. "I hope to see you again soon."

"Likewise." I glance at Alexander and gesture to the sink. "I'm going to handle these dishes, and then I'll be out of your hair too."

"No!" Giuliana wraps her entire body around my leg. "You can't go until you see my room. And I want to show you my homework. My handwriting is really neat. And then you can read me a bedtime story. I'll show you all my stuffed animals. Can you sleep over?"

"Easy, tiger." Alexander pries her hands from around my leg and lifts her into his arms. "Aarya can see your room, but then she has to go. You have homework, and you have to take a bath."

She groans and her body goes limp in his arms. "Why does she always have to go?"

Guilt pricks my stomach. "Why don't you come by the gallery after school tomorrow? I can take you on a private tour."

Her curls bounce around her face as her head whips around to look at me. "Really?"

I shrug. "As long as your dad is able to take you."

Alexander rubs the back of his neck. "I don't know if we're ready to go out just yet."

"Please, Daddy, please! I want to go!"

"I don't know if you'll ever feel ready," I say, lowering my voice. "But the paparazzi won't be allowed inside the gallery, so it'll be nice and quiet in there. You can even have Sam drive you around to the back entrance if you'd like."

His dark eyes bounce between me and his daughter. "I'll think about it."

Giuliana squeals and launches herself at me. "Come on. Let's go see my room!"

17

ALEXANDER

THIS IS A TERRIBLE MISTAKE.

Having Aarya in Giuliana's life only to rip her away at the end of our agreement.

She's *so* excited to show her new friend around her room, talking a mile a minute, telling her a story about each item she holds up.

Aarya goes along with it like a trooper, but I can see the uncertainty in her gaze. This is new for her, and it's not lost on me that this isn't the lifestyle she wants. The only reason she's in this is for the money.

A fact I need to remind myself of whenever we're together.

Yet she's here. She showed up with dinner knowing I'd need someone to lean on after that circus of a press conference. She did it of her own free will. And I can't pretend like that doesn't mean something to me.

Giuliana digs under her bed, attempting to pull out the trunk of old toys, and that's when I step in. "That's enough for tonight, Giuls. It's time for you to take a bath."

Her bottom lip juts out. "Five more minutes?"

"No more minutes. It's a school night. Now say goodnight to Aarya."

Her eyes fill with tears, but she blinks them away. "Goodnight, Aarya."

"Hey, don't be sad." Aarya crouches down beside her. "I can come back another time."

Giuliana makes herself at home sitting on Aarya's knee as if she's a human chair. "Come back on a weekend so I can stay up later."

Aarya chuckles. "Why don't we have a movie night? You can pick out your favorite Disney princess and I'll bring popcorn and snacks."

Giuliana's eyes light up as she flings her arms around Aarya's neck and squeals.

Aarya pushes off the ground and sets Giuliana on her feet. "Go take your bath and do your homework. Make sure you listen to your father so we can have that movie night soon."

"Okay!" Giuliana marches right past me and into the hallway.

I shake my head as I laugh. "Sorry about that."

Aarya waves me off. "Don't apologize. I'll get out of your hair now."

I step in front of her so she can't leave the bedroom. "Thank you."

For being here. For indulging Giuliana. For somehow knowing I'd need a friend.

She lifts her eyes to mine. "I just wanted to make sure you were okay."

My fingers tangle with hers, giving her hand a gentle tug to move her closer to me.

"Fuck, you want a hug, don't you?"

I hike a shoulder, a smirk playing on my lips. "You don't have to. I know you don't like them."

"I've met my hug quota for the month in just one day today." She heaves an exasperated sigh, and then without another word, she slides her hands around my waist and wraps them around my body.

I melt around her, engulfing her in my embrace. Resting my chin on top of her head, I can actually feel the tension leave my body as I inhale the deepest breath I've taken all day.

"Giuliana's life is about to change tomorrow," I say. "I don't know how to prepare her for any of this."

"Maybe you can't prepare her, but you can guide her through it."

She's right. I can't control what happens to us, but I can control how I react. Be there for Giuliana to hold her hand through this.

I lift my hand to cup her face, skating my thumb over her cheek, letting my touch say what my words can't seem to do justice. Regardless of the hardened mask Aarya keeps in place, she gave me a peek at the real woman underneath it today. I hope one day she'll be able to take it off completely for me.

"Daddy," Giuliana calls. "The water is getting high in the bath tub."

"Jesus," I mutter. "I should get in there."

"Go. I'll see myself out."

Before I bolt out of the room, I pull Aarya back in to me and press my lips to her forehead.

AFTER THE BATH, I run the comb through Giuliana's wet curls. "There's something I need to talk to you about."

Her big round eyes flick to mine in the mirror. "Am I in trouble?"

"No, not at all." I lean in and press a kiss to her pudgy cheek. "Something happened at work today, and it's important so I wanted to tell you."

Her little body straightens on the sink counter as she squares her shoulders. "I like when you tell me about work."

My face softens. "Well, that's good because I'm going to be talking to you about work a lot more now."

"Really? Why?"

I section her hair into three parts, preparing for a French braid. "I've tried to keep you away from all the people with cameras who are always taking pictures of me. And because of that, I haven't been able to take you many places the way Annie does. I was trying to protect you, because you're the most important thing to me in this world. You know that, right baby?"

She nods.

"But I think by keeping my work life separate from my home life, that hasn't been very fair to you. And I really want to take you out to places like all the other moms and dads do with their kids."

Her eyes widen. "Like Aarya's art gallery?"

I laugh. "Yes, like the art gallery. Or the park. Or Chuck-E-Cheese. And I want to bring you to the stadium when I have a game so you can see all the behind-the-scenes stuff."

She bounces on her bottom, shaking left and right. "Yay!"

Once I steady her, I use my pinkies to hold each strand of the braid as I twist each piece of her hair over the other. "But those people with the cameras, sometimes they can be very rude and not respectful of our personal space."

"The pepperoni?"

My head tilts back as I let out a loud laugh. "The paparazzi, yeah."

"Why are they so rude, Daddy?"

"They get paid for taking photos of us, so they try to get as close as they can to get a good shot. But it can be loud, and the camera flashes a lot. I took Aarya out to dinner the other night, and they were there."

Concern etches her features. "Was Aarya scared?"

"No, and I was there to protect her, so everything was okay." My fingers move down her braid. "I'm going to be hiring a security team to keep us extra protected too."

"Will the pepperoni hurt us?"

"No. They just get close and it's hard to walk around them to get where we're going."

Her nose scrunches. "Their parents have to teach them some manners."

I chuckle. "Yes, they do."

"So, does this mean we can go to Aarya's art gallery tomorrow?"

I pull the hair tie from around my wrist and twist it at the end of her braid to secure it. "You really like Aarya, huh?"

She nods vigorously. "You never have friends over the house, especially pretty ones like Aarya. And she doesn't treat me like I'm a baby. I like her."

Warmth spreads out from my chest. "Me too."

She turns her head from side to side and checks out her hair in the mirror, and I suck in another deep breath before dropping an additional piece of information on her.

After racking my brain about how I'm going to explain why Aarya's living with us, I landed on the safest lie.

"Aarya's apartment is undergoing construction, and she needs a place to stay for a while. Since you like her so much, I wanted to ask you if it's okay if she comes to stay with us for a while in one of the guest rooms."

Her mouth falls open and her eyes dart to mine. "Wait, really?"

I nod. "Would you like that?"

She squeals her ear-piercing squeal, and she flings herself off the counter. "Yes!"

I laugh as she jumps into my arms. "You really have to stop jumping around with this broken arm, you little spider monkey."

"Are we going to decorate her room for her?"

"No, I think we'll let her decide how she wants her room to look." I shoot her a wink. "But I do have another idea I think you can help me with."

18

AARYA

THE HIGH SCHOOL ART CLASS THAT VISITED THE MUSEUM TODAY was perfect for Giuliana to tag along with.

She insisted on walking beside me and holding my hand, and she took it upon herself to tell the class she was my assistant.

This kid is a trip.

Alexander stayed at the back of the group, watching and listening, taking it all in like the quiet observer he is. But it doesn't matter how quiet he is—when his eyes are on me, it speaks louder than any words he could say. I'd bet every penny of the hundred grand that he could recite each fact I've taught the group today—not because it's important to him, but because it's important to *me*. His attention is quickly becoming something I bask in, something I crave...and I don't know how to feel about that.

Several people recognized him throughout the day, asking for pictures and autographs. He accepted with a smile, though his gaze kept returning to Giuliana. I know he's nervous about how she's going to handle all of this, but I think it'll affect him more than it will her.

"I guess word got out that the great Alexander Krum is here." I glance out the window by the exit, noting the small crowd gathered on the sidewalk.

"News always travels fast." He finishes buttoning Giuliana's coat, and pushes to his full height as he lifts her into his arms. "Sam is pulling around back for us."

Giuliana pulls the lollipop I gave her out of her mouth. "You're coming to live with us tomorrow, right?"

I nod, answering her question for the fourth time today. "I am."

She smiles so big, her cheeks bunch up around her eyes. "I can't wait for you to see the surprise."

My eyebrows hit my hairline. "A surprise?"

Alexander presses his index finger to her lips. "No spoiling it, remember?"

She giggles and bites the tip of his finger like a piranha before sticking the lollipop back in her mouth.

I arch a brow. "A surprise, huh?"

Alexander smirks. "Only the good kind. Promise."

"Mr. Krum, I hope you enjoyed your tour today."

Both of our heads whip around as my boss strides toward us.

Alexander's jaw clenches before he forces a polite smile. "We did, thank you. We had a wonderful tour guide."

"Yes, well, the tour guide has to get back to work now." Carter glances at me with a blank, unreadable expression. "Aarya, I'd like to speak with you in my office before your three o'clock tour arrives."

I don't miss the way Alexander's eyes bore into the side of Carter's head.

I nod as I turn my attention to Giuliana. "See you tomorrow. Movie night, don't forget."

She sticks out her arms, and Alexander leans over so she can reach me, happy as a clam with her candy as she hugs me. "Bye, Aarya."

I hesitate as I gaze up at Alexander, unsure of how much PDA he wants to show in front of his daughter.

"Eddie will pick you up tonight since I have a game," he says, wrapping a hand around my waist as he presses his lips to my forehead. "And then I'll come get you with the SUV when I get back tomorrow so we can load up your boxes."

I shoot him a wink. "Good luck tonight."

He flashes me a smile, and carries Giuliana toward the exit. Her voice echoes as they head out, and I find myself wondering what she's saying.

Nerves eat at my stomach as I watch the two of them. I've never lived with anyone other than my mother. How will it feel living with Alexander and his daughter?

Am I ready for this?

For a hundred grand, I need to be.

Carter escorts me to his office, and closes the door with a click behind us.

"Boxes," Carter says as he rounds his desk to sit behind it. "Are you moving?"

I clear my throat and lower myself into the chair opposing his desk. "Yeah, I'm moving in with Alexander."

He arches a brow. "A little soon to be moving in, don't you think?"

My personal life is none of his business. I want to tell him that, but instead, I bite my tongue and tell him, "We've been dating for a while. We just haven't let anyone know about it."

He nods. "There are some things I'd like to discuss."

"Is everything okay?"

"I just wanted to make sure the promotion is something you're still interested in."

My chin jerks back. "Of course. Why wouldn't it be?"

He hikes a nonchalant shoulder. "I don't know. You have a rich new boyfriend. You seem preoccupied. I'd hate to see you throw away everything you've worked for."

My mouth flaps open. "Preoccupied? I'm sorry, but I'm not sure what you mean."

I've busted my ass at this job, bending over backwards to do anything and everything Carter has asked of me, staying later than any of the other employees and taking on more tours. He finds out about Alexander, and suddenly he thinks I'm *preoccupied*?

"The promotion means more hours; a higher work-load. I need to be confident that you're willing to put this job first. Taking on a relationship with a high-profile athlete who has a young child might get in the way of that." Carter slides a sheet of paper across his desk. "You recently put in for a few upcoming days off."

I glance down at my schedule for next month, several of Alexander's away games highlighted in yellow. "With all due respect, Carter, I rarely take off."

"I know, and now that's changing." He presses his lips into a firm line. "I noticed those are game days."

My eyebrows press together. "You looked up to see when his games are?"

"I'm a fan of the team. It was nothing against you."

My lips tug downward. "Carter, this job is everything to me. Having a relationship doesn't change that. I can do both. I can have a personal life and a career at the same time."

"I hope so."

This conversation feels like a threat, or a punishment for being with Alexander. Maybe it was a mistake inviting him here with Giuliana today. Or maybe Carter's jealous that I'm not single anymore, and he knows he can't cross the line like he used to.

Either way, I want to stand up and tell Carter to go fuck himself. That he can't tell me how to spend my given days off. That my relationship status shouldn't affect my consideration for a promotion.

Most of all, that he shouldn't be flirting with his female employees.

But I can't. I just need to find a way to honor both of my commitments, to my job and to this fake marriage agreement until the day comes when I can leave this place, and my boss, behind.

I FLOP onto the couch and glance around at the boxes stacked by the doorway.

"Well, Dash, this is it. We're moving tomorrow, and I don't know if you're going to like it." I run my fingers through his silky fur as he snores beside me. "You'll have a lot more room to roam around, but I just hope you get along with their dog."

I know this isn't the last night in my apartment *forever*, but it's the first time I'm moving in with someone else, and I can't help the nerves swarming in my stomach.

It'll all be worth it in the end when I have that money in my bank account.

My eyes follow Alexander as he skates across the TV screen, effortlessly passing the puck to McKinley between two opposing players in the replay from tonight's game. Since I spent the night packing, I watched his game from my apartment. He's talented. It's easy to see why he's the captain. It's like he controls every move on the ice, making each play bend to his will. He commands attention, taking the puck and putting it exactly where he wants it.

It's sexy as hell.

He's sexy as hell. But I can't touch him. Can't kiss him. Can't have him the way I want to. It's frustrating as hell. I want no-strings attached, and he wants monogamy. I don't catch feelings, and he wants to fall in love. We couldn't be more opposite. And the last thing I want to do is hurt him, so I have to respect his wishes. I need to put my physical feelings aside and remember that we're just two friends helping each other out.

After the game ends, my phone buzzes on the nightstand beside me, pulling me out of my thoughts. I swipe my thumb across Alexander's name before his face fills the screen.

"Hey, Big Man. Shouldn't you be out partying with the rest of your team?"

He rests against the headboard in his hotel room. "Not in the mood to party."

"Why not? You played a great game tonight."

His eyebrows shoot up. "You watched?"

"In between packing."

"How did that go?"

"Easy. I don't have much." I flip the screen so he can see the three boxes across the room before flipping it back to my face. "Dash is a little nervous though," I whisper. "Between me and you."

He chuckles. "Tell Dash he has nothing to worry about. We're going to make his stay as luxurious as possible."

I grin. "I bet Giuliana is excited."

"Annie sent me a video of her jumping on the bed like it was Christmas Eve." He shakes his head. "You're officially as cool as Santa."

I toss my hair over my shoulder. "Obviously."

"Giuliana loved being at the gallery today." A soft smile tilts his lips. "She was very intrigued by all the naked people in the rain-and-sauce era."

My eyes squeeze shut as I choke out a laugh. "Oh my god. That's what I'm calling the Renaissance from now on."

His shoulders shake with laughter. "I love when she gets words wrong."

"You should write them all down in a book and give it to her when she goes off to college."

"That's actually a great idea." He arches a brow. "Who knew you were so sentimental?"

I roll my eyes. "I have to keep you on your toes."

His smile fades as he tilts his head, those keen eyes of his boring into mine. "How are you doing?"

"I'm fine. Why do you ask?"

"I know this is a big deal for you, moving in with someone—especially someone who has a four-year-old."

I purse my lips. "So that's why you called me. You think I'm going to back out of our agreement?"

"Not at all." He pauses. "If I'm being honest, I called because I wanted to see your face."

"You just saw my face at the gallery today."

"It's a good face. I'd like to see it often."

I laugh off his compliment. "Well, good because you're about to see it a lot starting tomorrow. You'll be sick of this face in no time."

He lets his head fall back against the headboard as he grins. "Impossible."

"So, what is this surprise you have planned?"

"Why don't you tell me the reason you don't like surprises, and maybe I'll tell you."

I roll my eyes. "You won't tell me."

"You're right. I won't." His voice softens. "But you can still tell me."

My fingers smooth over Dash's fur, stopping to scratch behind one of his ears. "I don't like being caught off guard. My mom kept the truth about my father from me until she blurted it out one day while we were arguing. I guess that's where it stems from. Then, I'd be surprised to find an eviction notice on our door of each new apartment we lived in. And one day, she surprised me by kicking me out after a stupid fight." I shrug. "I've never been surprised by flowers, or a present, or good news. So, I guess that's why I hate surprises."

Alexander's lips tug downward as his eyebrows collapse. "She kicked you out? How old were you?"

"Seventeen."

"Where did you go?"

"I stayed with Cassidy until I was eighteen. Then I found an apartment in Newark. It was in someone's attic. No windows, poor ventilation. The owners of the house were dealers, and there was always an addict passed out on the front steps. I had to carry pepper spray with me everywhere I went, just in case someone tried to push his way inside the house."

The same pepper spray I had from living with my mother's revolving door of sleazy boyfriends.

He shakes his head. "That's why you're not scared to walk home alone from work every night."

"It's like a walk in the park compared to where I used to live." I pause. "I never did get to use the pepper spray though. Kind of disappointed about that. I'm dying to see how it works."

Alexander shoots me a look. "Let's keep it that way. I don't want you to be in a situation where you need to use it."

I waggle my eyebrows. "Maybe I can try it on you. What do you say?"

One corner of his mouth curves up. "This isn't the time for jokes. We're having a serious conversation right now."

"That's how I have serious conversations—deflection with a dark sense of humor."

He heaves a long sigh as he stares at me through the screen. "Well, I can promise you that this surprise is a good one. You have nothing to worry about."

And the funny thing is, I actually believe him. I don't think Alexander would do a damn thing to upset me or blindside me. He's so careful about what he says and does, so in tune with how I'm feeling.

I hate it.

Or I hate the fact that I don't hate it. I actually kind of like it.

I trust him, and fuck if that isn't the biggest surprise of all.

19

ALEXANDER

GIULIANA BOLTS OUT OF THE HOUSE THE SECOND SHE SEES US pull into the driveway.

Aarya smiles in the passenger seat, and it's the first sign of emotion from her all morning. She was quiet while we packed her boxes into my SUV, and she hasn't said much aside from whispering words of comfort to Dash inside his travel case.

I feel awful, as if I'm forcing Aarya to live with me—despite the fact that she chose to do this, and is being compensated. Nerves eat away at my stomach.

Will this plan work?

Will my grandfather believe the façade and leave us alone?

How will Giuliana handle this when Aarya moves out?

My daughter hops on her bare feet in the driveway waiting for Aarya to step outside. She's been so excited to meet Dash, and I can't help but chuckle as she peers inside the carrier when Aarya holds it up in front of her.

"He's beautiful," Giuliana whispers.

Aarya crouches down in front of her. "He's a little scared right now. He might need some time to get used to his new living space."

"Then I can hold him?"

"Then you can hold him."

Giuliana tugs on Aarya's hand as she stands. "Come on. We have to show you the surprise."

"Hold on, baby girl." I pop the trunk as I round the vehicle. "Let us get settled first. Then you can do the big reveal."

Giuliana squeals, her tiny hands balling into fists as she shakes. "Hurry!"

"Keep her out of the room, Annie," I call as she stands waiting in the doorway.

Annie grins. "On it."

I carry everything inside and stack Aarya's boxes in her new room. I debated on which of the three guest rooms to give her, and ended up opting for the one farthest from Giuliana's room. Sometimes she wakes up from a nightmare, or cries out for me if she's scared, and I'd hate for Aarya to get woken up in the middle of the night.

Aarya's eyes bounce around the room as she sets Dash's case on the bed.

"I hope this is okay." I scratch the back of my neck. "Feel free to decorate it in any way you want. Hang pictures on the wall, or change the comforter."

"It's fine the way it is." Aarya looks at me for what feels like the first time today. "Don't stress it."

I heave a sigh and shake my head. "I—"

"It's time for the surprise!" Giuliana bursts into the room and bounces on the bed, sticking her nose against the metal door separating her from Dash. "Hi, kitty! You're so pretty. You look so soft. I can't wait to hold you. Ellie wants to meet you too. I hope you get along, not like Tom and Jerry."

"Giuls." I kneel down at the foot of the bed. "What did we talk about? You can't barge into Aarya's room. You have to knock first."

Giuliana's big eyes fly up to Aarya. "Sorry."

"It's okay." Aarya holds out her hand for Giuliana. "Let's see that surprise you've been telling me about."

My stomach clenches as I follow them into the hallway, nerves eating away at me in anticipation.

"Close your eyes," Giuliana says.

Aarya glares at me over her shoulder before she complies. "Don't let me walk into a wall, kid."

Giuliana giggles. "I won't."

They stop in front of the closed door of one of the other guest rooms, and Giuliana counts down from three.

"Three, two, one." She twists the doorknob and flings open the door. "Open your eyes!"

Light floods in from the windows on the opposite side of the room, and Aarya squints as she steps inside.

"It's an art room," Giuliana explains, gesturing to the easel. "You can paint in here."

I wait for Aarya's reaction, watching as her eyes bounce from the different brands of paint on the wooden work table, to the dozens of paint brushes standing in the holder I found at the craft store, to the blank canvases stacked against the wall. I didn't know there were so many kinds of paint, and wasn't sure which kind she preferred...so I bought them all.

"I don't..." She blinks up at me. "I haven't painted in so long."

"I know." I swallow, slipping my hands into my pockets. "You said you used to love it, so I figured you could have your own creative space to do it again. Maybe even make a piece to hang in your own gallery one day."

She walks over to the table and runs her fingers over the bristles of the paint brushes.

"Maybe we can paint together one day," Giuliana blurts out, and I know she's been holding back that question this whole time.

Aarya smiles down at her. "That would be fun. We can get you a little easel of your own."

Her smile is so wide, her cheeks bunch up around her eyes. "Okay!"

Aarya put that smile on her face, and damn if that doesn't do something to my heart.

I hold out my hand for her. "Come on, Giuls. You can help me with lunch while we let Aarya unpack in her room."

"I can help her unpack."

I answer before Aarya can say anything. "Give her some space so she can organize her stuff. Plus, Dash needs to calm down."

Her bottom lip juts out, but she doesn't fight me on it. "Okay."

I squeeze her hand as she slips it in mine.

I glance at Aarya, who's still staring at the assortment of art supplies. "Let me know if you need anything."

She nods and offers me a smile.

It's a small one, but I'll take it.

AARYA DIDN'T COME out of her bedroom for lunch, much to Giuliana's dismay, but she ate with us for dinner.

I made her favorite spaghetti and meatballs as a *welcome to our home* kind of meal. More like a *thank you for agreeing to live with me and marry me so that I don't lose my parents' villa even though this is entirely too much to ask of you* meal.

After dinner, we introduced Giuliana and Ellie to Dash. Giuliana held out her hand to let Dash sniff her, and he let her pet his head until he decided he was over it. That wasn't nearly enough attention for my daughter, but she's being patient. Ellie is a gentle giant; she sniffed the cat curiously, but didn't jump or bark. Dash, on the other hand, hissed and then squirmed to get out of Aarya's arms before bolting inside his travel case to hide.

"It's movie time." Giuliana slides off Aarya's bed. "I picked a good princess movie for you."

I ruffle her curls. "Go get your pajamas on first."

"Can I help make the popcorn?"

"Of course."

She runs out of the room with Ellie hot on her heels.

I flick my eyes to Aarya. "I'm sorry. I know she's a lot."

"You don't have to keep apologizing for her." She shrugs. "She's just a kid."

"I know, but I also know this isn't the kind of life you're used to, and I just want to make sure—"

"I'm fine, Big Man." She tucks her hair behind her ear. "And thanks for the art room. You really didn't have to do that."

"I wanted to give you something that felt like yours."

"You're giving me plenty."

We stare at each other, and I have to ball my hands into fists at my sides to keep from reaching out and pulling her into a hug. The need for physical touch when she's around has become increasingly inconvenient. I've gone years without the touch of another woman, yet whenever I'm around Aarya, it's all I crave. Her arms wrapped around me, her body against mine, her nearness.

But that would be crossing a line, and I have to keep that boundary solid.

Giuliana appears in the doorway wearing her favorite pink onesie pajamas. "Do you have feetie pajamas, Aarya?"

She chuckles. "No, but I'm thinking I might have to get a pair now."

Giuliana's eyes light up as they step into the hallway, leaving me behind like I'm chopped liver.

I make three bowls of popcorn and pull out the fleece blankets from inside the ottoman. Giuliana takes the spot next to Aarya on the couch, insisting on sharing a blanket. She's practically in her lap, and I don't know how Aarya feels about it, but if she's annoyed, she doesn't let it show on her face.

Ellie curls up with me on the opposing recliner, and I pat her head as I push play.

As the music starts and the ice harvesters collect the cubes of ice from the lake, Giuliana explains the premise of the movie *Frozen* to Aarya.

"But the prince doesn't save the princess in the end," she finishes. "So, I think you'll like it."

"Don't spoil the movie," I warn.

"I won't." Giuliana sticks out her tongue at me, and Aarya sticks out hers too.

I chuckle to myself. Something tells me those two are going to be thick as thieves, and that worries me as much as it brings me joy.

"Hey, Aarya? What's wrong with the prince rescuing the princess?" Giuliana asks.

Aarya takes a deep breath before answering. "I just think the princess should try to save herself instead of waiting for someone to come and rescue her."

Giuliana nods as she takes in her answer. "But sometimes she needs help. She can't always do it by herself."

"Out of the mouths of babes," I mutter, unable to conceal my smile.

Aarya glares at me before bringing her gaze back to Giuliana. "You're right. Everyone needs help sometimes. But don't forget that the princess can be her own hero too. She doesn't always need a man to save her."

"She can even be the one to save him," I add.

Aarya's face softens as she offers me a smile, and I know she understands the underlying meaning within my words.

Giuliana beams. "They can help each other. And then they fall in love."

My daughter, the hopeless romantic.

Just like her father.

Aarya watches the movie with rapt attention, and I even catch her giggling at some of the quirky things Anna says. I do think my daughter picked the perfect movie to serve as an introduction to Disney movies. You have the self-isolating ice queen who has to learn how to stop pushing away the people who care about her; the brave, headstrong sister who fights for what she believes in; the deceitful man—which goes along with Aarya's jaded views—and the good guy who goes above and beyond to help the sisters. Plus, who doesn't love Olaf and Sven?

I even caught Aarya wiping a tear from her eye when she thought Anna had died.

"Well, what do you think?" Giuliana asks when the credits appear on the black screen.

"I loved it." Aarya's watery eyes flick to mine. "The princesses saved each other."

Giuliana smiles proudly at me, pleased with herself for picking the right movie.

I push off the couch, and Ellie jumps down with me. "Brush your teeth, and I'll read you a story before bed."

"Can Aarya read me a story?" Giuliana whips her head around. "Aarya, will you read me a bedtime story?"

Aarya glances at me looking unsure. "Uh, sure. If that's okay with your dad."

I feign sadness, slumping my shoulders and pouting. "I guess I've been replaced. No one loves me anymore."

Giuliana runs along the length of the couch and dives into my arms. "I love you, Daddy. Don't be sad."

I chuckle as I squeeze her tiny body, being careful around her cast. "I know you do. I was just joking." I lower my voice as I whisper, "I don't think

163

Aarya has ever read someone a bedtime story before, so you might have to show her what to do."

She nods. "Got it, boss."

"Boss?" I arch a brow. "You really need to stop hanging around Uncle Mac so much."

She giggles as I set her on her feet and darts into the hallway.

I turn to Aarya as she stands and folds the blanket before stuffing it back inside the ottoman. "You don't have to read to her if you just want to go to bed."

"I don't mind, as long as you don't."

"Of course not. I just..." I pause. "I don't want you to feel obligated to do something if you're not comfortable with it. She's going to ask for things, and it's okay for you to say no."

She nods. "I know."

I try to give the two of them privacy while Aarya reads the book Giuliana picked out, but I sneak a few peeks as I purposely pass her room in the hall. Giuliana insisted Aarya get on her bed and sit against the headboard while she read, and Giuliana laid her head in her lap. If Aarya is uncomfortable with it, she doesn't let it show. She looks more comfortable with Giuliana than I thought she would, to be honest.

At one point, Giuliana fell asleep, but Aarya didn't move. She closed the book, and gazed down at Giuliana while she played with her curls. I'd have given up a lot of money to hear her thoughts in that moment.

The sight had my throat burning, and I had to walk away to find something to busy myself with while I waited for Aarya to slip out of her bed. Giuliana has always had Annie, but she doesn't look at her like a mother; more like a grandmother if anything. Her preschool teacher is older, as well. Aarya is the only younger woman in her life, and I just hope she doesn't develop any feelings for her that could be problematic later on.

Giuliana once asked why she doesn't have a mother like the other kids at school, and all I could bring myself to tell her was that God decides what kind of family you have. That seemed to quell her questions, but I know as she gets older, it'll come around again.

After twenty minutes, I crept into the hallway to check on Aarya again —only to find her passed out with Giuliana in her arms.

I tiptoe into the bedroom and lift Aarya off the bed, careful not to jostle

Giuliana too much and wake her. I shut the lights off on my way out, and close the door behind me.

Aarya's eyes blink open as I carry her into her bedroom. "What's happening?"

"You fell asleep in Giuliana's bed. I'm just taking you to your room."

Her head falls back against my shoulder, and she nuzzles into the crook of my neck as she hums.

I peel back the comforter and lower her onto the bed. She scoots under the sheets, and curls up in a ball on her side.

I lean down and brush her hair away from her face. The moon shining through her window casts a sliver of light across the room.

"Thank you," I whisper, letting my fingers graze her cheek.

For agreeing to do this.

For being so patient with Giuliana.

For supporting me so I don't feel so alone.

I move toward the door, but stop when she calls my name.

"Alex?"

I glance over my shoulder.

"The art room was a good surprise."

Pride swells in my chest. "I'm glad you like it."

A faint smile touches her lips, and as I watch her drift off to sleep, I'm certain I'd do anything at all just to see her smile.

20

AARYA

THE FIRST FEW DAYS LIVING WITH ALEXANDER AREN'T AS awkward as I thought they'd be.

With his busy hockey schedule, we don't see each other around the house too much, and when we do, Giuliana serves as a good buffer. She certainly keeps things interesting. It's amazing how many questions her brain can conjure up.

Who was the first person to create pancakes?

How does electricity work?

What happened to the dinosaurs?

What would happen if a cat and dog had a baby? Which of course led to the inevitable, *Where do babies come from?*

It was fun watching Alexander field *that* question.

But raising Giuliana is a constant job—one I admire Alexander for. He never complains, and always does as much as he can on his own without having to ask Annie to help. Being a professional hockey player and a single parent is demanding on their own, yet he somehow finds a balance. It makes me wonder how much pressure he feels underneath the surface of his calm façade that he doesn't talk about.

And it makes me want to help out as much as I can.

Which is why I let Giuliana sneak into my room at 1AM when she tells me she's scared.

"Can I sleep with you?" she whispers, tiptoeing to the side of my bed.

I dig the heel of my hand into my eye as I stifle a yawn. "What's wrong, kid"

"I had a nightmare and now I can't fall back to sleep."

I switch on the lamp on my nightstand before patting my comforter. "Come on up."

Giuliana climbs onto the bed and scoots herself underneath the covers, glued to my side. "I had a dream that I was lost. It was really dark, and I couldn't see anything. I kept calling out for Daddy, but I couldn't see him."

"That does sound scary."

The parenting websites I've been on say to validate the child's feelings instead of telling them something logical, like, *There's nothing to be scared of.*

"I used to be scared of the dark when I was little too."

Her eyebrows shoot up. "Really?"

I nod. "I slept with a flashlight until I was twelve-years-old."

"Wow. That's old."

I smile. "And I didn't have a big, strong dad like you do to protect you. It was just me and my mom, and half the time she wasn't home because she had to work late hours."

"So, what did you do when you were scared?"

"I'd draw. I had a sketchbook filled with the things that made me feel happy, so I could take my mind off the scary things in my head."

"What did you draw?"

"Flowers, kittens, the beach." I shrug. "Whatever I could think of."

"Are you still afraid of the dark now?"

I shake my head. "Nope, not anymore."

"What are you afraid of?"

I pull a sleeping Dash onto my lap so Giuliana can pet him. "Nothing really."

Alexander's voice has both of our shoulders jumping. "Ah, come on. Everyone's afraid of something."

Dear God, the man is shirtless. Smooth olive skin. Broad shoulders and chest. Perfectly sculpted abs. Muscle upon muscle. His body is the result of endless hours of training and an athlete's diet. And fuck if I'm not going to stare and appreciate all the hard work he's put into it.

But my mouth drops open when I spot the glint of a silver barbell poking through one of his nipples, and black ink on the left side of his ribcage.

Damn. A motorcycle, a nipple piercing, *and* a tattoo? Color me surprised.

And turned on.

Wearing a pair of low-slung basketball shorts and nothing else, he strides into the room. His hair is disheveled, smushed up on one side, and he rubs at his tired eyes.

Thank God there's a child in the bed, otherwise I don't think I'd be able to control myself.

Giuliana pats the bed like I did for her. "Come sit with us, Daddy."

"Why are you up, little one?" He lowers himself onto the edge of the mattress, shooting me an apologetic glance.

"I had a nightmare and I didn't want to wake you up because I know you have to get on the plane early in the morning."

My heart. This little girl is a thinker and a worrier just like her father.

He smooths a hand over her hair. "Aarya has to get up for work tomorrow too, though, baby."

"It's okay," I say, giving Giuliana's hand a reassuring squeeze. "We were talking about the things I used to do to help me when I got scared as a kid."

"And you're not scared of anything now?" he asks me. "Not one single thing?"

"Probably sharks. I wouldn't want to be in the ocean with one of those." I hike a shoulder. "But nothing irrational like heights or spiders."

"How is a fear of spiders *irrational*?" His eyes narrow. "That sounds like a pretty rational fear to me."

"Spiders are amazing. They kill all the other harmful insects. Plus, they're adorable."

"Adorable?" He scoffs. "Dogs are adorable. Bunnies. Baby chicks. Anything that doesn't have eight legs and the ability to crawl into your mouth while you're asleep."

I roll my eyes. "They want nothing to do with your mouth."

"Think about it. Why do they need so many legs, hmm? Dolphins have none, and they're awesome. Dogs have four, and they're the best animals ever. Why do you need eight legs? It's not for anything good, I'm telling you."

"Just look at the way they build their webs, and capture their prey. They're so intelligent."

"Spiders are pretty cool, Daddy. Just like Charlotte from *Charlotte's Web*." Giuliana giggles. "He cried watching that movie."

"I don't doubt it." *The big softie.* I bite my bottom lip to keep from laughing. "Maybe if you learned more about them, you wouldn't be so scared. They're as fascinating as bees."

Alexander closes his eyes and shudders. "I *hate* bees."

I arch a brow. "Big Man is afraid of a little sting?"

"Those stingers hurt. People lie when they say *they won't bother you if you don't bother them*." He swings his arms out wide. "And they have the whole earth to roam around. Why do they always find my ear holes?"

"You liked *The Bee Movie*, didn't you?" Giuliana asks.

"Yes, but that was a cartoon." He heaves a sigh like he's stressed just talking about it. "Anything with a hive mentality is terrifying."

"That's what makes them so amazing. They protect the colony at all costs." I jump up to my feet and pull Giuliana up with me, lifting her into my arms. "Isn't that right, Giuls?"

"Protect the colony!" she shouts as I spin her around.

I jump off the bed and fly her into her room, flipping on the lights before I give her a crash-landing on her bed.

She squeals and scoots under the sheets. "Can you lay with me for a little while? Just until I fall asleep?"

Alexander starts to tell her no, but I interrupt. "Sure." I point my index finger at him. "And you get your butt back in bed because you need your rest."

"Yes, ma'am." He backs out of the room with his hands at either side of his head. "Maybe I should be scared of *you*."

"You should." I shoot him a wink and flip off the lights.

I lie with Giuliana until I hear her breathing even out, and then I slink out of her room and close her door.

Alexander is waiting in my room when I get back, with Dash curled up in his lap.

169

"She's asleep." I lower myself onto the foot of the bed beside him. "As you should be."

"I'm really sorry about that."

"Don't be. I'm up a lot throughout the night, so it's not a big deal."

Years of being woken up by my mother's flavors of the week—whether it was the sound of them having sex, fighting, or trying to get into *my* room— has turned me into a light sleeper.

He shakes his head. "All the more reason she shouldn't be waking you."

"It's okay if you're jealous that she wants me and not you." I nudge him with my shoulder, attempting to pull a smile out of him. "I'm pretty awesome. It's not her fault."

All I get is a smirk. He's quiet as his gaze remains on his hands in his lap.

"If you're worried about being away these next few days, don't be. We'll be fine here."

He nods. "I know."

"Then what's on your mind, Big Man?"

"We need to discuss when we're going to get married."

Nerves squeeze my stomach. "Sooner than later is probably best."

"I looked it up online. We need to have a witness there when we sign the paperwork. It seems pretty simple."

I pop a shoulder, trying to be nonchalant. "I can call tomorrow and make the appointment."

"That would be great, thanks." Still, he doesn't budge.

"Anything else?" I stifle a yawn. "You need to get some sleep before your alarm goes off."

He reaches into his pocket and pulls out a small black velvet box. "If you still want to do this, then I'd like you to wear my mother's ring. If that's something you're okay with."

My eyes widen as I stare down at the box like it's a live bomb. "I didn't even think about rings."

He nods as he flips open the top. "I always imagined I'd use my mother's ring when I proposed."

"Is this your proposal?" I try to laugh it off, but it gets caught in my throat.

His eyes flick to mine. "You'd hate it if I got down on one knee."

I grin, ignoring the fact that he knows me well enough to know that.

"Considering this is the only proposal I'll ever get, I'd say it's a memorable one."

His eyebrows pinch together, ignoring my joke. "You don't think you'll ever get married?"

"Nope. You're the only one locking me down."

The corner of his mouth tips up, as if that idea pleases him.

I gaze down at the ring between us. "It's beautiful, Alex."

There's a pear-shaped diamond in the middle of a thin gold band. It's not flashy, and the diamond isn't overly big. It's classy and simple.

I'm not into jewelry, but I don't mind this, knowing it means something to Alexander, knowing it's a piece of his parents that he's sharing with me.

"If you want me to buy you a new ring, I will. I just figured—"

"No." I wrap my fingers around his hand that's holding the box. "I would be honored to wear your mother's ring. We're doing this for your parents, after all."

He slips the ring out of the box and takes my left hand in his. The ring slides over my finger, but isn't tight enough to stay on it without the diamond spinning to the inside of my hand.

"I'll have it resized when I get back," he says, tucking the ring back inside the box. "Annie will be here in case you need anything. I cooked enough meals for the next two days, but I'll leave my credit card in the kitchen if you want to order anything."

"Stop thinking, and go to sleep, Big Man. Everything is going to be fine." I rise from the bed and tug on his massive arm, making Dash jump onto the floor. "Come on. Do you need me to tuck you in, too?"

He chuckles. "Yeah, read me a bedtime story."

He lets me pull him all the way down the hall and into his bedroom. I shove him onto the mattress and pull the comforter up around him. "Once upon a time, there was a giant hockey player who worried too much. One day, all of his hair started falling out, which was a damn shame because he had a nice head of hair. The end."

He squeezes his eyes shut as he laughs. "That is the worst story ever."

"It teaches a valuable life lesson: Don't worry so much or you'll go bald."

"Stick to art and leave the books to Cassidy." He reaches out and clasps my hand before I walk away. "Seriously, thank you for helping with Giuliana tonight."

"I didn't do anything special."

"You don't need to. Being you is enough." His thumb draws lazy circles against mine. "You're great with her."

Warmth blankets my body, something unfamiliar tugging at my heart. "Anybody would be. She's a great kid."

It's a shame her mother didn't stick around to see that. She's missing out, yet she'll never know.

I push away the sadness and squeeze Alexander's hand. "Have a good game tomorrow, Angel Food Cake."

With those big puppy eyes on me, he brings my palm to his lips and presses a kiss in the center of it before letting go of my hand. "Goodnight, spitfire."

"Don't let the bed bugs bite." I toss a wink over my shoulder when I reach the door. "Or spiders crawl into your mouth."

A pillow hits me square in the ass on my way out.

21

ALEXANDER

Being at away games are always hard.

I hate not being there for Giuliana, and I'm always worried something bad is going to happen. But between the added security, and the text updates from Aarya this weekend, I've been happy knowing Giuliana is having the time of her life with her new favorite person.

> Aarya: I gave Annie the day off and took Giuls to buy her a kid-sized easel
>
> Aarya: We're going to paint today
>
> Aarya: *insert picture*

> Me: Is that chocolate on her face?

> Aarya: I told her it was too early for chocolate, but she looked me dead in the eyes and said, "It's never too early for chocolate."
>
> Aarya: I couldn't argue with that kind of logic

Aarya will have to learn the hard way why I don't give my daughter sugar before lunch.

Another series of texts come in at noon, with pictures of Giuliana at a fast-food burger joint.

> Aarya: She has the same damn puppy eyes that you have

> > Me: What did she convince you to buy her?

> Aarya: This ice cream cone that's entirely too big for her

> Aarya: *insert picture*

> Aarya: I don't even know how it's possible to get ice cream on your ear

I laugh, knowing exactly how messy Giuliana gets when she eats.

> Aarya: There's a boy who isn't playing nice in the ball pit

> Aarya: If he touches her, I'm going to have to get in there

> Aarya: I'll shove his head under the balls and hold him there until he squeals

> > Me: So violent. Where are his parents?

> Aarya: Mom is talking her friend's ear off. Completely oblivious that her son is terrorizing the other children

> > Me: Some parents are like that

> Aarya: I just told Giuliana to hit him with her cast if he comes too close

> > Me: You can't teach my daughter to hit the other kids

> Aarya: The fuck I can't. She needs to know how to stick up for herself

> Aarya: We should put her in karate

My stomach clenches at the word *we*. As if Giuliana is ours. As if we're a team. I know she didn't mean it that way, but I can't ignore the way it makes me feel.

The texts continue as the day goes on, and I check my phone as I'm getting ready for tonight's game.

> Aarya: She just told me she wants a baby brother
>
> Aarya: Kid is barking up the wrong tree

> Me: LOL she is dying for a sibling
>
> Me: I thought the dog would be enough

> Aarya: Have a great game, Big Man. We'll be watching
>
> Aarya: *insert picture*

My heart swells at the sight of Giuliana and Aarya snuggled on the couch—in matching onesie pajamas—ready to watch me play. Ellie rests her head in Giuliana's lap while Dash lounges on the back of the couch behind Aarya.

"Look at those two."

My head spins around to catch McKinley peering at the picture on my phone over my shoulder. "Aarya spent the day with Giuliana. They had so much fun."

He plops onto the bench beside me and shoves his foot into his skate. "Things seem to be going well."

"It's only the first week, but yeah." I shrug. "Things are going much smoother than I thought they would."

Between the woman who doesn't want to be tied down playing house with the single dad, the kid with entirely too much energy, and an anti-social cat...I'd say the first week has gone amazing.

He lowers his voice. "When are you going to tie the knot?"

"She couldn't get an appointment until next month."

"I need everyone's attention." Jason stands and waits for the locker room to quiet down. "As you all know, Kourtney, Celeste and I aren't allowed to get married according to the state. But we want to exchange vows and have a ceremony, even if it's not recognized by the law. We're taking a trip to Greece next weekend since we don't have a game, and we'd love it if you could all join us. I know it's last minute, but—"

"We'll be there!" McKinley shouts.

The team cheers and surrounds Jason, clapping him on the back and congratulating him. After everything he has been through coming out in a polyamorous relationship, it makes me happy to see him being supported by our teammates.

I scratch the back of my neck, wondering how I could swing an impromptu trip to Greece with a four-year-old. I wouldn't want to leave her behind, and we have yet to be on a vacation. She'd be elated to get on an airplane and see another country. But I'd have to take her out of school for a few days. I've never traveled with a child before. Maybe I should just skip the trip and spend the time with her at home.

Thoughts speed through my mind, until Jason slaps my shoulder pad. "We'd love it if Giuliana could be our flower girl."

A huge smile stretches across my face. "She would absolutely love that."

"Yeah? You and Aarya would bring her?"

What's stopping us? The world knows about Giuliana now, and we can go wherever we want. Greece would be the trip of a lifetime, and she's always upset about being left out of the things I do with my friends. Taking her with me would mean the world to her.

I nod. "We'll be there."

I check my phone once more before the game starts, and one text from Aarya is waiting for me:

> Aarya: I think your daughter is my new best friend.

WE LOST THE GAME, but it was a close one.

I drag my tired ass into the hotel bed, wishing I could snap my fingers and be home with my girls.

My girls.

I pinch the bridge of my nose and blow out a long breath through my lips. Aarya is anything but *my* girl. It's ridiculous how often I have to remind myself of this.

Yet here I am, tapping on her name on my phone to call her so I can see her beautiful face before I go to sleep.

She's wearing a tired smile when she answers the FaceTime. "Hey, Big Man. Sorry about the game."

"It's okay. Denver is a tough team."

"You played great." She pauses. "I think."

I chuckle. "I'll take the compliment, even though you don't know the difference between great and shitty plays." She stifles a yawn, and I arch a brow. "How was *your* day?"

"It was great. Busy." She grimaces. "I'm exhausted and my whole body hurts."

"Kids will do that to you. You really should've let Annie help out. Today was a lot for you."

"It was fine."

"Giuliana looked like she had a great time with you."

That makes her smile. "Oh, by the way: You're going to Greece next weekend."

My eyebrows shoot up as I feign surprise. "I am?"

She nods. "Jason, Kourtney, and Celeste are getting married. They want Giuliana to be the flower girl. She's going to be so excited. You guys are going to have so much fun."

I tilt my head. "Don't you mean *we* are going to have fun?"

"Oh, no. I can't go. I could never afford a trip to Greece. Plus, my boss would kill me if I tried to take off on such short notice. He's already pissed about the amount of time I took off for your away games."

Bile rises in my throat. "What do you mean he's already pissed? What did he say to you?"

She slaps her palm against her forehead. "Did I say that out loud?"

"Aarya..."

"He brought up the fact that I took off specifically for your games, and made a comment about how work should be my priority." Her eyes flick up to the ceiling. "And he may have threatened to not give me a promotion if I don't take this job seriously."

This piece of shit. "Quit."

A laugh bubbles out of her. "I can't quit. I already told you."

"I don't care. I don't want you working for this asshole anymore. He doesn't have the right to tell you what to do with your personal time, and he certainly doesn't get to threaten you like that."

"Calm down, Big Man. I've got everything under control."

My jaw clenches. "And secondly, you are coming to Greece. I'm paying for you, Giuliana, and Annie. We're going together."

She shakes her head as she starts to argue, but I cut her off. "You're coming, and that's final."

She purses her lips like a brat. "You can't make me do anything I don't want to do."

"Good thing you want to come to Greece then."

The corner of her mouth twitches, and I know I've got her. "Fine. If you want to be my sugar daddy, who am I to say no?"

I cough out a laugh. "I'm not your sugar daddy. I'm your fiancé."

She lets her head fall back against the headboard of her bed. "It makes me uncomfortable that you keep paying for everything."

"I know it does, but that's only because you think you don't deserve it."

She says nothing in response to that.

"I want you to come to Greece. Giuliana wants you to come to Greece. And these are your friends—they want you to be there for their wedding, and so do you. I would never let you miss out on that."

She blinks at me with heavy eyelids. "You make it sound so easy."

"It is that easy." I roll over onto my side and stretch out my arm to prop the phone against the extra pillow. "When it comes to you, I don't have to think or try. I do the things I do because I want to."

She scoots down and mimics my position on her side. "I've never met someone like you before."

"Someone like me?"

"Someone who's selfless. Someone who does the right thing. Good things. Someone who wants to make other people happy, and doesn't ask for anything in return." Her eyes droop closed. "I didn't think people like you existed."

Emotion lodges itself in my throat, and I don't say anything in response, afraid to ruin the intimate moment.

Instead, I stay on the phone with her, watching her until she falls asleep.

She lives inside an impenetrable fortress, her emotions locked inside. I want to break down her walls, to rip out the nails holding up her misguided convictions.

But then I realize, no, I don't want to take her by force. I want her to trust me enough to let down her drawbridge and invite me inside.

I want her to hand me the keys to her heart.

And I'll earn them.

22

AARYA

"Excuse me. What the hell is that on your finger?"

My cheeks burn as I stick my hand behind my back. "Nothing."

"That's definitely not nothing." Chanora darts around the counter and lunges for my arm. "Did you get engaged and not tell me?"

I grimace. "Maybe."

She gasps as she wrestles my arm out and sees the diamond sitting on my finger. "Oh my god, this is beautiful."

I smile a genuine one because it is a beautiful ring. "It was his mother's."

She clutches her chest as she swoons. "That's so romantic." Then she smacks my arm. "Bitch, how could you not tell me this as soon as you walked in this morning?"

I rub my arm. "I'm still getting used to being...engaged."

"Didn't I tell you? I knew you'd meet *the one* and put an end to your single girl days." She pulls me into a hug, and squeezes me tight. "I'm so happy for you, Aarya."

I fight the frown that's pulling at my mouth. I didn't realize how shitty it would feel lying to people about this. The world thinks I've found my happily ever after, but all I've found is a big fat paycheck.

"How did he propose?"

I clear my throat. "Uh, he's a really private person so he did it at home."

"Did he get down on one knee?"

I lie and nod. "Yup."

Chanora squeals and throws her arms around me again. "This is so exciting."

Carter strides into the lobby, and my stomach clenches in a tight ball. "What's so exciting?"

I had wanted to hide this from Carter for as long as I could, mainly because I don't want him to tell me that I'm not making work a priority just because I'm wearing a ring on my finger.

Too late now.

"Aarya got engaged." Chanora thrusts my hand out in front of him. "Look."

His eyebrows jump as he glances from the diamond to me. "Congrats."

The word is as insincere as it can get coming from him, but I force a smile and thank him anyway. He's been giving me the cold shoulder since I asked for time off for Greece, and as uncomfortable as it is, I prefer this to the sexual harassment.

He slides his arms into his jacket and digs into his pocket before pulling out his keys. "Chanora, I'll see you in the morning."

Once he's gone, Chanora blows out a low whistle. "He is not happy with you."

I roll my eyes as I laugh. "Good. I prefer him when he's pissed at me. At least he's not groping me anymore."

She groans. "Hopefully he doesn't start groping me next."

I gesture to her very pregnant belly. "He'd have to be pretty fucking sick to grope a pregnant woman."

"I wouldn't put it past him."

Me either.

As we're closing up the gallery, Brittany, one of the newer hires walks into the lobby. She keeps her head down as she wraps her scarf around her neck.

I step around the front desk to catch up to her. "Hey, Britt. How was your day?"

"Fine." She sniffles, barely glancing up at me. "See you tomorrow."

"Hey, wait." I move in front of her, blocking the door. "What's wrong?"

"It's nothing. I'm just not feeling well."

Chanora and I exchange a knowing glance, and a bad feeling settles in my gut.

"You're upset." I dip my head, forcing her to look at me. "What happened?"

Her watery eyes bounce between me and Chanora. "It was...it's..."

"It was Carter, wasn't it?" Chanora blurts out.

A sob escapes her as she nods, and the tears stream down her face. "He told me not to tell anyone. He said he'd fire me."

I grip her shoulders. "What did he do?"

"He kissed me. And when I tried to get him off of me, he pushed me against the wall and did it again." She covers her face with her hands. "I was afraid to tell him to stop because I need this job, and I didn't want to make him mad."

"Son of a bitch." I spin around and run my fingers through my hair. "He can't keep doing this."

"Has he done this before?" Brittany asks.

Chanora nods. "To quite a few different employees."

"We have to put a stop to this." I pace the length of the windows, gazing outside at the people walking by. "We have to do something."

"We don't have proof," Chanora says. "It's our word against his. You know this."

"Then we need more than just our word." An idea takes form in my mind, one I'm positive could work against the creepy fucker. "We'll get video evidence."

"How are we going to do that?" Brittany asks.

Chanora shakes her head. "No. I don't like that idea."

I swing my arms out wide. "What other choice do we have? We need proof. If we can get a video of him doing something inappropriate, then we can use it against him."

Chanora folds her arms over her chest. "And how do you propose we get that video?"

I gesture to Brittany. "She and I can do it. One of us records it while the other..."

"While the other acts as the bait," Brittany finishes.

I nod. "He can't fire us with that video hanging over his head. And he wouldn't dare to take a chance harassing anyone else."

Chanora smooths her hand over her belly. "How are you going to get the video without him catching you? That sounds dangerous."

"I don't know." I press my fingers against my temples and rub small circles against my skin. "I'll figure it out once I get back from Greece. While I'm gone, you guys have to look out for each other. Don't let Carter get anyone alone in his office."

Chanora wraps her arm around Brittany's shoulders. "I got you, boo."

Brittany wipes her nose with the back of her hand. "Do you really think this will work?"

I nod. "I do."

It has to.

"It looks beautiful on you."

I stare down at the ring I forgot to take off my finger when I got back from work. "This isn't real, Annie."

She clicks her tongue against the roof of her mouth. "Don't say that. This might not be a marriage out of love and passion, but it's a real commitment. This thing you're doing for Alexander? It's real. And I'm so grateful for you. I couldn't bear to watch that boy lose the villa." She places her palm against my cheek. "And I know his parents would be grateful for you too."

"I wish they were here to see how wonderful his life is." My eyes dart to Giuliana, who's shoving clothes into the open suitcase on her bed. "I wish they could've met their granddaughter."

I hate that his parents had to die, while my shitty ones are running around doing whatever the hell they want with their shitty lives.

Annie nods, her eyes following my gaze. "She's something special, isn't she?"

"She is." I smile. "I can't believe how easy it's been living here with her."

"Were you worried it wouldn't be?"

"I don't know the first thing about kids." I let out a sardonic laugh. "And I didn't exactly have a great role model growing up either."

Annie frowns. "Are you not close with your parents?"

"My father left when my mother told him she was pregnant, and my mother kicked me out when I was a teenager. So, no. Not close at all."

"Jesus," she mutters. "I had no idea. I'm so sorry."

"Please, it's fine." I watch as Giuliana tries to fit her whole doll house into the suitcase. "I see myself in Giuliana. My father left me like her mother left her. It feels like there's this empty space where the love I should have for my parents is supposed to be, and I don't want her to feel like she's missing anything in her life."

Annie takes my hand and sandwiches it between both of hers. "That empty space? You'll fill it when you have a family of your own to love."

I scrunch my nose. "I don't think I'll ever have that."

"My husband and I didn't want children." A smile tugs at her lips as she gazes at Giuliana. "But loving that little girl ended up being the greatest joy of my life. Sometimes you don't know what you want until it smacks you in the face."

I don't bother arguing with her. Everything will go back to the way it was when this marriage is over, because that's the deal.

Alexander's footsteps in the hall pull my attention. "Hey, how was work?"

My eyes drop to his shirtless torso, snagging on that damn nipple piercing. Under the hallway light, I get a better view of his tattoo. Two stick figures—one tall with a hockey stick and one short with a dress—hold hands above the word *DADDY* written in shaky kid handwriting.

Everything about this man is sexy. He's got that biker boy edge, wrapped in leather with piercings and tattoos, and slams grown men into the boards on the ice. Yet he braids his daughter's hair, cooks chicken noodle soup, and cries when he watches *Charlotte's Webb*.

"Hmm?" I literally have no idea what he just asked me.

He smirks as he tips my chin, bringing my eyes up to his. "Work. How was work?"

I clear my throat. "Good. Fine. It was fine."

Guilt gnaws at my conscience. He would be livid if he heard about what happened to Brittany today, and there is no way in hell I'm telling him about my plan to catch Carter in the act. He'd tell me not to go through with it, and I refuse to be talked out of it.

"Good." He wraps an arm around Annie's shoulders, and drapes another around mine, peering into Giuliana's room to see what we're looking at. "Anyone going to tell her she can't bring her doll house to Greece?"

"That's all you, Big Man."

He heaves a sigh like he figured as much, and steps into the bedroom. "Hey, baby. Don't think that doll house is going to fit in your suitcase."

She pouts. "What if I take some clothes out?"

"Twenty bucks says he lets her take the doll house," Annie whispers.

I cover my mouth with my hand as I laugh. "I wouldn't be surprised."

I return to my room to finish packing, and after Giuliana falls asleep, there's a soft knock at my open door.

Alexander leans against the doorframe, the bastard still shirtless as if he knows exactly what that sight does to me. "You all set?"

"I think so." I press a kiss to the top of Dash's head before setting him down on my bed. "Just worried about being away from this guy."

"I've kept Ellie at this place before, and they're great with her. I think Dash will be fine." Alexander steps into my room and lowers himself beside Dash on the bed, stroking the fur on his back. Dash rolls over and gives him his belly, a sight I don't think I'll ever get used to seeing.

I reach out and trace the outline of the tattoo on his ribs. "Didn't expect you to have a tattoo."

He glances down at it. "I got it last year after Giuliana drew it for me."

"And this?" My fingers move along his chest, grazing the metal barbell.

He shudders. "When I was eighteen."

I arch a brow. "You have a wild streak in you."

"I used to be a lot more carefree before I became a dad."

"Hard to picture now."

He takes my wrist and turns my hand to gaze down at the ring on my finger. "My father always lived in the present. He never worried about the future, or the what-ifs. He's the reason I love riding so much. He surprised me with my first bike when I got my license, and we used to ride together. It's one of my favorite memories of him."

"I always viewed bikers as reckless adrenaline junkies. But you're not like that."

"It gives you an adrenaline rush for sure. There's always that element of danger there. One wrong move and it's all over. Yet, I feel so alive when I'm riding. It's raw, unfettered freedom. The feeling of the wind whipping against you; the power of the engine roaring under you. It's exhilarating."

Nothin in *my* life has ever made me feel that way.

I chew on my bottom lip. "Will you take me on a longer ride one day?"

His eyebrows shoot up. "You'd want to?"

I do, and it takes me by surprise as much as it does him. But I want to know him. To see the other side of him that no one else gets to see. I want to peel back his carefully guarded layers and crawl inside. He doesn't put on a show, doesn't pretend to be someone he's not. He's real and true and honest, and the more he tells me, the more I want to know.

Alexander keeps his circle small, his life private—and I feel lucky to be part of it.

I nod. "As long as you promise not to kill me."

He lifts my hand and presses a kiss to the top of it. "I'd never let anything happen to you."

23

ALEXANDER

THE ONLY THING BETTER THAN BEING IN GREECE IS SEEING Giuliana's reaction to being in Greece.

The wedding ceremony took place atop a balcony draped in white overlooking the Aegean Sea. Giuliana's wide eyes bounced around, so different from our home in the city. I love getting to see the world from her eyes, like everything is a wonder.

In her pale-pink dress, she performed her flower girl duties with a smile —which she'd practiced before we left, sprinkling fake flower petals all over the house.

And now, she's hopping around the dance floor with Annie and Aarya by her side, having the time of her life at her very first wedding.

Aarya is different here. Carefree. Since the moment we stepped off the plane, she seems more relaxed. It makes me wonder if she's ever been on a vacation prior to this. From the stories she's shared with me about her past, it doesn't seem likely.

"How is everything going between you two?"

I glance down at Cassidy beside me. "Great. Better than I expected, actually."

"She seems to be getting along really well with Giuls."

"She is."

"And how are *you* doing?"

"I'm fine."

She arches a brow. "You forget, I was in a fake relationship too. I know how blurred the lines can get."

"They're only blurred when you act out scenes for your romance book."

Her eyes widen as she swats at my shoulder. "You're not supposed to know about that."

I chuckle as I dodge her hand. "Your husband was very excited to share that with the team."

"The whole team knows?" She groans before shooting Trenton a glare across the dance floor. "He's lucky I love him."

My eyes flick back to Aarya. "The lines aren't getting blurred. I'm making sure of it."

Maybe if I say it out loud enough, it'll become true.

"Would it be so bad if they got a little blurry?"

"I have too much on the line to let that happen."

"Giuliana," she says.

And my heart.

Watching Aarya with Giuliana only makes me like her more. The way Giuliana lights up when she's with her; how patient Aarya has been with her; living with this beautiful woman, having her in my space every day and not being able to touch her and kiss her and hold her the way I want...it's all eating away at me.

It feels like I'm drowning, but I don't want to swim to the surface. I don't want to fight this. I want to slip under the surface and let Aarya consume me.

But I can't. I have to stay afloat—not only for me but for Giuliana.

"Sometimes things have to get a little blurry before you can see properly." Cassidy squeezes my shoulder before she leaves and makes her way over to her husband.

The music changes, and couples break off from the groups on the dance floor.

I head for my girls.

I kneel down to Giuliana's height and hold out my hand, palm facing up. "May I have this dance, young lady?"

She giggles as she throws herself at me. "Pick me up and spin me around."

Aarya smiles as she turns to leave us, but I reach out and clasp her hand, tugging her close to me. "Where do you think you're going?"

Her eyes dart to Giuliana before returning to me. "I was letting you have a dance with your daughter."

"Dance with us, Aarya," Giuliana says as she lays her head on my shoulder and yawns.

With one arm around my daughter, I wrap the other around Aarya's waist, sandwiching Giuliana between us. Aarya surprises me by lowering her head to my other shoulder and resting her palm against Giuliana's back.

My heart nearly bursts from my chest with how full it feels in this moment.

To Aarya, it's just a dance. To me, it's everything I've ever wanted.

One slow song bleeds into the next, and Giuliana's body hangs limp in my arms.

"She's asleep," Aarya whispers.

"I should get her to bed."

"I'll come with you."

"No, stay. Enjoy the rest of the party."

Annie appears beside me. "Both of you stay. I'll take her to bed. This old lady is tired too."

I give her a grateful smile. "Thank you."

She shoots me a wink as she carefully lifts Giuliana into her arms.

I spin Aarya out before pulling her back in, holding her body against mine as we continue to slow-dance.

Her eyes are on the newly married trio as they dance together several feet away from us. "I'm so happy everything worked out for them."

"Me too. It would've sucked if Jason got traded."

Someone tipped off the team's General Manager, and sent him videos of Jason, Kourtney, and Celeste having sex on Kourtney's website. Their faces were covered, but the rumors were enough to do some damage. Jason was about to be traded until we came together as a team, and figured out a way around it.

Aarya smirks. "I'm still in shock that the team posted videos of themselves on Kourtney's website."

"It was a great plan. The GM can't trade the entire team if we all post a video, right?"

She laughs, but then her eyes snap up to mine. "Wait, we? *You* posted a video?"

I nod. "Why do you sound so surprised?"

Her mouth flaps open. "I didn't think...I figured..."

"I had to do it in solidarity." I hike a shoulder. "I'm the captain, after all."

Her eyes bounce between mine. "Who did you have sex with?"

Heat trickles in to my cheeks. "Myself."

Her words come out in a hushed whisper. "You jerked off on camera?"

"I didn't want to show my face in case it somehow gets back to Giuliana when she gets older." I glance around to make sure no one can hear us. "But, yeah. I guess I can check off *star in a porno* off my bucket list."

Aarya's head tips back as she laughs. "Oh my god. I told you: You have a wild streak in you, Big Man."

I grin. "I just did what any good friend would do."

The smile drops from her face. "Is the video still up on the site?"

I hike a shoulder and avert my eyes. "Maybe."

She lets out an exaggerated yawn and tries to pull away from me. "Well, I'm super tired. I'm going to my room now. Goodnight."

I yank her back to me. "Uh-uh. No way are you looking up that video."

"I didn't say I was looking up your video." She rolls her eyes. "I'm just *really* tired."

I smirk. "Tired my ass."

"You do have a great ass." She pauses. "Is that in the video too?"

I laugh. "You're relentless."

"Come on, Big Man. I'm celibate because of you. You've gotta throw me a bone here."

The song ends, and I flick her nose with my index finger. "You are *not* watching me jerk off. End of conversation."

As much as the thought of her touching herself while watching that video makes my dick jump.

We hang out with our friends for another hour, and then we drag ourselves back to our hotel rooms.

I swipe the card over the lock, but stop when the door cracks open.

"Shit."

Aarya peers around the door of my hotel room. "What's wrong?"

When I booked the rooms, I got two adjoining rooms: one with a king-sized bed, and the other with two queens. I figured I'd sleep with Giuliana in one bed, while Annie and Aarya shared the other room.

But it looks like Annie didn't get that memo, as my bed is completely empty.

"Annie must have taken Giuliana back to her room instead of leaving her in mine."

Sure enough, when I crack open the door that connects our rooms, I spot the two of them sound asleep in each of the queen-sized beds.

Aarya shrugs. "It's okay. We can share a bed, Big Guy."

"Are you comfortable with that?"

"We're about to be married. I think I can handle sleeping next to you."

Well, that makes one of us.

24

AARYA

I PRETENDED TO FALL ASLEEP NEXT TO ALEXANDER, AND WAITED until I heard the sound of his steady breaths before I swiped my phone off the nightstand and crept into the bathroom.

There's no way I can sleep knowing that there's a video of Alexander jerking off floating around on the internet.

I don't bother to turn on the light, not wanting to chance waking him up, and I type the name of Kourtney's website into the browser. I click around, searching for what I'm looking for. As tempting as it is to click on my friends' videos—if you tell me watching Jason, Celeste, and Kourtney have sex wouldn't be the hottest thing you'll ever see, you're lying—I scroll past them. I also scroll past Cassidy's blonde hair, which is equally as tempting to click on because I know she and Trenton are into some freaky shit.

But there's only one video I'm interested in, and I won't stop until I find it.

Then I spot a familiar nipple ring.

I wouldn't have recognized it had I not had the absolute pleasure of seeing Alexander without his shirt on. I tap on the thumbnail, and click the button on the side of my phone to make sure the volume is turned down low.

The video begins with him holding the camera out in front of him, from the neck down, cutting off just above the V-shape leading down to what I'm waiting to see. He reaches out to turn on the water overhead, revealing those veins along his forearm that I've dreamed about licking.

And then the camera tilts downward.

My mouth falls open.

Huge feet and muscular tree-trunk legs are there, I'm sure of it, as are perfectly sculpted abs. But all I can focus on is the hand as it wraps around his long, thick cock.

"Holy fucking shit," I whisper, unable to contain my surprise.

I knew it'd be big. That's a given with a man of his size—at least one would hope, for his sake. But expecting it doesn't compare to seeing it.

It's beautiful.

Absolutely perfect.

It should be a work of art in a museum—nothing like those unfortunate Italian Renaissance sculptures.

Alexander's hand moves along his cock, slow at first, stroking it like he's warming up. A low groan echoes over the sound of the water hitting the floor, and my pussy clenches. What I wouldn't give to be the one eliciting his pleasure. He swirls his thumb over his crown and gives it a squeeze, the precum glistening in the dim light.

No one else would know it's him, but I do, and that notion makes this even hotter, being the only person to know his scandalous secret.

His hand moves faster, and I'm completely mesmerized. The way his hips thrust into his touch; the way his forearm flexes with each pump; the deep timbre of his grunts. I watch with rapt attention, my thighs squeezing together to subdue the ache between them.

Alexander shifts the camera out to the side, angling it to provide a full view of his lower body. Water drips down his thighs as his balls slap against them. This man is well-groomed, with only a dusting of dark hair covering the base of his cock. I lick my lips, my mouth literally salivating as I imagine wrapping my tongue around him, attempting to swallow the length of him and undoubtedly choking on his size.

Wetness pools in my panties as I watch him make himself come. His jerks get rougher toward the end, his head swollen and ready for a release. He draws out a long moan right before he spills his load onto the wall.

Fuck, that was hot.

What was he thinking about when he came? What turns him on? What does he like?

I watch the video two more times, unable to put my phone down and get myself together. My heart races and my skin heats, knowing he'll be touching himself under the same roof for the duration of our agreement.

Leaning against the sink counter, I replay the video and slip my hand inside my underwear. I'm so turned on, this won't take long. A moan escapes me, and I bite my bottom lip to keep my mouth shut. Once I get my release, I can go to sleep, and Alexander will have no idea—

The door bursts open.

And I'm caught with my hand *literally* in the cookie jar.

Those dark eyes of his take in the sight before him. He's wearing nothing but tight black boxer briefs that hug his hips like a second skin. My gaze snags on the bulge between his legs, now knowing *exactly* what it looks like.

He says nothing, and I know I should come up with something, but he knows what I'm doing, and what I'm watching—*who* I'm watching.

I slip my hand out of my waistband, ignoring the wetness coating the tips of my fingers.

He arches a brow. "Don't stop on my account."

"You kind of killed the mood, Big Man." I gesture to his dick. "You should be very proud, by the way. That thing is fucking magnificent."

Nice, Aarya. Real smooth.

One corner of his mouth turns up the slightest bit.

I push past him and make my way back to the bed, but he scoops me up from behind and carries me the rest of the way.

He drops me onto my back, and his shoulders rise and fall with his breaths. "Why did you watch the video?"

"Because I was curious." I shoot him a dubious look. "If I posted a video on a porn site, you mean to tell me you wouldn't watch it?"

"You'd want me to watch, wouldn't you?"

I tip my chin. "Yes."

His large frame towers over me. "Then do it."

"What?"

"Touch yourself, and let me watch."

Heat spreads like wildfire over my skin. "Right now?"

He leans over me, grips my neck in that massive hand, and pulls my lips against his as he speaks. "Right fucking now."

Then he claims my mouth in a searing kiss. He crawls on top of me, pressing his body against mine, wedging himself between my legs. I spread them wide to accommodate him, digging my heels against his ass and rolling my hips. With nothing but underwear between us, I can feel him, hard and thick.

Without warning and entirely too soon, he tears his mouth away from mine and pushes off the mattress. He drags the desk chair over to the foot of the bed, and then he yanks me by my ankles to the edge of the mattress before lowering himself into the chair like it's a front row seat.

He palms himself over his boxers with those dark eyes locked on me. "Remove the shirt."

My hands immediately go to the hem of the T-shirt. I should feel embarrassed or shy. I've never done anything like this in front of someone. But with Alexander watching me, telling me what he wants, I only feel bold.

Excited.

Obedient. *That's a new one for me.*

I tug the cotton material up and over my head, tossing it to the floor. Alexander's eyes drop to my chest, and his tongue skates out to wet his lips. What I wouldn't give for him to put that tongue on me and relieve this ache himself. But that's not the game we're playing right now, and he's in charge, so I wait for his next instructions.

"Touch those beautiful tits." He tips his chin. "Show me how you like it."

Arching my back, I cup my breasts and give them a squeeze before swirling my fingertips over my nipples—the entire time, my eyes locked on Alexander's heated gaze.

He lets out a low, satisfied grumble, slipping his hand underneath the waistband of his boxers. "You're beautiful."

I let one of my hands travel farther down my body, skimming over the front of my lace thong. A small moan escapes me, my body so turned on under Alexander's stare that I feel like a live wire ready to explode.

He fists his cock, giving it a few hard tugs. "That's it, Aarya. Touch yourself. Let me see you make that pretty pussy feel good."

I drag the material down my legs, and kick it off so I can spread myself wide for him.

"Fuck," he hisses. "Look at you."

My middle finger dips into the wetness seeping out of me, and I slide it over my clit in slow circles. Completely bare and spread out on the bed for him, I get off on watching the crazed look in his eyes as he watches me, pumping his dick like he can't help but touch himself to the sight of me.

"Alex," I moan, rubbing myself for him. "Tell me what you were thinking about when you made that video."

"You, Aarya. I was thinking about you." He squeezes himself at the base as he locks eyes with me. "All of my thoughts are consumed by you."

I moan again, working myself faster as I dip two fingers inside. "Fuck, Alex. I need you closer."

With a growl, he grips my hips and yanks me closer to him. My ass teeters over the edge of the bed into his lap as he places my feet on his shoulders. I can feel his hand moving over his cock, just inches away from where I'm playing with myself. His free hand roams over my breasts, squeezing them and rolling my nipples between his fingers. We're crossing lines, and I want to inch as close as he'll allow me to go.

"Alex, please." I arch into his touch, crying out and begging for more, for anything he's willing to give me.

"God, I love the sound of you begging. What is it you want, spitfire? Tell me one thing you want right now, and I'll give it to you."

I know he doesn't mean sex. We still have to keep his rules in place. Which is fine at the moment, because all I can think about is one singular thing after watching his erotic video.

"I want to watch you come." I flick my eyes to his. "On me."

I want to witness him unravel, and spill the evidence of his undoing onto me.

His head falls back as he lets out a loud groan. "You want me to come on you, baby?"

"Yes." I rock my hips, lifting myself up to get closer to where he's fucking his hand. "Please, Alex. Come all over me."

His dark eyes watch my fingers as they move in and out of me, his lips parted, tongue snaking out to wet them like he's dying for a taste.

I pull out my fingers and lift them to his mouth, seeing how far I can push him.

He grips my wrist and wraps his tongue around my fingers, sucking off my arousal with a long, satisfied moan. "So fucking delicious." He hits me with a lust-filled gaze, hunger in his eyes, as if he wants to devour me.

I wish he would.

The muscles in his forearm flex as he pumps himself in harsh strokes, his hips jutting into me. "You're perfect. Every inch of you."

I match his pace with my fingers, bringing myself to the edge and waiting for him to break.

Then this steady, controlled man loses control. Deep, guttural sounds of pleasure rip through him as he comes, and he never breaks eye-contact, calling my name over and over again like a prayer.

His cum spills onto my stomach and my breasts, covering me in him. It's sexy and dirty, and I've never been with anyone like this, but with him, I want it all.

My fingers slide through the moisture, swirling it over my skin before bringing it down to my clit. Alexander watches intently while I use his cum to get myself off, and within seconds, the mounting pleasure explodes between my thighs. I come harder than I've ever been able to make myself come before, the feeling amplified by his gaze. I call out for him, my body trembling as the waves roll over me.

We're both out of breath, our bodies warm and sated for the moment. Neither of us speaks. I expect him to push me away, to try to put space between us. Instead, Alexander pulls me onto his lap and kisses me. It's a mixture between a gentle press of his lips against mine, and deep, passionate strokes of his tongue, like he's at war with himself, knowing he should end this, yet not wanting to stop.

His rational side wins, and he carries me into the shower. He's quiet as he washes my body, taking his time until I'm clean. I'm turned on by the feel of his soapy hands roaming over my body, but I won't dare cheapen this moment with lust. The way he handles me with care, the way he looks at me with such reverence, like I'm this special thing that needs to be protected. No one has ever treated me like this before, and I'm not ready to let go of it just yet.

I wash him the same, letting my gaze eat up every inch of him, letting my hands feast on his incredible body.

After the shower, we don't bother to put our clothes back on as we crawl into bed and fall asleep wrapped around one another.

But in the morning when I wake, I'm alone in the bed.

Like I knew I would be.

25

ALEXANDER

"WOULD YOU QUIT IT?"

McKinley's shoulders droop. "I'm just trying to lighten the mood here."

Aarya pats him on the shoulder. "Read the room, dude."

He's been singing, "Chapel of Love," by The Dixie Cups, "Let's Get Married," by Jagged Edge, and Prince's, "Let's Pretend We're Married" since we got to the courthouse.

But this isn't a happy moment. We aren't two lovers about to pledge our lifelong love to each other. A beautiful woman wearing my mother's ring sits beside me, yet everything about this moment is all wrong. This day is only a reminder of the piece of shit my grandfather is, forcing me to make an insane decision to marry someone in order to keep my parents' villa.

I don't mean to take out my frustration on McKinley. He's doing me a favor by being our witness today. Still, I can't shake this awful mood I'm in.

It doesn't help that people are snapping pictures and asking for autographs, no doubt posting the news of our marriage for all the world to see.

Anxiety sits heavy on my chest, constricting my throat, and the tremor in my hands has me pushing out of the chair. "I'll be right back."

I head to the bathroom and splash some cold water on my face. I brace my hands on the counter, and let my head hang down between my shoulders as I breathe in.

One, two, three, four.

Out through my lips.

One, two, three, four, five, six, seven.

I jump at a gentle touch along my back.

"You're okay, Big Man. Just keep breathing."

I lift my head to meet Aarya's concerned gaze in the mirror. "You're in the men's room."

She smirks. "Nothing I haven't seen before."

"I'm sorry I—"

"Don't apologize." Her palm makes small circles between my shoulder blades. "I know this is a weird day, but remind yourself why we're doing this. We're taking control. You hold the power, and you hold the key to your parents' villa."

She's right.

I'm in control. Not my grandfather.

I turn around to face her, and brush my knuckles against her cheek. "You look beautiful, by the way."

She glances down at her cream-colored sweater dress. "I had to buy something for the occasion. I didn't realize how many black clothes I owned until I had to find something white to wear."

"You look stunning in any color." I drop my hand from her face, resisting the urge to pull her in for a kiss.

Something I've been having a difficult time doing since we got back from Greece.

I *knew* she was going to sneak off and look for that video I posted on Kourtney's website. But I didn't expect to walk in on her touching herself while she watched it. Catching her with her fingers in her panties, the heated flush on her cheeks, the look of lust in her eyes...my restraint snapped. We crossed a line that night, yet I can't find it in myself to regret it. The image of her completely naked in front of me with her ankles on my shoulders while she rubbed my cum on her pussy—how could I ever regret that? It's like the rational part of my brain shut down, and now that I've gotten a taste of her, I only want more.

I shake the memory from my mind so I don't give myself a raging hard-on before we stand before the judge. "I was thinking, since it's not too cold out today, maybe I can take you riding before I have to get Giuliana from school."

She waggles her eyebrows. "And I was thinking we could consummate our marriage."

I huff out a laugh and shake my head. "You're relentless."

"But it made you laugh." She grins. "Sure, I'd love to take a ride—on the bike, but to be clear, I'm down to ride you as well."

My shoulders shake with my laughter. "Come on, spitfire." I swat her on the ass. "Let's go make an honest woman out of you."

When it's our turn in the courtroom, we face each other, hold hands, and recite the vows to make this arrangement legal.

To have and to hold.

From this day forward.

For better or worse.

For richer, for poorer.

In sickness and in health.

To love and to cherish.

Until death do us part.

They're generic vows, yet they wrap around my heart when I say them as I look into Aarya's big brown eyes. What's more is the earnest way she looks at me when it's her turn to repeat after the judge. I know this is fake for her, a means to getting one-hundred-thousand-dollars deposited in her bank account. But for the mere seconds she holds my gaze and promises to love and cherish me, I let myself believe that she means it.

Because I want her to mean it.

Because I mean it.

Because no matter how hard I've tried to keep my heart safe, I'm falling in love with the woman I'm marrying.

Fully aware that she may never feel the same way.

"YOU'RE NOT GOING to go too fast, right?"

I spin Aarya around and collect her hair in my hands. "You're safe with me."

"Funny how that doesn't answer my question."

"I'm not going to push my bike to the limit with you on the back."

"I don't like the idea of you pushing it to the limit at all."

"I don't anymore. Not like I used to."

She pauses. "Are you...are you braiding my hair?"

"It'll get tangled if I don't."

"Perks of being a girl dad, I guess."

I chuckle. "I had to YouTube a lot of videos when Giuliana was younger. Thank God for the internet."

"If you need a hair tie—"

"Got one." I slip the black hair tie off my wrist and wrap it around the end of the braid. Then I take the helmet off my bike seat and carefully push it over the top of her head.

As a wedding gift, I bought Aarya a riding jacket and gloves so she didn't have to keep wearing mine, and had a new helmet fitted to her size.

Her eyes flick up to mine as I tilt her head and adjust the buckle under her chin. "Promise me you won't let me die?"

I tug the bottom of her helmet and bring it until it clinks against mine. "If you feel unsafe or scared at any time, you can tell me to slow down and I will. But I promise, I will always be careful with your life in my hands."

She nods. "Okay."

I turn to my bike, gesturing to the electronic screen between the handlebars. "So, once you turn the key and everything lights up, you're going to hit the kill switch over here. This is what turns the bike on and off. And then this button underneath ignites the engine."

She leans over to glance down at everything I showed her. "Can I start it?"

"Go for it, spitfire."

She reaches out and goes through the steps I just showed her, and then the bike roars to life. I mount the bike and lift the kickstand before holding out my hand for her. She steps onto the peg and swings her leg over to the other side, sliding her hands around my waist.

"I'm going to teach you how to be a good backpack."

"A backpack?"

"That's what it's called when someone rides as a passenger, because you're clinging to me like a backpack. So, you don't want to lean too much against me, especially when I'm stopping. You can brace one hand against the gas tank here." I take one of her hands and plant it in front of me. "When I lean into a turn, we won't fall over. Just go with the motion of the bike. And when I tap you like this," I reach my hand back and tap her knee, "You hold on tight."

I hear her say, "Got it," through the Packtalk speakers in my helmet.

I pull out of my driveway and onto the main road. I take my time, weaving in and out of traffic, and make sure she feels comfortable.

"How are you doing back there?" I ask several minutes into the ride.

"Good. You can go a little faster if you want."

I chuckle, and then I twist the throttle to accelerate.

Riding always calms my nerves. The world and all of its problems fade away as everything blurs around me. Riding takes concentration and control, and it quiets my mind. With Aarya holding onto me, it's like I've unlocked a new level of peace. Her body pressed against mine, holding onto me for security, trusting me to protect her with her life in my hands.

It's intimate. It means something.

When I reach the destination about twenty minutes later, I slow down and pull off the road to park. We stand and stretch, hanging our helmets off each handle.

Aarya scans the area. "So, where are we?"

"It's nowhere really. It's not a park or a well-known spot. I accidentally stumbled upon it right after I signed with the Goldfinches. I needed the quiet, away from the chaos of it all."

We disappear between the trees, our shoes crunching on the dead grass beneath us.

"What's that?" Aarya visors her eyes with her hand as she squints against the sunlight.

I bite back a smile as we walk over to the plaid blanket laid out on the ground with a picnic basket sitting on top of it. "It's our post-wedding celebratory lunch."

Her mouth drops open as her eyes fly up to mine. "You planned this?"

"I know it's not our real wedding day, but I wanted to do

something...special." I shrug, suddenly feeling foolish for thinking this was a good idea. "It's silly, but—"

"Stop." She rushes over to the blanket, and pulls out the bottle of champagne sticking out of the basket. "We're pretending, right? So why not pretend that we're a pair of happy newlyweds having a picnic under the Eiffel Tower in Paris?"

I laugh as I lower myself to the blanket beside her. "Okay, I'll play along. I'll be Anthony Spinelli, founder and CEO of a billion-dollar tech company."

Her eyes light up. "I'll be Regina Spinelli, world-renowned fashion designer."

I pop the cork, and pour each of us a glass of champagne. "To my beautiful wife. Thank you for marrying me and making me the happiest man alive."

She giggles as she clinks her glass against mine. "And to my handsome husband, thank you for taking me on the honeymoon of my dreams around the French riviera."

"Anything for you, shnookums."

She tosses her head back as she laughs, and my heart bursts at the sight of it. She'll smirk, or give me a smile every now and again. But the sound of her laughter is something I don't take for granted.

And after the weird morning we had, it feels good to be silly and let loose a little.

After we finish the sandwiches I made us, I hand her a napkin. "So how does it feel to be a married woman?"

Aarya holds out her left hand in front of her, gazing down at the sparkling diamond on her finger—now coupled with my mother's thin wedding band. "You know, darling, everyone says they feel no different when they're married, but I don't know. I feel different. Like I'm more mature. More elegant."

I stifle a laugh, trying my best to play along with the ridiculous charade. "You are very elegant, my little sugar plum." I press a kiss to the top of her hand before taking a bite of my sandwich.

"I'm so glad you were able to get away from the office, dear." She pouts. "I hate when you work those long hours."

I lift my thumb to her plump bottom lip and give it a tug. "I'm sorry, baby. I do wish I could be home with you."

She nips at my thumb, giving me those seductive dark eyes. "I get so lonely in that big house all by myself."

My gaze drops to her mouth, and I can't bring myself to pull my hand away. "I should make more of an effort to spend time with you."

"You should." Her tongue skates out and grazes the tip of my thumb. "I would make it worth your while."

"I have no doubt." My dick throbs in my pants as the memory of Greece flashes through my mind again. "One night making love to you would be worth all the damn money in the world."

She wraps her lips around my thumb, and I push it further into her mouth. Her tongue swirls around it as she hums.

"Every day I'm with you, the weaker I become in resisting you," I whisper, letting the truth slip free.

She pops my thumb out of her mouth and draws me closer with her hands around the back of my neck. "You don't have to resist your wife."

I shouldn't.

I don't want to.

These false pretenses have real consequences, yet I can't find it in myself to care with the way she's looking up at me, wearing *my* ring on her finger, after she took *my* last name.

When I look at her, all I see is *mine*.

And after seeing her sprawled out for me on the bed in Greece, marked with *my* cum, I seem to have lost all of my self-control.

Without warning, I scoop her up in my arms and carry her away from the picnic blanket. We're too out in the open here, and anyone wandering by could catch us. So I stalk over to my bike, parked and hidden behind a patch of trees, and plant her ass on the seat sideways, facing me.

I lean down and kiss her hard, my tongue surging inside in search of hers. She clings to me, teetering back on the seat as I ravage her mouth, licking and sucking and nipping at her like a man starved.

I *am* starving for this woman.

I have been since the moment we met.

I kneel down in front of her, and slide my hands up along her bare thighs, under her dress and hooking my thumbs on the sides of her panties before dragging them down her legs.

She leans back on the bike seat, spreading her legs wide.

"Goddamn," I murmur, gazing up at her while she watches me in anticipation. "Look at you, with your bare pussy on my seat, legs spread for me. I'm never going to get this image out of my head."

She tips her chin. "Good."

Good. Because she wants to be mine as much as I want her to be, whether she admits it or not.

I slide my thumb over her, swirling her arousal over her clit in slow circles. "So wet for your husband."

Her hips rock against my featherlight touch as she lets out a breathy moan. "Please, Alex."

"I've got you, baby. I'm going to take care of this for you." I grip onto her hips as my tongue glides over her, teasing her with soft strokes at first. "You gave me a small taste of you in Greece, and I haven't been able to stop craving you."

She lets out a loud moan, gripping onto the back of my head with one of her hands while the other keeps her propped up on the seat as she rolls her hips against me, pressing me exactly where she wants me.

She wants more, and I intend on giving it to her.

"Hold on, baby." I toss her legs over my shoulders and bury my face between her thighs, feasting on her like she's my last meal, rubbing my tongue all over her.

"Fuck, Alex. That feels so good."

It's my name that does me in. Not *Krum Cake.* Not *Big Man.* To her, I'm not just a famous pro athlete. She has seen behind the walls I've carefully constructed around myself. For so long, I've been comprised of hockey and fatherhood. I've devoted my life to those two things, and while I wouldn't trade them for the world, I want to be more than that. I *am* more than that.

I want someone to love all that I am. Not just the team captain, not only a dad. I want someone to see my heart and my soul. All of me.

And I want *her* to be that someone.

I curl a finger inside of her, matching the rhythm with my tongue.

Aarya gazes down at me, her fingers gripping my hair as she grinds herself against my face. "Right there, Alex," she whimpers. "Just like that. On your knees for me like a good boy."

I bask in her praise, groaning loud as I devour her. I curl a second finger inside of her, stroking her exactly where she needs me, and then she breaks apart, legs shaking as she screams my name into the sky.

I rub my tongue in slow strokes against her pussy as she comes down, lapping up every last delicious drop of her. Then I press soft kisses along her inner thighs and down each leg as I slide her panties back on for her.

She wobbles on her feet as she stands, clinging to me until she steadies herself.

She wears a sated smile as she reaches up to kiss me. "That was...incredible."

It was, and I won't be able to stop myself from tasting her again. I'm addicted.

"I know we should keep our boundaries set in place, but every time I'm around you, all I want to do is tear down every fucking one," I confess.

"Would it be so bad? To let ourselves enjoy each other while we're pretending?"

Pretending. I hate the word as soon as it leaves her mouth.

"This isn't pretending." I cup her face and stare into her eyes. "What we just did? What happened in Greece? It's not fake to me."

"I know. I... I shouldn't have said that." Her throat bobs as she swallows. "It's not fake for me either. The way I want you is *very* real."

But is it the same way I want her?

Maybe it's because we just got married. Maybe it's because we're wearing my parents' rings, and their lives were taken too soon so it feels like I should be living my life to the fullest in honor of them. Maybe having her for a while is better than not having her at all.

I stroke her soft cheek with my thumb. "You're wearing me down, spitfire. I'm defenseless against you."

That earns me another smile. "Good."

26

AARYA

"How's it going?"

I grimace as I prop my phone on the bathroom counter and rip off my T-shirt. "Have you ever seen someone projectile vomit before? I don't even know how that much vomit can come out of a child her size."

Cassidy wrinkles her nose on the other side of the FaceTime call. "The poor baby."

"I'm the one who got puked on. *I'm* the poor baby." I pull on a clean shirt—the second one I've had to change into today, and re-twist my hair into a bun on top of my head. "She just keeps crying, saying her stomach hurts. I feel so bad."

"I think you should call Krum. He'd want to know that his daughter is sick."

"He won't be able to concentrate at the game if he knows she's sick. Hell, knowing him, he'll charter a plane and fly it himself to come home."

She nods, and I know she understands because Trenton would be the same way. "At least you have Annie there to help you."

"That woman is a literal angel. I don't know what I'd do without her."

An hour after Alexander left for Denver this morning, Giuliana spiked a fever and started throwing up. It's scary seeing her like this, but Annie swears it's normal for kids to get the stomach bug and that everything will be over by tomorrow.

"The kid has been clinging to me all day. The only time I've been able to do anything is when she falls asleep. I know she needs the comfort of her father, but I'm doing the best I can until tomorrow when he returns."

"You're doing more than enough just being there for her," Cassidy says. "I'm really proud of you, babe."

I swipe my phone off the counter. "All right, I have to get back out there. I'll call you later."

"Let me know if you need me to drop off anything to you."

"I will. Thanks."

I head back out into the living room and find Giuliana still asleep on the couch. *Good, she needs to rest.* I'm about to drop down into the recliner and take a nap myself when the sound of heaving echoes from the bathroom in the hallway.

No, no, no.

I bolt into the hallway and crack open the bathroom door to find Annie hunched over the toilet. "Shit, Annie. Not you too."

She wipes her mouth with a wad of toilet paper and reaches up to pull the handle and flush. "You better get out of here before you catch it too."

As tempting as that thought is...

"I can't leave you like this with a sick kid. Come on." I lean over and help her to her feet. Her skin is hot to the touch. "Get on the recliner, and I'll bring out a garbage pail for you."

She's so weak, she doesn't even argue with me.

I spend the afternoon making sure Giuliana and Annie drink enough fluids, checking their temperatures, and cleaning out their puke buckets. One of the mommy blogs I searched up said this should only be a twenty-four-hour bug, and that all I can do is make sure the they both stay hydrated.

When Giuliana wakes up from another nap, she crawls over to me and lays her head against my chest. "I miss Daddy."

"I know, kid." I rub soothing circles on her back. "We can watch him on TV soon. You can give him some good luck vibes through the screen."

"Okay." Her little voice sounds so sad, it breaks my heart. "Do you love him?"

My body stills at her question. "Who?" I ask, to buy me more time.

"My dad. Do you love him?"

"I care about him very much." I pause, knowing that's not exactly answering her question. "Why do you ask?"

She lifts her head up to look at me, with her rosy cheeks from the fever and her curls a matted, sweaty mess. "Because if you love him, and he loves you, then maybe you can be my mom."

Oh.

I glance at Annie but she's no help, passed out on the couch.

None of the mommy blogs prepared me for this.

"I, well…" I pause, trying to think of the right words to say as unease twists my gut. "Do you want a mom? Have you been sad that you don't have one?"

She shrugs. "All of my friends have moms, so I think I'd like to have one. And you take care of me like their moms do."

"Friends take care of each other too, you know."

"Yeah." She lays her head back down. "But I like you living with us."

Affection squeezes my heart. "It was very nice of your father to give me a place to stay while my apartment is getting worked on."

I want to remind her that this isn't permanent. That I'm going to move out eventually. That her father and I aren't going to live happily ever after.

But I can't bring myself to burst Giuliana's hopeful bubble.

Or maybe I don't want to burst my own.

"I don't have a dad," I say, my voice low as I continue to rub her back. "And my mom wasn't the nicest mom either. But I learned that it doesn't matter what you call people. Mom, dad, brother, sister. The names we call them don't matter. What matters is how they treat you. So, it's more important to have good people around you who love and support you. Does that make sense?"

She nods. "I have lots of good people in my life."

"You do." I wrap my arms around her. "And I'll always be one of those people, okay? Even if I don't live here anymore, you'll always have me."

"Good." Then she lets out a whimper. "Aarya, I think I'm going to—"

Warm liquid spews from her mouth onto my lap.

I close my eyes and blow out a breath.

It's going to be a long fucking night.

GIULIANA WAS able to keep down a few crackers with some applesauce for dinner while we watched Alexander's game.

This is the longest she's gone without puking, so I'm hoping she's on the tail end of this wretched thing. I opted to sleep with her in Alexander's bed in case she needs me in the middle of the night, and I sent Annie home so she could get some solid rest without being woken up by Giuliana.

It's only nine o'clock on a Saturday night, but after the day I had, I'm wiped and ready to crash with a sick child, and two furry animals curled up at our feet.

My, how my life has changed.

But my phone buzzes on the nightstand and Alexander's name lights up the screen. My stomach twists with unease, worried about how he's going to react to me not telling him about Giuliana being sick.

Annie didn't tell him either, so at least we'll go down together.

I tiptoe out of the room so Giuliana doesn't wake up, and swipe my thumb across the screen. "Hey, Big Man. Great game tonight."

The smile falls from his face as soon as he sees me. "What's wrong?"

Damn, this guy is good.

I flop onto the couch and scrub my face with my free hand. "Please don't hate me, but Giuliana and Annie have been throwing up all day. I think they have a stomach bug."

"What? You're kidding. Why didn't you tell me?"

I grimace. "I didn't want to worry you before the game."

He groans as his head falls back. "Stomach bugs are the worst. How are they doing now?"

"I sent Annie home so she could get a solid night's rest. Giuliana is passed out in your bed with the animals. Her fever is down, and she ate some crackers for dinner. We'll see how tonight goes."

His eyebrows pull together. "I'm so sorry, Aarya."

"Please don't be sorry. Everyone is fine."

"This isn't your problem. Giuliana is my responsibility. I should be there with her."

"Hey, stop. Don't spiral. Shit happens. I have everything under control."

He pinches the bridge of his nose. "Was she asking for me?"

"She did, but I kept her in good spirits." I chew my bottom lip. "We had an interesting conversation before."

"Oh, yeah? What about?"

I scratch the back of my neck. "She may or may not have asked me to be her mother."

His face falls. "Really?"

I nod. "I did the best I could, but it might be a good idea for you to have a talk with her."

His eyes move somewhere off screen, and I know he's retreating into his own head filled with anxiety.

"I used to wish that I had a dad like my friends did growing up. Hell, I wished that I had a mom like theirs too." A humorless laugh escapes me. "I know how it feels to be on the outside looking in. To feel like you're different from everyone else—like they've got a leg up on you because they have something you don't."

Alexander frowns. "Do you still feel that way?"

"I don't think it ever fully goes away, the feeling like you're missing out on something. The curiosity of what my life would be like now if I had a different family growing up. But there's nothing I can do about it, so I remind myself that family isn't the end-all-be-all in life. Finding amazing friends and building a life you love is important too."

He's quiet for a moment. "I hate that Giuliana's mother walked away from her."

"But it's better than sticking around and being a shitty mom."

His eyebrows jump. "That's a really good point."

"I read a few articles about how to talk to your kid about a parent who walked out on them. I can send you the links if you want." I laugh. "These mommy blogs have been really helpful."

"Mommy blogs?"

"Apparently, all these moms get together on the internet and chat about motherhood. They post questions and everyone weighs in with advice and ideas."

An amused smirk plays on his lips. "Why are you reading mommy blogs?"

I scoff. "Because I have no idea what the hell I'm doing over here. Everyone was throwing up today. It was like a scene out of *The Exorcist*. I wasn't sure what was considered too high for a fever, or if I had to bring your daughter to the hospital. Last week when you were away, I had to Google, *What happens if your poop is blue?* because Giuliana showed me her turd and it was legit blue. Turns out it was blue because of the dye from the icing on a cupcake she had in school."

Alexander squeezes his eyes shut as he laughs. "I've had to Google countless questions just like that. One time when she was two, she shoved a marble up her nose. I couldn't get it out for the life of me, but I really didn't want to sit in the hospital for hours with a cranky toddler. I found this post online that recommended sucking it out with the vacuum hose. Worked like a charm."

"That's ingenious." I chuckle. "I'd love to see pictures of Giuliana from when she was a baby."

"There's a couple of albums inside the cabinet on the TV stand." He tips his chin. "Go grab them."

I crouch down and stack three photo albums in my arm, and bring them to the couch, scooting under a blanket and reclining the chair back.

I gasp when I flip open one of the covers. "Oh my God. She was so tiny."

It doesn't help that baby Giuliana is lying in her giant father's arms in the photo.

"She was tiny," Alexander says. "She came a week earlier than we expected. But the doctor said she was healthy. She was just ready to come out into the world. I'm so lucky I was there to see her the day she was born."

I'm reminded by what happened after she was born, and my heart wrenches for the father who thought his baby girl was ripped away from him.

"Fucking Rachel." My top lip curls in disgust. "Where is she now? I want to find her and hit her with my car."

Alexander grins. "I was angry with her for a long time, but I've learned to appreciate her for what she did. She gave me the best gift in the entire world."

My heart swells. "You're a really great dad, Alex. I don't think you hear that nearly enough, but it's true."

"Thank you." The smile falls from his face. "Sometimes I wonder if I'm not there enough for her. This job takes me away a lot, and I hate missing things."

"You're here when it counts, Big Man."

"She loves you, you know. I'm worried about how she's going to react when it's time for you to move out."

The thought of moving out hits me like a sucker punch to the gut. I've made myself at home in this house, more than I ever thought I could be. I've fallen into the routine of Alexander's life, got swept up in the whirlwind that is living with a four-year-old with real-life responsibilities. I went from having one-night-stands with strangers to reading bedtime stories to a little girl and five of her stuffed animals.

But I don't miss my old lifestyle, and the idea of going back to it fills me with dread.

"I guess we'll have to cross that bridge when we get there," is all I can say.

"If I'm being honest, I like having you at the house too." Alexander pauses. "I like coming home knowing you'll be there. I like the smell of paint when you're locked away in your studio. I like being able to see you before bed, and first thing when you wake up."

Emotion lodges in my throat like a rock, making it hard to swallow. "I like seeing you without your shirt on."

He laughs, low and raspy. "I know you do. I see the way you look at me."

My cheeks heat. "I keep thinking about what we did in Greece, and on your bike."

"Me too, beautiful."

We stare into each other's eyes, letting unspoken words fill the space between us.

"We should get some rest."

I nod, not wanting him to hang up yet, though we're both exhausted. "Okay."

"Goodnight, wife."

I smile. "Goodnight, husband."

I look through the photo albums for a little longer before heading back to Alexander's room to check on Giuliana. She's passed out on her back, arms overhead, and mouth open. I lie on my side and watch her as she sleeps, too innocent and precious for this world. I want to be there for her, be a part of her life, be here as she grows up. I want to be everything she needs, everything she's missing.

I just don't know if I can be enough to fill that empty space inside of her.

27

ALEXANDER

"Daddy!"

I drop my bag and brace for impact as Giuliana flings herself at me, Ellie not far behind.

"Hi, my girl. How do you feel?"

"Better."

I hold her tight to me. "Yeah? Your belly doesn't hurt anymore?"

"Nope. I haven't *frowed up* since yesterday."

I press my lips to her cheek. "I'm so sorry I wasn't here to take care of you."

"It's okay. I missed you, but Aarya helped me feel better."

I step into the living room, and spot Annie on the couch with Dash. "Hey, Annie. How are you feeling?"

She smiles as she pushes off the couch. "A lot better than yesterday."

I set Giuliana down, and she runs over to play with Dash. "I'm so sorry you had to handle all that while I was gone."

I know better than anyone how tough it is dealing with a sick child, especially when vomiting is involved. I'm reeling from the guilt of not being here for her.

She waves me off. "It was mostly Aarya."

I glance around the room. "Where is she now?"

Annie grimaces. "Poor thing isn't feeling well herself now."

My eyebrows lift. "She's sick?"

She nods. "She's been throwing up since this morning. I wouldn't have known if I didn't come by with groceries. I swear, she would've tried to take care of Giuliana by herself until you got home."

I let out a sigh and run my fingers through my hair. More guilt pours into my gut.

"Why don't you go and check on Aarya while I get dinner started? I don't know how much she'll be able to keep down, but the broth from the chicken soup might be a good start."

I shake my head. "You don't have to—"

"Stop." She squeezes my arm. "Go be with her."

I nod before stepping into the hallway. I crack open Aarya's bedroom door, and find her curled in a little ball at the edge of the bed with the garbage pail from the bathroom on the floor beneath her.

She can barely lift her head off the pillow as she peels her eyes open. "Alex, get out of here. Save yourself."

I lower myself onto the bed, trying not to jostle the mattress too much. Her hair is damp around her forehead, and her skin is a sallow color.

"I'm so sorry you're sick, baby." I press my wrist against her hot forehead, glancing at the empty nightstand. "Have you had anything to drink?"

"I can't keep anything down." She covers her face with her hands. "Seriously, don't look at me. I'll be fine by tomorrow."

"You need to drink and stay hydrated," I say, ignoring her request to leave her alone.

"And you need to go wash your hands. You can't afford to get sick."

"You're sick because you were taking care of my daughter. I'm going to take care of you now."

"There's nothing you can do for me. It just has to work its way out of my system." She reaches down for the garbage and groans. "Seriously, Alex. Get out."

I pull her hair back away from her face as she heaves into the pail. My chest aches for her, laden with guilt. After the wave of vomit is over, I place the pail back on the floor and wipe her mouth with a tissue off the nightstand.

She buries her face under the comforter. "I don't want you to see me like this."

"Like what, sick?" I peel back the covers and force her to look in my eyes. "We took vows, remember? In sickness and in health."

"We also said *until death do us part*, and we know that was a lie."

I heave a frustrated sigh. "You just spent the weekend getting puked on by my daughter—so I'm going to take care of you whether you like it or not."

She pouts. "I don't have the strength to argue with you right now."

I clutch my chest. "That's the best thing you've ever said to me."

She lifts a feeble hand and flips me off.

I chuckle as I rise from the bed and take the garbage pail with me, closing the door on my way out. I rinse out the pail, and line it with a garbage bag so I can change out the bag each time she throws up. I grab a Gatorade from the fridge, and stick a damp washcloth in the freezer to chill.

Giuliana is helping Annie in the kitchen, stirring a spoon in the pot over the stove. "We're making chicken soup for Aarya." She frowns as she looks up at me. "I gave her my germs, Daddy. I didn't mean to."

"It's okay, baby girl. It's not your fault." I ruffle her curls. "What do you say we have a daddy/daughter movie night tonight? I want to spend some time with my girl."

She beams. "Can I pick the movie?"

"Of course."

I return to Aarya's room and place the cool washcloth on her forehead.

She groans. "That feels so good."

"I want you to take a few sips of this Gatorade." I twist the cap and bring the bottle to her lips, tilting it so she can reach it. "There you go, baby. Just a few sips for me."

"God, why do you have to be so sexy right now when I look like roadkill?"

My eyebrow arches. "How am I being sexy?"

"*There you go, baby. Just a few sips for me,*" she mimics in a deep voice. "Jesus Christ. Now I have to change my underwear."

I chuckle as I shake my head. "Well, for the record, you don't look like roadkill. Now, get some rest and I'll be in to check on you in a little while.

And if you tell me I don't have to check on you, I'm going to ignore you, so save your energy and your breath."

She peeks up at me from under the washcloth. "Thanks, Alex."

"Anything for you."

And I mean it. Anything she wants, anything she needs...it's hers.

Including my heart.

"WOULD YOU LIKE MORE TEA, King Alexander?"

"Why yes, I would love some more tea." I hold out the tiny pink teacup, and Giuliana pretends to refill it. "This is a lovely tea party you're hosting, Princess Giuliana."

"Thank you, sir." She beams as she sets down the teapot. "Do you think Aarya wants to play with us?"

"She's resting, baby girl."

I went in her room periodically to put a fresh cool compress on her head, and change out her puke bucket. I made sure she sipped the Gatorade I gave her, and laid with her so she knew she wasn't alone.

"But listen, I wanted to talk to you about something." I adjust my ass on the tiny wooden chair underneath me. "Aarya said you asked her to be your mother."

Giuliana looks up at me with those big, round eyes. "Am I in trouble?"

"No, of course not." I reach out and clasp her hand. "I love that you say what's on your mind, and in your heart. It's one of my favorite things about you. But I don't want you to get the wrong idea about Aarya living here with us. She's my friend, and now she's your friend too. That's all."

She nods, looking down at the table. "Aarya said her mom wasn't nice to her. Why did she do that?"

"I honestly don't know. Some people aren't very nice."

"She doesn't have a family." Giuliana blinks up at me. "I think *we* should be her family."

Emotion clogs my throat, making it hard to swallow. "Friends can be just like family."

Friends. Because that's all Aarya will ever be to me.

"Do you love her, Daddy? She said she cares about you a lot. I think that means she loves you too."

I let out a soft laugh. *My daughter the matchmaker.* But before I can answer her question, the door cracks open and Aarya steps inside.

Her tired eyes bounce between Giuliana and me before her eyebrow arches. "I like the outfit, Big Man."

I glance down at the red cape tied around my neck, knowing full well how ridiculous I look wearing a bedazzled crown. "That's King Big Man, to you."

She offers us a weak smile. "Having a tea party?"

Giuliana nods. "How does your belly feel?"

"I think I'm going to try to eat some crackers."

Giuliana swings her gaze to me. "Can I have a snack too?"

"Sure, let's go."

We take off our tea party costumes, and head for the kitchen. They sit at the island eating crackers with jelly, watching me while I prepare Giuliana's lunch for school tomorrow. My Spotify playlist plays on shuffle in the background, like it always does when I'm busy in the kitchen.

Then a familiar song comes on, slower and quieter than the rest of my usual songs.

Aarya side-eyes me. "This song? Seriously?"

I press my palm against my chest like I'm offended. "What's wrong with *American Pie*?"

"Nothing. I just didn't expect it in the middle of all the ragey rock music you had playing."

"My father loved classic rock. He used to sing to my mom while she was in the middle of cooking." I smile, remembering a specific moment from my childhood. "Anytime *Brown Eyed Girl* came on, he'd sing to her, and she would have to stop what she was doing and dance with him."

Sadness pricks my heart, for the love they shared that was taken too soon. But a new sadness also settles into my chest.

A feeling of longing for what they had.

Longing to have that with *her.*

Aarya smiles. "That's nice that you got to see them like that."

Because she never saw anything close to that growing up in her childhood home.

Giuliana's voice echoes in my head. *I think we should be her family.*

"Come on." I wipe my hands on the dishtowel and hold out a hand for each of my girls. "Dance with me."

Giuliana stands on the stool and climbs into my arms. Aarya stares down at my outstretched hand.

"Come on, spitfire. One dance."

She pushes to her feet, and I wrap my hand around her waist, drawing her close. We sway to the sad song, and Giuliana gazes between the two of us, wearing a content smile on her face. And when the chorus comes on, Aarya and I belt out the lyrics, sending Giuliana into a fit of laughter.

It's in this moment that it hits me for the first time: Aarya doesn't need a prince or a knight in shining armor to rescue her. She's so strong and capable, she can do anything she sets her mind to. What she needs is to feel loved. To feel safe. To be reminded of all that she is.

She doesn't need a hero.

She needs someone to be her home.

I could be her home, if only she'd let me.

28

AARYA

"I HAVE A BAD FEELING ABOUT THIS."

"Don't worry." I pace the floor of the break room, holding my phone out in front of me. "Everything is going to happen according to plan."

Brittany nods from her seat at the table. "Don't stress, Chanora. We got this."

Tonight's the night Brittany and I are going to catch creepy Carter red-handed. While he was out running an errand earlier, we snuck into his office and scoped out the perfect spot for me to hide while still being able to record the video from my phone. Brittany is dressed in her usual work attire —high-waisted black slacks and a silky pink button-down—so as not to draw attention with anything overtly sexy.

Not that it should matter what a woman wears. Men shouldn't take a cute outfit as an open invitation to touch a woman.

"Well, I'm not letting you do this without backup," Chanora says. "Call me from Brittany's phone and keep me on the line while you record the video from your phone. Just in case anything goes wrong."

"Nothing's going wrong." I square my shoulders and lift my chin. "We're taking this guy down, and that's it."

"Come on, you don't want to make me worry when I'm with child."

I roll my eyes. "I'll call you once it's over, I promise."

"Just be careful."

We end the FaceTime, and I glance at Brittany. "You ready for this?"

She nods, pulling at her collar.

"Are you sure you want to be the bait? I can do it if you'd rather—"

"No." She stands from the chair. "I can do this."

"Okay. Let's go. Carter should be back any minute."

I lie and let Eddie know he's off duty for the night because Alexander will be picking me up from work. Then I head into Carter's office, and tuck myself inside the closet behind his desk. I'm able to hide behind one of the walls inside, and peek my phone's camera through one of the slats in the closet door.

Brittany hands me her unlocked phone before scurrying out of the office to wait for Carter.

While I wait for them to enter the room, I make sure my phone is set to silent so it doesn't go off and alert Carter that I'm in here. Luckily, New Jersey has a one-party consent law, meaning we can record Carter without his consent and use it as evidence in a case against him. I've thought of everything. There will be no surprises. This plan is fool-proof.

We're finally going to nab this asshole.

After several minutes, Carter invites Brittany into his office, closing the door behind her.

Show time.

Carter remains standing, facing Brittany, instead of asking her to take a seat. "I'm so glad you waited for me to get back so we can talk."

If she's nervous, she doesn't show it. She tucks her hair behind her ear, acting coy. "I just wanted to tell you how much I love working here. I'm so grateful you hired me."

His back is to me, so I can't see the look on his dumb face, but he reaches out his hand and lays it on her shoulder. "You've been doing a great job. I can see that you're willing to put in the work to move up the ranks."

"I am," she says as she nods. "I'm a hard worker. I'll do anything you need me to do to help out around here."

Ha. Way to bait him right into that one.

"Hard-working and beautiful." His hand moves off her shoulder, and his fingers trail down the buttons of her blouse. "That's a deadly combination."

My stomach lurches, and I have to bite the inside of my cheek to stop myself from gagging.

Brittany's throat bobs as she swallows. "Sir, I've been thinking. I know you kissed me the other day, but I want to keep things professional between us. I don't think you should do that again."

Good job bringing up the kiss for the camera, Britt.

"Ah, come on." Carter pops open the top button on her blouse, and moves to the next. "It'll be our little secret. We can still maintain a professional relationship."

She takes a small step backward, and puts her hand up. "I don't feel comfortable with that. You're my boss."

"That's right. I am your boss. And don't you want to please your boss, Brittany?" He inches forward with each step she takes away from him. He reaches out and grips the back of her neck. "I think we can make this a mutually beneficial partnership."

Brittany told me to wait until after he kisses her to make sure we have it on camera. I told her she didn't have to take it that far, that I didn't want her to do something she wasn't comfortable with, but she insisted.

I keep the camera pointed at her while Carter kisses her, and then she pushes him away. "Carter, please. Stop."

But he doesn't stop. He lunges for her again, shoving her against the wall like she said he did the last time.

I make sure to get the struggle on video before bursting out of the closet. "Gotcha, motherfucker."

Carter spins around, eyes wide as the realization of what's happening sinks in. "You stupid little bitches."

"I don't know, Britt. We just caught our boss sexually harassing us with video evidence. That doesn't sound too stupid to you, does it?"

She grins. "Nope."

I expected Carter to get angry. I expected him to beg us not to release the video to anyone. What I didn't expect was for him to slap the phone out of my hand, and wrap his fingers around my neck.

Brittany screams as Carter slams me against the wall, his hand like a vice. I point to my phone on the floor, trying to tell Brittany to grab it and keep recording.

But I don't know what Brittany does next. I barely register what Carter's threatening in my ear as he crushes my windpipe. My vision gets hazy, and my limbs feel heavy.

The last clear thought I have is: *Chanora was right.*

And I don't know if I'll get to tell her that.

My eyelids droop closed, but then the hand around my neck releases me.

"Get your fucking hands off my wife."

My eyes pop open as I fall to the floor, clutching my neck and gasping for air. I blink to clear my vision, but when I look up, I blink again because I can't believe what I'm seeing.

Alexander is punching the shit out of Carter.

"Alex," I choke out, struggling to push to my feet.

Brittany tosses her arm around me and helps me up. "Come on, let's get out of here."

"No. Wait." My throat is raw and my voice sounds like I swallowed gravel. "Alex, stop."

Alexander stands over Carter, who's barely able to keep his arms up to shield his face as Alexander's fist connects with his jaw again.

"I'm going to break every bone in your body if you ever come near my wife again. Do you understand me?" he shouts.

Carter's only response is an agonizing groan.

Fuck.

"Alex, enough!" I shout as loud as my throat will allow and move to stand in his line of vision. "Think of Giuliana. Please, you can't do this."

At the sound of his daughter's name, he freezes. His hand, raw and bloody, drops to his side as his wild gaze flicks to mine.

Guilty tears roll down my cheeks as he steps over Carter's body and crashes into me, pulling me into a suffocating hug. "Are you okay? Fuck, baby, tell me you're okay." His hands come up to cradle my cheeks, his eyes bouncing around my face before he tilts my chin to inspect my neck. "I got here as soon as Chanora called me. She said you were in some kind of trouble. What the hell is going on?"

I swallow, my throat dry, as a sob bubbles out of me. "I'm okay. You weren't supposed to be here."

Brittany steps closer, and holds out my phone. "The screen is a little cracked, but the video is there."

"Video?" Alexander echoes.

I can't bring myself to look at him. "I was trying to catch Carter harassing Brittany. We came up with a plan, and—"

"You *planned* this?" His voice is too calm, too quiet.

Another tear rolls down my cheek as I nod. "It worked. I got the video. Now he can't harass us anymore. Now—"

"You put yourself in danger. On purpose." He pauses. "And you didn't talk to me first."

I wrap my hands around my midsection, hugging myself for comfort. "I just wanted to put a stop to this."

"Where's Eddie?"

My chin hits my chest. "I sent him home."

He glances around the room, taking a minute to speak again. "I'm parked out back. Take Brittany and go wait in the truck. I'm going to have a chat with Carter."

"But—"

"Go wait in the truck, Aarya."

I clamp my mouth shut at the sound of his clipped tone, and lead Brittany out the door. We don't say anything, but she clings to my hand as we walk outside and get in Alexander's SUV.

I twist around to look at her in the back seat. "I'm really sorry I involved you in this, Britt."

She shakes her head, wiping at her tear-stained face. "I wanted to do this with you. I wanted to catch Carter just as much as you did."

"I shouldn't have put you in this situation. He came on to you like a monster. Are you okay?"

"I'm okay, really." She lifts her eyes to mine. "What do you think is going to happen now?"

"I don't know."

Several minutes later, two police cars and an ambulance pull around the back entrance of the gallery, without lights and sirens. Alexander must have told them to keep things quiet so as not to alert anyone passing by of what's happening inside. The last thing we need is the media to get their hands on a picture of what Alexander did to Carter's face.

After Brittany and I give our statements and show the cops the video of what Carter did, he's arrested. The sight of him being shoved into the back of the police car brings me only a sliver of satisfaction.

The EMT examines my neck, and then the three of us are back in Alexander's SUV.

He doesn't look at me the entire ride to drop Brittany off at her apartment, or on the way back to his house.

I'd rather him yell at me, or tell me how stupid I am, or lecture me about my safety. Anything but this crushing silence.

I wait until we pull into his driveway and he kills the engine before I turn to him. "Please, say something."

His head falls back against the headrest and he releases a long sigh. "It doesn't matter what I say."

My lips wobble. "That's not true."

"Isn't it? I told you I wanted you to quit that job because of your boss. I told you I worry about you when you're alone in there with him, or when you'd walk home alone." He finally turns those stormy eyes to me, and I see the tears brimming. "I care about you, Aarya. About your safety. About your well-being. You matter to me. And I know you've never had anyone care about you like this before, so I understand that fierce independence you have. But what I don't understand is why you don't value your life the way I do."

A lone tear rolls down his cheek. "Do you know what it was like for me to walk in that office, not knowing what I was going to find? Seeing him choking the life out of you? Only to find out that you put yourself in that position. To find out that you took matters into your own hands instead of coming to me and talking to me." He sucks in a shaky breath, like he's struggling to keep his composure. "We were supposed to be a team. I thought we were in this together."

"We are," I start to say.

"No." He shakes his head. "Tonight, you made yourself very clear. You keep pushing me away, yet I don't fucking listen."

Tears stream down my face. "We *are* a team. I'm sorry I scared you. I'm sorry I put myself in a dangerous situation. I swear, I didn't see it going the way it did."

"You're only sorry because you got caught. And what would've happened if I couldn't get to you in time? If I was out of town at a game? God, he had his hand around your throat, Aarya. What if he took you from me? From Giuliana?" His booming voice reverberates within the closed space. "How could you think that this is okay?"

"I'm sorry." A sob escapes me and my shoulders shake. "I'm sorry, Alex." I crawl over the console and climb onto his lap, wedging myself between him and the steering wheel, burying my face in his neck.

His arms snake around me, and I fall apart in the safety of his embrace.

Coming down from the adrenaline and the fear, reality sets in. I went behind Alexander's back and did something I knew he wouldn't want me to do. I allowed myself and Brittany to get into an unsafe situation with Carter, and we're lucky it didn't end up worse. I even put Alexander in danger— because he could be in jeopardy of losing his daughter with assault charges.

I can't remember the last time I cried like this. Not since I was a child, because I learned early on that tears don't fix anything. But right now, clinging to Alexander, the only real, true, solid thing in my life, I let it all out.

His disappointment in me is the worst thing I've ever felt.

Once I quiet down, Alexander speaks. "I have to get Giuliana settled for bed. You can go through the garage so she doesn't see you. I don't have the energy to answer her questions about the marks on your neck."

I lean back and take his right hand into mine, inspecting his swollen knuckles. "She's going to have questions about this."

"I'll tell her I hurt it during practice." He reaches out like he's going to brush my hair away from my face, but he stops himself and lets his hand fall into his lap instead.

He doesn't want to touch me. He can barely bring himself to look at me, and it stings.

I move off of him and scoot back into the passenger seat.

Without another word, he gets out of the truck and heads inside.

I TAKE A LONG, hot shower while Alexander puts Giuliana to bed.

I wish I could see her, and tell her goodnight. I could really use one of her hugs right about now.

How would she have felt if something worse had happened to me tonight? How would it have affected her? I'm not used to having someone to miss me, to depend on me.

How could I be so reckless?

There's a cup of tea sitting on my nightstand when I get out of the bathroom with two white pills beside it.

Even when he's mad, Alexander can't help but take care of me.

I down the pain relievers and let the tea soothe my throat before tiptoeing down the hall toward his bedroom. The door is cracked open, and a dim light shines from the lamp on his nightstand. I peek my head inside, and the sight of him nearly breaks me.

Fresh out of the shower with damp hair, he's hunched over the edge of the bed with his elbows on his knees and his head in his hands.

My gentle giant.

He looks so tortured, so crestfallen. My heart aches for what I put him through tonight.

I move to stand in front of him, hesitant and afraid he'll tell me to leave.

But then he lifts his head and reaches out for me, wrapping his hands around the backs of my bare thighs as he pulls me close. I straddle him, positioning my knees on either side of his waist, and he engulfs me in his arms, squeezing me so tight.

He's shaking, the aftermath of tonight taking a toll on his nerves.

He presses his lips to the marks along my neck, peppering me with tender kisses. I don't deserve his kindness right now, don't deserve him treating me like this when I'm the one who screwed up. But after what happened tonight, this is exactly what I need from him, and somehow, he knows it.

He always knows what I need.

He drags his lips up along my jaw, blazing a trail to my mouth. He kisses me with such fervor, such need, yet there's nothing sexual about this moment. This is the only way we can express how we feel right now, desperate for each other in a way that words can't make sense of.

This isn't fake. This isn't us pretending to be together. It's real, true, raw emotion, and it consumes me.

Tonight, Alexander saved me. That irony isn't lost on me. But he didn't save me from a fire-breathing dragon, or an evil queen.

He saved me from myself.

I've spent my life convincing myself that I don't need anyone, that I can do it all on my own. Yet Alexander has spent these last few months pulling at the threads of every conviction I've ever had, until I stand before him now. An unraveled mess of the person I used to be lays at my feet. I can choose to pick it up and keep going down the path I've been on, or I can leave it behind and start weaving myself into a better version.

I lose track of time, lost in all that this man is, and we kiss until our lips are swollen and our eyes are tired. And when he whispers, "Stay with me tonight," I tell him *yes*, and we crawl under the covers together. I lay my head on his chest, and he wraps his arms and legs around me.

I care for him, more than I've ever cared for anyone in my entire life.

I don't want to push him away.

The realization sits heavy on my chest, but his steady heartbeat serves as a comforting lullaby as I drift off to sleep.

29

ALEXANDER

"You okay, Krum?"

I keep my head down as I nod, lacing up my skates. "I'm good."

Trenton lowers his voice as he leans in. "Cassidy told me what happened. You should've called me."

I lift my bruised hand. "I didn't need backup."

"Still." He blows out a breath through his lips. "Aarya okay?"

I've tried to shake the image of Carter choking her out of my mind, but it's all I see when I look at those red marks around her neck. If I would've gotten there just two minutes later, who knows what he would've done to her.

"She's alive."

Trenton nods. "I would've lost my mind if someone put their hands on Cass like that."

I did lose my mind for a minute there. Had Aarya not stopped me...

"What's happening with the scumbag?"

"We met Brittany at the precinct this morning, and they filed restraining orders against him."

"Are they pressing charges?"

"They didn't want to, but everything is on record, including the video."

I swallow. "And hopefully the fucker doesn't try to come at me with assault charges."

He shouldn't, as I was quite convincing before I left the gallery last night.

As soon as the girls left Carter's office to wait in the truck, I dialed 911 and then I dragged him off the floor and propped him up in a chair. Blood dripped from his split lip, as well as from a gash along his cheekbone. His face was swollen and bruised, and the evidence of my rage turned my stomach.

I haven't lost control like that since a fight I had on the ice when I first started playing. Since then, I've learned to keep my anger in check. But when it comes to Aarya's safety, apparently all bets are off.

I threatened to slap him with a lawsuit and take him for everything he's worth if he even thinks about coming after me or Aarya. I hate using my celebrity status, but in this case, it came in handy. I told him I have friends in high places because everyone in this city is a Goldfinches fan, and they're eager to see me take my team to the playoffs this year. So, he'd be wise to tuck his tail and take responsibility for his actions against the women in his gallery.

I also threatened to kill him if he lays another unwanted finger on my wife ever again. I think he got the message loud and clear. Still, you never know what a slimy bastard like him will do when faced with jail time.

"I'm glad you're all okay." Trenton claps me on the back. "Let's get a win tonight. Our girls are out there watching."

My head snaps up to him. "Aarya is here?"

Trenton smiles wide. "Along with someone else."

My eyebrows press together. She didn't tell me she was coming to the game tonight. I figured she'd want to stay home and rest after last night.

And who is she with?

As soon as I'm announced onto the ice, I skate out and make a beeline for Cassidy's usual seats behind the goal. I spot Aarya next to her—wearing my jersey with a yellow scarf wrapped around her precious neck—and then I spot a little curly-haired girl bouncing on her lap.

Wearing the same exact jersey, only in a much smaller size.

"Daddy!" I can hear her shouting as I get closer.

I stop right in front of the boards and place my gloved hand against the glass. "Hi, baby!"

Giuliana points to her jersey. "I'm wearing your number!"

I laugh. "It looks so good on you."

My girls are here, wearing *my* number.

I have people in the crowd here for *me*.

My eyes dart to Aarya. She knew I needed this. She knows what it means to me.

Thank you, I mouth.

She shoots me a wink, and a smile sweeps across her face, wide and unbridled and genuine. My heart nearly bursts from the sight of it.

God, I love this woman.

In spite of what she did, as angry as I am about her sneaky plan to catch Carter, I can't turn my back on her. She's been on her own for so long, unloved and unappreciated by her parents, unaware of all that she is and deserves. She needs to see that no matter what, I'm always going to be here for her. I'm always going to have her back. She can trust me. She can lean on me. She can count on me to hold her hand through anything.

I think she's beginning to understand the way I feel about her.

And I think she might feel the same way about me.

I only wonder if she knows it.

GIULIANA IS sound asleep by the time I get home, sandwiched between a giant dog and a skittish cat.

She was a trooper until the third period when she fell asleep on Aarya's lap. I'm sure the copious amounts of snacks she ate prior to that aided in her sugar coma.

Aarya isn't in her room, her bed still made up from the morning, and when I reach my bedroom, my dick practically jumps out of my pants.

She's still wearing my jersey, but her thick thighs are bare, garnering all of my attention.

I drop my duffle bag onto the floor and close the door behind me, making sure to lock it before I step into the room.

Aarya gazes up at me, her dark hair fanned out on my pillow wearing a playful smirk on her lips. "You won."

"I did." I kick off my shoes and pull my T-shirt over my head. "Are you my reward?"

"I am." Her knees fall apart, giving me a glimpse of the most perfect pussy I've ever seen.

"Fucking Christ," I hiss, yanking down my pants and boxers at the same time. "I'll make sure to win every game if this is what I get to come home to."

She runs her hands along her thighs, and that's when I notice her bare ring finger.

I tip my chin. "Where are your rings?"

Her eyebrows knit together as she looks down at her hand. "Oh, I took them off before I took a shower. I guess I forgot to put them back on."

I arch a brow. "You *forgot*?"

She bites her bottom lip as she nods.

"We'll have to make sure you never forget again." I tip my chin toward the nightstand. "Put those rings back on your finger. Then I want to see you crawl to me."

She scrambles to swipe her rings off the ring dish sitting on the nightstand, and then she prowls across the mattress toward me at the foot of the bed.

I know how much she loves it when I take control. She can be the dominant spitfire outside the bedroom, but in here, she gazes up at me with those eager eyes, waiting for my next command.

I fist my cock in my hand and tap the crown against her lips. "Open for me."

Aarya takes me between her plump lips, and the wet heat of her mouth surrounds me.

"Oh, *fuck*."

Her tongue twists around me in a mind-numbing rhythm, her mouth providing the most blissful suction. She grips my balls and gives them a squeeze as she works her other hand around the base of my cock, making up for the space her lips can't reach.

I tangle my hands in her hair, and my hips jut into her, moving of their own volition. She gags as my dick hits the back of her throat, and I pull back quickly, trying to regain control of my body.

But Aarya moans like she likes it.

I should've known my spitfire wants it rough.

I fist her hair in my hands and thrust my dick into her again, diving deep into her throat before pulling back to give her a second to breathe.

"Let this serve as your reminder." Holding her head, I drive back into her mouth. "You don't forget to put *my* rings back on your finger. Understand? Better yet, never take them off."

I fuck her mouth like a man unhinged, and she moans in between gags like she can't get enough.

Seeing her on all fours sucking my cock is enough to bring me to my knees, but gazing down at *my* last name stitched across her back, the pair of my rings nestled on her finger, and knowing she brought my daughter to watch me play tonight...it breaks me wide open.

I yank her off me by her hair and guide her up on her knees until her lips meet mine, and I crush my mouth against hers. Sliding my hands under her jersey, I squeeze two overflowing handfuls of her ass and press her against me, rubbing my dick between her legs.

She presses her thighs together, trapping me where she wants me. "Fuck me, Alex," she begs against my lips. "Please. I can't wait anymore."

"Oh, I'm going to. I've been dreaming of this moment since the first night I laid eyes on you." I drag my lips down her neck, sucking at the sensitive skin behind her ear. "You were wearing that backless little scrap of a dress. I wanted to haul you into a dark corner of the club and fuck you against the wall."

She hums as her head falls back, granting me better access to her neck. "I wanted you to."

My hands travel up her body, lifting the material of the jersey until I can pull it off and toss it on the floor. "And the night of the air hockey game at Mac's house, I wanted to spread you out on the table and bury my tongue in your pussy."

She grins. "You should've."

I bend down and suck one of her pert nipples into my mouth. "I wanted to sink my fingers inside of you when we were at the MET. Stand behind you and make you come all over my hand while you were staring up at the paintings."

Her back arches and she releases another sexy moan as my tongue swirls around her nipple. "God, I wanted that too."

I graze my teeth against her sensitive skin before making my way to show her other breast the same attention. "I've imagined fucking you against every square inch of this house. Do you know how difficult it has been to have you here, right under my nose, and not have you?"

"You have me now, Alex. We don't have to wait anymore. Take me. I'm yours."

Pride and possession rip through me.

Mine.

I clutch her jaw and speak against her lips, making sure she feels the verity in my words. "You are fucking mine."

She whimpers, her body shuddering against me.

I nip at her bottom lip before taking a step back. "Now lie down."

She scrambles to obey as I reach into the nightstand for a condom. She watches with rapt attention as I tear the wrapper and roll it over my length.

I climb onto the mattress and kneel in front of her, pumping my dick in lazy strokes while I gaze down at her. With her knees hiked up to her heaving tits, she waits for me, her pussy glistening in the dim lighting.

I lean down and slide my tongue over her, unable to stop myself from having a taste. I groan against her, lapping her up until she's a writhing mess under my tongue.

I'll never get enough of her.

I line up my cock at her entrance and tease her, pushing my crown inside in shallow pulses.

Her hands fly over her head, palms flat against the headboard as she pushes against it trying to sink down and urge me further inside.

I flash her a sinister grin. "You ready for me, baby?"

"Yes." She's breathless and desperate. "Yes, please. I need you inside me."

I lean over, propping myself up with my hands on the mattress on either side of her head so I can be closer to her. I stare into her eyes, glazed over with desire as they lock with mine, and I push myself all the way inside of her, inch by slow, agonizing inch.

She murmurs a string of expletives, and I'm only able to make out phrases like *huge*, *so good*, and my personal favorite, *best dick ever*.

Her pussy clenches around me, so tight and wet, and a long groan releases from my chest. "Oh, fuck, Aarya. You feel incredible."

We're still for a moment, our breaths mingling, her body adjusting to my size while I try to rein it in so I don't fuck her senseless and it's over in thirty seconds. It's been so long since I've been inside a woman, and I'm beyond happy that my first time is with Aarya. It's pure ecstasy being inside her, being this connected to her. This feels like more than sex, more than just a means to a release that we've been longing for. This is more than physical.

It's everything I've ever wanted.

With her. Only her.

"Tell me you're not pretending," I whisper. "Tell me you feel this."

She cups my face, letting me see the truth in her eyes. "I'm not pretending, Alex. This is real for me. It's me and you."

My chest cracks wide open.

Emotion strangles me, my throat thickening as my vision blurs. "It's real for me too, baby."

I am wholly yours.

My heart belongs to you.

I love you.

Then she starts moving, letting me know she's ready. I grip onto her hips, and pull myself out of her before plunging right back inside. I fuck her in slow, deep strokes, loving the way she moans each time I slam inside of her. I lick into her mouth, kissing her in sync with the punishing rhythm of our hips.

"You're so beautiful," I whisper in her ear while I pump in and out of her. I need her to know, need her to feel how perfect I think she is, how much I want her. I glance down and watch the way her pussy swallows me, mesmerized by the way she takes me—in awe that this is finally happening.

"You feel so good." Aarya's eyes flutter closed as one hand leaves the headboard and grips onto my lower back, her hips meeting me thrust for thrust. "It's so right with you."

I relish in her words, understanding the magnitude of them. This isn't one night; this isn't something you get from a stranger. We're connected on a deeper level. This means something.

"You woke me up and breathed life back into me," I tell her, our breaths mixing as we kiss. "I was so lonely before you came into my life."

"You don't have to be lonely anymore," she whispers against my lips. "We're in this together. I have you."

Our pace picks up, and she wraps her arms and legs around me, holding on while I pound her into the mattress. We're panting into each other's open mouths as the sound of our skin slapping together echoes throughout the room, pouring everything we've got into one another.

And then Aarya comes, with the sound of her throaty moan in my ear, my name falling from her lips over and over again.

I go over the edge right after her, succumbing to the pulsing waves crashing into me.

The last time I was inside a woman, I don't even remember it. I was most likely drugged, and taken advantage of. She stripped my control from me. The times before that were meaningless—purely physical fun because I was young.

But this? Sex with Aarya?

It's on another level of intimacy, like her soul has tethered itself to mine.

As we come down and catch our breath, I brush her hair away from her face and pepper her with gentle kisses.

Her fingers draw idle circles along my back as she smiles. "I'd say that was worth the wait."

I chuckle into her hair as I pull her close. "That was worth everything."

"I meant what I said." She pauses. "I want this to be real. I want you to be my boyfriend."

"You want your husband to be your boyfriend?"

She jabs me in the ribs. "Yeah, I do."

I pull out of her and roll onto my back, taking her with me so her head is resting on my chest. "I'd love that."

She lifts her head to look at me. "Thank you for being so patient with me."

I tuck her hair behind her ear and let my fingers linger on her cheek. "Thank you for being so good with my daughter."

"She makes it easy." Aarya laughs. "It was probably worse for you dealing with me."

"Yeah." I shake my head. "You've been a real pain in the ass."

"Hey!" She jabs me in the ribs again. "You weren't supposed to agree with me."

I laugh and then crush my mouth against hers. She opens for me and moans when my tongue slips in side, and we lose ourselves in another explosive kiss.

"Make me come again, husband."

I flip her onto her stomach and slap my palm against her ass. "As you wish, wife."

30

AARYA

After three rounds of mind-blowing sex, Alexander is passed out in bed.

I'm too wired to sleep, so I'm pouring my creativity into a painting. My mind races as I brush the paint across the canvas in light strokes, and I smile as the vibrant hues I mixed closely match the color of the sea in the photograph I'm referring to.

It feels good to paint after so many years of stifling that creativity. Now that I'm no longer working at Carter's gallery, I feel a sense of freedom. No more excuses as to why I can't open my own gallery. No more putting off my dream. It's time to pursue the things that make me happy.

My eyes flick to the giant, shirtless man leaning against the doorway.

He makes me happy.

My heart rate kicks up at the sight of him. This feeling is so foreign, so new, so unlike anything I've ever felt before. Life with Alexander is a life I never dreamed of because I didn't think I could have it. But he's here and he's mine, and I don't want to give any of this up.

"How long have you been standing there?" I ask, setting down my brush.

"Not nearly long enough to get my fill." He shrugs. "Though I'm not sure I ever will."

I let out a contented sigh. "I love it in here."

"I love seeing you in here." He pushes off the frame and steps into the room, making sure to stop before getting too close to the painting I told him I won't let him look at until it's finished. "The way your eyebrows push together while you work; the way you bite your bottom lip while you're mixing the colors. You're so focused, yet so at peace. I can't wait to see what you'll look like when you're standing in your own gallery one day."

I stand and pull the apron over my head, laying it down on the wooden work desk beside me. "I think I'm ready to go look at some spaces."

His eyebrows jump. "Yeah?"

"I've been looking up vacant spaces in the area." I walk over to him and slip my arms around his waist, resting my chin on his chest as I look up at him. "Will you come with me?"

An expression of what can only be described as joy takes over his face as he smiles. "Of course."

I might not need someone to do things for me, but I sure as shit wouldn't mind this man holding my hand while I do it.

"Bye, Aarya!"

I spin Giuliana around before setting her back on the porch. "Bye, kid. Have fun at your sleepover tonight." I lower my voice and add, "And don't break your other arm, or else your father will blow a gasket."

She giggles as she glances over my shoulder at her father waiting for me in the driveway. "Blow a gasket."

Annie ushers her inside and wishes me good luck before locking the door behind them.

I turn to the man dressed in all black waiting for me on his black and yellow motorcycle—a BMW s1000rr, according to the Big Man, as if I have the slightest clue what that means.

He flips up the visor on his helmet and his coal eyes meet mine. I can't help the tingles that spread throughout my body at the sight of him straddling the seat.

Forget the knight in shining armor all women dream of. I want the dark knight on a bike.

I walk over to him and twist my hair into a low bun before pulling my helmet over my head.

His deep voice comes through the speakers. "Stop eye-fucking me, or we won't be going anywhere tonight."

"Being out on your bike didn't stop you last time."

The memory of being spread out on Alexander's bike with his tongue between my legs flashes through my mind, and my thighs clench to suppress the ache.

"You're walking a little funny," he says in an amused tone. "Everything okay?"

I hop on the back of the bike and wince. "Let me see you get fucked by your anaconda dick and try walking without a limp the next day."

He chuckles, totally pleased with himself.

I slide my hands around his waist, giving him a squeeze to let him know I'm ready.

We're visiting three vacant spaces in Brooklyn today, and I'm equal parts nervous as I am excited. One of these could be my future gallery.

The first place we visit is small and simple. White walls in a long, rectangular room. It would be a great place for someone just starting out like me. The second space is a little larger, with a wall separating two different rooms. That could work for separating different artistic mediums.

But nothing *excites* me.

We pull up to the curb and I tear off my helmet, glancing up at the last space of the day. Tall windows line the front of the building separated by three columns of bricks.

"Last stop," Alexander says, clipping his helmet to the strap on the seat.

Maybe the third time will be a charm.

Alexander swings open the front door, and all of the breath whooshes out of my lungs when I step inside.

My eyes travel from the maple wood floors, up along the industrial steel columns, to an upper-level mezzanine area. The high open-beam ceiling has three large skylights giving a natural light to the huge space. It looks nothing like the first two, modern mixed with vintage, and my heart thrums with excitement.

"Wow," I say on an exhale.

A tall, slender man with blond hair walks over to us and smiles. "It's beautiful in here, isn't it?"

"It's so open."

His hand shoots out between us. "I'm Mark. You must be Mr. and Mrs. Krum."

I shake his hand before Alexander. "Thanks so much for meeting with us today."

"Of course. You mentioned about turning this place into an art gallery over the phone. Did you know it was once a gallery a little over a decade ago?"

"No, but I can see it." I imagine paintings hanging from the brick walls, and sculptures on tables upstairs. "How many people does this place hold?"

"A little over 350. The neighborhood is great, as are the business owners on either side of you. This place gets a lot of traffic." Mark slips his hands into his pockets. "Why don't you take a look around and check out the view from upstairs. Then you can let me know if you have any other questions."

"Thank you."

I tug on Alexander's hand, and we spend the next ten minutes wandering around the vast space. I point out random things, talking out loud as I envision where I'd hang certain types of pieces. All the while, Alexander remains quiet, allowing me to take it all in without giving me his opinion.

To get upstairs, there's a floating staircase on one side, and a lift at the back of the room giving it a fun, studio vibe.

I lean over the black railing overlooking the entire space, and take it all in. "It's awesome up here."

Alexander's hands slip around my waist as he stands behind me, resting his chin on my shoulder. "Kind of reminds me of the American Wing at the MET."

I smile. "It does."

This place is *so* much nicer than the first two we visited. But it's also a bigger undertaking. Nerves buzz around my stomach like bees, filling me with doubt.

"What are you thinking?" Alexander asks.

"The first two had better price points. But this one..." I chew my bottom lip as my voice trails off, trying to find the words. "I don't know. I feel something special here."

He spins me around to face him. "Don't think about the money. That's not what's driving your decision. Go with your gut."

I hook my hands around the back of his neck. "My gut says this the one."

"Then it's yours," he says, as if it's just that simple.

"But what if it fails? What if I can't find artists to work with, or what if I spend all this time and money to open it, but nobody comes here? What if—"

"What if it works out exactly the way you want it to?" He leans down and presses his lips to my forehead. "Living with anxiety, I've learned that the things we worry about are just that—worries. They're not real. They're not factual. So, let's stay in the present and look at what's in front of us right now. There's a beautiful space for a gallery available. If you want it, it's yours. You'll handle everything else that comes along with it, one step at a time." He laces his fingers with mine. "And I'll be right here with you."

I let out a long breath and nod. "That helps. Thank you."

"Want to go tell Mark?"

A slow smile spreads across my face. "Are you sure? It's your money we're spending."

He pulls back as he gazes down at me. "This money is yours to do what you want with it. We made this deal when we agreed to get married, and that hasn't changed, even though our feelings did."

I'm so gone for this man.

His honesty, the way he communicates, how he puts me at ease. He makes me feel secure, and that's something I haven't felt since...ever.

I slept with pepper spray under my pillow when I was growing up, for Christ's sake.

I head back downstairs to let Mark know that I'm interested in renting this space. After we finish up and exchange information, Alexander holds my hand as we walk outside to his bike.

I'm bursting with so much energy and excitement, I can hardly contain myself.

This is it. The moment my dream turns into reality.

Once we have our helmets on, Alexander tugs me close by the back of my neck. "I'm proud of you, spitfire."

"Thank you for making this possible for me." Then I flip his visor down like a brat. "Now take me home so I can properly thank you."

"I thought you were sore from last night?"

"Not too sore to do it all over again." I grin. "It's like dessert. There's always room for more."

We have about a thirty-minute ride, all of which I tease him relentlessly.

When we stop at a red light, I slip off my gloves and stuff them into my coat pockets. Once we start moving again, I let my hands roam, massaging his thighs, squeezing his muscular quads and trailing my hands up along his groin.

A deep rumble comes in through the speaker. "What are you doing?"

"Enjoying myself."

I unzip his jacket so I can slip my hands under his shirt, letting my fingers slide over the smooth, hard ridges of his muscles. I swirl over his nipple piercing that I love so much, and feel his stomach contract under my touch. He leans back, taking one hand off the handle bar and wrapping it around my leg, granting me better access.

Then I travel south, my fingers dancing back and forth along the waistband of his pants.

He lets out another low groan while he cruises, and I slip inside his pants and wrap around his cock, giving him a few short pumps in the tight space.

I know it's killing him to not be able to touch me, to keep his eyes on the road and control the bike to keep us safe—which makes it all the more fun for me.

As soon as Alexander pulls into the garage and the door closes us in, he kills the engine and tears off his helmet. I barely get mine off before his mouth crushes mine. His kiss is hot and needy, his tongue sweeping into my mouth and forcing my jaw open as he steals my air.

Then without warning, he spins me around and bends me over at the waist. "Hands on the seat."

He yanks down my pants, leaving them pooled at my ankles, trapped by my shoes, and his tongue blazes a trail along my inner thigh. He tears at the strings on my thong, ripping it in half and tossing it onto the floor before rubbing his tongue all over my pussy.

I arch my back and moan, sticking out my ass further as he spreads me apart. My legs tremble at the feel of his warm, wet tongue lapping me up hungrily as he devours me.

"So sweet," he murmurs. "You taste like mine."

He plunges a finger inside me while his tongue continues circling my clit, that thick finger curling and stroking me at a languid pace. I glance behind me to see him on his knees, loving the way he worships my body and knows exactly how to please me.

"Alex, yes," I say breathlessly. "That's so good."

He moans against me, enjoying my praise. "Come for me, Aarya. Let me hear how good I'm making you feel."

Knowing we have the house to ourselves, I don't hold back. I cry out his name as my orgasm slams into me. My thighs shake and I grip onto the seat to hold myself up as the euphoric feeling takes over.

Alexander toys with me while I ride it out, sliding his tongue lightly over me, sending tingles throughout my entire body.

Then his tongue disappears and he pushes to his feet.

His breath is hot at my ear. "I'm going to fuck you just like this, spitfire, so you better hold on."

"God, yes. Please," I beg, gripping onto the seat of the bike.

He fishes a condom out of his wallet and rolls it over his length, wasting no time before slamming inside of me. He's so big, I'm completely filled, full of him. His fingers dig into my hips as he pulls back out and does it again, and again. He fucks me hard over the side of the bike, owning my body, slapping my ass and pulling my hair. I love how he takes control, dominating me in the way I crave. Like I'm at his mercy, and all I can do is submit to him because I know he'll give me everything I need.

He *always* knows what I need.

His words become more possessive with each passing second. "This pussy is mine. *You* are mine. I'm going to fuck you like this every day. I want you so sore that every time you move, you'll remember it was *my* cock who did that to you."

I get off on how unhinged he is, loving the way he unravels for me. He makes my body come alive, with every touch, every kiss, every word uttered.

"Give me another one." He leans forward and his fingers slide around to my clit as he whispers in my ear. "I want to feel you come around my cock."

With one hand on the bike, I lift the other to grip onto the back of his neck, arching my back and meeting each of his wild thrusts with my own. "Harder, Alex. Fucking wreck me."

He buries himself inside me, giving it all to me. With his fingers between my thighs, I detonate like a bomb, another orgasm exploding throughout my body.

I'm barely able to catch my breath before Alexander's release rips through him, and he lets out a thundering groan that I feel deep in my bones. He shudders against me, his pace slowing as he rocks in and out of me. And then he leans down and presses his forehead between my shoulder blades, fighting to catch his breath.

My legs are barely able to hold myself up after that earth-shattering orgasm.

Without warning, he pulls out of me and sweeps me into his arms, my pants still hanging around my ankles. "Giuliana won't be home until tomorrow morning, which means we only have tonight."

"For what?"

"For me to fuck you on every surface of this house."

31

ALEXANDER

"The limo is here."

Aarya's muffled voice comes from behind the bathroom door. "Almost ready!"

The door cracks open and Giuliana slips out before closing it behind her. "Wait until you see her. She looks like a princess, Daddy."

"I bet she does." I scoop her up into my arms and press my lips to her pudgy cheek. "You going to be a good listener for Annie tonight?"

She rolls her eyes. "I'm always a good listener."

I arch a brow. "No waiting up for me?"

Her shoulders slump forward. "Can I at least sleep in the big bed while you're gone?"

"You have Ellie and Dash to keep you company in *your* bed."

"But *your* bed is *so* much more comfortable," she whines.

"Tell you what: If you sleep in your own bed tonight, I'll take you to the movies tomorrow to see the new Disney movie."

Her eyes light up as she gasps. "Deal!"

I planned on taking her to see the movie regardless, but she doesn't have to know that.

A flash of red in the corner of my eye pulls my attention as Aarya steps out of the hallway and into the living room.

My jaw drops, and Giuliana giggles. "Told you she looked like a princess."

Aarya in this curve-hugging satin gown looks like anything but a princess. More like a tantalizing siren ready to lure me to certain death—and I'd go willingly.

Aarya does a slow spin, giving me a glimpse of the backless cut of the dress that stops just above her tailbone. Her hair is swept into an elegant low bun. I don't often get to see her with her hair up, and my lips are already itching to kiss the nape of her delicate neck.

I blink and clear my throat. "You're flawless."

She grins as her eyes trail down my tux. "You don't look so bad yourself."

We say goodbye to Annie and Giuliana, and make our way to the limo outside.

"You did good picking out this dress, Big Man." She arches a brow. "Do I even want to know how you figured out my size?"

"I went through your closet while you were in the shower a couple of weeks ago. Then I went to a few stores until I found this one." My hand rests on her low back, my fingers skimming the soft skin there. "I knew it'd look perfect on you."

She shivers against my touch. "Keep touching me like that and we'll have to find a coat closet when we get there."

My dick twitches at the thought as we get inside the limo.

She rests her head on my shoulder as the driver pulls away, as if showing me affection is the most normal thing in the world. I don't know if I'll ever get used to it though. Since the night she got attacked by Carter, it's like something changed in her. As if she needed to know I'll stand by her even when she messes up; as if she finally realized that I mean it when I say I'm not going anywhere.

As if maybe, she's falling in love with me too.

She hasn't said it, and neither have I. I don't want to scare her off being too much too soon. But the words are at the tip of my tongue every time I look into her eyes.

"I've never been to a charity event before," she says.

"This one is pretty standard compared to other galas, but there's a two-drink maximum at this one."

"That's a great idea. There shouldn't be an option for people to get drunk at an event with people who lost their loved ones to drunk driving."

I've been supporting this charity since I started making money with the Goldfinches. A drunk driver took my parents away from me, and while there's anger and resentment there, I also feel sorry for the person who was has to live with that mistake on his conscience for the rest of his life. That's what I love the most about this charity. Not only do we help the victims' families, but we provide assistance to substance abusers who need help. If my money can make a difference in someone's life, then I'll happily donate anything I can.

As the limo approaches the venue, I squeeze Aarya's hand. "It might be a little chaotic when we arrive. The paparazzi aren't allowed in, so we'll have to take a few pictures, but then we can relax once we're inside."

She lifts her head off my shoulder and watches out the window as we get closer. She hasn't complained about being in the spotlight once since we started this thing. She hasn't complained about being photographed, or being hounded everywhere she goes, and she hasn't given security a hard time about following her. She has truly taken this whole unlikely situation in stride, and I couldn't be more grateful for it. For *her*.

Throngs of people crowd the entrance as the limo rolls to a stop, and the camera flashes intensify when I step outside.

I keep Aarya close as we step out onto the path leading to the entryway door. We smile and pose, and I answer a few questions, some of them geared toward tonight's event or the hockey season—but most of them are about Aarya.

"Did you two set a date yet?" one reporter asks.

Aarya holds up her left hand and grins. "Surprise. We already got married."

The cameras flash around us like a million bolts of lightning, and questions erupt from every angle. We answer as many as we can, tag-teaming the reporters as if we've been in the spotlight together for ages. Then I tug Aarya's hand until we're safe inside the building.

Before we enter the main ballroom, Aarya stops beside an easel holding up a large sign—with my face on it.

Her eyes dart to mine. "You're the *guest of honor*?"

I shrug. "I am every year."

She smacks my arm. "Why wouldn't you tell me that?"

"I didn't think it was important."

"What makes you the guest of honor?"

"I donate the most amount of money, and I pay for the event."

"Oh, you're right. Totally no big deal at all." She shakes her head. "You're so fucking modest."

I press my lips against her temple and whisper, "You're so hot when you curse."

She purses her lips as she scowls at me. "Don't try to distract me with your sexy voice in my ear."

My tongue skates out and traces the cusp of her ear. "You make my dick hard when you glare at me like that."

Her grip on my hand tightens. "Then it'll really send you over the edge when I tell you I'm not wearing any underwear."

She lets go of my hand, and waltzes toward our friends standing by the bar, glancing over her shoulder to flash me a devious smile.

Yeah, we're going to have to find a coat closet.

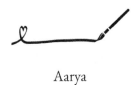

Aarya

"How are you feeling?"

I shrug before taking a sip of champagne. "Fine."

"I'm your best friend, and I've barely talked to you in weeks since everything happened at the gallery." Cassidy's eyes drop to where the marks have faded away on my neck. "That was pretty intense."

"I know it was. I think I'm still processing." I lean my elbows back on the bar as I gaze out at the beautiful ballroom. "I didn't think of the consequences. I just did it. I didn't expect Carter to react like that."

"You've always been that way. You react on impulse, and ask questions later." She squeezes my hand. "I'm really glad you're okay."

My eyes find Alexander talking to a group of people across the room. "I don't know what would've happened if he didn't get there in time."

"Don't think about that. He did, and that's all that matters." She lowers her voice as she leans in. "I heard he hurt Carter pretty good."

My eyebrows lift. "You have no idea."

"Good." Cassidy shakes her head. "That asshole is lucky I don't stab him in the dick."

"Who are we stabbing in the dick?" Celeste asks, walking up to us with Kourtney on her arm. "I love a good dick stabbing."

I chuckle. "No one. Keep the sharp objects away from Lorena Bobbitt over here."

"You and Krum Cake look awfully close tonight," Kourtney says. "How are things going for you newlyweds?"

"He's on the other side of the room. How do we look *close*?"

Kourtney arches a brow at me. "Oh, I don't know. Maybe it's because I saw you both coming out of the coat closet in between the first and second course."

Celeste and Cassidy gasp. Loud.

"Shh." I clamp my hand over Cassidy's mouth because she'll be the one to scream exactly what everyone's thinking. "We were...looking for something."

"Yeah, Alexander's dick," Celeste blurts out. "Bet your vagina found it too."

She sure did.

No longer able to keep up the charade, my shoulders slump forward. "He has the most perfect dick I've ever seen."

"I knew it!" the three of them shout in unison.

Celeste shoves my shoulder. "You owe us fifty bucks, bitch."

I hold up my index finger. "No, you bet that we'd have sex within the first month of living together. So, *you* guys owe *me* fifty bucks."

"She's right," Kourtney says.

"Of course I am." I flash them a triumphant grin. "I accept cash, Venmo, or PayPal."

Cassidy side-eyes me. "And what about the other bet we made?"

I feign ignorance. "What other bet? There was no other bet."

Three pairs of eyes stare me down in silence.

I lower my voice, glancing around me to make sure no one else is within earshot. "I'm not in love with Alexander. We're just..."

But I can't finish the sentence.

"Just what?" Kourtney asks, her expression softening.

"I don't know. It's weird. You ever meet someone who gives you such good orgasms, you get the urge to cook him a meal?"

Cassidy tips her head. "What do you mean?"

"Have you ever been like, damn, this man has the most magnificent dick, I want to make sure he's fed?" I heave a frustrated sigh, unable to get the right words out. "The other night, I gave Annie the night off so I could hang out with Giuliana. I knew Alex was on his way home from an away game, and he's always starving when he walks through the door, so I..." I blink. "I cooked him dinner. As in, I had dinner waiting for him when he got home."

Cassidy bites her bottom lip in a half-assed attempt to hide her smile.

"And then, the other day, I saw that his laundry was piling up." I shrug. "So, I did it. I did a grown man's laundry because I knew he'd be tired when he got home."

"Let me get this straight," Celeste says. "You are doing things for him because you care if he's hungry and tired. You're taking care of his kid when he's not around." She pauses. "And you think it's because he's good in bed?"

I shrug like it's simple math. "How else would you explain it?"

"You care for him," Kourtney says.

"Well, yeah. I care."

Duh. That's obvious. We've grown into something closer than friends over these last few months.

Cassidy sniffles, and dabs at the corner of her eye.

My chin jerks back. "Why are you crying?"

"Babe, you're in love." She sniffles again. "That's why you want to do all of these things for him. And that's why he's been doing all these romantic things for you—because he's in love with you too."

I shake my head before she even finishes her sentence. "No way. That's not what this is."

Celeste rolls her eyes. "Don't do this. Don't do the whole *ignoring you're in love* thing. You're not a delusional romance book character."

"I'm not ignoring anything." My chest squeezes, and I struggle to suck in my next breath. "We've only just started dating. Sure, we have feelings for each other, but..."

We can't be in love, can we?

253

"But, what?" Cassidy asks, those keen eyes of hers looking right through my façade like only best friends can do.

"I just don't know what this is, honestly."

I've never been in love before. How would I know what it feels like?

Kourtney gestures with her index finger. "Then tell me how you feel about that woman hitting on Alexander right now."

My head whips around. "Who's hitting on him?"

A tall, beautiful blonde-haired woman is talking with Alexander at the edge of the dance floor. The way her body is angled toward him, the flirty smile pulling at her lips, and the fuck-me eyes she's giving him tell me everything I need to know.

He says something, and she throws her head back as she laughs, placing a palm on his shoulder.

Oh, hell no.

I slam my champagne flute down on the bar, and strut over to them.

Celeste barks out a laugh. "Go and get your man!"

Alexander sees me coming before the woman does, and I don't miss the brief smirk that twists his mouth to the side.

I don't slow down as I approach him, and he removes his hands from his pockets as he turns his body toward me. Without thinking twice about it, I slam into him and wrap my arms around the back of his neck.

I hug him.

I fucking *hug* him.

His arms wrap around me so tight, I can barely breathe, and he twirls me around in a circle before setting me down on the floor again.

"Louise, this is my wife, Aarya." He keeps his arm securely around my waist as he introduces me.

Louise-who-touched-my-man reaches out her hand to shake my outstretched one. "It's so nice to meet you. Alexander was just telling me about your new gallery. I have several pieces of art that I recently procured, and I'd love for you to take a look at them. Maybe you'd want to show them in your space when you're ready."

"She's an art curator," Alexander explains.

In other words, *that's* the reason he's talking to her.

For *me*.

"That would be great. I'd love to chat with you sometime." I let out an awkward laugh. "I feel so overwhelmed opening up my own gallery. I don't know where to start."

She reaches into her clutch, and pulls out a business card. "Here's my number. Please, call me any time. We can meet up and have lunch, or I can come by the gallery. Whatever works for you."

Okay, maybe Louise can keep her well-manicured hand attached to her wrist.

We chat for a few more minutes until the DJ announces that it's time for dessert, and then we say goodbye to Louise.

Alexander trails his fingers along my lower back as he leads me to our table. "What do you think of her?"

"I think she's lovely." I flash him an innocent smile. "As long as she keeps her hands off my husband."

"Yours are the only hands I want on me, spitfire." He chuckles as amusement sparkles in his eyes. "But I kinda like this jealous version of you."

Jealous.

I don't get jealous.

I take what I want and then I leave. There has never been room for jealousy, because I don't get attached to things that aren't mine.

But it feels like Alexander *is* mine.

Moreover, I want him to be.

His head dips down as he speaks close to my ear. "You never have anything to be jealous over. You are all I see, all I want, all I crave. You are it for me. The sooner you accept that, the sooner we can be on the same page. So, I'm gonna need you to catch up."

His words wrap around my heart, causing a deep ache in my chest.

I pull back and gaze up at him, those honest eyes of his showing me everything I need to see like he's laying it all out on the table for me.

And it hits me.

This feeling, this overwhelming emotion consuming me...I know what it is.

Shit.

The girls were right.

I fucking love him.

32

AARYA

"Mrs. Krum, you have visitors."

"Eddie, you don't have to keep calling me—" I set down the box I'm carrying. "Wait, visitors?"

My bodyguard smiles. "Come and see for yourself."

I wipe my palms on my leggings as I walk out of my new office and into the hallway. Cassidy, Celeste, and Kourtney are waiting in the lobby, holding bottles of wine and coolers in their hands.

My eyebrows shoot up. "What are you guys doing here?"

Cassidy's smile is so wide, it almost splits her face in half. "A little birdie told us that you've been working so hard at the gallery all week that you keep forgetting to eat. So, he asked us to bring you dinner."

Celeste holds up a bottle of red wine in each of her hands. "And booze!"

"A little birdie, huh?" I arch a brow. "Does he happen to be a Goldfinch?"

Kourtney laughs. "He made dinner for all of us and said you might need a girl's night to celebrate." Her smile softens. "This place is beautiful, Aarya."

My heart thunders in my chest at the thought of Alexander going through all the trouble to cook for the four of us, and reach out to the girls on my behalf. I tend to self-isolate when I'm stressed, and he knows it.

He knows *me*.

"You look surprised." Celeste winks as she waltzes past me. "You know that man is head over heels for you, right?"

I roll my eyes. "I officially own this place, you know. I can kick you out if I want to."

She chuckles and sets down the bottles on the front desk. "Give us a quick tour, and then we can eat. This food smells fucking amazing, and I'm starving."

Cassidy sets down the cooler and practically jumps into my arms. "I'm so happy for you."

I say, "All right, enough with the hugging," but I squeeze her tight in my arms in spite of myself. "I can hardly believe this is my life."

A year ago, I never would've imagined I'd be the owner of my own gallery.

Or married.

Or helping take care of a four-year-old.

Or falling in love with the man who made all of this possible.

I walk the girls around the empty gallery, telling them some of the plans I have for each area.

"You can use my parents to cater for your grand opening," Kourtney offers.

"Thanks, Kourt. I can't even think about a grand opening at this point. It's overwhelming thinking about how much needs to get done in order for that to happen."

Cassidy squeezes my shoulder. "You'll get there."

We grab the food and wine, and head upstairs to eat so we can overlook the gallery.

"Sorry I don't have a table or chairs for us. I wasn't expecting company."

Celeste lowers herself onto the floor and crisscrosses her legs. "It's fine. We're bendy, aren't we, Kourt?"

Kourtney's cheeks burn.

"Okay, you have to tell me what you're referring to," I beg.

Celeste's eyes light up. "Last night, we—"

Kourtney's hand clamps over Celeste's mouth. "No!"

Celeste's shoulders shake with laughter. "All I'll say is, you ladies should invest in a swing for your bedroom."

Cassidy and I glance at each other with wide eyes. "Yeah, I don't think I'd be able to explain that one to Giuliana," I say.

We eat and drink, and most of all, we laugh. The stress I've been under melts away, and aside from my friends, I have Alexander to thank for that.

"I'll be right back. I have to grab something from my purse." I jog down the stairs and run right back up with my wallet in hand. Once I'm seated again, I pull out a crisp fifty-dollar bill for each of them. "I think I'm in love with Alex."

Cassidy kicks her feet as she holds up the money like it's baby Simba. "I knew it! I freaking knew it!"

Celeste clinks her wine glass against mine. "Congrats, girl. Welcome to the club."

"This is terrifying," I groan, burying my face in my hands.

Kourtney rubs her palm along my shoulder. "It's scary, but it's the most wonderful feeling in the world. You deserve this."

Cassidy nods. "Alex is a great guy, and an amazing dad. You love Giuliana, and you're great with her. This couldn't have worked out any better."

"What if he doesn't feel the same way?" I ask.

"That's not possible." Celeste shakes his head. "That man has been in love with you for a while now. I can see it all over his face when he's with you."

Does he love me too?

His caring gestures.

His attentive ways.

Is that love?

It feels like it is, like he does.

"You should tell him how you feel," Cassidy says. "Remember what you told me when I was falling for Trenton while we were still fake dating?"

"I'm not going to give you advice anymore if you're going to use it against me."

She laughs. "I'm being serious, Aarya. Tell him how you feel."

I nod. "Maybe."

I don't know how to do this. My mother never told me she loved me. We certainly never expressed our feelings, not unless they were the kind we spat at each other out of anger.

The thought of telling Alexander how I feel terrifies me, and it plagues my mind for the rest of the night, until he walks through the door of the gallery to pick me up and we say goodnight to the girls.

"How was your night?" he asks, wrapping his hands around my waist and pulling me in for a kiss.

"It was great. I really needed that." I blink up at him. "Thank you for doing that for me."

He gazes down at me, nothing but sincerity in his eyes. "You know I'd do anything for you, right?"

Emotion clogs my throat, my own feelings wrapping around my vocal cords, so I nod instead of speaking.

Trusting someone is scary after being let down your whole life. But looking up at this man before me, not trusting him seems so foolish. How could I not give him my heart? How could I not give him everything I have in me?

I only hope it's enough for him.

He deserves the world. Am I capable of that? Could I be what he deserves?

Questions bombard me, so I stuff those three words back down under the surface for a little longer.

I'll tell him another time.

As Alexander pulls back, it's now that I realize he's holding a shopping bag in his right hand. "What's that?" I ask.

He reaches inside and pulls out a small square package wrapped in shiny gold wrapping paper. "This is for you."

My eyes narrow. "For what?"

He laughs. "Just open it and you'll see."

I arch a brow. "A good surprise?"

"Definitely." He pauses. "Why would I wrap a bad surprise in gold wrapping paper?"

"That's the thing about bad surprises—they're always wrapped in a pretty bow disguised as a present."

Before I can snatch the gift out of his hands, he tips my chin, forcing my eyes upward again. "Hey, look at me. You're not going to get any bad surprises from me, okay?"

I want to tell him he can't promise me that, but I don't.

Because I want to believe him.

"Got it, Big Man."

He releases me, and I tear open the package he brought for me. Inside a square box is a black picture frame. In the middle of the glass is a small, rectangular piece of white paper with blue lettering that says: *A dream you have will soon come true.*

My eyes widen. "This is the fortune from my cookie the night I brought Chinese food to your house."

He nods. "I figured you could hang it behind your desk in your new office as a reminder that you're making your dreams come true."

"You saved it?"

He nods again. "I've always believed in your dream. Now it's your turn to believe in it."

I bury my face against his chest. I definitely don't deserve this man. I don't know how I could ever live up to the woman he deserves.

But I know that I want to try like hell to be that woman.

When we get home, we say goodnight to Annie and walk down the hall to kiss Giuliana goodnight while she sleeps.

Only, she's not in her bed.

We creep into Alexander's room and find her fast asleep in the middle of his bed, with Ellie and Dash at the foot of the bed like her protectors.

Alexander heaves a sigh as he smiles. "She's obsessed with my bed," he whispers.

I shake my head. "It's not the bed. It's her father when he's in it."

He tangles his fingers with mine as he leans down and presses his lips against my cheek. "Sleep with us tonight."

I glance at Giuliana before swinging my gaze back to him. "But what will she think when she wakes up and sees me in bed with you guys?"

"She'll think she has her family with her, and that she is loved."

Family.

Something I've never felt like I was a part of.

Until now.

I nod and give him a small smile. "Okay."

After we wash up and change, we slip into bed. Alexander takes the left side and I take the right, sandwiching Giuliana between us. He reaches over and presses a kiss to the top of her head, her messy curls sprawled out over the pillow. Then he reaches for me, stroking my hair away from my face and caressing my cheek. His soft touch lulls me to sleep, despite my racing heart ready to jump out of my chest and lay at his feet.

Each beat sounding more and more like the words I can't bring myself to say.

Maybe tomorrow.

I'll tell him tomorrow.

33

AARYA

"Yes! Score!"

Cassidy jumps to her feet and screams with me. "Let's fucking go, Goldfinches!"

The score is officially 1-0, and we have home advantage. The crowd is electric around us, cheering on their team and booing the shit out of Philadelphia.

Alexander's teammates slap him on the shoulders as he skates by after putting points on the board, and then his eyes find me in my usual seat behind Trenton's goal. I blow him a kiss and he pretends to catch it with his glove before returning his attention to the game.

"Keep your eyes on numbers four and five," Celeste says. "They're notorious for playing dirty and causing a lot of fights."

Cassidy groans. "Why do they have to fight? Why can't they just play?"

Both Cassidy and Celeste have seen their husbands take some mean hits on the ice, and Jason even got taken out on an ambulance once. My stomach hurts just thinking about something like that happening to Alexander, but I know it's the name of the game. Hockey is an aggressive sport.

Going into the second period, I notice the two players Celeste pointed out getting bolder with their hits. They each end up in the penalty box a couple of times, but it doesn't seem to stop them. Each time they slam into one of the Goldfinches, the crowd lets out an audible gasp in unison. McKinley is visibly pissed, and at one point he ends up throwing off his helmet and gloves to fight number four. Both of them come away with bloody faces. He's up McKinley's ass again in the next play, but Alexander slams him into the boards and shouts something at him before skating away.

Heat flushes my skin. There's something about watching my man take charge on the ice that gets me all hot and bothered.

"You're turned on, aren't you?" Celeste asks.

A devious smirk twists my lips in response.

I can't wait to get him home later.

I'm going to tell him tonight. I'm going to tell him I love him.

Philadelphia has yet to score, and the tension between the teams only continues to rise in the third period. They take a shot, but Trenton blocks another goal attempt and passes the puck to Jason, who manages to get it to Alexander.

"Go, baby, go!" I scream, cupping my hands over my mouth.

Alexander flies like lightning across the ice, and I'm in awe at how fast he gets to the other side of the rink. Philly's defense is strong though. Alexander passes to McKinley, and he quickly fires it back. Alexander takes it behind the goalie's net to escape, but number five is right behind him, running him into the boards and trying to steal the puck. They fight for possession, when all of a sudden, number four skates down the ice toward them.

"Shit," Celeste mutters as we all rise to our feet.

"Get out of there!" I yell, as if Alexander can hear me over the roar of the crowd.

He's looking down at the puck, trying to get it away from the asshole behind him. He comes away with the puck, picking up speed and getting in position, but right before he can shoot for the goal, numbers four and five slam into him—one from the front and one from behind, sandwiching him between them. Alexander's helmet flies off as they tumble.

And his head smacks against the ice.

Hard.

My hands fly up to my mouth as I gasp, the sound swallowed by the eruption of the people screaming around us.

There's a frenzy of fighting, gloves and sticks flying around the ice.

Players from both teams take swings at each other, but all I can see is Alexander's lifeless body lying on the ice.

"Why isn't he moving?" I ask. "Why isn't he getting up?"

Celeste clutches my left hand. "He probably just got the wind knocked out of him."

A whistle blows and a medical team is signaled by one of the refs. Both teams freeze, realizing something is wrong.

Alexander's arms and legs are splayed out and he's not moving, but I'm too far away to see anything else.

"Are his eyes open?" My heartbeat feels like it's in my throat, and bile rises in my stomach. "Can you see anything?"

Cassidy laces her fingers with my free hand. "Give him a minute."

Come on, Big Man.

Get up.

Please get up.

My heart plummets when the stretcher comes out onto the ice. The medical staff secures Alexander's neck in a brace and they carefully haul his giant body onto the stretcher and off the ice.

"Where are they taking him?" I reach down and grab my jacket and my purse. "Where is he going?"

"To the medical room. They'll asses him there." Celeste pulls out her phone and her thumbs fly across the screen. "One of my friends works in there. I'll have her text me with updates."

Trenton's head hangs downward as he skates toward us to take his spot at the crease.

He lifts his eyes to mine when he skids to a stop. "Just breathe," he mouths before putting on his helmet.

Then the game continues as if nothing happened.

I blink. "They're just going to keep playing?"

Cassidy tugs on my arm. "Come on. Let's go take a walk to the bathroom. I'm sure we'll hear something soon."

Celeste follows us out, and it's like I'm walking through a fog. I can't see anything in front of me, and the voices around me sound muffled.

I pull out my phone to check in with Annie, and see if Giuliana was watching the game. My stomach sours at the thought of her watching her father get carted off the ice like that.

> Me: You guys aren't watching the game, are you?

> Annie: No, why?

> Me: Alex got hurt. I don't know what's happening yet but I'll keep you posted.

In the time it takes us to walk to the bathroom, Celeste's friend calls her with an update.

She presses the speaker button before she answers. "Hey, Sarah. What's happening?"

"He's still unresponsive. They're taking him to Jersey Shore Medical."

Unresponsive.

Hot tears burn my eyes, but I blink them away as I spin around and walk right out of the bathroom, mindlessly going through the motions as I try to find my way out of the stadium.

Unresponsive.

I shoot a text to Annie to let her know where we're going, and then to Eddie who's waiting outside to let him know we'll be needing a ride to the hospital.

The girls stay silent on the way, and I'm grateful for it because I don't have any words to say. Not until I find out what's happening to Alexander. Instead, I type *head injuries* and *concussions* and *unresponsive* into the Google search, attempting to prepare myself for what's to come.

At the hospital, I fill out the forms to the best of my ability, but I have to ask Annie for specifics that I don't know.

I don't know his social security number.

I don't know his insurance information.

I don't know his blood type.

I don't know anything, because we're not a *real* husband and wife.

I return the clipboard to the woman behind the desk, and she lets me know that someone will come out to speak with me once they know something.

Celeste wraps her arm around my shoulders, and walks me back to the chair. "Now we play the waiting game."

Unresponsive.

"Are you hungry or thirsty?" Cassidy asks. "Want me to get you some coffee or water?"

I shake my head as I lower myself into the chair.

And I stare at the doors, willing Alexander's doctor to walk through them with good news.

"Mrs. Krum?"

I jump to my feet as soon as I hear my name, making a beeline for the tall blonde doctor walking toward us. "Is he awake? Is he okay?"

"I'm Dr. Kelly," she says. "I have some updates about your husband. Would you like to sit?"

I shake my head. "How is he?"

The doctor glances around at the waiting room, now filled with giant-sized hockey players. "Your husband had some internal bleeding that needed to be drained. That's common with head trauma. I hear he took a nasty hit on the ice tonight."

The vision of his head bouncing off the ice flashes through my mind, and I cringe. "So, now what?"

"Now he's in recovery, and you'll be able to see him soon. But we're not out of the woods yet."

"Why?" McKinley asks before I can get the word out.

"We'll need to monitor him to make sure we can keep the brain from swelling further."

"They said he was unresponsive when they brought him in." I swallow. "Will he be conscious now that he's had the surgery?"

"The brain is a tricky thing," she says. "Everybody's recovery is different."

"So, what does that mean?" Trenton asks, reading my mind.

Dr. Kelly nods, turning to glance at him. "Right now, he's in a coma."

A coma.

Alexander is in a coma.

"When will he wake up?" I ask, even though I know it's a stupid question.

Dr. Kelly offers me a sympathetic smile. "That's up to your husband."

I hate when people say that. As if Alexander is choosing to not wake up. "When can I see him?"

"Once we get him settled in his room. It shouldn't be too long."

After the doctor heads back behind the double doors, my friends surround me.

"He just needs to recover," Celeste says.

"Everything is going to be okay." Cassidy.

Trenton squeezes my hand. "He's a strong motherfucker. He'll be fine."

But they don't know any of those things. Not even the doctor does. We don't know if Alexander will be okay, or if he'll wake up at all.

He's in a coma.

"I have to call Annie." I push out of the chair and head outside, needing the cold air to soothe my clammy skin. My fingers shake as I press the call button, and I swallow down the bile in my throat.

"Hey, what's happening?" Annie answers.

"H-he had surgery to drain the bleeding in his brain, and now he's in recovery. B-but he hasn't woken up yet. The d-doctor s-said she doesn't know when he will."

If at all. I leave that part out because I can't bring myself to say it out loud.

It's quiet for a moment before she responds. "Oh, God."

I nod even though she can't see me. "The doctor said she'd let me in to see him once he's settled in a room."

She sniffles. "All right. Keep me posted when you see him."

"What are we going to tell Giuliana?"

"Nothing. Not yet. When she wakes up in the morning, I'll tell her he had an early meeting before practice, and that you're at the gallery." She pauses. "No need to upset her."

Tears sting my eyes. "But what if—"

"No. Don't think about that. We take this one moment at a time, you hear me?"

"One moment at a time," I echo.

After the call ends, I blink up at the night sky to will the tears away.

One moment at a time.

The emergency room doors slide open behind me, and McKinley steps out. Out of all his teammates, he's the closest with Alexander, and I know this is difficult for him.

"How are you holding up?" he asks.

I'm glad he's keeping his hands in his pockets, because if he tried to hug me, I'd probably break down in his arms and I can't do that right now.

I have to stay strong.

My tears won't bring Alexander out of his coma.

I shrug. "This fucking sucks."

"Yeah, it fucking does."

"Any chance you can find out where numbers four and five live?"

He arches a brow. "I'm sure I can."

"Good." I ball my hands into fists. "Let's pay them a little visit."

He lets out a humorless laugh. "Trust me, it's gonna be bad for them the next time we play against them."

I turn my head to look him in his crystal-blue eyes. "Mac, what if he doesn't wake up?"

"Don't think like that. He just got out of surgery. Give him some time." One corner of his mouth turns up. "He's too much of a control freak to let this take him out. He's probably fighting like hell in that head of his."

A half-laugh, half-sob bubbles out of my chest. "Definitely."

He dabs at the corner of his eye. "I'm going to wait here with you, if that's okay. They might not let me in to see him, immediate family and all, but I want to stay."

I nod. "Of course. We can tell them you're his brother."

He runs his hand through his coppery curls and chuckles. "Adopted brother."

Some of the team heads home while our small circle stays to wait it out. It's another thirty minutes before a nurse comes out and lets me know that I can see Alexander.

She places her palm against my back as we walk down the long corridor. "I don't know if you know anything about comas, but studies have shown that people can hear their loved ones. So, feel free to talk to your husband. Some people sing to them, some people read."

I nod. "W-what is he...what does he look like?"

"He's breathing on his own, so he's not hooked up to a ventilator. But he does have a feeding tube in. That can be a little jarring when you walk in."

She pauses outside room 504. "His head is also wrapped in a bandage from surgery."

"Thank you."

My pulse pounds against my neck, my blood pumping so loud, I can hear it in my ears.

I open the door and inch my way into the dimly-lit room, the sound of rhythmic beeping greeting me before the sight of Alexander does.

I clamp my hand over my mouth when I lay eyes on him, my insides twisting in anguish.

My big, beautiful man lies motionless on the bed.

I don't recognize this version of him, pale and void of the passion and life that makes him who he is.

His dark eyes don't meet mine.

His lips don't curve into a smirk.

His hands don't reach out for me.

Remembering what the nurse told me, I make my way over to the chair beside the bed and lower myself into it.

I clasp his hand between both of mine. "Hi, Alex." I clear my throat. "It's me, Aarya. I don't know if you can hear me, but the nurse said you can. This feels silly talking to you while you're clearly unconscious." I roll my eyes, and a lone tear slides down my cheek. "But if there's a chance you can hear me, I guess I'll have to try."

He doesn't answer, because of course he doesn't, but I stare at him as if he'll miraculously open his eyes and ask why I'm crying.

He'd hate to see me cry.

"You promised me." My voice shakes as one tear turns into two. "You said there would be no bad surprises."

And then the floodgates open. I lay my head on his lifeless hand on the bed, and I let it all out.

Please come back to me, Alex.

34

AARYA

I STAYED AT THE HOSPITAL UNTIL GIULIANA GOT OUT OF school the next day.

Annie picked her up and we're meeting at the house so we can tell her about her father together. He hasn't woken up yet, and we don't want to keep lying to her about where he is.

But as I sit in the driveway, staring up at the house, I can't get out of the car.

I spent the majority of the night Googling what to say to children in situations like this, trying to figure out what I'm going to say to Giuliana. The mommy blogs say it's best to tell the truth, in the simplest form. To leave out your own emotions, so you don't impart them on the child.

Eddie glances at me in the rear-view mirror. "You okay, Mrs. Krum?"

"That kid is going to be devastated." I pause. "She's going to have so many questions, and I don't have answers for her."

He heaves a sigh. "Maybe it's not about having the answers. Maybe she just needs you to be there for her."

"Thanks, Eddie."

I suck in a long, deep breath, and blow it out through my lips, digging deep for any courage I might have stored inside me somewhere that I'm unaware of.

Then I get out of the car and head inside.

"Aarya!" Giuliana comes running for me before I can shake off my jacket, jumping into my arms. "You're home early. How's the gallery?"

I force a smile. "It's good. I came home early because I wanted to see you."

"You did?"

"I did."

Ellie bumps me with her nose, so I reach down and pat her head. She takes her time sniffing me, no doubt trying to figure out the scent of the hospital on me.

"Listen kid, Annie and I need to have a talk with you about something."

"Something important?"

I nod. "Let's go sit down on the couch."

I set her on the floor and she scampers into the living room to wait for me with Annie. I hang up my coat and toe-off my shoes, taking my time to prolong the inevitable a little longer.

Giuliana sits between me and Annie on the couch, her wide eyes bouncing between us.

I clear my throat and clasp my hands together, one squeezing the other. "Last night, your dad got hurt at his hockey game. He...fell down on the ice and hit his head."

"He had-ed his helmet on, right?"

"He did, but it got knocked off." Acid climbs up into my throat, and I attempt to swallow it down. "He went to the hospital so they could help him, and that's where he is right now."

"Can we go see him?"

I glance at Annie before returning my gaze to Giuliana. "We can. But there's something you need to know. Your dad..." I pause, clearing my throat again. "He's asleep. And the doctors don't know when he's going to wake up."

"Is he really tired?" she asks.

Tears burn my eyes. "Yes, he's resting because his brain needs to heal."

Annie clasps her tiny hand. "He has a big booboo on his head."

Giuliana stares at us with those big round eyes like she's processing. "We should bring the Elsa band aids to the hos-bit-al. He always puts them on me when I have a booboo."

Annie sniffles and turns her head away to conceal it with a cough.

"That's a great idea." Another fake smile strains my face. "I went to visit him last night, and he looks a little different right now. He has a bandage wrapped around his head, and a tube in his mouth so they can feed him while he's sleeping."

"They feed him while he's sleeping?" Her nose scrunches. "That's weird."

I can't help but chuckle. "It is, right?"

She hops off the couch with Ellie right behind her. "I'll go pack the band aids."

Then she runs into the hallway, and disappears.

I let go of the breath I've been holding. "Well, that was easier than I thought it would be."

"She doesn't understand the magnitude of the situation just yet." Annie reaches over and pats my knee. "You did good."

"I don't know what I'm doing. This is..."

This is too much. I'm out of my depth. Alexander should be here. He'd know what to do.

"We have to stay strong for her. She needs us to stay hopeful," Annie says.

Hopeful? I'm no good at that. Alexander himself told me I was a jaded pessimist when we first met. How am I supposed to stay positive when I saw him hooked up to all those machines with a tube stuffed down his throat?

"What if he doesn't wake up, Annie?" I whisper, my voice shaking. "What are we going to do?"

I need answers. I can't live in this limbo of not knowing what's going to happen. It feels like my heart is being ripped apart from the inside.

Annie shakes her head. "We can't think like that. He's going to wake up, and everything is going to be fine. That boy is a fighter."

My lips tremble. "I kept putting off telling him I love him. I kept telling myself, *another time, another day.* But now that day might never come."

"He knows, Aarya. He knows. You didn't have to say the words because he felt it." Annie scoots across the couch cushion and wraps me in her arms. "But you have to stay strong. You have to believe that he will be okay. He needs your strength right now. You can't give up on him."

I could never willingly give up on that man.

I only hope life doesn't force me to.

WHEN WE GET to the hospital, my brave little curly-haired girl looks up at me and asks, "Can you pick me up like Daddy does?"

"Of course." I bend down and scoop her into my arms, just as happy as she is to have someone to hold in this moment.

She scrunches her nose. "It smells weird in here."

"I know. But that just means it's clean."

We stop in front of room 504 and I glance over at Annie. "You ready?"

Annie nods. "You ready, Giuls?"

"Yes." Her voice sounds curious yet wary.

We step inside the room, and I watch Giuliana's face to gauge her reaction. Her eyes flick from the machines to the wires, to the tubes where everything is hooked up to her father.

She squirms to get out of my arms, and I set her onto the floor. She doesn't run like she normally does, taking tentative steps toward his bed.

"Hi, Daddy," she calls.

He doesn't answer.

She glances back at me. "Can I climb onto the bed?"

"Just be careful with those tubes coming out of his arm." I walk up behind her and lift her onto the bed, patting the space beside him. "Here looks like a good spot."

She places her tiny hands on either side of his face and leans in, inspecting the tube coming out of his mouth. "Does this hurt his throat?"

I shake my head. "No."

"Hi, Daddy," she says again, only this time she whispers it. "I have your favorite Elsa band aids for your booboo."

Annie clutches my hand while we watch Giuliana dig into the tote bag she brought, and pull out the box of band aids, selecting one with Olaf on it.

"I'm giving you an Olaf one because you love him so much, and you like warm hugs just like him."

Alexander does love his hugs.

I miss his hugs.

After she places a band aid over the bandage wrapped around his head, she begins pulling out everything else from inside the bag.

"Animals aren't allowed in the hos-bit-al, so I brought you little Ellie instead. She can keep you company in case you get scared at night." She sets the stuffed animal by his hip before pulling out white paper along with a box of crayons. "I'm going to draw you a picture so when you wake up, you can see it."

On the ride over, Annie and I explained to Giuliana that even though her father is asleep, he can still hear her. We encouraged her to talk to him, despite the fact that he won't respond, and now she's doing exactly that.

I expected her to cry. To be upset about the fact that her father is hurt. But I don't think the magnitude of the situation has set in yet. And how could it? She's only four.

She's only four.

Too young to lose her father. Too young for any of this.

Giuliana begins working on a picture as she tells her father about her day, like she would if we were home. Annie and I drop into the chairs beside the bed, and force smiles on our faces to keep the mood light.

After an hour, Giuliana looks up at us. "Why isn't he waking up yet?"

I chew my bottom lip. "I think when your body is healing, it puts you to sleep until it's finished."

"So, when he's finished healing, he'll wake up?"

The harsh truth gets stuck in my throat, but luckily Annie takes one for the team and lies for me. "Yes."

"This is a really long nap, Daddy." Giuliana shakes her head, looking exactly like her father when he gives her one of his disapproving head shakes. "You're going to have so much energy when you wake up."

When he wakes up.

If he wakes up.

No matter how hard I try to keep my mind on the positive track, it keeps yanking me back to the negative thoughts.

I can't live in a fantasy land. I never have, at least not until I met Alexander. He convinced me that love and romance and good men do exist. He even convinced me that I could have those things, that I could be loved by a man like him.

Is this my punishment for believing it? Is this what I get for playing house in this fake life that I don't belong in?

Maybe I never should've agreed to this arrangement in the first place.

But when I glance over at that little girl sitting on Alexander's bed, I erase that thought from my mind.

Maybe *that's* the real reason I'm here. To help Giuliana through this.

Maybe I'm not destined for an epic love story after all.

35

AARYA

THE NEXT FEW DAYS ARE LIKE *GROUNDHOG DAY*.

I keep Alexander company for as long as visiting hours will allow me. My time is spent talking to him and filling him in on how Giuliana's doing in school, and telling him all the funny questions she's had, because I know how much he hates missing out on time with her.

My evenings are for Giuliana, helping her with homework, making sure she feels surrounded by the people who love her, and trying to make things as normal as possible in her father's absence. McKinley has been over a lot too, making sure to keep the smile on Giuliana's face.

Nighttime is the hardest. That's when I Google all the possible outcomes of a man in a coma. Everyone keeps telling me to stay positive, to keep the faith that Alexander will wake up and everything will be okay. But I can't delude myself. I have to keep my feet on the ground. There's a chance Alexander might not wake up. There's also a chance he wakes up and suffers from amnesia, or lifelong complications. The longer he stays in a coma, the worse it gets.

Of course, I want him to wake up. I wish for it with every fiber of my being. But I have to prepare myself for the worst.

Saturday morning, I open my eyes in Alexander's bed and spot Giuliana beside me. Every night, she starts out sleeping in her own bed—only because

I know her father would want her to maintain her routine—but every morning when I wake up from a broken night's sleep of tossing and turning, she's always here beside me.

I drag myself out of bed, and Ellie trots behind me while Dash stays curled up with Giuliana. I take the dog for a walk, feed her, and then down a cup of coffee so I can get back to the hospital.

"Aarya, you have to eat." Annie casts me a dejected glance. "You can't survive on black coffee all day."

"I'm not hungry."

She heaves a sigh. "Listen, I need to talk to you about something before Giuliana wakes up. Can we sit down?"

The tone of her voice has the bile churning in my empty stomach. "What's wrong? Did the hospital call while I was asleep?"

She shakes her head. "No, but I need to show you something."

There's a manila envelope sitting on the dining room table, and Annie slides it toward me as we take our seats. "This is Alexander's will."

I almost vomit on the spot. "Oh, fuck. I don't want to see this."

"I'm not showing you this because I think he's going to die. I'm showing you this because I think you could use a pick-me-up."

I stare down at the envelope, too scared to open it. "This feels morbid."

Annie ignores me and flips it open, and points to one of the bottom paragraphs. "We discussed this about a month ago."

My eyes scan the page until my vision blurs. "Why would he do that?" I shake my head. "I can't...I can't..."

"He wants you to be Giuliana's legal guardian should anything happen to him. It used to be me, but..." She huffs out a laugh. "I'm getting old, and I think this is the best decision for her."

Me?

Me.

Giuliana's legal guardian.

"Why wouldn't he talk to me about this first?"

She chuckles. "Probably because he knew you'd say no, like you are right now."

Panic licks up my spine. "I... I'm not a mom. I'm no good at this," I stammer. "Look at me. I don't know what I'm doing."

"Sweetheart, you have been the most wonderful addition to this family.

That little girl looks at you like you hung the moon. You've done everything you can to ensure her health, happiness, and safety. And you give her love. At the end of the day, that's all that matters."

"How is this supposed to cheer me up?" This is overwhelming at the very least.

"Because it shows you how highly that man regards you." Annie swipes away a tear. "He has fallen so deeply in love with you, and it has been an honor to sit here and watch it all unfold. So, hold onto that reminder. Hold onto the hope that he's going to come back to you."

The sound of Dash's meow pulls my attention to the hallway, where he and Giuliana step out into the dining room.

I push my lips into a smile. "Hey, kid."

But she doesn't smile back. Her tiny sniffle gives her away.

Fuck.

"I miss Daddy."

I open my arms wide, and she crashes into me. Her little body shakes as she cries, and I hoist her onto my lap so she can koala herself around me.

"Why is it taking so long for him to wake up?" she wails. "Isn't he done healing already?"

My throat burns. "I know it's taking a long time."

I can't deny her frustration. It *is* taking a long time, and this really sucks. She's allowed to feel it. She's allowed to throw a tantrum if she wants to. I'm surprised it took her this long.

It's in this moment, holding Giuliana as she breaks down in my arms, that it hits me.

It doesn't matter what I think of myself. It doesn't matter if I think I'm a good mom, or fit to take on this role. I'm here regardless. I'm in it. And this kid needs me. So, I'll be whatever I need to be, do whatever I need to do, in order to ensure that she has everything.

Even if it means being her mom.

"You have a visitor in the waiting room," the nurse says, standing in the doorway.

I glance at my phone, wondering if it's McKinley or Cassidy, though neither of them texted me.

Annie pushes out of the chair and takes Giuliana with her. "We'll go get some dinner."

"Bye, Daddy." Giuliana waves at Alexander's lifeless body. "We'll be right back, okay? Maybe you can wake up and have dinner with us."

Another knife slices through my heart.

The nurse walks out with Annie, and I tell Eddie to follow them instead of staying with me.

Several minutes later, footsteps sound in the hall. I glance over my shoulder, but I'm not greeted by McKinley's orange curls, or Cassidy's hopeful hazel eyes. A tall, frail man stands in the doorway wearing an expensive-looking suit. The fluorescent lights shine off his bald head, his face covered in wrinkles.

"Nope." I stand and point my index finger at him. "Get the fuck out of here."

He arches a bushy gray brow. "Excuse me?"

"I know who you are, and you're not welcome here, Lorenzo."

A smirk plays on his thin lips. "Is that any way to speak to your grandfather-in-law?"

I open my arms wide. "We're surrounded by lots of pointy objects, so unless you want one jammed in your eye socket, then I suggest you turn around and leave. Cancer will be the least of your worries when I'm through with you."

A surprised chuckle leaves his mouth as he strides into the room. "Well, you're a charming young lady, aren't you?"

I grit my teeth. "I swear, I'll call security and have your ass throw out of here."

His feet halt, and he holds up his hands on either side of his head. "I just wanted to see how my grandson is doing."

My eyebrows hit my hairline. "Your grandson? You mean, the one you've ignored for the last twenty-nine years of his life? The one you're trying to con out of his parents' villa? That grandson?"

He smirks. "And you must be the wife he's arranged to con me out of the stipulations in my will. Tell me, how much is he paying you? I can offer more."

I make a gagging sound and scrunch my face. "Eww, you want me to marry you? Sorry, but I'm not into sugar daddies."

He chuckles. "You know what I mean, Aarya."

The sound of my name in his mouth sends an eerie shiver down my spine. "I'm only going to say this one more time: Leave. Now."

I slip my phone out of my back pocket and tap out a quick text to Eddie telling him I need his assistance in the room, but to keep Annie and Giuliana away.

"I'm not here to cause trouble. I feel for you, truly. And I can offer you a way out. You didn't sign up for all this." He waves his arm, gesturing to Alexander. "You thought it'd be easy, didn't you? He buys you an art gallery in exchange for a marriage agreement. You go on a few dates, you spend some time acting like a couple. But this is too much of a commitment. Are you prepared to stick by his side for as long as this lasts?"

His insinuation is insulting. "I will stay by his side for as long as I have to, because I am his wife and I love him." I lower my voice and clench my fists as I inch toward the old bastard. "Maybe a heartless piece of shit like you would pretend to marry someone just to get one over on your dying grandfather, but Alexander would never do that. He's a better man than you ever were."

He ignores my jab. "How long do you plan on staying married? Six months? One year? It'd have to be at least that to make it look legit. Or maybe you're just waiting for me to die."

"How could you do that to your own daughter?" I ask, turning the questions around on him. "Do you ever think about her? Do you regret the way you treated her while she was alive? Do you wish you could have a second chance to make things right with her?"

"Would that make you feel better, to know that a father regrets not being in his daughter's life? Do you wonder if yours thinks about you at all?"

This motherfucker.

For a split second, I envision jumping on him like a spider monkey and clawing his eyes out of his face. But that's what he wants. That's why he's here, to get a reaction out of me.

Instead, I smile. "No, I don't think about my father at all actually. Just like Alexander won't think about you when you're gone. It's amazing how the trash always ends up taking itself out."

He heaves a sigh. "This is my final offer, Aarya. Name your price, and you can get out of this mess."

This mess. Alexander's life hangs in the balance, and he's referring to it like an inconvenience.

"Take your money and shove it up your ass, Lorenzo."

Eddie strides through the doorway and wraps his hand around Lorenzo's arm. "Time to go."

"One more thing." I stand in front of the old man and square my feet as I look into his soulless eyes. "I hope the cancer eats away at your insides, and you die a slow, painful death. And I hope the last thought that crosses your mind is the fact that no one on this earth gives a shit that you're dead."

Lorenzo shakes his head and turns to leave without another word.

Alone in the room with Alexander once again, I return to my chair beside his bed. I lift his hand and place his palm against my cheek, closing my eyes and wishing his thumb would stroke my skin like it used to.

"I hope you heard that, Big Man. Because I meant what I said to your scumbag grandfather. I love you, and I'm not going anywhere. And if you would just wake up, I could tell you that. I'll wait here for as long as I have to, but the coffee here sucks and this chair is really uncomfortable, so if you could hurry this along, that'd be great." A manic laugh bubbles out of me as I start to cry. "I miss the sound of you laughing at my sarcastic jokes. I miss you calling me spitfire. I miss riding with you. I miss...I miss everything about you. If you don't come back to me, how am I supposed to go on? You've engrained yourself into my life, and now I don't know how to do this without you. You changed everything for me, and now I need you to come back. Giuliana needs you. Your team needs you. So, I'm gonna need you to open those puppy dog eyes of yours now."

I stare at him, willing his eyelids to flutter. Willing his hand to twitch against my face. Waiting for a sign, for *something* to give me even a spark of hope.

But he doesn't, so I bury my face in his blanket and cry.

Several minutes later, Eddie returns to the room. "All clear, Mrs. Krum."

I turn around and give him a feeble smile. "Thanks."

He glances down at me before he goes, and says, "Remind me not to mess with you. You're terrifying when you're angry."

36

AARYA

"I THINK YOU SHOULD GET OUT OF HERE FOR A WHILE."

I ignore Cassidy and continue with my routine. I fluff Alexander's pillow, roll some chapstick over his dry lips, and change the water in the vases from the flowers that continue to show up from random strangers.

"Aarya." She comes up behind me and touches my shoulder. "Seriously, this isn't healthy for you. It's been seven days. You need a break."

"I take a break every night when visiting hours are over."

"No, you don't, because you go home and take care of a four-year-old. And Annie said you haven't been sleeping because you're painting all night." She moves in front of me so I can't pass her. "Why don't you go to my apartment and sleep? Trenton's at an away game, and no one's there."

I shake my head. "I'm not tired."

"Okay, well, I can take you to the gallery if you want. Maybe that'll take your mind off—"

"I don't want to take my mind off of him." My voice comes out harsher than I intend it to. "I want to stay right here, and wait for him to wake up. He needs to hear me. He needs to feel me. He needs to know I'm here. I don't want to leave him alone."

"The doctor will call you if there's any change."

"No."

The words are on the tip of her tongue, but she doesn't let them out.

She wants to ask, *What if he doesn't wake up? How long will you continue this?*

I know because she's my best friend, and it's what I'd be asking her if the roles were reversed. But I can't bring myself to leave until visiting hours are over.

And I can't even *think* about the gallery, let alone go there. I only have that place because of Alexander. Maybe things will change in time if he doesn't wake up, but right now, after a week of this mind-numbing torture, I'm not ready to let go.

My stomach breaks through the silence with a loud grumble.

Cassidy arches an eyebrow. "Not hungry, huh?"

I hike a shoulder. "I guess I could go for something."

She sighs. "I'll go grab us some cheeseburgers from the cafeteria."

"Hey." I reach out for her arm before she can turn away. "Thank you for being here for me."

She's been here every day. She brings her laptop and works on her next book while she keeps me company.

She clasps my hand. "You'd do the same for me."

And I would.

I wait for her to leave before I take my seat beside Alexander's bed, and run my fingertips along his forearm. "Well, it's day seven. I took Giuliana to get her cast taken off today. The doctor said the fracture healed just fine. I made sure to ask a hundred questions because I know that's what you would've done." I lift his hand and press my lips to his knuckles. "I love you, Alex. I wish I would've told you sooner. I wish I wasn't such a stubborn ass. But I hope you can hear me in there. I love you."

I swipe my phone off the armrest and click to open the Spotify app. I've been shuffling through his playlist for him, hoping the music helps stimulate something in his brain.

Brown Eyed Girl comes on first, and I smile, remembering the story Alexander told me about how his father used to sing this to his mother while they were cooking in the kitchen. Then the memory of us dancing with Giuliana in the kitchen flashes through my mind, and hot tears sting my eyes.

"Please, Alex." I lower my head against his palm as I sob. "Please, wake up."

I lie there until the song ends, needing to release the emotion before Cassidy returns with dinner.

But right before the song switches to the next, Alexander's fingers twitch against my cheek.

My head whips up as I gasp.

Did I imagine it?

I stare down at his hand until I see his fingers twitch again.

"Alex? Can you hear me?" My eyes flick up to his closed ones, waiting to see if they'll open. "Alex, you just moved your fingers. Do it again, baby. Come on. Come back to me."

I hit the button to call the nurse's station, and within seconds, one of the nurses I've become friendly with shows up in our room.

"Jerome, I felt his fingers move. I was sitting here, and they twitched. Then they twitched again. Does that mean—"

Alexander's eyelids flutter.

I gasp, and my hands fly to my mouth. "Tell me you see that."

"I see it, sweetie." Jerome moves around the bed and checks the screen displaying Alexander's vitals. "He might be disoriented at first, so we have to give him time to come out of this. Sometimes, patients are agitated. Other times, they fall right back to sleep. We have to be patient. It's not like it is in the movies."

I clasp Alexander's hand and stare at him, waiting for him to make the next movement.

"I'll go page the doctor," Jerome says.

I nod and lower myself back into the chair, afraid to blink, afraid to miss something.

"Alex, I'm here, baby." I keep my voice low and even. "I'm here waiting for you to open those beautiful brown eyes of yours. Take your time. I'm not going anywhere. Everything is going to be okay."

My heart races, and I can barely suck in a breath as I wait.

Dr. Stephens enters the room several minutes and two hand twitches later. "Good afternoon, Mrs. Krum. I hear our hockey star is finally waking up."

"I think so. His fingers keep twitching and his eyes are moving."

"All good signs." He leans over Alexander and lifts each of his eyelids up, shining his small flashlight into his eyes. "He's responding to light."

I watch the doctor as he moves around Alexander's body, performing tests for responsiveness. I have so many questions, but I keep them bottled inside because right now, all I want to focus on is Alexander waking up.

Cassidy strides into the room holding a brown paper bag in one hand while balancing two soft drinks in a cup holder in the other.

Her eyes go wide as soon as she looks at me. "What? What's wrong?"

A lone tear trickles down my cheek. "He might be waking up. H-his fingers... they moved. And his eyes..."

My voice trails off, hope getting caught in my throat.

Cassidy quickly sets down our dinner and scampers to sit on the chair beside me. "Come on, Krum Cake," she whispers.

"This is a gradual process," Dr. Stephens says. "Slow and steady."

I nod, wiping away the evidence of my tears. "How long does this process usually take?"

"Every patient is different, but we'll get the feeding tube out of him and see how he does over the next twenty-four hours."

After he leaves, I call Annie and fill her in. We agree to hold off on telling Giuliana until we know what state Alexander wakes up in.

I try to contain my excitement, but my insides feel like they're about to burst.

This agonizing wait might finally be over.

THE NURSING STAFF lets me stay overnight.

Jerome is a huge Goldfinches fan, and when he convinced everyone on the floor to keep a secret and let me stay, I told him I'd get him free tickets to thank him.

Annie let Giuliana sleep at Makayla's house so I don't have to explain where I am. I feel guilty not going home to see her, but I also don't want to leave Alexander's side in case he fully wakes up.

It's impossible to sleep in this place, so I'm in and out of cat naps in this uncomfortable chair. Jerome offered to get me a cot, but I want to be as close to Alexander as possible. I need to feel him move again, even if it's the slightest of movements.

I'm watching a muted Goldfinches game on my phone when I feel Alexander's hand squeeze mine.

My gaze shoots up to his, and I'm greeted with dark-brown puppy eyes.

My phone clatters to the floor and I swallow down a gasp. "Alex."

He squeezes my hand again, blinking slowly and keeping his eyes locked with mine.

So many words bubble to the surface, so many things I want to say, but the only thing that comes out of me is, "Please tell me you don't have amnesia and you know who I am, or so help me God, I'm going to fucking scream."

The corner of his mouth twitches, and I hold my breath waiting for more, but it doesn't come.

I lift his hand and press it against my cheek, pressing my opposing palm hand against his handsome face. "I missed you so much. I'm so happy to see your eyes open looking at me."

A tear escapes me and rolls down my cheek, and his thumb moves to catch it. He makes a raspy noise in his throat, but no words come out.

"It's okay, these are happy tears." I turn and grab the cup of water waiting on the portable table on the side of his bed. "Here, your throat is probably so dry."

I lift the straw to his lips and watch as he attempts to take a sip.

"There you go, baby." I lean down and press my lips against his cheek, peppering his face with kisses. "You were in a coma for seven days. But you're going to take it easy, and everything is going to be okay."

Everything is going to be okay.

His eyes flick around the room like he's searching for something.

"Giuliana is at a sleepover tonight. She was here earlier today." I smile. "She got her cast off. She's excited to show you."

His eyes water, and my heart wrenches at the sight.

"It's okay, baby. We're all okay. You just scared the shit out of us, but we're all good. I've been taking care of Giuliana, and so has Annie. I've even been taking Ellie on her daily walks. That dog takes such massive shits, it's unreal. Also, McKinley might've taught Giuls the word *fuck*, but I made her swear to never repeat it until she's thirty."

Something in his chest wheezes as he attempts what sounds like a laugh, but then he starts coughing.

"Okay, okay. No more jokes." I let him have another sip of water. "God, Alex, I'm so fucking happy you're awake right now."

He squeezes my hand, tugging me closer to him.

"What's the matter? What do you need? More water?"

He pulls me until I'm in an awkward position, half leaning over him on the bed.

"You want me to come lie down with you?" I ask, searching his eyes for the answer.

He nods, the slightest movement, and my heart soars.

I kick off my shoes and climb onto the bed, maneuvering around the tubes in his arm. I settle my head against his chest, and he rests his free arm on my waist.

He's awake.

He's holding me.

A wave of relief floods me, and the tears start falling from my eyes without permission. I bury my face in his neck so he doesn't see. The last thing I want to do is upset him further right now.

"I really hope this means you remember me," I say, choking back a sob. "Otherwise, I'm going to have to kick your ass for letting some random woman get in bed with you."

His shoulders shake as he quietly laughs.

37

ALEXANDER

AARYA IS THE FIRST THING I SEE WHEN I OPEN MY EYES.

Which is fitting, because she was the last thing to flash through my mind right before I cracked my head on the ice.

Waking up, it takes me a while to understand where I am, as well as what happened, but my brain slowly pieces it together. I can't talk right away either, which is so frustrating because all I want to do is tell Aarya how much I love her.

How sorry I am for worrying her.

How awful I feel for leaving everything on her shoulders.

I was out for a *week*. I missed a whole week. It kills me to know I scared my daughter like that. Aarya tells me she was a trooper, but I hate that I put her through something like this.

"Daddy!" Giuliana's voice pierces through the quiet as she comes dashing into the hospital room. "Daddy, you're awake!"

Aarya hoists her up onto the bed, whispering a reminder to be gentle, and then my baby girl is in my arms. Tears prick my eyes as I hold her little body, sick to my stomach over what she must've went through while I was in a coma.

"Daddy, you slept for a really long time. Is your brain all healed-ed now?"

"I think so." I tap the band aid on my head. "I think it was Olaf's magic that did it."

She giggles. "No, it wasn't. It was the doctors and nurses."

God, the sound of her laughter soothes my aching heart. "I heard you were the best girl for Annie and Aarya this week."

"I was the bestest." She pulls away to look at me and pauses. "Why are you crying, Daddy? Did I hurt you?"

"No, baby. Not at all. I'm just so happy to see you."

"You missed me while you were sleeping?"

I nod. "I did."

"I missed you too. Could you hear me talking to you?"

"I heard your voice, but I didn't know what you were saying. It was like I could feel you there with me, wherever I was."

She purses her lips like she's trying to make sense of what I said. "I got my cast off. Look! And I made you a picture while you were sleeping." She points to the paper taped on the wall above my bed, but I can't turn around to look at it.

Aarya reaches over and pulls it off the wall, a small smile on her lips as she hands it to me.

Four stick figures stand beside a tree—one a tall man; the other a little girl with curly hair; the third a woman with long, dark hair; and the fourth is a shorter woman with grayish hair.

Even Ellie and Dash made it into the picture, sitting together under the tree. Each of our names are written in perfect capital letters underneath our bodies, but it's the one under Aarya's stick figure that has my heart filling with emotion.

MOMMY.

"This is the most beautiful picture I've ever seen," I whisper, unable to speak around the ball of sentiment in my throat. "I love it."

Giuliana leans in and cups her hand around her mouth as she whispers. "Aarya took really good care of me, just like a mommy. She was so sad while you were sleeping. I heard her crying a lot at night. She doesn't know I heard her, but I did."

A tear slips down my cheek. I never want to be the reason that woman cries, and I hate that I was, even if it was out of my control.

"Thank you for keeping her company," I whisper back. "I'm sure you helped her feel happy when she was sad."

Giuliana nods. "When can we go home? This hos-bit-al smells bad, and I don't want to come back here anymore."

Annie laughs as she comes to stand beside my bed. "We'll leave as soon as the doctor gives us the okay."

I reach out and clasp Annie's hand. "Thank you so much. For everything."

I know she must be exhausted after this last week. Having Giuliana full-time is a lot for anyone, let alone someone at her age.

"You don't have to thank me. I'm just so glad you're okay." She sniffles as she squeezes my hand. "Your parents were watching over you, and they guided you back to us."

Giuliana reaches for Aarya, and I melt at the ease in which Aarya scoops her up into her arms.

"Why does everybody keep crying?" Giuliana whispers loud enough for us to hear.

"Sometimes, people cry when they're happy. It's how we show our emotions." Aarya nuzzles her nose against Giuliana's hair. "Plus, your dad's a big softie."

Giuliana giggles. "Like a giant teddy bear."

"I can hear you, ya know," I tease. "I'm not in a coma anymore."

Annie turns to Giuliana and holds out her hand. "Come on, let's go see if they refilled the candy in the vending machine."

"Yay!" She squeals as she lets Annie lead her out of the room.

I let my head fall back against the pillow, lifting my hand for Aarya.

She laces our fingers together as she stands at my side. "So, your grandfather was here a couple days ago."

I lift my head again and my body goes rigid. "What?"

"I debated on whether I should tell you now, or when you're home, but decided it was best to have a medical staff around in case your blood pressure spiked."

Oh, it's spiking. "What the hell did he want?"

"He tried to pay me off." She drops my hand. "And he actually made a pretty good offer, so I'll be seeing you."

I grip her wrist before she spins away, and yank her back to me. "It's not nice to play games with a man in my weakened condition."

She grins. "He still thinks we're faking this marriage, so he offered me money if I gave up the act. I told him to shove his money up his ass."

"And...?"

"And... I said some other choice words, and now we might need to hire a new bodyguard because I think Eddie is scared of me."

I laugh. "I think we're all a little scared of you."

"Good." She shoots me a devious wink before her eyes drop to Giuliana's drawing in my lap. "So, Annie showed me your will."

I pat the space beside me, and motion for her to climb up.

Aarya nestles in close and we get as comfortable as we can in this uncomfortable bed. "Why didn't you talk to me about being Giuliana's legal guardian?"

I run my fingers through her hair. "Because you'd find any reason as to why you wouldn't make a good guardian and fight me on it."

She heaves a sigh. "I probably would've."

"Definitely," I correct. "So, how do you feel about it now?"

"Well, I hope I never have to raise her without you again, but...I'm good with it."

I smile with pride. "You make a really great mom."

Aarya pushes to sit up so she can look into my eyes. "I've been doing a lot of thinking this week."

"Oh?"

She glances down as she fidgets with the wedding rings on her finger, so I tip her chin to bring those beautiful eyes back to mine.

"What's on your mind, spitfire?"

"I've been wanting to tell you this for a while now, but I kept chickening out. And then when you got hurt, I didn't know if I was ever going to get the chance to tell you. So, now seems like a really good time because I don't know if I can wait another minute to say this."

"Tell me what, baby?" I swipe away the tears falling down her cheeks. "Why are you crying?"

It takes a lot to make her cry. She looks so nervous, I can't imagine what she's going to say next.

Until she blurts it out. "Alex, I'm in love with you."

The beeping on the machine I'm hooked up to speeds up. "You are?"

She nods as more tears fall. "I've never been in love before, and I don't know if I'm going to be any good at it. You're so incredible, I don't think I'll ever be able to live up to that. But I love you and I love Giuliana, and I never saw this coming but I want to be in this with you guys." She sniffles, the tears now streaming down her face. "I want spaghetti dinners and tea parties and movie nights on the couch. I want our little family. I want *you*, Alex. I love you."

I cradle her face, bringing her lips to mine. "I love you, Aarya. So much that I don't know how I've held it inside all this time. But I don't want to hold it in anymore. I want you to know how happy you make me. I want you to know how hard I've fallen for you. You keep saying that you're not good at love, and that you're not a good mom, but those are the two things you've blown me away with. You've showed up for me, time and time again. And you've been there for Giuliana, which means more to me than you'll ever know." My voice cracks. "I've dreamed of finding someone for not only myself, but for her; someone to love her and care for her; someone to teach her new things, and answer her incessant questions."

"God, does she ask a lot of questions."

"The kid is relentless." A teary laugh comes out of me. "But I couldn't have dreamed up someone better than you. Aarya, you're everything I've ever wanted, so I need you to stop doubting yourself. Stop doubting your worth. Stop telling yourself that you don't deserve everything I want to give you, because you do. You deserve the moon and the stars, and every single good thing in this world. And I'll spend the rest of my life convincing you of that."

She trembles as she rests her forehead against mine. "I love you so much. I was so scared this week. I was terrified that I'd lost you."

"I'm sorry, baby. I'm so sorry that you had to go through that. But I'm here now. I'm here and I'm not going anywhere."

She sobs, and it feels like a week's worth of agony rolling out of her like the tide after a storm.

I hold her while she lets it out, and I cry with her. The pain and the heartache we've both endured, separately in our past, and since we've been together, has come to an end.

We're together now.

We have each other.

Giuliana skids to a stop as she bursts into the room.

"More crying?" She shakes her head and throws up a hand. "What the fuck?"

I'm definitely going to kill McKinley.

38

AARYA

"Alexander Thomas Krum."

His shoulders bunch up around his ears as he makes a slow turn to face me. "Whoops."

I step into the garage and give him my best glare. "*Whoops* is right. The doctor said you need to rest."

He grimaces. "I'm getting antsy sitting in bed all day."

I tip my chin toward his bike. "So, whatcha doin'?"

"Just tinkering." He drapes a rag over the seat. "I don't know what to do with myself."

My tone softens. "I know you miss riding, and playing hockey."

He nods, the corners of his mouth tipping downward. "I hate knowing the guys are out there on the ice without me."

"You'll be out there with them soon."

As much as that thought bothers me, I shove it down. Athletes don't have the luxury of taking their time to recover. Once Alexander is cleared to play by the medical team, he'll go right back to playing as if nothing happened.

But something *did* happen.

Something I never want to relive.

And he reads it on my face like he always does, reaching out a hand for me. "Come here."

I slip my hand in his, and let him tug me close. He presses a kiss to the top of my head as he wraps his arms around me.

"How are *you* doing?"

"I'm fine," I start to say. "Just feeling overwhelmed with the gallery, and—"

"The truth, baby." Alexander's grip around me tightens. "Tell me what's wrong."

I let out a long sigh. "I'm terrified of the thought of you putting on those skates again." I pause, forcing out the words I've been holding inside for the last two weeks. "Every night before I fall asleep, I see you lying there in the hospital all over again; that bandage around your head; the tube down your throat; your body hooked up to machines." Emotion stings my eyes. "I can't get it out of my brain."

He pulls back just enough to tip my chin, and I lift my gaze to those puppy eyes of his. "I'm sorry you had to go through that. I can't imagine how I'd feel if the situation were reversed. But I'm okay. *We're* okay. I don't want you to torture yourself with the memory of what happened. We have to keep moving forward."

I nod. "I know."

"But you don't have to pretend to be okay for me. You can talk to me. I want to hear what's going on inside that beautiful head of yours. I want you to tell me when you're worried, when you're scared. I want to carry that load with you. We're in this together."

I close my eyes as he rests his forehead against mine. "I love you, Alex."

"I wasn't sure I'd ever hear you say those words." He presses his lips to mine. "I hoped for it. I dreamed of it. But I didn't know if you'd allow yourself to feel it."

"You didn't leave me much choice." I smile. "Your love made it impossible for me to keep my guard up."

"You never need to have your guard up with me." He leans in for another soft kiss. "I love you."

Warmth rushes over me, spreading from my chest out to every nerve ending in my body. I tilt my head and open my lips, my tongue sweeping inside his mouth, needing to deepen the kiss and pour myself into him.

"We don't have much time," I murmur, knowing we have to pick up Giuliana from school this afternoon.

"I know." Alexander sweeps me into his arms and carries me into the house. "I just need to be inside you. Now."

We've been insatiable since Alexander got released from the hospital. It's like we can't get enough of each other, can't get close enough, trying to make up for lost time, or for the time we almost didn't get to have.

We don't make it past the kitchen as Alexander sets me down on the island. We're frantic as we claw at our clothes, ripping off each piece and tossing it onto the tile.

"No condom," I breathe against his lips. "I'm on the pill."

He pauses, letting his forehead fall against mine as he catches his breath. "Are you sure?"

I nod. "I want to feel you. All of you."

He gives his dick a slow pump as he swallows. "I'm clean. I got tested after—"

"I'm clean too." I gaze up into his eyes. "Please, make love to me, Alex. And don't stop until you come inside me."

His mouth drops open and his eyes dilate. He runs the smooth head of his cock through my wetness, coating himself in me and teasing us both, notching himself at my entrance. I spread my legs, resting my heels against the edge of the counter while I lean back on my palms.

Then he pushes himself inside, in one agonizingly slow motion.

We both moan, unable to contain the feeling of being skin to skin with nothing between us.

"Fuck, you feel incredible." He clutches my face and draws me in for a mind-blowing kiss, ravishing my mouth while he buries himself all the way inside me.

His hand slides down to cup my breast, squeezing it while the other hand grips onto my hip to hold me steady as he pulls himself almost completely out of me before plunging back in.

I roll my hips to meet him stroke for stroke as he fucks me in a slow, sensual rhythm, letting me feel every bare inch of him.

I lift my eyes to his, overcome with love and devotion to this man. "I love you, Alex."

"Say it again," he whispers.

"I love you." I lift my hands and cradle his face. "I love you more than I've ever loved anything or anyone."

His eyes close, as if he can't believe the words I'm saying. When they open and meet mine again, they shine with emotion, so much adoration emanating from the depths of those dark eyes.

"I love you, Aarya. Forever and always, I will love you and cherish you, every day of my life."

We rock against each other, moving as one, losing ourselves in the moment.

"I love the way you take me," he murmurs. "Love the way your pussy wraps around me, like I belong inside of you."

My head falls back as I press my palms into the countertop. He leans down and captures one of my nipples in his mouth, licking and sucking and making me wetter by the second. The sound of him sliding in and out of me fills the room, along with my moans of pleasure.

Then he brings his thumb to my clit, rubbing slow circles while he fills me.

I reach up and wrap my hands around the back of his neck, needing to feel him closer. "Don't stop, Alex."

"You gonna come for me, baby?" His hips move faster, fucking me in deliberate, firm thrusts. "I can feel you tightening around me."

I'm pulled under by a wave of bliss, only able to mutter a string of nonsensical words, like *yes* and *Alex* and *more.*

"That's it. Come on my cock. Soak me." Alexander doesn't stop moving in and out of me, letting me ride out the orgasm for as long as I can while talking me through it.

My body trembles, my pussy spasming around him, and then Alexander releases a guttural groan as he comes, releasing inside of me.

By the time we're done, we're breathless and clutching to one another, basking in the sated calm that blankets us.

Alexander's forehead falls against mine as his chest heaves. "I love you, Aarya. I'm going to love you forever, do you understand me? You *own* me. I'm yours, and nothing is going to take me away from you, so you don't have to worry, because I'll always fight my way back to you."

Tears sting my eyes as I squeeze them shut. "I can't believe we're here. I can't believe the way you've changed my life over these last few months. I never thought I'd find someone like you. I never knew something could feel this good."

His large hands come up to hold my face, forcing my gaze to lock with his. "Believe it, baby. Believe it and know that you deserve it. You deserve to be loved the way I'm going to spend my life loving you."

My heart pounds a furious rhythm in my chest as I look up at this beautiful man, and I have no doubt in my mind that he will live up to his words.

He backs up and pulls himself out of me, and we both look down as the evidence of his release oozes out.

His lips part, and his eyes darken on the spot as he watches it. His tongue skates over his bottom lip as he swirls his thumb over the cum, rubbing it all over me. I watch as he pushes it back inside, pumping in and out of my pussy in short pulses.

He's mesmerized by the sight of it.

I arch a brow. "You good, Big Man?"

"Yeah." His voice is raspy. "I like seeing my cum inside you."

I smirk. "I kinda like knowing your cum is inside me."

He flicks his eyes to mine. "Do you think...have you ever thought about having kids one day?"

My eyebrows jump. "You saying you wanna put a kid in me?"

"I'm just asking if you'd ever want to, in the future—in general, not just with me."

"I've never wanted a kid. Or a husband. Or a boyfriend, for that matter." I lift my hand and caress his jaw. "But that was before I met you."

He leans into my touch as I continue.

"A lot has changed for me, and now I want all the things I thought I didn't want." I pause. "Being with Giuliana has altered who I am as a person. I didn't know I had this much unconditional love inside of me to give. I didn't expect to ever be in this role—a step-mom; a caretaker; a nurturer. I didn't think I'd be any good at it."

"You're *so* good at it, baby."

"And watching you be her father? It's the most beautiful thing I've ever witnessed. It's one of the things that made me fall in love with you." I smile. "Plus, it's hot as fuck."

He chuckles. "So, what are you saying?"

"I'm saying, I think I'd like to make a baby with you one day."

Alexander crushes me in a hug, wrapping his strong arms around me and holding me against his warm body. "I'd put a baby in you so fast."

"Okay, okay. Relax, Big Guy." I push his chest and give him a playful shove. "I said *one* day, not *today*."

"THIS PLACE IS INCREDIBLE. I'm so happy for you."

I beam at Chanora. "Thanks. I really love it here."

She rubs her belly while she gazes around the gallery that's finally coming together. "Have you heard anything new about Carter?"

"A few of the other girls came forward and corroborated our sexual harassment claims. That along with the fact that he assaulted me will give him some jail time." I glance at Brittany and hike a shoulder. "I just hope he doesn't continue to do this to anyone else in the future."

"Well, everyone quit." Brittany huffs out a laugh. "So, good luck to him trying to keep that gallery afloat without any employees."

"About that." I chew my bottom lip, my eyes bouncing between them. "Do you think anyone would want to work here?"

Chanora's head whips to mine. "You'd hire us?"

"Of course. Once I get this place up and running, I'd be honored to have you here with me."

Brittany reaches out and clasps my hand. "That would be amazing."

"Absolutely." Chanora's eyes well. "Look at you, Aarya. Look how beautiful your life is."

I chuckle. "I can't wait for you to have this baby so your pregnancy hormones stop making you cry over everything."

She flips me off before swiping away a tear. "I'm happy for you. Sue me."

The truth is, I'm happy too. Truly and irrevocably happy. My life is blossoming in the most incredible way, and most of the time, I sit here in awe watching it happen, as if it's someone else's life and not my own.

The front door swings open, and Annie strides into the gallery.

"Annie, hey. What are you doing here?" My heart drops into my stomach. "Oh, God. Is everything okay?"

"Yes, yes." She stops in front of me and clutches my arm. "Everyone is fine, I'm sorry. I didn't mean to scare you."

I blow out a relieved breath. "Shit. I guess it's gonna take some time to get over the trauma of this whole thing, huh?"

"Healing always takes time. Nothing we can do about it."

"What are you doing here?"

"I wanted to show you my husband's paintings. Figured you could sort through them and pick which ones you want, if any."

"Are you sure you want to part ways with them?"

She nods and offers me a smile. "I kept his favorite at the house, but these will serve you better than they will me. It'd be a pleasure to see them hung in your gallery."

Affection warms my heart. "Thank you. I'd love to take a look at them."

Her smile widens. "Alexander had Sam pull the SUV around back."

"Great. Let's bring them into my office."

Chanora and Brittany follow us to the back door and we carry the covered paintings into the gallery, and set them carefully against the wall in my office.

I uncover the first canvas, and gasp. "This is a Jackson Pollock."

Annie bites back a smile as she watches me.

"That's an *original* Jackson Pollock," Chanora says.

I glance at the next painting, lifting the protective covering. Another original.

"Annie... I can't accept these. They cost a lot of money, and I don't have—"

"They're yours," she says, cutting me off. "I don't want the money."

I'm at a loss of words, flipping through each canvas and realizing that each and every one is an original piece from very well-known artists.

"Are you sure?"

Annie steps forward and takes my hands in hers. "They're yours. Alexander's parents can't be here to meet you, to love you, but I am. And I want to watch you make your dreams come true. So, take these paintings and love them like I know you will."

My own mother couldn't muster the effort to provide a safe, loving environment for me growing up—the bare necessities from a mother to a daughter. But like I told Giuliana, your family doesn't always run blood-deep; sometimes, it's the people you meet along the way who show you the meaning of the word.

I don't know what else to do other than wrap my arms around this sweet woman and hug her.

Where words fail me, I'm noticing that hugs can go a long way.

"Thank you," I whisper.

"Thank *you*, for making that boy so happy."

My eyes flick to Alexander, who's watching us with a content smile on his lips.

And then I glance at Chanora, who's wiping her eyes, again, with the backs of her hands.

I shake my head at her. "Again? Jesus."

She flips me off.

39

ALEXANDER

"All right, birthday boy. Here's your present."

Aarya struts out of the bathroom and drops her towel. "I hope you're ready because I'm about to rock your world." Her feet falter halfway to the bed. "You're not naked. You're supposed to be naked. Why aren't you naked?"

"Sorry." I chuckle, holding up the letter in my hand. "I got momentarily distracted by this. But now that you're in here looking like *that*, I'm distracted by something else entirely."

She snatches her towel off the carpet and wraps it around her body. "What's that?"

I hand her the letter from my grandfather's lawyer as she lowers herself to the mattress beside me. "He's dead."

"Lorenzo?" She gasps as her eyes fly across the paper. "So, the villa...?"

"It's mine."

Aarya jumps to her feet and pumps her fist in the air. "Fuck, yeah! Take that, motherfucker. He's dead and the villa is yours! Justice is served."

I toss my head back and laugh at her reaction, mainly because she dropped her towel and is metaphorically dancing on someone's grave while butt-ass naked.

Aarya covers herself with the towel again. "Damn, I can't compete with that kind of gift. This is one smokin' hot bod, but it's hard to top a dead evil grandfather and a villa in Italy."

I tug the towel until she's standing between my legs at the foot of the bed. "This smokin' hot bod blows everything else out of the water."

I almost feel an odd sense of gratitude to the dead bastard. If it weren't for him, I'd never have ended up where I am today, completely in love with this gorgeous woman—someone who stands beside me and holds my hand throughout life's ups and downs; someone my daughter can look up to; someone who makes my soul feel whole and at peace.

We'd never be married or living together if it weren't for Lorenzo.

But then a thought crosses my mind, sobering me immediately as the smile drops from my face. "So, uh... I guess we should talk about things now."

Aarya tilts her head. "What do you mean?"

"Now that my grandfather is out of the picture and the villa is mine, we don't exactly have to stay married." I clear my throat, my eyes dropping to my hands in my lap. "You know, if you don't want to. We don't have to pretend—"

Aarya leans down and cuts me off with a kiss. "You want a divorce, Big Man?"

I shake my head. "No."

She drops her towel and tosses the letter somewhere behind her. "You sure about that?"

"Positive."

"Good." She climbs on top of me, straddling me as she pushes me onto my back. "Because I don't want a divorce either."

My hands fly up to her hips, gripping her tight. "Are you sure? I know we did things a little backwards."

"Do I look like someone who is unsure of what she wants?"

"No." *Not my spitfire.*

She reaches down between us and palms me over my sweatpants. "Maybe you just need some convincing then...?"

My lips curve into a smirk. "Now that you mention it, I'm not feeling too convinced."

She hums in response, lowering her lips to my nipple ring and sucking on the sensitive skin there. "Then let me make myself crystal-clear." Using her tongue, she toys with the metal barbel. "You are my husband." Her hand slips underneath the waistband of my pants, and she pulls out my dick, giving it a few firm pumps. "We took vows. In sickness and in health." She glides her slick pussy over my length, coating me in her arousal. "In good times and bad." The head of my cock notches at her entrance, teasing us both. "Until death do us part." She stills and her eyes lift to mine. "And I wouldn't have it any other way."

My hips jut up to hers, and I cup her beautiful face in my hands. "Me neither, baby."

Then she sinks down onto me, burying my cock inside of her, and we both cry out in relief. She pulls back and sits up, riding me like the goddess she is. I can't take my eyes off of her. The sway of her tits, her mesmerizing eyes, the curve of her hips, the way her pussy swallows me whole...I'm consumed by this woman. I'm at her mercy. She has me, now and forever.

She runs her fingers over my shoulders and down my chest, and that's when her eyes land on my tattoo—the new addition to it.

Her mouth drops open. "What...when did you do this?"

"This morning." I grin. "A small birthday gift to myself."

I knew I wanted to get the tattoo as soon as I saw Giuliana's family picture in the hospital. Adding Aarya's stick figure, accompanied by the word *MOMMY* in Giuliana's handwriting was a no-brainer for me. I needed to have our little family on my body forever.

Aarya traces around the raw skin with her index finger, her eyes wide with admiration. "You permanently tattooed me on your ribs, yet you asked if I wanted a divorce?"

I chuckle. "I had to ask to be sure this is what you wanted."

"Always asking for consent, since the first day I met you." She flashes me a smile. "And all I wanted was for you to fuck my brains out."

I wrap my arms around her and roll us both over until she's flipped onto her back beneath me. "Then you'd better hold on because I'm about to fuck my wife."

"FUCK, YEAH! OUR CAPTAIN IS BACK."

McKinley slaps my shoulder pads as we shuffle toward the locker room exit. "Man, it feels good to have you back."

I grin. "It feels good to be back. I was going crazy sitting on the bench."

The announcer begins calling each of us onto the ice while we wait our turns in the tunnel. Adrenaline courses through me, those familiar nerves buzzing just under my skin, pumping through my veins.

I love this game. It's a delicate art, despite the physical toughness of the things we push our bodies to do, and there's an unprecedented level of talent required to maneuver on sharp blades of steel. It's constant, fast-paced action with the speed in which we fly across the ice, combined with the agility it takes to control a small puck into the back of a net. Not knocking any other sport, but I just don't see how anything can compare to hockey.

It takes control. It takes precision.

It's a lot like riding a motorcycle, ironically enough.

Furthermore, I love my team. We can't play this game without each other, without assisting and giving one-hundred percent to each other. These people are my friends. My brothers. And I'm proud to lead them.

I glance up at the quote painted on the wall—*Great moments are born from great opportunities*, from the late Herb Brooks—and I tap it three times with my stick, as I do before every home game. Then I step up to the entrance, and the announcer's voice booms over the speakers.

"And now, returning to the ice, let's hear it for the captain of the Goldfinches—who's celebrating his thirtieth birthday with all of us tonight —Alexander Krum!"

The cheers from the crowd shake the stadium as I glide across the ice. Lights flash, and people jump from their seats as they hold up their homemade signs welcoming me back after a terrifying injury. Their support means so much to me, yet there's only three people in this crowd who are truly here for me and me alone.

I lock eyes with my curly-haired baby girl, standing on her seat holding up a foam finger that's bigger than she is. She is my whole heart, my reason for living. She made me a father, and taught me the meaning of unconditional love.

Annie holds her steady from the seat beside her, beaming at me like a proud mother would. I got through some of the toughest times in my life because of that woman, and I am eternally grateful for her.

And then my gaze drifts to the spitfire next to them, donning my jersey and looking like the sexiest woman I have ever laid eyes on. From fake wife, to step-mom, to the love of my life, Aarya has engrained herself into the fabric of my soul. How we ended up here, I'll never understand, yet at the same time, it feels like we were inevitable.

I'm one lucky bastard.

Looking back at the loss of my parents; Rachel's betrayal; my conniving grandfather—it all feels like another lifetime. Everything is different now. Everything I've been through has led me to this moment, and there's no other place I'd rather be than where I am right now.

We play a great game, and come away with another win. Annie takes Giuliana home, while Aarya and I head out to a bar with the rest of our friends to celebrate.

"To Krum Cake's triumphant return!" Jason raises his shot glass in the air, and I clink my water bottle against it.

"Happy birthday, Big Man." Aarya squeezes me with her arm around my waist.

I press my lips against her cheek, and then whisper, "How did you feel watching me play tonight?"

"I was nervous at first, but it went away by the second period."

I tuck her hair behind her ear. "Thank you for being there, despite it being hard for you."

"I wouldn't have missed it. I'm proud of you for getting back out there."

McKinley wedges himself between us and rests an elbow on each of our shoulders. "Look at you two. Head over heels in love." He side-eyes Aarya. "Correct me if I'm wrong, but the last time we were here, you were having a very serious conversation about love being *bullshit*."

She rolls her eyes, a smirk curving her lips.

My eyebrows jump as I shove McKinley out of the way, and move to stand in front of her. "You think love is bullshit?"

"I didn't say *love* is bullshit. I just don't buy into all that romantic crap. No guy is going to do the things you read in a book."

I cross my arms over my chest, recreating the conversation we once had in this very VIP room months ago. "Men can be romantic."

She lifts her chin like a brat. "I've never met a man who has done *any* of those romantic things."

"Then you haven't been spending time with the right kind of men."

Her smile slips free as the façade fades, and she lifts her hands to wrap around the back of my neck, stretching up onto her toes to reach my mouth. "I only want to spend my time with one specific man."

My hands skate around to her lower back, pulling her flush against my body. "Lucky man."

"He is." She nips at my lower lip. "But I'm also a lucky woman."

"That so?"

"Mhmm." She presses her lips against mine. "You showed me what it feels like to be cared for."

"I will always take care of you." My grip tightens around her. "You will always feel loved, and appreciated, and safe with me."

Her eyes flutter as she gazes up at me from under her long lashes. "I love you so much, Alex."

"And I love you."

She kisses me again, and this time I deepen the kiss, slipping my tongue between her lips and wrapping it around hers. Our friends whistle and clap around us, and we break apart wearing sly smiles.

We spend some time with our friends, and we dance. But it's not long before we're ready to go home and spend the night together—just the two of us.

"Remember when you told me you don't want to be tied down, just tied *up?*"

Aarya waggles her eyebrows. "I do."

I bring my lips to her ear. "I have some zip ties in the garage."

Her body shudders against me. "Take me home."

I take her by the hand, and I do what I wanted to do the night we first met.

I take her home.

But this time, it's *our* home.

40

AARYA

SIX MONTHS LATER

"How do you feel?"

I smooth my shaky palms down my black dress. "Like I'm going to puke."

Louise laughs and gives my shoulder a squeeze. "That's totally normal. But you have nothing to be nervous about. The gallery looks amazing. The art pieces you've chosen are perfect. You've worked hard these last several months to get everything ready for tonight."

I *have* busted my ass to make sure the gallery was ready for tonight's grand opening. I've gone over everything a hundred times, ensuring there isn't a single thing I've left out.

I just can't believe this is happening.

"Thank you for all your help." My eyes bounce around the room. "I really enjoyed working with you."

"I'd love to continue working with you. I think this gallery is going to do great." Louise smiles as she glances over my shoulder. "It looks like you have it all. The career. The man. The kid."

I follow her gaze and lock eyes with Alexander, who's watching me from across the room with Giuliana in his arms.

"I do have it all." I shake my head in disbelief. "I don't know how, but I do."

"Cherish it." Louise offers me a sad smile. "It doesn't happen for many of us."

I didn't think it would happen for me. If I'd never agreed to fake marry Alexander, I'd still be stuck at Carter's gallery. A shiver runs through me, shaking me to my core. I often wonder how he's doing in jail. If he regrets the choices he made. If he feels remorse. If he'll be any different when he gets out.

I block out the thoughts of my old life and return my attention to Louise. "It could still happen for you. Trust me, I never thought this would be my life. I was *not* this person you see before I met Alexander."

"You were." Alexander's hands slide around my waist as he steps behind me. "You just didn't know it."

Louise places her hand over her heart. "You two give me hope."

"Do you mind if I steal my wife for a minute?" he asks.

"Of course not, go." Louise waves us off.

"There's champagne over there!" I yell as she walks toward the back of the gallery.

Alexander tugs my hand toward the corner near the entrance, and he points up at the painting on the wall. "This is unbelievable."

My cheeks heat as I blink up at my finished painting. "You think so?"

"I know so." His brown eyes bounce around the canvas as he shakes his head. "You are so unbelievably talented."

Pride swells in my chest. I worked on that painting for months, trying to make sure it was just right before letting Alexander see it tonight. When we were in Greece, I snapped a photo of Giuliana standing on the balcony overlooking the Aegean Sea. The colors of the water, mixed with the sunset in the sky, and her bouncy curls blowing in the breeze made for a stunning picture.

Giuliana runs up to us and tugs on my hand. "Hey, that's me."

I bend down and lift her into my arms. "It is you. So pretty."

She squishes my cheeks together, making my lips pucker like a fish. "*You're* so pretty."

"Watch her makeup," Alexander warns, flashing me an apologetic grimace.

Giuliana lifts her hands up like a thief who's been caught. "Oops. Sorry."

"That's okay." I smack my lips against her cheek, leaving an outline of red lipstick on her creamy face. "You want to help me cut the ribbon?"

She gasps as her brown eyes widen. "Yes!"

She wriggles out of my grasp and bolts over to McKinley and Trenton. "Uncle Mac! Uncle Trent! I'm going to cut the ribbon!"

I grin as I watch her. "She gets so excited over the smallest things."

Alexander spins me around and pulls me flush against him. "She really makes you appreciate everything."

"I appreciate *you*." My fingers weave through his hair at the back of his neck. "I couldn't have done this without you."

"You could've. I just helped you a little."

"A little?" I arch a brow. "I forgot you have hockey player money. Our idea of *a little* is very different."

"*We* have hockey player money. What's mine is yours. You're my wife, remember?"

I smirk. "I remember."

"Look at this." He waves his arm around the room. "This is all you. Your vision. Your dream. I'm simply an investor. So, tonight, make sure you take the time to pat yourself on the back for what you've done here, and celebrate the woman you are. Because I'll certainly be celebrating you."

"Oh, yeah?" I slide my hands down along his muscular arms. "I think I like the sound of that."

He grins as his head dips down, and he runs his lips along the side of my neck. "I bet you do."

Goosebumps fly along my skin as his teeth graze my earlobe. "You think anyone will miss us if we slip into my office for a few minutes?"

"Considering you're the woman of the hour, yes, I think they'd miss us." His laugh is low and raspy. "Plus, I'm going to need more than just a few minutes to worship you tonight."

My thighs clench in anticipation.

He lifts his wrist and glances at his watch. "I think it's time we get started."

I suck in a deep breath and straighten my dress as we break apart.

I walk over to where Giuliana is standing with our friends, and hold out my hand for her. "You ready, kid?"

"Ready, Mommy."

Alexander

One year later

"You remember the plan, right, Giuls?"

My girl nods fervently. "After you exchange the rings, I read the letter to Aarya."

I hold up my palm and she smacks hers against it. "How are you feeling?"

"Excited." She grins wide, revealing her missing bottom tooth. "And you should be excited too, because I saw her dress and she looks better than a princess."

"You know who looks like a princess?" I scoop her up into my arms and spin her around. "You."

She squeals until I set her shoes on the floor again. "Daddy, you can't pick me up like that anymore. I'm too big."

My eyebrows shoot up. "You're too big for your dad to pick you up?"

She nods with wide eyes. "I'm five now. Things are different."

I swallow down the laughter climbing up my throat, wanting her to know I hear her and I'm taking her seriously. "Am I allowed to hug you, then?"

She thinks on it for a second, and then she hikes a shoulder. "Sure."

I kneel down in front of her and clasp her hands. "You look absolutely beautiful, baby girl. I am so proud of you, and I'm constantly impressed by your bravery."

"*I'm* brave?"

"Absolutely." I coil one of her curls around my index finger. "You say what's on your mind, and you ask questions. You're so smart and so capable. You can do anything."

A small smile tugs on her glossed lips, and I hope she always remembers my words.

Cassidy knocks on the doorframe. "We need to steal the flower girl."

"It's my time to shine!" Giuliana darts across the room, the tulle on her white dress bouncing around her as she runs.

I chuckle. "See you out there."

She glances at me over her shoulder and waves. "Bye, Daddy!"

Tears prick my eyes as I watch her follow Cassidy down the hall.

"She's growing up way too fast," McKinley says with a heavy sigh.

I arch a brow. "Even more so when you keep teaching her all these grown-up phrases."

He holds up his hands on either side of his head, feigning innocence. "Hey, man. This is a happy day. Let's not talk about it."

I grunt.

"Come on." He claps me on the back. "Let's go get you married—again."

Trenton and Jason are waiting for us outside on the veranda with the rest of our friends. It's a warm July day in Tuscany, and the sun streams across the courtyard of the villa I used to play in as a child. Today, Giuliana gets to create her own memories here.

The warm breeze rustles the leaves on the tall tree beside the garden my mother used to spend her time in, while my father looked on from the bench swing hanging from the branch. I can feel my parents all over this place, and it serves as a reminder that they're still with me.

I take my spot under the archway, alongside McKinley—who convinced us to let him officiate our ceremony, God help us all—and the music begins to play.

Cassidy, Celeste, and Kourtney each walk down the aisle, taking the spot mirroring their husbands standing behind me.

Even though we're already married, my stomach clenches in anticipation as I await Aarya's walk down the aisle, just as it did when I got down on one knee and asked her to marry me—again—last summer. I wanted to do all of this for real, instead of acting under false pretenses. That was what brought us together, but this is a decision to love each other from the bottom of our hearts until death do us part.

Giuliana sprinkles white rose petals down the aisle, her big brown eyes on me as she skips down the aisle. I kneel down to hug her when she reaches me, and then stand and clasp her hand as we wait for Aarya.

Aarya asked Annie to walk her down the aisle. She said she didn't have parents who were worthy of performing the honor, and that Annie deserves to give her away. Annie cried, of course, and hugged her—and Aarya hugged her back.

I knew we'd break down her *no hugging* rule eventually.

The music changes, and I suck in a sharp breath as Aarya emerges from the villa, her elbow linked with Annie's.

Emotion strangles me, constricting my lungs and burning my eyes. I blink to clear my vision as Aarya floats down the aisle in a white floor-length gown, the strapless lace bodice hugging her voluptuous figure and giving way to a flowy tulle skirt that matches Giuliana's.

My God, she is the most exquisite human I've ever laid eyes on.

And she's walking toward *me*.

To marry *me*.

She loves me so much she's marrying me *twice*.

I don't know what I did to deserve her, but I'll do it every day for the rest of my life to ensure that I keep her.

Annie places Aarya's hand in mine when they stop before me, and sandwiches our joined hands between her own as she suppresses a sob. "I love you both so much."

I wrap Annie in a tight hug, whispering, "Thank you for everything," in her ear before we break apart and she takes her seat.

Aarya reaches up and thumbs away a tear from my cheek. "Hi, Big Man."

I lean into her touch. "Hey, spitfire."

She holds out her fist. "Good job on the flowers, kid."

Giuliana beams as she bumps her fist with hers.

McKinley rubs his palms together and then opens his arms out wide. "We're gathered here today to bear witness to the union of these two beautiful humans. I was already the witness to their first nuptials, so I think we all know who the favorite friend is here."

Trenton and Jason roll their eyes while the crowd chuckles.

"But today, we're witnessing more than just a ceremony. We're witnessing the creation of a family. We've all seen Alexander raise his little girl on his own, and what an amazing person she is growing into." He reaches down and ruffles Giuliana's curls. "But Aarya came in and stepped into their family as if she belonged there—as if there was an empty space waiting for her to fill it."

To my surprise, McKinley wipes his eyes with the back of his hand. "I can't tell you how much it means to me to know that my best friend has someone looking out for him and his daughter the way you have."

Aarya swallows as she blinks back tears, nodding to McKinley.

He gestures to me, letting me know it's time for my vows. I clear my throat, and clutch Giuliana's hand in my left hand while clasping Aarya's in my right.

"I knew I wanted you from the moment I laid eyes on you, but I didn't think I could have you. You were a skittish black cat, and I was the overeager dog. We came from different worlds, with different beliefs. Yet we fit together so perfectly, finding in each other the very things we were both missing. Love. Trust. Companionship." I swallow past the thick ball of emotion in my throat. "Watching you with my daughter has brought me more joy than I ever thought imaginable. I always dreamed of being in this very spot with Giuliana, in the place I grew up, with a woman who loves us. You've made my dream come true. You settle my soul. And I promise to spend the rest of my days making sure you know how loved you are."

I lift her hand to my lips and press a kiss to her knuckles.

Aarya's eyes brim with unshed tears, and her lips part as she releases a breath. "It's no secret to anyone here that I wasn't looking for you when I found you. I kept pushing you away, convinced that I didn't want the things you stood for. But it turns out, I needed every single thing you offered me, and I was just too fu—" her eyes flick to Giuliana for a moment, "messed up to realize it. You've given me a life I never knew I could have, and I'll be eternally grateful for you for being so patient with me while I figured it out." She squeezes my hand. "You taught me the meaning of love. You and your amazing daughter, and I love our little family so much."

I nudge Giuliana, and right on cue, she pulls out a folded piece of paper from her now-empty basket. "Daddy told me I could say something, so I've been practicing."

She reaches up and hands Aarya the picture she drew while I was in a coma last year, the same one with the word *MOMMY* under Aarya's stick figure that I had tattooed on my ribs.

Aarya smiles as she gazes down at it.

"Daddy asked you to be his wife." Giuliana looks up at her with those big brown eyes of hers. "So, now I'm going to ask you: Will you be my mommy?"

Aarya's eyes fly to mine before she drops down to her knees in front of my daughter. "You want me to adopt you?"

Giuliana nods and then throws her arms around Aarya's neck. The dam breaks and Aarya's tears overflow. We've discussed it several times, long after Giuliana had fallen asleep, while we snuggled together in bed. Aarya wanted to adopt Giuliana, but she wanted to make sure it was something Giuliana wanted to make official. She didn't want to give her the wrong impression and make her think she *needs* a mother. Every family is different, and our blended one has been getting along just fine.

But being able to call Aarya her mother is something Giuliana has wanted for quite a while.

I bend down and wrap my arms around my girls, holding them as we all cry.

Until Aarya pulls away and turns around, looking to Cassidy behind her. Cassidy reaches into her bouquet and pulls out a long white stick, and hands it to Aarya.

Aarya sniffles and her eyes return to me. "I guess this is the perfect time to tell you both." She holds out the white stick in front of Giuliana, with the word PREGNANT in the middle of the digital screen. "You're going to be a big sister."

Giuliana looks from me to Aarya with wide eyes, her little lips forming an O shape.

Then she rips the stick out of Aarya's hand and holds it over her head as she shouts, "Hell yes!"

And I can't even find it in myself to glare at McKinley for teaching my daughter that phrase, because I'm too overcome with shock and joy.

I clutch Aarya's face and pull her in for a kiss. "We're having a baby?"

She nods, more tears streaming down her cheeks. "That's the only plausible reason for all these damn tears."

I chuckle, and pull her in for another kiss as my own tears free-fall from my eyes. "Oh, my God. I can't believe it. We're having a baby."

"I know it's a little sooner than we'd hoped for, and I know it's inconvenient because the gallery just got off the ground, but—"

"But nothing. Aarya, I'm so fucking happy."

A baby. We're having a baby.

Our friends surround us to congratulate us, and Giuliana starts rattling off baby names, and plans of where the baby will sleep, and all the things she wants to show the baby when he or she comes.

McKinley cups his mouth with his hands. "All right, settle down everyone. We have one more part left, and then we can party."

Everyone takes their seats, and Aarya and I clasp hands as we face each other.

"By the power vested in me," McKinley announces, "I now pronounce you husband and wife—and mommy, and big sister. Alexander, you lucky bastard, you may kiss the bride."

I grip Aarya's face and kiss her with all the love and devotion in my soul. And then I lift Giuliana in my arms—because she's never going to be *too big* for me to carry her, no matter what she says—and we sandwich her between us while we kiss her cheeks.

The familiar tune of *Brown Eyed Girl* starts playing through the speaker I set up earlier, and I close my eyes as I hold my own brown-eyed girls in my arms.

THE END

Want to read Trenton & Cassidy's story?
Click here to read Heart Trick

Curious how Celeste, Jason, and Kourtney got together?
Click here to read Odd Man Rush

Come stalk me:
Facebook
Instagram
TikTok

Want to be part of my warrior crew?
Join Kristen's Warriors
A group where we can discuss my books & where friends will remind you
what a badass warrior you are.

ALL OF MY BOOKS ARE FREE ON KU:

Collision (Book 1) – Reverse grumpy sunshine
Avoidance (Book 2) – Reverse grumpy sunshine
The Other Brother (Book 3 – standalone) – Grumpy sunshine
Against the Odds (Book 4 – standalone) – MMA fighter workplace
romance

Hating the Boss – RomCom standalone – Enemies to lovers workplace
romance
Back to You – RomCom standalone – Second chance workplace romance

Inevitable – Contemporary standalone – Bodyguard forbidden romance
What's Left of Me – Contemporary standalone – Best friend's brother
grumpy sunshine

Someone You Love – Contemporary standalone – Forced proximity grumpy sunshine
Bring Me Back – Contemporary standalone – Next door neighbor cop romance

Dear Santa – Fake dating holiday novella
Trick or Truce – Age gap grumpy sunshine single dad novella

Heart Trick – Fake dating hockey novella
Odd Man Rush – FFM hockey romance

ACKNOWLEDGMENTS

To my dream team beta babes: Dorthy, Mary, Becca, and Taylor, thank you for reading through my process of this story and for always giving me your honest feedback. You are the reasons I can push through the impostor syndrome and finish writing. I appreciate you more than you know!

To Matt: Thank you for letting me bother you incessantly with biker questions, and for matching my excitement about this book. I hope you enjoy seeing all the little pieces of you sprinkled throughout the main character.

To my readers, I love you unconditionally. Thank you for your support in everything I do, and for hyping up my books. I'll never be able to thank you enough for being the reason my writing dreams came true.

Printed in Great Britain
by Amazon

39892638R10185